Marco Vozzolo

The Last Soldiers of Rome

Vexillatio – 476 CE

VENTUS

To Margherita, my daughter
To Michele, my son
To Pumba, Legionary
To the Legionaries

Prologue

I believe it is necessary, before beginning the reading of this historical novel, to provide some context about the time period in which the story takes place.

We are in the year marking the end of the Western Roman Empire. In this temporal context, the events described mainly take place in two locations: Duro Catalaunum, and the region of Vescinae, the latter name derived from ancient texts referring to the Roman spa area located along the banks of the Liris River, now known as the Garigliano, which divides Lazio from Campania.

Duro Catalaunum was a Roman settlement near the site of the famous Battle of the Catalaunian Fields, won by the last great general of the Western Roman Empire, Flavius Aetius. Today, the city built on the ruins of this ancient settlement is called Châlons-en-Champagne, in the Marne department of France—a thriving tourist center with an agricultural vocation.

In 476 CE, it was still under Roman control. These were times of crisis for the Empire, especially at one of the last outposts of Roman expansion, where a massive barbarian attack was expected at any moment. Other centers had already been ravaged by the barbarian hordes coming from the north and east.

Until that point, the settlement had been spared by the invasions of the Thuringians and Burgundians, mainly due to its advanced yet isolated position, shielded by forests and the terrain. However, it was clear that this fortunate situation could not last much longer. Around it, villages and towns had been burned after being plundered. Eventually, the barbarians would turn their attention to this small fortified village as well.

Fortunately, until then, the migrating tribes' focus had been on the wealthier provinces of Provence and Burgundy, leaving the domains of the Visigoths in the western part of Europe untouched. By avoiding conflict with the Visigoths, who were costly adversaries, the barbarian tribes did not engage with them, instead establishing control over every city they conquered and imposing a form of governance through the Roman administrative system.

By 476, Duro Catalaunum mirrored the decline of the entire Western Roman Empire, characterized by corruption that had impoverished the finances of the state. In this environment, the imperial delegates showed little interest, and everything was left in a state of neglect—from roads and postal stations to aqueducts requiring constant and expensive maintenance, as well as the upkeep of agricultural and commercial resources.

The town of Duro Catalaunum was not exempt from the Empire's decay. Roman tax collectors demanded payment without providing any benefits, while the Church did the same, further complicating the management of public affairs.

A story lingers about the decline of Arvando[1], the Praetorian Prefect for Gaul, who suddenly fell out of favor with the Emperor and paid dearly for it. He was condemned as a traitor, although

---

[1] *Arvando*: A Gallo-Roman who, in 464 CE, was appointed by Emperor Libius Severus as Praetorian Prefect for Gaul. This appointment was approved by the *magister militum* Ricimer, who was, in fact, the true power behind the Western Roman Empire. Arvando's task was extremely difficult: he was tasked with restoring order in a region increasingly squeezed between the barbarian kingdoms. After the death of Libius Severus, Arvando was confirmed by the new emperor, Anthemius. However, shortly thereafter (in 468 CE), he was brought to Rome without his office and as a prisoner. This led to a trial during which witnesses (nobles from Gaul) presented a letter in which Arvando urged Euric, the king of the Visigoths, not to recognize the new emperor and to show tolerance toward the Burgundians, with the aim of dividing the expansive territory of Gaul. It was Sidonius Apollinaris who saved him from the death penalty, reducing his punishment to exile.

there is suspicion that the Church played a part in his trial, particularly because he had sent a letter to the Visigoth king Euric urging him to attack the Bretons and to be less hostile toward the Burgundians in order to divide an expansive domain over Gaul.

Thus, in addition to the barbarians, there were internal plots aimed at eliminating political and military opponents, sometimes even physically. What was happening in the frontier town of Duro Catalaunum reflected the broader reality of the Western Roman Empire.

Vescinae, on the other hand, was a Roman spa area favored by Emperor Septimius Severus. He paved an ancient road that followed the Liris River, starting from Minturnae and reaching the area where the thermal waters of Vescinae emerged. The name Vescinae is derived from "Vescia," an ancient city in the Pentapolis Aurunca, destroyed by the Romans.

Vescinae was a settlement connected by a bridge across the river, the remains of which are still visible when the river is low. The Garigliano valley was an area with strong commercial interest, thanks to its navigability and its proximity to the port city of Minturnae at the river's mouth. Along the road built by Severus, various locations and profitable activities related to river navigation thrived. The names of some of these places have been passed down through the centuries, such as Porto Galeo and Taverna Cinquanta.

It has been my intention to connect these two locations, so distant from one another, as both represent key turning points in the course of history. Like Duro Catalaunum, Vescinae was deeply affected by the changing times. As Europe was divided into domains, the Garigliano valley was about to become a critical point at the beginning of a new era.

The "transition" from the Empire to the medieval phase was marked by events that made this region economically and militarily significant. It was inevitable that such interests would lead to political plots and historical upheaval. The arrival of the Saracens, followed by the Lombards and Normans, changed the entire landscape and fate of the region.

During the Middle Ages, this area was the "border," even though the maps indicated the real boundary further north, above Gaeta. Three fortresses—Ventosa, Castelforte, and Suio—were built to guard the "limbo," a natural boundary marked by the river's course.

In short, even though there were 1,413 kilometers—approximately 954.85 Roman miles—between Duro Catalaunum and Vescinae, the fates of these two locations seemed so similar that it felt appropriate to set the pages of this novel in both places.

A final brief note on the division of Europe in the years when the Western Empire was on the brink of collapse is necessary to give a complete picture of the temporal space we are entering. Nomadic tribes, composed of various populations, were settled to the north of the famous Teutoburg Forest, pressing from the east. The Iberian Peninsula and North Africa were under the control of the Vandals. The Alamanni had seized lands as far as Helvetia[2]. The Gallo-Romans were already independent of Rome, and Britain had long been abandoned.

For years, one emperor after another was murdered within a year of their coronation. It had been a long time since the assassination of Valentinian III and the Sack of Rome by Alaric. The imperial court had become a nest of spies and conspirators.

In 476, the year in which this novel is set, Odoacer, king of the Heruli, had been elevated to the rank of general. However, this did not change his barbaric nature or his hostility toward the sacred person of the Emperor. Thousands of refugees fled from the cities plundered by the barbarians, escaping horrific tortures, while the senators of Rome and the entire court of the Sacred Palace were concerned only with grandeur and feasts to display extravagance and power.

Enjoy your reading,

Marco Vozzolo

[2] *Elvezi*: Refers to the ancient region of Switzerland.

Chapter I – Departure

The small church dedicated to Saint Pantaleon[1] stood on bricks the same color as the earth, raised above the nearby sulfuric baths. Slivers of light filtered through the long, narrow windows, illuminating the stone floor. The censer, suspended from chains, emitted a haze that dissolved shortly after appearing.

A woman, small in stature, sat curled up in front of the Cross, her nails digging into the stone pavement, crying over the loss of her son, even though he was still alive.

Outside the church, the woman's son, devastated by grief, watched a heron glide over the riverbanks. His name was Vatinius Auruncus, and he closed his eyes, enjoying the light breeze that cooled the water before brushing his face. He barely noticed the presence of the other boys around him, who were celebrating the *toga virilis*, the rite of passage from adolescence to adulthood.

He paid little attention to the ceremony, even though it was an important event in the life of every young man, as it brought with it responsibilities and marked the end of carefree youth. Despite the fact that this tradition had fallen into disuse with the advent

---

[1] *San Pantaleo:* Saint Pantaleon (ca. 305, Nicomedia) was the personal physician of Galerius (Gaius Galerius Fulcinus Maximianus). He suffered martyrdom during the "Great Persecution" initiated by Emperor Diocletian, during which edicts were issued revoking the rights of those practicing Christianity. Alongside Saints Cosmas and Damian, Pantaleon was considered one of the "Fourteen Holy Helpers." In the thermal bath of Suio Terme, located in the municipality of Castelforte (LT), a zone still bears his name, as reflected in the local toponymy.

of Christianity, it was still officiated in the region of *Vescinae*[2], and all the boys wore the toga, symbolically, for that single day. Even though they had reached fifteen springs, none of them felt grown-up.

Once the rite was over, the group of boys walked along a paved path and reached the remains of an old tavern. The ruins spoke of life on the banks of the *Liris*[3] River, from a time long past. With a leap, Vatinius Auruncus perched himself on a funerary stele.

"MY AMPHORAE WERE THE BEST OF NOT ONLY *MINTURNAE*[4], BUT ALSO OF FORMIA AND CAPUA. MY NAME IS CALPURNIUS AUGUSTALIS, AND NOW I AM WITH MY SON. WE MAKE AMPHORAE EVEN IN HADES. THIS IS WITHOUT A DOUBT THE MOST BEAUTIFUL ONE."

He repeated aloud the words that had been inscribed there during the time of the once-great Rome. They told the life story of a potter who had his workshop near the tavern. It was here that the boys had played since childhood, and it had become their meeting place.

Growing up along the riverbank, which flowed lazily, winding its way to the sea, this was where they recreated adventures and games with their imagination.

"Tomorrow they'll come for us..." Vatinius Auruncus spoke first.

No one answered. They stood there, staring at each other, trying to withstand the weight of their unease. Each of their parents had received two gold *solidi*[5] for the delivery of their sons.

---

[2] *Vescinae:* A thermal bath situated between *Minturnae* and *Trifanum*, corresponding today to Minturno (LT) and Cellole (CE), respectively.

[3] *Liris:* The Garigliano River, historically called *Liris*, serves as the dividing line between the Lazio and Campania regions. Its banks witnessed significant events during the Roman era, as well as the Medieval and Renaissance periods. In World War II, it marked the infamous "Gustav Line," a critical front in the conflict.

[4] *Minturnae:* A Roman town established along the Garigliano River. Its modern equivalent is the area of Marina di Minturno, part of the municipality of Minturno (LT).

[5] *Solido:* A Roman gold coin introduced by Emperor Diocletian around 284 CE.

"We won't see our families or homes for many, many years," began Severinus Majorianus.

The bold air he had carried since childhood was gone now, given the emotion that Fulcinius Agricola Statius was visibly displaying. "Many of us won't survive the campaigns we'll be part of," he said.

Between one sentence and another, a long silence passed. They were there, for the last time, at the place where they had always met for their games.

The last to speak was Ulzio Dacianus: "I tried to hide so I wouldn't have to leave, but my father found me and beat me like he does with eels before cooking them. I don't think we'll be able to escape our fate."

After that, no one spoke again. They stood in silence, staring at the sluggish water flowing by.

At dawn the following day, a contingent of soldiers arrived in Vescinae.

The meeting took place on the banks of the Liris River, shrouded in a milky haze. Horses snorted through their nostrils, irritated by the morning chill.

The sun rose behind the trees lining the river, casting slanted beams of light through the foliage.

The flapping of wings from a flock of waterfowl caught the attention of children huddled in coarse woolen cloaks.

Mounted soldiers followed behind three wagons already nearly filled with somber-faced boys.

A decurion[6] dismounted and approached four children standing close together, clinging to one another.

"What are your names?" he asked.

"Vatinius Auruncus."

"Severinus Majorianus."

"Fulcinius Agricola Statius."

---

[6] *Decurion:* a public administrator of a city. Primarily responsible for tax collection, as well as supplies, maintenance, and organizing entertainment events.

"Ulzio Dacianus."

The soldier studied them for a long moment, then wrote their names on a sheet of papyrus.

"Get on the wagon," he ordered.

Vatinius Auruncus cast his gaze over the surrounding area, committing the scene to the most precious corner of his memory.

When he turned back to his father, he saw the man already walking away, his back turned.

The contingent set off southward. They needed to fill the wagons with more boys to train for the army.

Just before crossing the bridge, Vatinius saw her: his mother, watching him from behind a clump of reeds. He raised a hand to wave, and she broke into sobs. It was a moment Vatinius Auruncus would never forget.

The creaking of wagon wheels over the bridge's paving marked the point of farewell.

They reached Suessa[7] before the *Hora septima*.

Outside the city's walls, the same scene from the morning unfolded: more boys, most of them frightened, waiting to be taken by the soldiers.

The decurion dismounted again and approached the children.

From atop the wagon, Vatinius Auruncus watched, this time from a different perspective.

The soldier bore no resemblance to the Rome of old—the one etched into columns, carved into steles, or immortalized in sarcophagi.

No helmet with rounded cheek guards, no transverse crests, no banded lorica.

Instead, he wore a plate cuirass over a coarse woolen tunic.

The *cingulum militare* had been replaced by a wide belt that held a sword at his waist.

Even the sword was a long one, its hilt markedly different from the old gladii, long out of use.

---

[7] *Suessa:* The modern town of Sessa Aurunca (CE), known historically as Suessa.

Only the cloak retained its deep red, a common mark of all the soldiers in that cursed contingent.

Vatinius tried to imagine his life with the Roman armies and silently vowed never to forgive his father for selling him like this.

He glanced at his friends, who were watching the scene with terrified expressions.

An hour passed before they set off again, this time heading north along the Appian Way.

By evening, they had already passed Fundi and stopped for the night at an old caravanserai.

Around the fire, the boys began to talk, breaking the silence they'd kept out of fear.

"I'm Christianus Caligatus, and I can hunt boars," one began.

"My name is Gaius Octavianus, and I'm good at hiding so no one can find me," said another.

"I'm Tarquinius Glaucus, and I'm a shepherd."

"I'm Drusus Variatus," another followed.

"My name is Auctus Tullius Sextus, and I freely admit my fear!"

An awkward silence hung in the air for a moment before the boys erupted into laughter.

"I'm Gallienus Lars Gracchus, and...I'm not from around here. My father needed money to repair the dromon, so..."

They laughed again.

The decurion noticed the laughter and exchanged a glance with the other soldiers warming themselves by the campfire.

"I've watched them carefully. They'll make fine soldiers. But I'll hand them over to Aristarchos—they need to fetch a good price when sold. I expect to earn at least triple what they cost me."

The others nodded in agreement. After all, the more the decurion earned, the more they would profit as well.

At first light, the caravan resumed its journey.

This time, the travel lasted nearly a month, ending only in Arles, where the boys were taken to a military barracks.

Awaiting them were two young officers, dressed in the equipment of legions that had once made every border tremble.

The two *campidoctores*[8]—army trainers—stood tall, observing the young recruits. They gathered the boys together and stood before them. The age gap between the trainers and the recruits was no more than a dozen years.

One of the trainers climbed onto a stool and shouted, "Here, you'll become legionaries!"

A murmur arose, which the other trainer quickly silenced by striking Drusus Variatus and Fulcinius Agricola Statius with a vine-wood stick.

After exchanging a brief look of understanding, the first trainer resumed speaking:

"I am Aristarchos Themistocles, and I am the *principales*[9] in command of this unit.

I, along with this other officer, will oversee your training until you join the ranks of the Imperial Army."

The other young officer then stepped forward. "I am Antoninus Tacitus, second *principales*.

I will assist Aristarchos until I see you fall, one by one, in the battles we will face.

But we will fall with honor, which you will learn, and with courage, which we will instill in you."

Vatinius Auruncus' gaze locked with that of Aristarchos Themistocles for a long moment.

They recognized each other—both were from the same region, as was the other trainer, also hailing from the banks of the Liris.

Without breaking eye contact with Vatinius, Aristarchos continued, "Our roles are simple: I command, you obey, boy."

Vatinius Auruncus nodded, though his demeanor betrayed no sign of submission.

---

[8] *Campidoctor:* Roman military trainers, typically highly specialized. Examples of *campidoctores* for auxiliary troops have been documented, aligning closely with the circumstances described in this narrative.

[9] *Principales:* Junior-ranking officers in the Roman army.

Meanwhile, more wagons arrived, filled with boys conscripted from every part of the Italian peninsula and lower Gaul.

Vatinius noticed that each group was met by two equally young *principales*, who were, it seemed, from the same region as the boys they greeted—just as had happened with his own group.

By evening, the boys were served a hot meal, after which they were gathered in the center of the parade ground.

Shortly after, a *turma* of cavalry entered the torch-lit barracks, led by a general.

The high-ranking officer dismounted and was greeted by numerous field officers, all standing stiffly at attention in a military salute.

The general climbed onto the dais and began his *adlocutio*, the traditional address to the troops.

This time, however, his audience consisted of recruits.

"I am the Praetorian Prefect of Gaul[10], and I will make you into legionaries. There is one thing you must know from the very start: you will be trained as soldiers of Rome as it was at its peak. You will use the equipment of the old legions, you will learn to fight with the gladius, and you will maneuver using the techniques of the past. In this way, you will become deadly and invincible."

Once again, Vatinius Auruncus' gaze met that of Aristarchos Themistocles.

Antoninus Tacitus noticed and whispered to his fellow trainer, "Why does he keep staring at you?"

"Because he hates us more than anyone else," Aristarchos replied with a faint smile.

"But he will learn to love us and see us as brothers."

Vatinius Auruncus etched the faces of the young officers into his memory, fully aware that he would share many, many years of his life with them.

---

[10] *Petrus Marcellinus Felix Liberius:* Roman general and patrician, appointed Prefect of the Praetorium of Italy and the Gauls.

Chapter II – Vexillatio, 31 Years Later

Gallia Belgica, the small fortified village of Duro Catalaunum[1], Nones of September[2], 476 CE; Year 1229 since the founding of the Urbs.

Snow began to fall in large yet delicate flakes, seeming to hover midair as if defying the gusts of wind. On the ramparts, the sentries warmed their hands over brazier fires, their breaths forming long clouds of vapor in the icy air. Their eyes scanned beyond the walls of Duro Catalaunum, searching for what they fervently hoped would never appear.

That cold morning, several dozen refugees entered through the eastern gate. They were met by a contingent of legionaries led by the centurion in command of the *vexillationes*, the detachment assigned to guard this remote corner of the territory.

The soldiers watched the procession of men, women, and children, all emaciated and dressed in whatever they had salvaged during their flight from a sacked homeland. There were no elderly among them; they would have slowed the escape.

An *optio* guided the refugees through the cobbled streets and into the grand hall of the Governor's palace, the only structure large enough to accommodate them all. The Governor himself,

---

[1] *Duro Catalaunum:* A fortified city located in Gallia Belgica, corresponding to the modern city of Châlons-en-Champagne.
[2] *Nones of September:* according to the Roman calendar, this corresponds to September 5th.

however, was conspicuously absent, claiming to be in a meeting with the bishop. Everyone knew it was merely an excuse to avoid dealing with such problems.

Governor Attilius Faticus still harbored hopes of regaining favor with the Emperor and returning to Ravenna. That left centurion *primae spatha* Aristarchos Themistocles with the unenviable task of receiving the wretched souls that fate had spared from barbarian atrocities.

When the refugees saw Aristarchos, they halted. The centurion scratched his neck, momentarily relieved from the itchy rash caused by the dampness of this accursed place. A native of Minturnae, born to a Roman mother and a Greek sailor father, he had grown up accustomed to the sun and the sea—things he could no longer even recall the scent of.

With a glance, he signaled the soldiers, who promptly brought amphorae of fresh water to quench the refugees' thirst. Aristarchos scanned the group, searching for someone to speak with. An emaciated man, likely a scribe judging by his tattered yet once-refined garments, stepped forward to represent the group.

Despite the grime on his hands and the terror etched into his gaunt face, his eyes remained sharp, ever-watchful, as if expecting an attack at any moment.

The man began to speak:

"Centurion, we come from *Silvanectum*[3]. The city was besieged and then sacked by the Heruli—about three thousand of them. But from what we could gather, they were only a fraction of their full force. The garrison defending the city numbered barely a hundred,

---

[3] *Silvanectum:* The modern city of Senlis. A Roman city that developed in the second half of the 1st century BCE on a pre-existing Gallic settlement. Its founding was due to its strategic position at a crossroads. It was the ancient capital of the Silvanectes, who gave their name to Senlis (also known as Sulbanectes, meaning "autonomous"). Previously known as Augustomagus Silvanectum, in the 3rd century, it was surrounded by walls up to four meters thick for protection, sections of which can still be visited today.

and held out for only a few hours before they were all slaughtered. Many were tortured before their deaths.

"The archers had their fingers cut off before their eyes were gouged out. I myself saw a group of Heruli flay a soldier alive, stripping the skin from his back to his waist. Once the walls were breached, the barbarians unleashed horrors upon us. Women and young girls were violated and killed. The elderly were almost entirely exterminated.

"The men were butchered, save for those chosen to be sold in the slave markets of Persia and Dalmatia. Their leader paraded through the city streets with a woman on a leash, forcing her to crawl on all fours. He executed her on the steps of the church of *Saint Apollinaris*[4] before the stunned deacon, who tried in vain to intervene. They tore out his tongue and hung it from the church door. Then, after severing his arms, they disemboweled him."

The centurion *primae spatha* clenched his jaw, his body taut with anger as his pulse thundered in his temples. He wondered why the Fifth Ironclad Legion hadn't intervened. Could no messenger have reached General Marcellinus[5] advance forces, stationed not far from the sacked city?

Taking a deep breath, he finally responded:

"I will see to it that you are given as much sustenance as we can spare. Supplies have not arrived here in months, and even our reserves are running low. But you are safe now."

His words were firm, but hollow, as he feigned a confidence he did not feel. Aristarchos knew full well that with the meager

---

[4] *Saint Apollinaris:* Apollinaris of Ravenna (born in Antioch, 1st century – died in Classe), is considered the first bishop of Ravenna. His *dies natalis* (day of martyrdom) is July 23rd. Sparse sources suggest that he was ordained as bishop by Saint Peter, his reputed mentor. He was later sent to Classe, where he suffered martyrdom under Emperor Vespasian.

[5] *Petrus Marcellinus Felix Liberius:* Also known as Petrus Marcellinus Felix Liberius, a Roman general and patrician appointed Prefect of the Praetorium of Italy and Gaul.

forces left to him by the Legion's general, they wouldn't withstand a prolonged siege.

He had only his century and the assistance of another unit commanded by Centurion Vatinius Auruncus. Auruncus was a capable fighter, disciplined in carrying out orders and rigid in issuing them. Yet Aristarchos often felt he was better suited to being a *litterator*[6], given his fastidious demeanor. Still, Auruncus had proven himself in combat, particularly at the Battle of Arles, where he had distinguished himself with bravery and earned numerous scars as reminders of his valor.

Aristarchos signaled for an aide. The man approached, snapping to attention with a crisp salute.

"Your orders, Centurion?"

"Find Centurion Vatinius Auruncus and tell him to meet me."

The aide disappeared at once to carry out the command.

***

He strode briskly across the colonnade of the peristyle[7] and slipped through the door into the hall.

"Centurion..." he called to the man, who was gripping the woman's hips beneath him.

"Centurion, the commander wants to see you."

But nothing.

The man didn't hear him and kept rhythmically moving his hips, in perfect harmony with the woman.

Only when they had finished did the man collapse beside her, panting. Finally, he deigned to acknowledge the legionary standing there, clearly eager for his attention.

---

[6] *Litteratores:* Teachers of basic education in the Roman Empire. This role was common during the Imperial era, but disappeared by the late Western Roman Empire.

[7] *Peristyle:* A row of columns surrounding a defined space. In Roman architecture, it referred to the portico encircling the central garden of a *domus* (residence).

"Tell the *primae spatha* that I'll be there soon. Go!"

He began dressing, but not before passionately kissing the woman, who was already starting to drift off to sleep.

When the young centurion, Vatinius Auruncus, stood before Aristarchos, he snapped to attention with a rigid military salute.

"Greetings, Centurion!" he announced, almost at a shout. His gaze was fixed on a point beyond the commander.

Aristarchos studied him briefly, returning the greeting with a curt nod. The young man's appearance was immaculate: his polished armor gleamed, the purple cloak was draped elegantly over one shoulder, his neck was shielded by a neatly tied *focale*[8]. At his side hung his gladius, and under his left arm, he carried a crested helmet, striped in black and white.

He was nearly flawless. But nearly wasn't enough.

"You've come from Ravenna, I presume?"

Vatinius Auruncus cleared his throat before replying, "A bout of dysentery delayed me, Centurion..." he lied.

The commander didn't believe him, but it hardly mattered. He had orders to give and no time to waste.

"Centurion, Silvanectum has been sacked by a band of Heruli. From the reports, it seems they were only a fraction of their much larger force." He paused, ensuring the other understood the gravity of the situation. "However, there's something peculiar in the refugees' accounts. Marcellinus' Legion didn't intervene. Furthermore, no messengers arrived here in Duro Catalaunum to warn us about what was happening..." He trailed off, almost speaking to himself. "Why didn't even Marcellinus' auxiliary vanguard engage the barbarians?"

Vatinius Auruncus nodded slightly, but didn't interrupt his superior's reasoning. At the same time, he reflected on the string of bad news that had been arriving lately, and instinctively moved his hand to his groin for a superstitious gesture.

---

[8] *Focale:* A strip of cloth worn around the neck by Roman legionaries for protection, including from weather conditions.

The *primae spatha* continued, "In this godforsaken backwater where we've been stationed, something dark and dangerous is brewing. Gather a detachment of soldiers and head south in search of the Legion. It should be quartered near *Argentoratum*[9]."

Vatinius Auruncus received the orders with a sense of dread. This meant the barbarians were already dangerously close, and things were about to take a turn for the worse.

He was painfully aware that they were vastly underprepared to defend this remote outpost of the Empire where they'd been sent.

He detested the place. The cold, the perpetually gray skies—even in summer.

By contrast, he loved the Tyrrhenian coast and its warm, fragrant air. His hometown, though long razed centuries ago, was still known by the locals as Vescia, a name that persisted since the days of Septimius Severus.

For a moment, he could almost see the slow-moving river flowing toward the shores of Minturnae and feel the sun warming his face.

The commander's voice shattered the pleasant reverie.

Without revealing any trace of his thoughts, he nodded to show he had understood the orders.

He was about to leave when Centurion Aristarchos gave him one final warning.

"Be careful. If my suspicions are correct, the forests around here are crawling with barbarians, preparing to plunder these lands. Ensure you're well-escorted."

---

[9] *Argentoratum:* The Roman *castrum* (fort) near present-day Strasbourg, established as a military post in 12 BCE and a permanent legionary camp by 17 CE after Germanicus' campaigns in Germania (14–16 CE). It remained active until the fall of the Western Roman Empire. Notable units stationed there include: *Ala Petriana Treverorum* (Auxiliary Unit) from 12 BCE to 17 CE, *Augustus' Second Legion* from 17 to 43 CE, Auxiliary units from 43 to 90 CE, and *Augustus' Eighth Legion* from 90 CE until the empire's collapse. The auxiliary fort built after 12 BCE is thought to have housed the *Ala Petriana Treverorum* and supported the military campaigns of Drusus the Elder.

"Centurion..."

"What?"

"Our walls are still intact, but they won't hold them."

"I'm aware. So?"

"There's a chance we won't return home."

"That's the duty you accepted when you joined the Imperial Army: the possibility of never returning home."

"I didn't choose this. They bought me. I feel abandoned by the very Empire I 'chose' to serve."

"Those are dangerous words. I'll pretend I didn't hear them. Now go, complete your mission."

The young centurion repeated his military salute and left the room at the same brisk stride with which he had entered.

Reflecting on the grim prospect of not making it back home, he again made his superstitious gesture.

He headed to his century's barracks to inspect his men and decide who to take on the mission.

Along the way, he heard cries that caught his attention.

Turning, he saw Legionary Fulcinius Agricola Statius, tied by his hands and hanging from a tree.

The man's head was bowed, and he was cursing.

"Legionary...why have you been punished?" he asked, approaching.

Fulcinius raised his head, smirking weakly. His expression left no doubt that the flogging had left him in significant pain.

"I was punished for disobeying an order, Commander," he said through gritted teeth, then added, "...but I'll be freed at sundown."

"Who ordered your punishment?"

"The *primae spatha* himself. I disobeyed him. He ordered me to gather firewood outside the walls with four other men, but I sneaked into the armory instead, trying to dodge the task. One of his soldiers caught me, and...well, you can see the result for yourself." He even had the audacity to chuckle.

Vatinius Auruncus stifled his anger. He hated it when others punished his men, even if they were superior officers. But starting an argument with the centurion commander now would cause a major problem.

Still, he needed this scoundrel for the mission. The man was excellent in close combat.

"Have him released immediately. I'll personally secure the *primae spatha's* approval," he told the soldier guarding the punished man.

The guard hesitated, visibly nervous about carrying out the order.

"Centurion, if I do that and—"

"Perhaps I should tie you to that rope instead?"

"I'll obey, Centurion!" the man replied hastily.

He needed this unruly soldier, who would undoubtedly grumble and question every order, but who would never shy away from drawing his sword and fighting when needed.

Once freed, Fulcinius rubbed his sore wrists and arms.

He saluted the young centurion, muttered a few curses, then stepped to a corner and began to relieve himself.

Vatinius Auruncus watched in silence.

The legionary turned to him. "Come on, Centurion, piss with me!"

The centurion didn't reply, only raising a hand to his forehead in exasperation.

Fulcinius, still grinning, headed toward the armory to retrieve his gear.

***

The squad, a total of fifteen men, exited through the southern gate, urging their horses to a steady walk. The animals exhaled clouds of vapor from their nostrils with each breath, but they seemed calm enough—except for the horse belonging to Fulcinius Agricola Statius, which was restlessly kicking.

"Even the horse is as agitated as he is!" Vatinius Auruncus quipped, watching the legionary curse at the animal while trying to calm it down.

He turned back to ensure the squad was following and that their equipment was in proper order. Each soldier carried food supplies for two days, though with careful rationing, they could stretch it to four.

The guards patrolling the walls watched the small column pass by until it disappeared from sight. They returned to warming themselves by the lit braziers, discussing the uncertain future of the Empire and the city.

The group of legionaries was now on its way.

Riding a little apart and in silence was optio Severinus Majorianus, a veteran of the 22nd Legion. He had fought in the infamous Battle of Arles alongside the regiment the Gallo-Romans referred to as the "Italics."

A man of few words, he was among the best when it came to hand-to-hand combat.

The centurions respected him, as did the soldiers.

He had an ironclad memory, missing no details even in the most critical situations. It was said that during the battle in Sicily against the Vandals, under Marcellinus' command, he had held off five barbarians simultaneously, cutting them down one by one. Additionally, he had led a group of otherwise doomed legionaries out of an encirclement by maintaining a remarkably calm and detached perspective—almost as if he possessed an innate ability to view things from above, no matter the situation.

That evening, after passing through looted and burned farms and past the mutilated bodies of farmers and their families, the group decided to make camp for the night.

They took advantage of an abandoned postal station, of which only two walls remained standing. For centuries, postal stations had ceased to function as they once did.

The decline of the Empire, coupled with constant barbarian raids and the administration's neglect of public affairs, had significantly eroded what was once an efficient Roman communication network. As a result, the roads had fallen into complete disrepair.

A young soldier took charge of lighting the fire, gathering wood and stacking it inside a circle of large stones to contain the embers.

Severinus Majorianus left the soldiers busy with their improvised camp and wandered off to check for any barbarian scouts in the area. He vanished into the dense forest, moving with his usual caution.

Meanwhile, Fulcinius Agricola Statius was kicking apart a triclinium bed to use its wood as extra fuel for the fire.

"I don't want to freeze while I sleep," he justified himself when he caught the disapproving look of the centurion.

Vatinius Auruncus tried to stop him, recognizing the piece as a finely crafted piece of furniture. Judging by the intricate carvings and finishes, it was clearly the work of a skilled artisan.

The two argued heatedly for several minutes until the legionary gave up, throwing the broken pieces of wood aside. Only then did the young centurion let the matter drop.

Fulcinius, however, couldn't help muttering, "What's a rotten piece of wood worth anyway? Of course, I get stuck with a centurion who has a soft spot for art."

The centurion, overhearing him, rolled his eyes to the heavens.

The squad shared a makeshift dinner around the fire.

The soldiers, who viewed the arrival of refugees as the harbinger of even worse events, exchanged opinions on the Empire's state of disarray. Their commentary mixed political critiques with sarcastic jabs at the sacred figure of the Augustus.

To their surprise, the night passed without incident.

However, the centurion had strange dreams, which he attributed to the ominous signs weighing on his mind—in his gut, even.

The squad set out again just after the fourth watch had ended.

The pale winter sun began to highlight the peaks of towering fir trees.

Moments later, beams of light pierced through the trunks, dissolving the mist lingering over the ground.

After traveling only a few miles, the air grew heavy with the stench of death, becoming increasingly unbearable.

Flocks of crows fluttered everywhere, and the soldiers' expressions grew increasingly grim.

Optio Severinus Majorianus gestured with his chin toward the young centurion, Vatinius Auruncus, who immediately understood and nodded in return...

At that point, Severinus spurred his horse forward, pulling ahead of the group. Leaving the path behind, he disappeared into the forest once again.

The squad, however, continued its cautious advance, moving at a slower pace. Only the sound of the horses' hooves broke the tense silence.

Vatinius Auruncus looked visibly grim, his face tight with an expression of foreboding, as if bracing for an imminent threat.

He called over his most trusted men—Fulcinius Agricola Statius and Drusus Variatus, the two veterans of the group. Then, without a word, he raised his arm and clenched his fist.

The other legionaries, recognizing the silent order, formed a defensive position. Anxiety was palpable among them, fully aware of their small numbers and their disadvantage should they face a surprise attack.

Swords were drawn, shields made ready.

The tension affected the horses, making them snort and paw at the ground restlessly.

Meanwhile, Severinus Majorianus covered his face with his scarf as the stench of rot became unbearable. A wave of nausea caught him off guard, but he forced himself onward, determined to uncover what had happened.

When he came upon a Roman soldier tied to a post, his fears were confirmed. The man's skin had been flayed, leaving him a bloody spectacle from head to waist. He still wore his tunic and belt, though his head hung at an unnatural angle—likely from a broken neck.

"Gods of the underworld... What horrors must this man have endured?" he muttered under his breath.

Every sound heightened his alertness.

It would take only a single arrow from the shadows to send him to the afterlife.

He was beginning to believe the entire legion had been wiped out.

He dismounted and continued on foot, climbing a gentle hill. When he reached the top, the scene that unfolded before him was horrifying.

Thousands of bodies littered the vast battlefield. Many heads had been stacked into grotesque, rotting pyramids.

The once-proud Roman standards had been stripped of their honor, now planted atop one of these grim piles as a symbol of mockery. The weapons scattered across the ground were mostly broken, while others had been taken by the victors—mercenaries from unknown tribes.

This was the defeat of the northern army. The Empire's last potential resistance to the barbarian advance had been obliterated.

Severinus' disbelieving eyes scanned the plain. Hundreds of crows feasted on the remains of the dead, adding to the gruesome spectacle.

Finally, he spotted the legion's eagle standard. It had been impaled at the summit of one of the pyramids of heads.

Severinus approached it to retrieve it, but as he did, he recognized the battered face of General Marcellinus, the army's commander.

It was truly over, he thought, overwhelmed with despair.

He quickly returned to his horse and rode back to the waiting squad.

As he reached them, he advanced slowly, offering no greeting.

From the expression on Severinus' face, Centurion Vatinius Auruncus immediately understood the grim news he was about to deliver.

The optio halted his horse. "Centurion...the legion has been completely wiped out. Beyond those hills lies the battlefield—a vast plain strewn with corpses. Judging by the weapons and clothing of the barbarian dead, the attackers were Goths, Burgundians, Heruli, Thuringians, and Alans."

Vatinius Auruncus' mouth fell open in shock. The bitter taste of defeat filled him, and he lowered his gaze in despair.

Noticing the others watching him, he quickly composed himself, regaining a semblance of martial bearing, though he felt no such calm within.

"We must return to Catalaunum and defend the garrison—at least until reinforcements arrive. We'll send messengers to Ravenna in the hope that the Emperor will dispatch an army..." His voice was barely more than a whisper, and even he knew those hopes were futile.

The army was in shambles.

The high-ranking officers of the Italian forces, commanding contingents now largely composed of barbarian mercenaries, remained hidden in their quarters, waiting to see how events unfolded before deciding where to pledge their loyalty. For these men, loyalty to the Emperor—whoever he might be—was little more than a convenience.

One thing was certain: no army, not even the formidable forces of the Emperor of the East, would come to their aid in Belgica.

Despite the stark reality of the situation, Vatinius Auruncus struggled to accept it. A loyal soldier of Rome and its legions, he found it hard to believe that the Empire had truly fallen so far.

The squad set off toward Duro Catalaunum, hoping to avoid any ambushes from barbarian mercenaries lying in wait.

Barbarian Army Camp

The stench of horse dung mingled with the nauseating odor of animal hides—wolves, deer, bears, even hares and squirrels—that had been hunted, skinned, and left to dry atop the tents.

A mercenary sipped cider, lounging as a prostitute moved atop him, panting, her breasts exposed, nearing climax. Not far away, within other tents, the prostitutes were busy with their brisk trade, while outside, furious brawls frequently broke out among warriors struggling to maintain their place in the long queues. Although the kings of the tribes had forbidden the use of daggers during these scuffles, it wasn't uncommon for someone to be killed or severely injured regardless.

Rudulfus, king of the Heruli, rode his horse around the encampment of his tribe, inspecting to ensure that the sentries were truly vigilant—that is, sober and not playing dice—and that everything was in order. His chosen guards followed close behind, never leaving his side. Even when Rudulfus was in his tent, accompanied by one of his wives, his men stood watch outside, alert and eager. Among the Heruli, they were known as the most bloodthirsty, feared even by the barbarian mercenaries, who avoided dealing with them whenever possible.

One of these guards stood out: Cunipert, a former officer of the Gallo-Roman army once commanded by General Syagrius[10]. Cunipert had wisely decided to return to his people when he realized that Syagrius' forces had no hope of maintaining Roman governance over the northern territories.

Indeed, being at odds with the court at Ravenna, Syagrius had lost control of those regions. Still, he clung to the dream of the Rome that once was, ruling a strip of land between the Seine and the Loire, beleaguered by the Visigoths and Franks—a dream that would soon see its twilight. Cunipert proved himself a capable officer, climbing the ranks even within King Rudulfus' army.

However, his presence among the Heruli and his brazen ambition did not go unnoticed. It became clear to all that Cunipert sought to command the king's personal guard.

As Rudulfus rode, he spurred his horse harshly, making it snort and neigh in irritation. His reddish hair, braided in long plaits that

---

[10] *Syagrius:* Afranius Syagrius, a Roman general stationed in northern Gaul. The son of Aegidius, he was the last magister militum for Gaul. After the collapse of the Western Roman Empire, Syagrius ruled a Roman enclave between the Loire and Seine rivers, trapped between the Franks and Visigoths. Known as the "King of the Romans" by the Franks, he was assassinated in 487.

spilled out from beneath his helmet, swung across his shoulders with each of the animal's movements. His gaze was lofty and menacing, and a grin sat as if etched beneath his mustache—a grin that unsettled anyone who met him.

He wore a plated cuirass, adorned at its center with a golden bear's head. It was just one of the many exquisite suits of armor he owned, all spoils of plunder and raids carried out during their invasions. He didn't wear them merely to flaunt his superiority and rank, but also out of necessity.

It was far too dangerous for him to move about unprotected; doing so would make it easier for assassins sent by rival barbarian kings—or ambitious pretenders to his throne—to target him.

This constant threat had shaped Rudulfus' demeanor over time, leading him to adopt exaggerated behavior to intimidate. He wanted anyone who crossed his path to feel as if they were encountering a divine figure from the realm of souls. Even as he rode, he would abruptly jerk the reins to agitate his horse, making himself appear even more fearsome than he already was.

On his way back from his inspection, as he reached the center of the sprawling camp, which extended as far as the woods beyond, Rudulfus encountered an unwelcome sight.

It was Gargalico, king of the Thuringians, a figure equally feared and respected among warriors. Even the Augustan court in Ravenna had considered him a potential ally of the Empire—a reckless choice, given that Gargalico had, in fact, contributed to the Empire's collapse.

It was well known that in his youth, Gargalico had trained in the heart of the Sacred Palace of Ravenna. He had served as an official and had been close to the previous emperor, Glycerius[11], before returning to his tribe. However, these experiences made Gargalico

---

[11] *Glycerius:* A Roman Emperor of the West (473–474), chosen by the Germanic faction of the army. Deposed by Julius Nepos, he was later appointed Bishop of Salona.

unpopular among the barbarians, as did his Romanized manners. He was often seen wearing finely adorned dalmatics, threaded with gold, or reading classical works and philosophical essays. When his warriors got drunk, they would mock their king, staging scenes in which he was mounted by bishops and patriarchs[12].

The two kings locked eyes in challenge and slowed their horses to a light trot, which ended with them halting side by side. A moment of icy silence followed. The guards on both sides placed their hands on their sword hilts, feigning calm while their nerves bristled.

Cunipert moved behind his king, ready for anything. He knew all too well the importance of reacting first in such situations.

It was Gargalico who broke the tension:

"Greetings, Rudulfus. I see you've learned well from your father's lessons on commanding an army," he said, nodding as though ironically pleased. "It's a pity, though, that you've inherited so little of the courage that made him a great warrior!" he concluded with a mocking laugh.

Rudulfus responded with laughter of his own—a laugh laced with hatred that stretched on until his face suddenly darkened. He replied coldly, "Odoacer will have your tongue cut out for those words. That is, if I don't do it myself when I become governor of Gaul, of course!" His words hinted at his closeness to Odoacer, who had recently declared himself king of Italy.

Gargalico turned his horse in a circle before facing Rudulfus again. "I will be the one..." he emphasized the word, "...to become governor of Gaul, you damned bumpkin!" he snapped, before spurring his horse and departing, followed by his guards.

Rudulfus twisted his mouth in disdain and mulled over Gargalico's words. Could Odoacer have made a secret pact with Gargalico, promising him the governorship of Gaul? Had the Thuringian king sent envoys to Ravenna in secret, seeking to forge an alliance

---

[12] *Patriarch:* A title for the five leading metropolitan bishops: those of Jerusalem, Rome, Antioch, Alexandria, and Constantinople.

at Rudulfus' expense? His mind swirled with dark thoughts and ominous suspicions.

After a moment of reflection, unable to reach a logical explanation for Gargalico's claims, he shrugged and made his way back to his tent, muttering insults about his rival.

He resolved to unleash his spies within the sacred palace to uncover enough information about court affairs to anticipate Odoacer's moves. He would double their pay to prevent bribery by others. Then, he planned to hire propagandists to spread false rumors about Gargalico, tarnishing his reputation and making him fall out of favor with Ravenna. Once Gargalico became indefensible, Rudulfus would accuse him of treason and have him killed.

For a moment, Gargalico's face materialized vividly in Rudulfus' mind. As if clawing at it, Rudulfus' gloved hand slashed through the air, dispelling the vision.

"My king...we should leave now," Cunipert's voice advised from behind him.

Rudulfus cast him a cursory glance, but followed his suggestion, digging his heels into his horse's flanks.

Duro Catalaunum

When the squad returned from their mission, they were greeted by a city on the brink of starvation—after only a few days.

The granaries were nearly empty. Food was rationed, and long lines of people waited for a meager handful of spelt or grain from public stores.

Two squads of *vigiles* patrolled to keep order, often resorting to rough methods.

The soldiers of the *vexillatio*[13], left behind to guard the city,

---

[13] *Vexillatio:* A detachment of troops from its parent legion. The term comes from *vexillum*, the banner carried by the detachment.

trained as though they expected an imminent attack. Armorers polished weapons and greased chainmail to prevent rusting—an essential task, given the weather in this godforsaken place. Relentless rain and the mist rising from the ground corroded metals quickly.

Vatinius Auruncus and Severinus Majorianus were summoned by Commander Aristarchos Themistocles, where they recounted the defeat of the legion and the horrors they had witnessed. Their faces conveyed more than their words ever could.

Hearing their report, Aristarchos Themistocles closed his eyes, bracing himself for calamity. The truth was becoming painfully clear.

The Empire was falling apart, and they were on their own.

Barbarian incursions ravaged Europe almost unchecked. There was no longer any true control over what remained of imperial domains.

Aristarchos' thoughts turned to prominent military figures, searching for someone to whom he could send a desperate plea for aid. He found no one.

The *magister militum*[14], who should have been organizing defenses against the barbarians, had become the true wielders of power. Ironically, most of them were barbarians themselves, with the exception of the great Aetius, who had defeated the Huns at the Catalaunian Plains.

These same magister militum elevated puppet emperors, mere shields for their ambitions, only to dispose of them when they became inconvenient or resistant to their schemes.

Yet, brushing aside these grim musings, the centurion *primae spatha* allowed himself a fleeting moment of nostalgia. It wasn't so long ago that he had served in the army of Emperor Julius

---

[14] *Magister militum:* A high-ranking military commander in the late Roman Empire. They commanded Roman imperial armies and barbarian mercenary forces. Notable figures include Aetius, who defeated Attila's Huns at the Catalaunian Plains.

Valerian Majorianus, perhaps the last great emperor of the Western Empire.

A faint smile touched his lips as he recalled the Battle of Arles, where the legions had defeated the Visigoth armies[15].

The Emperor had been assassinated only three years later[16], and Aristarchos regretted this deeply. He knew that with Majorianus' death, the Empire had lost the last Augustus who genuinely cared for the Republic.

During the Battle of Arles, Aristarchos Themistocles had commanded the second century. Many of the legionaries now under his command in Duro Catalaunum had fought with him then—professional soldiers, not hastily armed peasants or unscrupulous mercenaries. His most trusted squad consisted of men who had enlisted with him, all hailing from the Gulf of Lestrigonia. Many had grown up playing on the banks of the Liris River, which flowed into the port of Minturnae.

They were men raised in the legions, bearing none of the glory of the Rome that once was. Yet he and his comrades hadn't seen those sunlit lands in decades. A pang of homesickness gripped his throat.

While the centurion was lost in thought, a legionary burst into the *principia*[17].

"Centurion...the barbarians...the barbarians..." he panted, breathless from running and clearly agitated. "They're beyond the forest—thousands of them. They appeared out of nowhere, hidden by the hills, and they're headed this way."

Aristarchos Themistocles shot to his feet. He knew the man standing before him well: Gaius Octavianus, nicknamed "the

---

[15] In 458 CE, the Roman army under Emperor Majorian (Majorianus) defeated the Visigoths at Arles.

[16] Emperor Majorian was assassinated in Italy in August 461, near Tortona, by Ricimer, the magister militum.

[17] *Principia:* The military headquarters.

Scout." His moniker came from his assignment as a reconnaissance specialist, gifted with the uncanny ability to blend into any environment and survive even the most extreme conditions.

The centurion motioned for him to continue.

"I was hiding in a tree..."

Aristarchos couldn't suppress a chuckle at the thought, but his expression quickly grew serious again.

Gaius Octavianus resumed, "At first, I saw their scouts. Hours later, I saw the rest of their column. Their line stretched beyond the horizon. I'm talking about Burgundians, Thuringians, Alans, Heruli, and Goths. Around ten thousand men, at least from what I could see before nightfall. They have no supply wagons, livestock, or families with them, so this is clearly just a detachment—likely part of a much larger force." Gaius swallowed hard, the weight of his statement evident.

"I ambushed one of their patrols, stole their clothes and weapons, and even took one of their horses. That's how I reached their main force for a closer look. Only then did I realize..."

The centurion *primae spatha* regarded him with admiration.

Vatinius Auruncus and Severinus Majorianus, their mouths agape, were eager to hear the rest of the scout's report.

"What did you realize?" Aristarchos Themistocles urged, gesturing for him to continue.

Gaius' eyes sparkled, as they always did when he felt his work was appreciated.

"I watched their camps for almost two days, using my disguise. I can confidently say that the various tribal leaders act independently. Each calls himself a king among his people, surrounded by trusted generals. The Goths seem to lead this expedition, but the other tribes, while subordinate, will fight for their own causes.

"Several times, I saw messengers with Burgundian or Alan standards hurrying to the Goth king's tent to report on their forces' activities. What's more, the kings avoid meeting each other to maintain their own prestige, communicating only through couriers," Gaius concluded.

Centurion Vatinius Auruncus nodded, exchanging a knowing glance with Commander Aristarchos Themistocles before speaking. "We agree—these are Goths, Burgundians, Heruli, Thuringians, and Alans. We deduced as much from the bodies on the battlefield. The legion was defeated by them."

Severinus Majorianus stepped forward. "I saw firsthand the horrors inflicted by these peoples. If the force Gaius Octavianus observed is only their vanguard, that means at least fifteen thousand more mercenary warriors will join them in a few days."

Everyone understood the gravity of his words. Severinus Majorianus was known for his foresight. In a matter of days, this mass of humanity would be at their gates.

Many thoughts crossed the minds of those present. Perhaps the wisest course of action would be to abandon the city and retreat south, where they could count on the support of the Gallo-Romans. But evacuating all these people was no small feat, especially with their limited provisions to sustain so many refugees.

The centurion *primae spatha* nodded, seemingly sharing the same thought as Vatinius Auruncus. For a moment, the possibility of abandoning the outpost of Duro Catalaunum with only his garrison to join what remained of the Roman legions flashed through his mind. However, he quickly dismissed the horrible thought. He was certainly not the type to flee and leave the local population at the mercy of the barbarians. But the resignation to the few alternatives available to him irritated him to the point of making his stomach churn.

He would have to deal with Bishop Calibertus and Governor Attilius Faticus, whom he considered a pair of syrupy hypocrites and empty-headed palace bureaucrats. He couldn't stand them. Two complete incompetents living in luxury, while all of Europe now knew nothing but hardship and ruin. Just the thought of having to speak with those individuals clouded his clarity.

He dismissed the soldiers and called for Centurion Antoninus Tacitus, responsible for the guard on the bastions. The centurion entered the principia scratching his backside. His gait was clumsy and amusingly cocky. His rough beard complemented his often furrowed expression. When he stood before the first centurion, Antoninus Tacitus stiffened in a military salute and removed his crested helmet. Then he asked, "I must prepare to welcome some stinking barbarians, am I right?" He had guessed the reason for his summons.

He was right, in fact. The first centurion of the spatha pretended not to catch the irony and gave him clear orders: double the guards at the walls and be ready for an imminent and certain attack. There needed to be a detachment of archers always on standby in case of an alarm. Patrols were to be sent to monitor the barbarians' advance.

When Centurion Antoninus Tacitus made to leave the room, he rubbed his head, muttering. Aristarchos Themistocles followed his gait to the exit. He glanced at some maps, looking for an idea that might help him escape this damned situation, but found nothing.

He dismissed everyone from the room. Finally, after finishing the discussions with his subordinates, he stood up, preparing in his mind the right words to persuade the governor and the bishop to comply with his requests, since he was the only one able to set up a defense for the city that could be considered at least satisfactory.

Then he took a deep breath, savoring the sharp air that entered through the open windows, and put on his purple cloak and helmet before heading to Governor Attilius Faticus' palace. In the center of the colonnade marking the perimeter of the cloister, he noticed his attendant. He was sitting on the capital of a column, writing.

The young litterator, who earned a meager salary writing dispatches and performing secretarial duties for the Duro Catalaunum military detachment, knew how to read and write, unlike most people. No one, except for the patricians and wealthy landowners, bothered to educate their children anymore, especially in a border region like this.

This legionary, however, knew how to read and do arithmetic. He didn't even try to hide his passion for poetry. His name was Auctus Tullius Sextus, but his comrades had given him the nickname "Plato".

When he saw his commander standing before him, he showed himself ready to listen. His face was focused.

"Legionary..." the centurion reprimanded him.

Auctus Tullius Sextus, aka Plato, jumped to his feet. "Yes, Centurion!" he remembered to say.

"Start writing, there's no time to lose. Send a messenger to Ravenna for the magister militum. Report the advance of the barbarians and request the intervention of the imperial army stationed in Southern Gaul as quickly as possible," Aristarchos Themistocles ordered. He then gave in to a moment of despair, reflecting to himself that it was likely the Southern Gaul army no longer existed.

However, it remained possible that whoever was governing the Empire at the moment would have kept an army in the Italian Peninsula, without which it would be impossible to demonstrate any authority.

The young man immediately set to work, writing on a scrap of parchment. Partly to follow the order, and partly because he understood the gravity of the news, which terrified him to death.

Exiting the principia, Aristarchos Themistocles sighed, resigned and bitter. Still lost in thought, he felt that it was very likely that the messenger, even if he managed to reach the capital of the Empire, would find neither a court nor a magister militum. He knew the sacred palace was the center of gossip regarding the Emperor, who loved luxury and surrounded himself with eunuchs and sly, incompetent politicians.

As if that weren't enough, conspiracies were a daily occurrence, and often the spies working for the Emperor were also working for the conspirators.

However, he thought, sending a request for help was an attempt that had to be made, though not to be pinned with all hopes.

Without realizing it, absorbed in his thoughts, he found himself at the door of the governor's palace. A ceremonial official invited him in and allowed him to skip the usual long wait, which was strange.

The palace's environment clashed with the reality beyond its walls. There was a certain opulence maintained inside, contrasting with the hunger visible on the faces of the people. The gracious concession of skipping the wait was possible only because the terrible news of the barbarian forces' presence had already reached within those walls; otherwise, his wait would have been much longer, as it often was.

Waiting to greet him in a room decorated with multicolored marbles with white veining was Governor Attilius Faticus, who nervously tapped his knee. The worry was clear on his face, but it wasn't concern for the people of Duro Catalaunum; it was for his own wealth and possessions.

Fortunately, seated on a wooden chair with intricate inlays on its extended backrest was Bishop Calibertus, who was plucking Egyptian dates off a glass tray.

Seeing him, Aristarchos felt relieved: he would be heard by both authorities at once. He took a deep breath to appear calm. Only the Almighty could know how much he despised both of them, and this was a circumstance he had never imagined he'd face: barbarians at the gates, and two foolish, arrogant, powerful men to whom he had to explain there was no escape.

At least he wouldn't have to waste time going to the curia to report to the high clergy.

What happened next was incredible. The bishop jumped to his feet, and as soon as he noticed the obvious attention of those present, he began to invoke the Blessed and Holy Virgin to protect the good Christians. Then he recited the passage from the Testament concerning the Great Flood, making sure to draw parallels with the current situation, entrusting all hope to heaven.

When he finished that dramatic performance, Bishop Calibertus sat back down, imperiously gesturing for a servant to bring him some cider.

Finally, as if he were a spectator at a play, he assumed a comfortable position, waiting for the performance to begin.

The performance, needless to say, was the report from the commander of the *vexillationes*.

Thus, Aristarchos Themistocles began to explain in great detail the situation and how he might contain it. But when he had finished, the response he received greatly irritated him. In fact, it devastated and disgusted him to the point that he barely restrained himself from throwing himself at those two insipid individuals and slitting their throats. For a moment, he imagined the scene and took pleasure in it.

The bishop, after listening with his white-gloved hands clasped, stated that faith would protect them from barbarian attacks and that any contrary thought would be akin to blasphemy. He was certain that there would be nothing to fear if every citizen of Duro Catalaunum went to church to beg for forgiveness for their sins and promise charity.

Aristarchos avoided responding, even going so far as to bite his lip. He simply sighed in discouragement, aware that debating with such a fool would lead nowhere.

The commander placed more trust in the governor's opinion, or at least hoped to convince him to follow his proposals. Unfortunately, this was not the case.

Attilius Faticus arrogantly assumed the role of a diplomatic expert. He believed that if he sent messengers to the barbarian leaders, promising adequate rewards and substantial gifts, they would abandon their plans to sack the city.

The protests of the centurion *primae spatha*, aimed at persuading him to abandon such futile ideas, were of no use. These proposals would only encourage the barbarians to plunder and destroy.

It would be like revealing the impotence of the city's defenses, showing the enemy that no army would come to oppose them.

The governor became so irritated that he threatened to personally speak with the magister militum, the commander of the army of Gaul, to arrange for exemplary punishment to be inflicted on him.

Aristarchos Themistocles decided to end that absurd conversation and stiffened into a military salute, pretending to bow to the governor's will.

But he did not immediately take his leave. Instead, he decided to make one last attempt and insisted a bit on the fact that there was probably no longer a magister militum or even an imperial army.

But this last attempt, too, was unconvincing.

Defeated, the commander turned and crossed the hall with long strides, hearing the muttered comments of the bishop and the governor behind him.

He cursed the fate that had allowed such people to reach those positions, before giving in to a moment of despair. Having participated in many campaigns and fought in countless battles, he had gained enough experience to foresee the trouble they were in.

The barbarians would not only conquer the city, but would also commit unspeakable slaughter and seize everything of value.

From their passage, only rubble, corpses, and columns of smoke would remain.

Once outside the palace, the commander headed to the barracks with a determined step.

The gloomy air betrayed a certain disgust; those who knew him well understood that it was always the same whenever he encountered the governor. With a heavy heart, he tried to find a solution to the unfortunate condition not only of his soldiers, but also of the city's inhabitants. Unfortunately, every thought dissolved in the face of the only certainty: they would all die.

When the soldiers saw him approach, they quickly passed the word to one another, so that within minutes they were all in formation, wearing their loricae over purple tunics, their focale tightly fastened around their necks, helmets under their right arms, and swords at their waists.

Vatinius Auruncus approached him: "Centurion..."

Without even looking at him and continuing his swift pace, Aristarchos Themistocles passed by, forcing him to turn quickly to follow his lead.

"Prepare the men. Let them sleep, eat, and always be ready, as if the assault could happen at any moment. Given the fortifications of this city, it's almost certain they will attack from the eastern side, where the walls thin and stretch out. So, keep them ready for possible sorties from the *porta dextra*[18], allowing us to strike the flanks of their troops, which will also buy us enough time to maneuver the maniples within the walls."

Vatinius Auruncus saw him quicken his pace, furious. He understood immediately what the centurion *primae spatha* meant. He had served with him in the Imperial army during the Battle of Arles and knew his tactics. He appreciated his tendency to exhaust the enemy with flank attacks before launching the frontal assault.

He also knew that when Aristarchos Themistocles was nervous, just before battle, he fell into a foul mood and was utterly irritable.

"Honor of Rome!" was Vatinius Auruncus' only response.

"Honor of Rome..." came the bitter reply, already distant.

He advanced, fighting off a blast of icy wind that cut through him, finally threading his way among the ranks of the soldiers, who shuddered.

When he appeared on the ramparts of the city walls, Aristarchos Themistocles realized that the night ahead would be an extremely cold one. Small clouds of condensation billowed from his mouth with each breath. The lit braziers did little to warm the air, and the soldiers on guard were frozen stiff with the cold.

He gestured to a soldier, who immediately sprang into action, signaling that he would carry out the order he was about to receive.

"Find Centurion Antoninus Tacitus and tell him to come to me."

The legionary disappeared along the walkway. A few minutes later, he returned with Antoninus Tacitus, who wore his helmet askew and scratched at his rough beard.

"Command me, Centurion!" he greeted, before coughing and spitting up phlegm.

"Organize guard shifts, no more than two hours at a time. Tonight, the temperature will drop sharply, and the soldiers

---

[18] *Porta dextra:* The *porta principalis dextra.* In Roman urban planning, this gate was located at the end of the *cardo maximus* (main north-south road).

won't be able to stand watch properly if they're frozen solid, not to mention the risk of frostbite."

Antoninus Tacitus nodded.

"When the time comes, use the archers from the Balearic Islands. Let them unleash a hail of arrows when the moment arrives..." he looked him straight in the eye.

Those last words made Antoninus Tacitus flinch. "Alright. I understand," he said, "...I truly understand."

The two men stared at each other for a long while until Antoninus Tacitus voiced his fears. "Commander, when will they attack?"

"Probably sooner than we think. We need to be ready, and when the time comes, we must sell our lives dearly."

"I...I heard about the 5th Ironclad Legion. Are there any survivors?"

"As far as we know, no. But we can't say for sure. If there are any, they're probably heading south to seek refuge in Gaul. I'd have done the same if I had been in that situation."

Antoninus Tacitus shook his head without trying to hide the despair that clutched his gut. When he looked up, he asked, "And the Imperial army?"

The centurion of the first cohort was determined to be honest: "No one is coming to save us. We shouldn't count on it, I'm sorry," he concluded, giving the centurion a firm slap on the shoulder, forcing his legs to remain steady despite the terror rising in his chest.

When it was clear that nothing more needed to be said, Antoninus Tacitus stiffened and slammed his fist against his lorica's chest.

"Honor of Rome!" said the commander, who would now prepare the city's defense.

"Honor of Rome!" was the reply from the centurion assigned to guard the ramparts.

***

Back in his *cubiculum*[19], Aristarchos Themistocles removed his cloak and placed it on a stool. He examined it, noting that the edges were worn, and the lower part was frayed in several places. Next, he took off his armor and set it on the floor. A slight dent reminded him of a blow from a Herulian that had nearly killed him at Arles. He unlaced the chinstrap of his helmet, pulling it off with both hands. The leather lining inside was worn, making him think that his discharge was near, something he would have achieved with the usual honors—if not for the fact that he probably wouldn't live to see the next spring.

He removed his neck cloth and slid off his short tunic and trousers. Finally, he took off his hobnailed boots. He collapsed onto his bed, trying to reflect. The barbarians were very close; he was sure of it. Most likely, the coming night would be the last peaceful one for Duro Catalaunum.

He called for his servant, asking him to bring some mead. Then he requested the presence of Placidia, the kitchen servant, with whom he had a far more intimate relationship. Despite trying to deceive himself, maintaining some emotional distance due to his rank, he loved her.

And not only that—he respected her. Although she had been his war prize, captured after he suppressed a rebellion of the Thuringii by killing their leader, her husband, she had never shown any resentment toward him. Quite the opposite. After an initial period of distrust, Placidia—whose real name had been Kungian before being Romanized—had even shown a certain complicity, never appearing submissive. Instead, she exhibited a combative temperament, at times even forceful.

And when she disagreed with any of his decisions, she pointed it out boldly, unconcerned with any punishment. That was what he admired most about her—the ability to stand up to him in any situation.

---

[19] *Cubiculum:* A room or lodging.

One day, the second after the calends of September, their relationship grew even closer. He remembered it well, as though it had happened just a moment ago. He remembered it like one remembers the most pleasant moments of life. Placidia was preparing the fire where she would cook a slice of wild boar stuffed with honey and figs when he entered the kitchen to check that everything was in order. He couldn't help but notice her for what she truly was: a woman so captivating that she even imposed herself in his dreams.

He saw her rummaging through spice containers and handling sharp knives with ease as she sliced through the meat. The tunic, cinched at the waist, struggled to hide her generous, alluring curves. When she noticed him, Placidia felt embarrassed, but quickly tried to suppress it. After all, he was the master, and she was the slave.

It was then that he ordered her to follow him to his quarters, and there he undressed her, his eyes fixed on her, despite the strong urge to avert his gaze. Placidia never stopped looking at him, like an untamed beast ready to strike. He guided her, placing his hands on her shoulders, until she was lying down.

At first, he was perplexed by her expression, devoid of any emotion. She showed neither hatred nor resentment, nor pleasure or desire. He felt the desire to possess her, but decided against it. Frustrated by her lack of involvement, he kept her in his bed for the rest of the night.

It seemed strange, yet almost absurdly, he felt desired by her. An odd sensation, considering she was a slave who would obey any of his wishes simply because of her position. Yet, he couldn't shake the feeling that she desired him. How could that be? he wondered.

Since that time, it became frequent for the two to make love, and not infrequently, it was Placidia who initiated it. However, that evening was different.

Placidia came to him with a serious expression, more concerned than curious: "What has become of the glory of Rome, soldier?" she asked.

She was an intelligent woman, and her gaze suggested that some rumor had made her realize how dire the situation in Duro Catalaunum had become.

"Little, it seems..." He lowered his gaze. "Very little, my dear Placidia," was his only reply.

She then approached him and took a small cup filled with scented oil, which she used to massage his shoulders, attempting to ease the tension that had built up. As her warm hands moved, she focused on the scars, the indelible marks of past campaigns.

"Placidia?"

"What?"

"Nothing..."

Perhaps this would be their last night together. He didn't want to ruin it with foolish words.

Late at Night (around 23:20)

The legionary rubbed his cold, aching hands over his closed eyes, trying to resist sleep. When he opened them again, he noticed several men emerging from the fog that hung over the land, enveloping everything. Within seconds, there were already hundreds of them. They were attacking.

He raised the alarm by waving his torch, and soon a dozen more torches began to wave from various positions along the ramparts.

The centurion of the first cohort was woken by a soldier already in battle gear.

"Centurion, the barbarians..."

He silenced him with a gesture of his hand.

"You're already wearing your armor..." he cleared his throat. "They must be very close. Run, check the *dormitories*[20], make sure everyone is ready, then go to the other centurions and tell them

[20] *Dormitories:* Small sleeping quarters.

I want them in battle gear immediately! Tell the horn players to sound the alarm before it's too late."

The soldier turned to run and carry out the order, but a strong grip clutched his forearm.

"That's not all. Finally, go through the streets and recruit as many citizens as you can. Set up a guard at the granaries. I don't want any scavengers inside these walls. They must arm themselves with whatever they can: pitchforks, sickles, stones, anything. Now go!" the centurion commanded, slapping him on the shoulder.

The legionary gave a martial salute and disappeared, determined to carry out his task.

When Aristarchos Themistocles appeared on the ramparts, all the soldiers fell silent. Ignoring them, he advanced, finding Centurion Antoninus Tacitus arguing animatedly with some soldiers. He was nervously scratching his beard. The archers had already been stationed along the entire perimeter of the walls. At their feet were dozens of bundles of arrows, the tips having been sharpened in advance.

The soldiers' gazes were all directed toward the thicket, from which groups of mercenaries were still emerging. Their faces were tense, as taut as their nerves.

"Commander..." Antoninus Tacitus greeted the arrival of his superior, his crested helmet already tight around his neck. He stepped aside to allow him a broader view of the walls.

"Centurion... How many?" Aristarchos asked simply, pointing beyond the walls with his knotted *vitis*[21], weathered by time.

"You can see for yourself, Aristarchos. At least seven thousand... and that's just the vanguard. The rest of the army, optimistically speaking, will take at least another day to arrive."

It was true. The barbarian army, made up of Goths, Thuringians, Alans, and Heruli, numbered at least fifteen thousand warriors. And that was just the soldiers, not counting their families, mer-

---

[21] *Vitis*: the command staff used by centurions in the Roman army.

chants, and others who had decided to join the massive migrating federation of people.

The legionaries began to hear the murmurs and strange noises produced by the enormous human mass in motion. It was like a vast breath, ominous and unsettling. The heartbeat of an army made up of thousands of cutthroat mercenaries.

Aristarchos Themistocles pressed his lips together. If they were lucky, the siege would last no more than a week. They wouldn't hold out longer than that. And no reinforcements were coming.

He reminded himself that the Fifth Legion had been completely wiped out, and the messengers probably wouldn't have made it to Ravenna. Or, in the unlikely event the dispatch had arrived, the Emperor wouldn't have had time to send the Imperial Army. Of course, assuming there was still an army. Or an Emperor.

They were doomed, and he knew it, but he was determined: they would sell their lives dearly. Or perhaps, they could negotiate with the enemy. The latter was more a product of his hope to survive than a realistic expectation. He considered himself foolish for having thought that.

He shook his head slightly, trying to dismiss the ominous thoughts. Just thinking about what awaited the people of Duro Catalaunum sent a shiver of sorrow through his body.

Two hours later, Governor Attilius Faticus and Bishop Calibertus made their appearance on the ramparts. The governor's guard kept the soldiers at a distance, as if there were any danger to him within these walls. The legionaries and archers had no interest in him. It was merely a theatrical performance.

Antoninus Tacitus didn't hide his sneer when he saw the bishop trembling like a leaf, supported by a skinny advisor with protruding teeth. The centurion's expression turned to disdain when his gaze landed on the governor, who, in addition to wearing an extravagant robe, had made sure to present himself with painted eyes.

"Attilius is made up like a courtesan," he muttered.

The first centurion laughed. "He must want to charm them... who knows?"

Antoninus Tacitus touched his testicles as if checking whether they were still there.

The newcomers, after taking a quick look over the walls, stepped aside, whispering among themselves. The result of their hasty consultation was the sending of a messenger to request a truce from the besiegers in exchange for the city's wealth.

Displaying an unexpected and ultimately futile boldness, it was Bishop Calibertus who volunteered as the envoy, convinced that his diplomatic skills would save the souls of Duro Catalaunum.

Centurion Antoninus Tacitus made an attempt to dissuade this reckless decision, using the best arguments at his disposal: "Your Excellency, if we send a messenger before the assault, they'll think we can't defend ourselves and it will give them the belief that they can crush us like ants, without much effort. Consult with the centurion *primae spatha*; his experience, gained from many campaigns, will help in your—"

"Silence!" Attilius Faticus, his face contorted with rage, interrupted him. With the corners of his mouth foaming, he stood before him threateningly. "Should I perhaps seek advice from a centurion? From someone of lower rank than mine?"

The centurion opened his mouth, hoping to respond, but was once again interrupted. "If I didn't value the presence of every Christian soul in this dire time for all of us, I would have had your tongue hung at the city's entrance to serve as a warning for everyone."

With these words, two of his *bucellarii*[22] stepped forward, gripping the hilts of their swords, ready to carry out any of their lord's orders. The sound of metal made it clear that a legionary had already drawn his gladius from its sheath, ready to defend the centurion if needed.

"Which of you wants to lose your head first?" Ulzio Dacianus' voice was flat, but his tone was unmistakably clear.

---

[22] *Bucellarii:* A private militia serving as bodyguards, often comprised of barbarian mercenaries, loyal to influential figures.

However, the two bucellarii didn't fully understand his threat. Both were of Gothic origin, and Latin was a language they didn't grasp well.

With a gesture, Antoninus Tacitus ended the tense situation. This was not the time to bicker on the walls.

"Every decision you make is unquestionable and correct, my lord," he muttered through gritted teeth.

Upon hearing these words, Governor Attilius Faticus turned away angrily, muttering something under his breath. He signaled for his men to lower their weapons.

He and Bishop Calibertus descended the stairs, continuing the consultation they had started.

As soon as they disappeared from sight, the centurion spat on the ground and farted.

Aristarchos took his leave with a chuckle, disappearing behind a small building.

When word spread through the fortified village about the intentions arising from the common agreement between the governor and the bishop, the citizens, seized with despair, sought to hide their possessions wherever they could. They buried them, bricked up walls, sealed tombs, and employed various other methods.

The women hurried to the church dedicated to the martyr Modestinus[23] and to other chapels within the walls, praying for the city to be spared from plunder.

The centurion Vatinius Auruncus cast his gaze over his century, carefully observing his legionaries. A light gust of wind stirred the transverse crest of his helmet. His glance could inspire courage in the face of adversity, but also strike fear into his enemies, who quickly realized he was a formidable obstacle to overcome.

---

[23] *Modestinus the Martyr*: Born in 245 CE in Antioch, he became a bishop and was arrested during Diocletian's persecution of Christians. In 311 CE, he was martyred at Praetorium of Mercogliano (AV), burned to death with heated armor.

Positioned at his side, outside the formation, stood the standard-bearer Gallienus Lars[24] Gracchus, a veteran of countless battles. Like many soldiers of the Duro Catalaunum garrison, he had fought in the infamous Battle of Arles under Emperor Majorianus. The scars on his arms—and one in particular that slashed across his cheek—bore testimony to his valor. He was the kind of man who would never back down, no matter the odds.

Rumors circulated among the ranks that he descended from Etruscan ancestors, who had passed on to him extraordinary knowledge. This much was true: he had Etruscan roots, though he was taken in as a boy in Minturnae, after his family arrived there aboard a dromon laden with jars of olive oil.

It was not uncommon to catch him performing mysterious rites, rituals undoubtedly rooted in ancient traditions. Such practices could have placed him in grave danger if any spy had reported his behavior directly to the bishop. Yet no one dared betray him—his intimidating demeanor was enough to quell any thoughts of treachery.

Some even accused him of murdering a presbyter under mysterious circumstances. The man's body had been found among the ruins of an old pagan temple. Whispers claimed the presbyter was a spy for Bishop Calibert, and the soldiers of Germanic origin—most of whom followed the Arian[25] faith—rejoiced in the rumor.

Within the century, Gallienus Lars Gracchus had assumed an almost sacred aura. In the heat of battle, it was not unusual to see him plant the staff of the eagle standard firmly into the ground

---

[24] *Lars:* An Etruscan term that likely referred to a title of nobility or social prominence.

[25] *Arianism:* A belief system established by Arius (c. 256–336), a priest of Alexandria. It denied the divinity of Christ and asserted the Son's subordination to the Father. This was the predominant religion among Germanic peoples such as the Burgundians, Ostrogoths, Vandals, Goths, Lombards, and Visigoths.

and charge into the fray, skewering any enemy in his path. There was no doubt he was a critical presence in combat.

When the youngest centurion of Duro Catalaunum, Vatinius Auruncus, approached him, Gallienus' face broke into a smile, the scar on his cheek stretching wide.

"Hold it high, my brother, so that all may draw courage from it," Vatinius said.

"I'd rather ram it up the backside of those barbarians—if you wouldn't have me flogged for it! This time, though, don't leave me holding this golden bird. Let me carve up a few of those mangy dogs. I promise to gift you their parts when I'm done," Gallienus replied with a hearty laugh.

"Save those for the tavern wenches you frequent. They couldn't expect much else from you!" the centurion shot back, gripping Gallienus' neck in a firm clasp.

Gallienus' grin widened, clearly pleased with the retort.

Vatinius' gaze then shifted to the optio, Severinus Majorianus, who stared ahead as if fixated on infinity, silent and deeply focused.

Nicknamed the "iron core" of the century for his lengthy service, he was among the strongest veterans of the Roman army. He was the kind of man capable of mounting an improbable defense of a camp surrounded by barbarians and set ablaze, as he had done in Arles some time before.

"This time will be tough," Vatinius said, stepping in front of the optio and locking eyes with him.

The optio, a seasoned soldier, barely flinched. "Then we'll die on the field of honor, Centurion."

"I wouldn't want to be in your enemies' shoes," replied the centurion, already heading toward the center of the formation, his eyes scanning his legionaries as they all fixed their gaze on a precise point ahead—all, except one.

Fulcinius Agricola Statius prayed silently to the pagan gods he worshipped, murmuring incantations and supplications for protection. He, too, hailed from the Aurunci Mountains, where he had grown up until he was conscripted, like nearly all his companions. He had a wife and a son he longed to return to after receiving his *honesta missio*[26], his honorable discharge.

He had met his wife in Arles and married her while on a long leave to recover from battle wounds. Now, she and their child lived in Vescinae, along the Liris River, and he yearned to rejoin them. He dreamed of starting a construction business, as his military campaigns had taught him to make architecture an art, both for fortifications and homes. No frontier fort had been built without his contribution.

Still, everyone knew he'd settle for any activity that matched his resolute nature; refinement was not his forte. He was infamous for burping loudly during a religious service, earning himself a flogging from Bishop Calibert.

But such were the veterans: men hardened by steel, chaos, screams, and blood, accustomed to marching side by side with death. They were not the ones Vatinius Auruncus worried about. It was the fresh recruits in his century, many of whom had never faced a real battle, that concerned him.

Among them was Auctus Tullius Sextus, nicknamed "Plato," facing only his second battle. His nervousness tightened his features, but he methodically adjusted his belt and ensured his helmet was securely fastened under his chin. Looking up, he saw the crest of the centurion moving among the upright javelins, approaching until it loomed directly before him.

Plato stiffened, trying to appear more martial than he truly felt. His unruly curls had already made him the subject of sighs from the matrons of Duro Catalaunum.

Vatinius Auruncus planned to address the inexperienced soldiers. He saw their pale faces, alabaster-like, motionless and rigid under the century's banner. Just as he was about to speak, the legionaries' attention shifted upward. Heads turned toward the walls.

---

[26] *Honesta missio:* An honorable discharge from the army.

The shouted orders from officers above made one thing clear: the barbarian mercenaries were advancing closer. The assault was imminent.

Realizing time was short, Vatinius Auruncus positioned himself before his century. The crest of his helmet towered above his men.

"Soldiers."

Not a sound was heard.

"You bastards!"

A murmur of laughter rippled through the formation.

"We've fought countless times during our careers in the legions. And yet, look at yourselves now..." He paused, ensuring he had everyone's attention.

"With rare exceptions, you barely know the comrade standing beside you. You come from every corner of the Empire, gathered here from disbanded legions—remnants of an Empire in decay."

His words were heavy, especially for men who were likely about to meet their fate for that very Empire. But his point was different, and he made it clear.

"This time, we fight for ourselves. Thousands of barbarians are pouring against the walls of this damned, forgotten city at the edge of an Empire that now exists only in the minds of bureaucrats and eunuchs who've destroyed the Rome that once was. The only reason we'll survive is the soldier at our side."

Many laughed at the sarcasm, catching his tone.

"This will be the battle that makes us masters of our own lives. We'll earn a place in Hades—or freedom as men!"

A few protested at his mention of Hades; the growing Christian faith, spread since Constantine's time, now dominated even among the soldiers. They believed in one great God who ruled over men, offering paradise, not Hades.

Vatinius Auruncus ignored the muttered objections and raised his voice over the devout murmurs.

"Out there, thousands of mercenaries eager to feast on our guts have set a trap for us, and will attack until we're worn down.

Unfortunately for them, they found us waiting—true Romans. I almost feel sorry for them..." His expression turned sardonic.

More laughter erupted.

"When the time comes, I'll ask one thing of you—just one. A single, resolute act. Form a wall of shields that will make those savages realize they're facing warriors without pity. They'll see they have the misfortune of confronting the strongest soldiers alive—the legionaries of the Third Century!"

The soldiers roared, javelins raised: "Third! Third! Third!"

Vatinius Auruncus surveyed his century with a satisfied glance, his face set in a daring grin.

"Be ready...be ready," he muttered to himself.

The Entrance of Duro Catalaunum, Tertia vigilia[27]

The scene that unfolded carried a bleakly comedic tone. Bishop Calibertus, dressed in his finest ecclesiastical robes to inspire awe in the barbarians, approached the city gates accompanied by a procession of deacons and servants.

The guards hesitated to open the massive doors until Centurion Antoninus Tacitus grumbled out the order amidst muttered curses and insults directed at the cleric. The small procession stepped out toward the vanguard of the invaders, who halted in astonishment.

Despite warnings from the centurion *primae spatha*, the bishop had decided to mediate personally, showing unexpected courage—perhaps believing that the barbarians would spare him if he could offer gold and riches without bloodshed.

The gates closed behind the diplomatic cortege, leaving them exposed to the barbarian vanguard stationed only a few hundred meters from the walls. A barbarian warrior knelt, feigning reverence for Bishop Calibertus, who began waving his hands

---

[27] *Tertia vigilia*: from midnight to 3:00 AM.

in solemn gestures, making the sign of the cross as if invoking divine protection.

The barbarian shouted something unintelligible at the Romans, in a tone that seemed mocking. The centurion *primae spatha* squinted, watching the scene with sharp focus, while the legionaries on the walls observed silently. Some relayed what they saw to those waiting below.

Meanwhile, Governor Attilius Faticus, standing at the battlements, was approached by his servant, who whispered something in his ear. Judging by the governor's suddenly relaxed expression, the message must have been reassuring—likely confirming the safety of his hidden treasures.

Tacitus sneered in disdain, muttering a comment loud enough for the governor to hear, who glared back with fury. Ignoring the governor's wrath, Tacitus returned his attention to the unfolding spectacle below.

"Give me permission to slit his throat and toss him beyond the walls," Tacitus quipped, half-serious.

Aristarchos Themistocles chuckled. "Let the Thuringians have him. They know some delightful torture techniques."

Tacitus gave a sideways glance. "I'd rather save them the trouble."

"Save your breath—you'll need it when you're barking orders to your archers," replied Aristarchos dismissively.

By the time Bishop Calibertus reached the Heruli warriors, he realized the grave mistake he had made. These men did not appear inclined toward negotiation.

With a trembling hand, he signaled to his interpreter—a Heruli slave he had bought at the Mogontiacum[28] markets—to step forward and translate his words.

At that moment, a group of mercenaries pushed through the Heruli ranks, shoving aside their own men with brutal force. They

---

[28] *Mogontiacum:* A Roman fortress and later fortified town, slightly north of Argentoratum, corresponding to the modern German city of Mainz.

were the personal guard of Rudulfus, leader of the Heruli tribes, and they positioned themselves in front of the bishop.

The most distinguished among them, a general, took a few steps toward Calibertus, listening to the proposal with what patience he could muster. As the slave finished translating the bishop's plea, a tense silence fell over the scene.

The general stroked his beard thoughtfully, feigning deep contemplation, before bursting into uproarious laughter. Without warning, he swung his double-headed axe in a diagonal arc, cleaving the interpreter in half. The slave crumpled to the ground, lifeless.

The general crouched to scoop up the man's entrails with his bare hand, then hurled them into the bishop's face. Calibertus recoiled, whimpering.

As if on cue, the Heruli mercenaries launched themselves at the bishop's entourage, slaughtering them mercilessly. The screams of agony reached the fortifications, where Tacitus struggled to suppress his fury.

One Heruli mercenary drew a dagger and gouged out the eyes of a young deacon, who staggered to his feet, blind and wailing, blood streaming from his empty sockets. Stumbling and reaching out for aid, he received only jeers, shoves, and spit from the barbarians. Another barbarian triumphantly brandished the severed head of the interpreter, while others busied themselves disemboweling an elderly priest pinned to the ground.

"Oh God... Oh God..." muttered Governor Faticus, his wide eyes fixed on the carnage below.

Amidst the massacre, Bishop Calibertus emerged, crawling on all fours. The barbarians took turns kicking him, laughing cruelly as they kept him from escaping. The sight infuriated Tacitus, who swore so loudly that one Heruli turned to shout something obscene in their own tongue.

At that moment, Rudulfus himself rode into view atop a warhorse. He raised a hand, instantly silencing his men. It was clear he commanded deep respect, earned through countless battles.

Aristarchos Themistocles regarded him with a flash of grudging admiration.

The Heruli leader dismounted, drew a dagger from a deerskin sheath, and, gripping the head of a slain priest, sliced out its tongue. Holding the bloody trophy, he approached the cowering bishop, who averted his gaze.

Two warriors growled and forced Calibertus to stand, gripping his head and making him watch. Rudulfus extended the severed tongue to the bishop and said, in passable Latin, "Take this to the commander of the city's garrison. Tell him to surrender now, or his tongue will be next when I'm done with his legionaries."

Calibertus nodded frantically, trembling so violently that he urinated on himself. He could not summon words; fear had stolen his voice.

"Go now, before I change my mind," Rudulfus growled.

Clutching the grisly relic, Calibertus staggered back toward the city, barely able to take one step after another.

Rudulfus turned his gaze toward Aristarchos Themistocles, as if he had already discerned him to be the Roman *vexillatio* commander left to defend the city.

He raised the blood-stained dagger and shouted in Latin, "Where are the legions now?" before bursting into laughter that echoed among his men. Moments later, a roar of laughter erupted from the vanguard of the barbarian army.

The taunts of the Heruli greatly irritated the centurion *primae spatha*, who glanced down and caught the eye of Vatinius Auruncus. A single look was enough to signal him to ready the Third Century. With steady, practiced movements, the young centurion tightened the chinstrap of his crested helmet. His eyes shielded by the cheek pieces, he looked at the hilt of his gladius, gripping it firmly, reflecting briefly on the many battles he had fought with that blade.

The shouts and jeers of the Heruli and other mercenaries from beyond the walls shook him out of his reverie. He fixed his gaze on his soldiers and bellowed, "Today, for us legionaries of the

Third, it will be toil, valor, and honor. Legionaries of the Third Century..." His men listened with rapt attention, their nerves taut as if ready to snap like the strings of a lyre.

"Third Century, prepare for battle!"

The optio Severinus Majorianus echoed the order, ensuring that every soldier had heard it, then fastened his own helmet securely beneath his chin. The legionaries of the Third Century stood rigid and fearsome, ready for the fight.

Meanwhile, the bishop's journey to the city's massive wooden gate was fraught with torment. Heruli archers began firing arrows in his direction, not aiming to hit him, but to mock him. With uncanny precision, their arrows struck the ground between his legs, pinning his fine robes to the earth and forcing him to tear them to continue forward.

At last, as he neared the gate, the hapless man was overcome by convulsions and collapsed, sobbing and curling into himself. A group of priests rushed out to console him. Seeing this, some enemy archers resumed firing, ostensibly for sport, but one arrow struck the bishop in the back, killing him instantly.

Rudulfus himself approached the offending archer and impaled him with his own sword. "Did I not command that he be left alive?" he growled.

Immediately, the city guards slammed the massive gates shut, securing them with a heavy crossbar.

The fragile truce afforded by the bishop's ill-fated mission was shattered by the chilling war cries of the barbarian vanguard, their voices slicing through the air like a blade. Aristarchos Themistocles donned his helmet, the brass-rimmed cheek pieces gleaming, and issued his first orders, firm and unequivocal.

"Antoninus Tacitus, prepare the archers..."

But the order was hardly necessary. The archers under Tacitus' command were already swiftly stringing their bows and adjusting the fletching on their arrows.

The assault was imminent.

The legionaries were prepared.

***

Rudulfus summoned his officers and issued precise commands to commence the siege. As his troops took their positions, reinforcements of Alani and Thuringian warriors emerged from the nearby woods.

Apprehension gripped the defenders atop the walls; it was palpable. Rudulfus, still mounted, waited for the other commanders to arrive. They conferred for what felt like an eternity. When their deliberations concluded, each commander returned to their respective forces.

Irritated by the tension, Rudulfus' warhorse began to rear and kick. After calming the beast, the Heruli leader raised his right arm skyward.

And silence fell.

It was as if the gesture had cast a spell, silencing thousands of barbarians now poised for a bloodbath. Time seemed to stand still.

When his arm dropped, the thunderous roar of battle cries and the pounding of thousands of feet shook the earth and sent a chill through the hearts of the Roman defenders.

The centurion *primae spatha* Aristarchos Themistocles shot a glare at Antoninus Tacitus, who responded by raising his gladius. The Roman archers nocked their arrows and drew their bowstrings taut.

The ground quaked under the advancing barbarians, and their ferocious cries echoed throughout Duro Catalaunum, freezing its citizens in terror. When the attackers came close enough to the walls, Aristarchos gestured to Tacitus, who mentally calculated the distance and gave the order:

"Archers, aim high. Be ready...choose your targets."

The Roman archers held their positions, disciplined and accustomed to waiting for precise commands.

The enemy drew nearer and nearer to the walls.

"Loose!"

The first rank of archers fired their arrows, then stepped aside to make way for a second rank, which immediately unleashed a new volley. The projectiles hissed through the air like serpents, arcing down upon the charging barbarians.

With a series of dull thuds, dozens of attackers fell, while others scrambled for cover behind shields of every shape and hue. Yet the Roman arrows pierced even the smallest gaps in their wooden defenses, driving into flesh and felling more of the assailants.

Since being entrusted with the defense of the walls, Antoninus Tacitus had meticulously devised strategies to fulfill his duty. At a distance of roughly twenty paces from the walls, he had arranged piles of stones to serve as aiming markers for the archers. He had even salvaged an old ballista abandoned by the Legion, its waterlogged wheels rendering it immobile. Tacitus had ordered it reassembled atop the walls, but intended to hold it in reserve for the opportune moment.

"Fire high!" he shouted again.

More arrows whistled hungrily through the air, plummeting into the enemy ranks, halting their advance as they fell, pierced and lifeless.

Among the Roman archers stood a woman, Vunxa. Initially unwelcome because of her Celtic origins, she had earned her place by bringing down a stag for roasting, becoming a sort of auxiliary to the troops. Skilled beyond measure with a bow, she never missed her mark.

Vunxa's practiced eye locked on her target, deliberately blurring the tip of the arrow to maintain focus on her prey. As her vision converged with precise timing, she loosed the bowstring with expert anticipation. It sang forward, sending the arrow straight into the throat of a Herulian warrior charging with a double-headed axe. His stride stopped abruptly as his legs kicked out from under him, his body collapsing into the mud.

Her free hand had already nocked another arrow, and her dark brown eyes fixed on her next victim. Known as the "Sagittaria", Vunxa earned her title for the icy precision and calm with which she wielded her bow.

She had grown up following the legions, the daughter of a Batavian cavalryman who ended his career in the *vexillatio* at Duro Catalaunum. Her golden hair glimmered beneath the crested helmet she wore, its black horsehair plume trailing behind her. Her torso was encased in a scaled cuirass, leaving her arms free to draw and fire with relentless strength.

One shot after another, her arrows claimed many lives. Around her, volleys from Roman archers spread death and terror among the mercenary ranks, though the relentless hordes still pressed forward. The sheer number of enemies rendered the archers' efforts insufficient to halt the advancing tide of warriors hungry for plunder.

For Centurion Antoninus Tacitus, the time had come to deploy the old ballista. Legionaries worked the cranks to charge the siege weapon, its groaning hinges and creaking beams straining under the tension. They loaded it with stones and timber fragments. A hammer struck the release, and the arm snapped forward, hurling its deadly payload.

A cluster of Herulian warriors charging the walls was obliterated. Limbs and torsos flew apart, scattering gore. One unfortunate fighter was gravely wounded when a severed arm struck him square in the face.

Another barrage of arrows descended on the barbarians, felling more of them. But it was clear that the Roman missiles would not be enough to stop the inexorable surge of thousands.

Watching the carnage from afar, Rudulfus sneered. "Do these Roman sodomites think they can stop us with a few arrows?" He beckoned an officer, who approached swiftly.

"Are your archers ready?" Rudulfus demanded, leaving no room for hesitation.

"They're eager to skewer those flabby Roman hides," the officer replied gruffly.

"Then let loose a rain of Herulian arrows upon them," Rudulfus ordered, unleashing his own archers.

The massacre among the Roman ranks began. The relentless barrage of enemy arrows made it impossible for Roman archers to return fire effectively, forcing them to seek cover while the barbarian forces resumed their advance.

A shaft zipped so close to Antoninus Tacitus that he felt its hiss against his ear. Moments later, another arrow struck the chest of a soldier beside him with a muffled thud. The man collapsed lifelessly.

Cursing under his breath, Tacitus quickly assessed the situation. The enemy was now at the base of the walls, and the archers would no longer suffice to repel them. Without hesitation, the rugged centurion summoned additional maniples of legionaries to reinforce the walkways, preparing to counter any attempts to scale the walls with siege ladders.

Chaos reigned on the parapets and stairs, as some soldiers scrambled to carry out their orders while others evacuated the wounded, shielding them from the relentless hail of arrows. The packed earth behind the curtain wall grew slick with blood, and the cries of the injured echoed through the fortified city's streets.

The barbarian horde's roars, like a deafening thunderclap, froze the blood of the townsfolk. Some prayed to God, others scrambled to bolster makeshift defenses, while a few brought water to the soldiers. The most virtuous among them tended to the wounded.

Aristarchos Themistocles, his crested helmet cinched tightly under his chin, surveyed the scene and realized he had to make a bold move. Two arrows struck the shield of the legionary beside him in rapid succession, and a third pierced the man's throat, killing him instantly.

Struggling to regain control amidst the onslaught of arrows, Themistocles called for Antoninus Tacitus. Raising his voice above the cacophony of battle, he issued an order: "Take command of the First Century! Lead my men and attempt a sortie with Vatinius Auruncus' Third. Your maneuver will buy us time to reorganize the defenses on the walls. When we're ready, I'll give the signal for you to retreat. Now go—before it's too late!"

Tacitus straightened, replying with grim resolve, "For the honor of Rome!"

"For the honor of Rome!" Themistocles echoed.

Descending swiftly from the parapet, Tacitus joined Vatinius Auruncus, his counterpart in the Third Century.

"We're launching a sortie," he announced bluntly.

"Care to elaborate?" Vatinius quipped.

"We're launching a sortie," Tacitus repeated, his tone final.

Vatinius knew Tacitus well enough to recognize his brevity as a sign of urgency. Without further protest, he nodded in agreement.

For many of them, this day would be their last. Perhaps for all of them.

Gallienus Lars Gracchus, the Etruscan standard-bearer, approached Tacitus and whispered, "Are we marching to slaughter? They outnumber us tenfold..."

Tacitus pressed his helmet tighter onto his head. "Gallienus, pray to your Etruscan gods for favor and strength. What we're doing is the only way to slow the barbarians. Take your position and rally the others. A brutal fight awaits us outside those walls."

Gracchus pursed his lips in disapproval but obeyed, slapping the shoulder of young Plato, who was looking skyward in silent prayer for survival.

"Hope you enjoyed some dalliance yesterday," Gracchus joked grimly. "You won't get another chance."

Plato shot him a glare, but said nothing.

He had proven himself reliable in previous skirmishes, but never had he faced odds so dire. This wasn't a battle with evenly matched forces—it was a desperate defense against a foe twenty times their number. Duro Catalaunum had become a death trap.

Fulcinius Agricola Statius gripped the hilt of his gladius tightly, his face twisted into a grimace of determination. He was fighting in yet another battle, a mere replica of countless others he had seen. His task was simple: cut down as many enemies as possible. If he were to fall, he would still earn his place of honor in the Underworld, as befitted a true warrior.

The faces of the legionaries were taut and resolute. Yet, within them, fear gave way to tenacity and a sense of duty.

When the *primae spatha* gave the order from atop the walls, the gates swung open swiftly. Massive timbers creaked as robust, powerful horses pulled them apart. The hinges groaned, the muscular beasts pawing and whinnying in protest.

On the left side of the towering wooden gate, one pair of horses reared up, kicking wildly. Their rippling muscles quivered with irritation as the handlers struggled to restrain them, tugging at the reins to calm their nerves. The beasts snorted and fumed, but at last, the gates stood wide open, revealing the centuries poised to confront the invading barbarians.

Severinus Majorianus, the optio, barely suppressed a curse, while Gallienus Lars Gracchus raised the centurial standard high for all to see, a rallying beacon of courage.

On the other side, the Heruli slowed their advance, puzzled by such an unconventional tactic.

They knew this Roman outpost couldn't possibly house an entire legion. At most, two or three centuries would emerge. Opening the gates in front of thousands of charging enemies seemed a reckless move that demanded caution.

The sentries at the entrance were vigilant, ready to close the gates at the slightest sign of danger.

Then, the First and Third Centuries charged out, taking positions to defend the city.

"Close ranks! Tighten up! Form into position!" barked Antoninus Tacitus to the First Century. The legionaries swiftly fell into formation, locking their shields together in a solid wall.

Vatinius Auruncus simply raised his gladius in the air, and the Third Century lined up behind their shield wall, poised for battle.

With a quick glance, the two centurions silently coordinated their strategy.

As the barbarians resumed their charge, roaring war cries, the centuries suddenly shifted their formation.

"To the testudo! Form the testudo!" Vatinius Auruncus shouted.

"Testudo! Testudo! Testudo!" echoed the optio[29], Severinus Majorianus.

The centuries broke apart, only to reassemble instantly into maniples forming the testudo. The rectangular shield formations protected the legionaries from all sides, even from above—a time-tested tactic of the legions, handed down from the days of the great Caesars.

Though largely abandoned by the modern Roman army, the three centurions stationed at Duro Catalaunum firmly believed that the strategies of Rome's glorious past were still highly effective.

The Heruli were familiar with the testudo formation, often described around campfires. But even so, they underestimated its power, believing the Roman legions no longer posed the fearsome threat of old.

They were wrong.

***

The city gates were sealed shut as the maniples stood motionless, bracing for the overwhelming wave of humanity that would crash against them in mere moments.

"Hold your ground! Stay still, and don't move your shields," growled Vatinius Auruncus to his men. Through a gap in the shields, he watched the enemy's advance.

"Tighten the ranks, soldiers of the First! Let them smash into the wall of courage our shields form. Once they hit, we'll carve them up with our blades. They'll leap onto our shields like grasshoppers, and we'll skewer them!" ordered Antoninus Tacitus to his century.

The ground trembled beneath the legionaries as the Heruli closed in, their bloodlust palpable. Yet the Romans stood firm, bracing themselves for the violent impact. Their resolve was unshaken, almost predatory.

---

[29] *Optio:* A subordinate officer in the Roman army, ranked below the centurion.

At the forefront of the Heruli, Rudulfus urged his warriors to slaughter as he sprinted forward, hurling curses at the Romans. His gaze locked onto the black-and-white transverse crest of the young centurion, Vatinius Auruncus, who met the challenge without flinching, pointing his gladius at the barbarian leader.

The barbarians were now only a few dozen meters from the centuries arrayed for battle. The short distance was all that separated life from death, a gap soon to be filled with screams, the clash of metal, blood, and iron.

Chaos erupted in an instant.

The Heruli crashed into the testudo formations. The impact created a thunderous crackling, like an unrelenting explosion. Shields and armor collided; shouts, curses, and the din of battle filled the air.

The Roman lines held impressively against the assault. Wherever a shield faltered, the centurions swiftly ordered it replaced, keeping the formation tight.

From the walls above, Aristarchos Themistocles watched with satisfaction. Training the centuries in the ancient techniques of Rome's legions had proven worthwhile.

Roman blades darted through the narrow gaps between the shields, cutting down numerous enemies. The Heruli, by contrast, flung themselves at the shielded formations, desperately searching for openings to thrust their weapons, only to find them ill-suited for such an attack.

The legionaries' short swords, on the other hand, were perfectly adapted for this style of combat. Years of grueling training ensured that each soldier knew exactly what the one beside or ahead of them would do, making the formation nearly unbreakable.

The barbarians struck the shields with ferocity, but failed to land any decisive blows. Meanwhile, the Romans ducked low, stabbing under the shields to sever tendons and bring their foes to the ground. Fallen enemies were then crushed with shield-bosses, their faces and skulls shattered.

Rudulfus stared in astonishment. Despite their overwhelming numbers, his forces suffered heavy losses, while the Romans stood resilient.

Yet the battle wasn't going the same way everywhere. Some maniples, especially those at the outer edges, bore the brunt of the barbarian assault and began to falter.

Antoninus Tacitus cut down two warriors to reach the northernmost maniple of his century, which was on the verge of collapsing under the Heruli onslaught.

In that corner, the battle had devolved into close combat, threatening to breach the defensive structure of the Roman formation and allowing the barbarian ranks to pour through. Tacitus couldn't let that happen.

Gathering twenty legionaries, he rushed to reinforce his struggling comrades. Reaching the embattled maniple, the centurion ordered his men into a defensive line with shields raised. Once the maneuver succeeded, the formation began a steady advance, step by step, creating an impenetrable wall of shields against the Heruli, who attacked with every weapon at their disposal, even throwing stones.

Among the legionaries in that line was Drusus Variatus.

Drusus was the son of an *argentarius*[30] from Suessa. His presence in the Roman legions was far from voluntary; he had been conscripted under the levy imposed by Emperor Majorianus. Despite his father's desperate efforts to spare him three years of mandatory service, all attempts had been futile.

Now, facing the barbarian horde, Drusus fought not for any great sense of duty, but simply to stay alive, compelled to defend the whims and commands of an emperor he had never seen—and whose name he barely knew.

Yet, with all the courage he could muster, he fought to protect his comrades' lives.

---

[30] *Argentarius:* A manager of a deposit and loan bank.

Such was the way of the legions. Each soldier was responsible for themselves and for the companion at their side, forging an unbreakable chain of warriors.

A warrior struck his shield forcefully with an axe, but Drusus Variatus stood firm against the blow. The enemy then attempted a downward strike at the legionary's head, a deadly attack that Drusus barely avoided by chance. Realizing the precariousness of his situation, he summoned all his strength and courage, fully aware that as the frontline of the battle, his life was most at risk. Gripping the hilt of his gladius tightly, he maneuvered the blade through the narrow gap between his shield and that of the soldier beside him. Yet his strikes seemed ineffective.

Fortunately, his helmet absorbed the persistent blows from the barbarian, who showed no sign of relenting. Then, almost surprising himself, Drusus saw his shield part to reveal his arm extending forward. The tip of his gladius tore into the Heruli warrior's abdomen. The blade ripped through flesh, and the man's intestines spilled onto the ground. Eyes wide, the barbarian fell to his knees, clutching at his wound. Without hesitation, Drusus fell back into formation, bracing for the next adversary.

Behind him, Gaius Octavianus, the scout, pressed against Drusus' lorica, ensuring he held his position and maintained the line.

"Well done, Drusus Variatus! Well done!" Gaius shouted encouragingly.

As the pressure on the legionaries in the frontline intensified, Centurion Antoninus Tacitus issued the order: "Switch the line! Switch the line!"

The optio echoed the command, striving to make it heard above the din of battle and clashing steel. With precision honed by training, the legionaries at the front pulled back into their maniples, replaced by those in the second rank.

Now face-to-face with the advancing mercenaries, Gaius Octavianus growled through gritted teeth, "Come on, then! For the honor of Rome!"

His sharp gaze, partially obscured by the imperial-style helmet, locked onto a mercenary charging with a long spear—one he had no intention of letting pierce him. Waiting until the foe closed in and believed he had the advantage, Gaius spotted an arrow streaking down from the walls. It struck the Heruli warrior in the clavicle, burying deep into his chest. The man crumpled at Gaius' feet.

Looking up, Gaius caught sight of Vunxa, the markswoman atop the walls, already notching another arrow with a satisfied expression. But the brief respite was short-lived. Three more barbarians were upon him, their long, peculiar swords battering his defenses.

The barbarians had reddish hair tied in braids, their unkempt mustaches marred by dirt. Clad in coarse, dark woolen tunics and chainmail, they radiated menace. One of them, likely an officer, wore a plated cuirass under a crimson cloak, with a conical helmet crowned by a horsehair plume. Barking commands in a harsh and guttural language, he spurred his comrades on.

Gaius parried and countered, yet fatigue gnawed at him. To his side, a legionary was speared through the side and fell face-first into the bloodied ground. Another stepped into his place but was swiftly decapitated.

Realizing the line was faltering, Gaius edged back, careful not to betray the fear tightening in his gut. He shoved one of his attackers back with his shield, only for the others to rain strikes from above. Forced to raise his shield, Gaius left his lower body exposed—a perilous vulnerability.

Desperate, Gaius made a daring move. Dropping low, he crouched beneath his shield just as a strike came down from above. The barbarian's blow missed, striking empty air. Exploiting their brief confusion, Gaius struck. His gladius swept low, slicing through the ankles of two warriors who collapsed, their tendons severed. The third, caught off guard, found the blade plunged into his groin, sealing his fate.

Exhausted, Gaius wavered. His legs felt weak, and he clung to his shield to stay upright. Relief came in the form of a ten-man maniple reinforcing his position, among them the young Plato, dispatched from the Third Century to bolster the embattled flank.

Plato immediately severed the arm of a barbarian attacking Gaius before throwing himself into a vicious duel with another invader. This allowed Gaius a moment to catch his breath, though it was short-lived as a towering warrior charged him.

The ensuing clash was brutal and animalistic, more akin to a gladiatorial bout than a military action. Bloodied and weary, Gaius sustained wounds to his calf and forearm, but refused to yield. When his foe made a critical mistake, arrogantly twirling his blade before delivering a finishing blow, Gaius seized the chance. He flung his shield, disrupting the barbarian's attack and leaving him vulnerable. With one swift motion, Gaius drove his gladius into the warrior's chest, ending the fight.

Drained of all energy, Gaius collapsed face-first onto the blood-soaked earth, the acrid-sweet scent of death overwhelming him.

Plato fought valiantly over his fallen comrade, stepping on Gaius repeatedly as he fended off the enemy. Finally, he managed to drag Gaius to the rear lines.

Nearby, Centurion Antoninus Tacitus had just dispatched several Heruli warriors. He panted heavily, his armor and face smeared with blood, sweat, and dirt. Wiping the blood from his face, he glanced toward the walls and locked eyes with the centurion *primae spatha*, who observed the battle's grim progression.

Antoninus shook his head, signaling that the tide of the battle was turning against them. Then, steeling himself, he returned to the fray, cutting down any enemy within reach.

Despite their fierce resistance, the Romans were vastly outnumbered, and the Heruli pressed relentlessly. Aristarchos Themistocles surveyed the battlefield with a grim expression. The situation was dire, as he had anticipated, yet the legionaries had performed far better than expected.

The First and Third Centuries, deployed in a semicircle with testudo formations, were now besieged. While some sections still held firm, others were beginning to falter under the relentless assault.

The Third Century's formation fared no better than the First. It was locked in bitter clashes. The frontline was faltering, but Centurion Vatinius Auruncus worked tirelessly to pull the ranks back together.

Despite the protection of the front line's shields, a sharp impact struck his helmet. The pain stunned him momentarily until he realized he'd been hit by an arrow. Shooting a fierce glare at Fulcinius Agricola Statius, who should have been covering that side with his shield, he barked:

"Keep that damn shield up!"

"Centurion, I was holding back the *cingulum*[31] of the soldier in front of me..." the legionary offered as a weak excuse.

In truth, Fulcinius Agricola Statius had been too eager to engage the barbarians, lowering his shield to peer ahead and assess the battlefield. The clash of battle was his natural element, and he'd served in Rome's army for many years.

He wouldn't have to wait long to join the fray. The mercenary barbarians pressed so hard that the front ranks began to buckle. In the center of the Third's formation, the maniples were forced to split apart, each engaging in chaotic hand-to-hand combat.

The battle intensified as the barbarians realized they had disrupted the Roman formations. A few steps behind his advancing warriors, Rudulfus, the Herulian leader, stood shouting commands. He was protected by an intricately-crafted cuirass, his left hand holding a shield etched with prayers to the gods, and a long sword gripped in his right. His voice carried over the thunder of thousands of charging feet, issuing orders to smash through the Roman lines and sow chaos.

Rudulfus, seeing his vastly superior numbers, realized the time was ripe to encircle the enemy now that their ranks had broken. He noted the Roman soldiers battling desperately to hold their

---

[31] *Cingulum militaris:* A belt worn by legionaries to hold weapons and often used for decorative purposes.

ground. Raising his eyes to the heavens, he laughed, imagining the gods relishing the Romans' defeat while sipping wine and eating honey-sweet grapes. Meanwhile, he savored the bitter taste of earth, blood, and bile. Victory or defeat now rested solely on his decisions.

Two arrows struck a soldier at his side, toppling him backward with a dull thud that disrupted Rudulfus' musings. More such impacts followed—the Roman archers were still targeting them. Rudulfus glanced toward the walls, spotting a woman with golden hair, radiant like the sun, loosing arrows with speed and precision.

The sight surprised him, though some of his warriors jeered, mocking her with crude gestures. Ignoring them, he quickly calculated how many men he might lose to the arrows—perhaps two hundred, at most, dead or wounded. A small price given his overwhelming strength.

Then, an arrow struck Rudulfus' shield, sending a sharp vibration through his arm. He was now close to the Roman shield wall. There was no time left for calculation. It was time to fight.

The hiss of arrows soared over the Heruli's advancing lines, targeting the Roman rear to avoid friendly fire. The persistent, dull thudding of arrows on armor and shields sounded unnervingly like a butcher's cleaver on meat.

In some places, the mercenaries broke through the lines, causing panic among the soldiers. Elsewhere, the Roman formations held firm, though the continuous pounding of shields left the rear ranks restless.

Vatinius Auruncus observed the Heruli advance, noting its disarray compared to his Third Century. The enemy pressed forward in chaotic clusters, driven by a bloodthirsty frenzy, despite their officers' sharp reprimands.

He seized the moment to act. "Reform ranks! Reform ranks! Close the line—don't move!" he growled, advancing and striking his sword against his soldiers' shields to command their attention. The shield wall had to be reestablished.

As he surveyed the young soldiers' faces, he saw some murmuring prayers, while others twitched nervously. He knew their fear well; he had felt it himself early in his career—a fear not of death, but of pain.

His orders were especially for them, sent to this godforsaken corner of the world to die for a reckless and immoral emperor. The veterans, on the other hand, needed no such guidance. They were seasoned, long accustomed to fear—or perhaps they no longer felt it at all. For them, it was simply a matter of raising their swords and striking the nearest enemy.

A shiver ran through the young centurion as a cold wind swept the grass, rippling through the Third's ranks.

Signifer Gallienus Lars Gracchus held the standard high and proud. The men drew strength, not even from seeing it, but merely sensing its presence. Vatinius Auruncus felt a surge of pride, offering a silent thanks to the heavens.

At that moment, an unexpected and forceful Herulian surge broke through the lines, catching him and the others off guard. Every soldier in the front ranks was now engaged in combat, striving to repel the assault.

Vatinius cursed his luck. Out of the corner of his eye, he noticed the far-right wing of the Roman formation stretching over nearly two stadia, effectively preventing the enemy from executing an encirclement. The crests of the *decurions* stood prominently at the front and rear of every maniple, indicating that this part of the formation had taken the initiative and was counterattacking.

But with that maneuver, the cohesion of the ranks, already severely tested by the barbaric onslaughts, had suffered further.

Not to mention that, in their attempt to keep up with their advancing comrades in the maniples, the legionaries of the unit to his right had also moved forward, leaving that side unguarded.

This recklessness left the soldiers near him dangerously exposed. It was a disadvantageous situation that absolutely needed to be remedied.

The centurion's worried eyes, protected by a helmet smeared with blood and mud, scanned the line of soldiers who were struggling to lock their shields together in an attempt to reform the formation, hindered by the insidious advance of the barbarian horde.

With a quick assessment, he realized that in many places the ranks of his century had been disrupted, leaving them to fend off the enemy's assaults in a scattered manner. They were in a position that would surely drag the Third to defeat unless something changed.

He had to come up with something before all hope of action became futile.

He scolded himself for his lack of initiative—spending too much time thinking and, as always, ending up battling his fears before battling his opponents.

"Enough hesitation! Stop overthinking... It's time to act," he berated himself.

He had just uttered those words when an arrow struck the shield of the legionary beside him. A sharp, ominous sound—a clear sign that the enemy archers were not hesitating to shoot, even at the risk of hitting their own comrades. Those arrows were so terrifying that they seemed like lightning bolts hurled by Jupiter himself.

He straightened to his full height to survey the situation once more, but an enemy came charging at him, brandishing a double-headed axe. They now faced each other, separated only by the centurion's shield.

Vatinius Auruncus blocked the incoming blow, crouching low behind his shield.

Staggering backward, he stumbled over the corpse of a fallen soldier, but managed to stay on his feet. The enemy, seizing on this moment of uncertainty, pressed him with a series of powerful strikes, each blow sapping his strength. Though the shield was between him and the axe, his whole body vibrated with every impact.

Sizing up his opponent's stature and skill, he decided to act swiftly, or risk being overwhelmed. With a sudden movement, he shifted the shield aside and thrust his sword forward, piercing through the plated armor and into the enemy's chest.

A crimson gush spurted from the wound made by the Roman blade. Even the *signiferi*, seasoned veterans hardened by years of war, widened their eyes in disbelief as the giant collapsed to the ground.

"He was a giant!" cried Gallienus Lars Gracchus.

The young centurion nodded, gasping for air, his mouth wide open in a desperate attempt to catch his breath. Staggering but resolute, the action sparked an idea in his mind—perhaps the only way to save his century.

Speed.

He needed to use speed.

"Form up! Square formation!" he shouted.

Immediately, a dozen soldiers surrounded him, forming a protective wall around their commander. They were visibly exhausted, their armor and faces smeared with blood, viscera, scraps of flesh, dirt, and sweat.

"Third!" they roared in unison, locking their shields together.

With this protection, the centurion could now calmly observe the battlefield and strategize.

The right flank of the formation had collapsed, but the optio Severinus Majorianus was rallying the remaining maniples to repel the enemy. On the opposite flank, the maniples in testudo formation had held firm against the barbarian advance, with both sides locked in a fierce stalemate.

The First Century, however, was completely scattered, succumbing to relentless attacks that were claiming many lives.

In some places, the fighting was so brutal that it was taking place atop the bodies of the fallen.

This was the moment to risk an assault maneuver that could take the enemy by surprise.

With that quick assessment, Vatinius Auruncus hurried to execute his next move.

"Break the testudo!" he shouted with all the strength he had left. "Form a wall!"

Optio Severinus Majorianus echoed the command, preparing for the next maneuver.

The young centurion issued another order: "Shields!"

The soldiers locked their shields into a long wall. At the same time, the unlucky Heruli trapped behind their lines were slaughtered.

A quick glance confirmed that Vatinius Auruncus now had a long shield wall, and his men were arranged in three rows.

The formation was now maneuverable.

Positioning himself behind the central legionary in the shield wall, he pushed forward.

"Third, advance in wedge formation!"

The century, now shaped like a cone, began moving toward their struggling comrades. With this formation, they would carve out the gap needed to save the First Century.

"Third Century: One step forward!"

The soldiers advanced a single step, shouting war cries.

"Two steps forward!" he bellowed again.

The crest of his helmet swayed as the compact formation surged forward two steps, driving the enemy horde back and thrusting their swords forward.

The first opponents began to fall.

The retreat of the Heruli mass caused many to be trampled by their own comrades.

Caught in confusion and unable to find space to strike effectively, they became vulnerable to the next assault by the advancing Roman force.

Indeed, the front line of the Romans would open their shields just enough to let in attacking Heruli, only for them to be stabbed by the Roman swords in the rear ranks.

The *signifer* Gallienus Lars Gracchus was now chanting the rites of battle and hurling impudent curses at the barbarians' gods.

"Two more steps forward!" came the next order.

The formation advanced, incorporating isolated groups of legionaries into the fight.

Optio Severinus Majorianus allowed himself a satisfied grin. He turned to check that his maniple was holding firm. His peculiar helmet, with its white crest so long it nearly dragged on the ground, served as a beacon for both officers and soldiers.

"Again! Advance two more steps!" the centurion shouted once more.

Caught up in the frenzy of a battle that now seemed to favor them, the soldiers began rhythmically striking their shields with their swords, marking their steps forward.

The Heruli ranks launched a desperate counterattack, trying to halt what now appeared to be an inevitable advance, but they had lost all cohesion. They hurled themselves wildly against the Roman shield wall, driven only by their recklessness.

The mournful clash of bodies and weapons against the shield wall echoed ominously across the battlefield.

The maneuver was complete. The Third Century had created a wide enough gap to allow the First Century to regroup and reestablish their ranks.

But they couldn't hold out for long, given the overwhelming numerical superiority of the barbarian horde.

It was time to retreat behind the walls.

But something disrupted the centurion's plans.

Fulcinius Agricola Statius, shield raised for protection, advanced a few steps deeper into the enemy ranks, striking down several warriors with his sword. He pulled his gladius from the shoulder of a Herul, kicking the lifeless body to the ground. In that instant, a large Burgundian lunged at him, knocking him onto his back. Fulcinius found himself face-to-face with what could only be described as a human mountain, with fiery red hair and eyes as cold and clear as ice.

The two were locked in combat on the ground, like a tavern brawl—only this time, one of them would not survive. The Burgundian said something in his harsh tongue, and Fulcinius understood it as a kind of victory cry. It seemed his opponent believed the fight's outcome was already decided. A series of punches to Fulcinius' face left him bleeding and dazed, but thanks to the padding of his helmet, he avoided losing consciousness.

At one point, the barbarian drew a dagger from his belt and slashed Fulcinius across the cheek, forcing him to twist sideways to escape his enemy's grip. Fulcinius unfastened the chin strap of his helmet and removed it, then used it to strike the Burgundian—once, twice, and again—until the man's face was buried in the mud.

Fulcinius Agricola Statius remained on his knees, panting and exhausted, oblivious to the battle raging around him.

At that moment, Tarquinius Glaucus, a legionary from a fortified village along the Liris River called Castro Forte, intervened. Using his javelin, he prevented another Burgundian from attacking Fulcinius from behind. Together, the two soldiers attempted to return to the Roman formation, but a hail of arrows descended on the century, forcing them to raise their shields in defense.

The impacts of the arrowheads against the Roman shields and armor resembled the sound of a hailstorm.

Taking advantage of the Romans' momentary stillness as they shielded themselves from the arrows, the barbarian horde pressed forward, attempting to breach the ranks once again.

Supported by Tarquinius Glaucus, Fulcinius Agricola Statius managed to rejoin the formation.

Vatinius Auruncus' eyes shot a piercing glare at Fulcinius before he peered through a gap between the shields. The enemy was advancing. At that moment, he decided to fall back toward the city gate.

The barbarians, having initially been driven back by the Romans, were now pressing up against the shields once more. Chaos erupted again—iron clashing, shouts ringing out, and a frenzy of bodies colliding.

A sudden strike knocked Vatinius Auruncus' shield from his grasp and dragged him out of the formation. He now stood unprotected, facing an enemy.

"Hold your position, no matter what happens!" he shouted.

The centurion's blade flashed, slashing across the lower part of the barbarian's face, sending teeth and blood flying. Watching the enemy collapse to the ground, Vatinius took a few steps back, gripping his gladius tightly with both hands. His arms stiffened, and his legs felt like reeds, barely able to support him. He needed to catch his breath—and he imagined the other legionaries felt the same.

"Fall back! Two steps!" he ordered.

The formation moved backward. The soldiers opened a narrow gap to allow him to reenter, but it was at that precise moment he noticed something.

Rudulfus, the king of the Heruli, was staring at him—and laughing!

Yes, laughing. A deep, demonic laugh that echoed across the battlefield.

Pointing his sword at Vatinius, Rudulfus called out: "Roman! Prepare to die!"

The young centurion replied without hesitation: "If you want the nut, you'll have to crack the shell first!"[32]

Rudulfus did not like the response. With sudden force, he raised his long sword and brought it crashing down on the centurion, who barely managed to block the blow. A series of thrusts from the barbarian king drove Vatinius Auruncus backward as he desperately avoided being sliced apart. Each strike made his arm and body tremble from the force.

But Vatinius' desperate counterattack proved effective, forcing Rudulfus onto the defensive.

The centurion noticed the fine craftsmanship of the barbarian king's armor, clearly the work of a skilled artisan. Its elegant design and intricate adornments made Rudulfus look almost like a Roman general. The armor was studded with dozens of metal rivets, perhaps trophies from past battles or campaigns. He also wore a coarse brown wool cloak and a finely made helmet. His long hair, surprisingly well-groomed for a man of a lawless and uncivilized people, added to his noble appearance.

---

[32] *Qui e nuce nuculeum esse volt, frangit nucem!:* "He who wants the kernel must break the nut!"

Rudulfus stumbled over a dead soldier's body and fell backward, pulling the young centurion down with him. The fight devolved into a vicious struggle in the mud, with neither side holding back. The Heruli king managed to pin Vatinius beneath him, straddling him, and delivered one, two, three powerful punches to the Roman's face.

Vatinius Auruncus, exhausted and on the verge of defeat, felt his vision blur with tears, and the sickly sweet taste of blood filled his mouth. But when he heard Rudulfus chuckle again, a surge of unexpected energy welled up inside him. Fueled by newfound determination, he reacted decisively, even surprising himself.

He drew his *pugio*[33] from its sheath and tried to stab the barbarian in the side. Rudulfus rolled away to defend himself, freeing the centurion, who quickly rose to his feet and reclaimed his gladius.

And then, the unexpected happened.

The king of the Heruli was called back by his officers. After exchanging one last look of hatred with the centurion, Rudulfus retreated into the ranks of his warriors.

The sounds of battle continued to echo in Vatinius Auruncus' ears—the cries of the wounded, shouts of encouragement, the clash of metal, and the whistling of arrows.

Raising his gladius, he commanded: "Third Century, to the standards! Reform the ranks under the standards! Reform the ranks!"

Optio Severinus Majorianus, who had kept an eye on him despite being engaged in many skirmishes himself, echoed the call: "Third Century, close ranks! Close ranks!"

The legionaries disengaged from their individual fights and regrouped, tightening their formation into a solid rectangle of raised shields.

At the center stood the proud standard of the Third Century, held high by the *signifer* Gallienus Lars Gracchus. Bloodied, sweaty, and gasping for air, he bore a deep axe wound in his thigh. Yet

---

[33] *Pugio:* A dagger carried by Roman legionaries, typically secured to the *cingulum*.

the Etruscan soldier made no complaint, his mouth set in a grim line, his lower lip jutting out in defiance of the pain.

Once the formation was restored, Vatinius Auruncus prepared his men for a retreat. They would not withstand the next wave of attacks.

The barbarian vanguard cautiously withdrew, realizing the Romans were about to fall back behind the city walls. They knew they would be vulnerable to the arrows of the archers stationed there.

A murmur rose from the Heruli's rear ranks as Rudulfus gathered his senior officers to plan the next assault.

What remained of the First Century had regrouped.

They had taken advantage of the maneuver executed by their comrades in the Third, which had successfully recovered them all.

Centurion Antoninus Tacitus had already cut down dozens of Heruli and Burgundians, but he was now utterly exhausted. His arms were weak, and his focus on controlling the formation was slipping. He had just pulled his gladius from the belly of a barbarian, whose lifeless eyes stared at him as the last traces of life ebbed away, when more Burgundians came charging at him.

The legionaries were all retreating now, bearing the weight of the blows they received and the exhaustion of relentless combat.

Drusus Variatus was struck in the chest by an arrow, but fortunately, it failed to penetrate his square-plated lorica. Suddenly, the cacophony of the battlefield dulled, as though everything around him was happening in another dimension.

Drusus Variatus found himself struggling to breathe. He unfastened his scarf in a desperate attempt to fill his lungs with air. The images around him began to fade, and then everything went black.

Auctus Tullius Plato hunched his shoulders with every arrow that struck his shield. There was no respite in this battle.

The retreat was taking place under a relentless rain of enemy arrows.

Then a voice shouted: "Step by step, fall back! Hold the front and fall back!"

The command was clear—they had to retreat without stopping.

As he carefully stepped backward, shield raised and perfectly aligned with his comrades, Auctus Tullius Plato saw him: his friend, Drusus Variatus.

He was on the ground, but still moving.

They had grown up together on the plains of the Liris and had been inseparable ever since. Even in the Legion, they had been assigned to the same units.

He couldn't leave him there at the mercy of the barbarians, who would subject him to horrific torture before killing him.

He turned to his fellow legionaries, searching for their approval, but found none. The overwhelming desire to survive, coupled with the fatigue of battle, had sapped the courage from even of the most seasoned veterans.

Plato even saw a soldier who had advanced too far get surrounded by the Burgundians. Aware of the tortures inflicted on Roman prisoners, the soldier stopped, removed his helmet and scarf, and, with his gladius, slit his own throat—a soldier's death, true to Rome.

It was that act of courage that spurred Plato to act. He broke from the line and rushed to his fallen comrade. Hoisting Drusus Variatus onto his shoulders, he cast a quick glance at the advancing enemy. The barbarians were closing in, but he still had a slight advantage. A few more seconds. He steadied his friend on his back and ran toward his formation.

The shields parted to let him in, closing just in time to absorb a barrage of arrows, which struck with dull thuds.

He had saved him. Plato was exhausted, panting, and his heart pounded in his temples from fear—but he had saved him.

Antoninus Tacitus was astonished. He knew he should punish him for disobeying orders—leaving the formation was strictly forbidden—but he couldn't help but admire what he had just witnessed with his own eyes.

The group regained their resolve, and finally, the First Century was aligned again. Now the two units retreated together.

From atop the battlements, Aristarchos Themistocles had never taken his eyes off the battle. Before unleashing a rain of arrows on the enemy, he needed to ensure his Centuries were safely inside.

The centurions in the field breathed a sigh of relief as they heard the gates creak open.

The Third Century was the first to retreat within the walls, followed by the First, which endured a barrage of hundreds of arrows as they made their way inside.

Finally, the gates were closed once more.

Vatinius Auruncus signaled to the legionaries to rest, gesturing with his hands, palms downward, to indicate calm. He didn't even have the strength to speak.

He unfastened his crested helmet, striped white and black, and sank to the ground.

The garrison soldiers began transporting the wounded to makeshift shelters, hastily prepared for the occasion.

The sickly-sweet smell of blood and the agonized groans of the injured filled the young centurion with a sense of despair.

The legionaries settled as best they could. Some lay down to catch their breath, while others searched for water to quench their thirst.

Some pulled sacred statuettes from their pouches and began to pray, ignoring the laws that forbade such practices. Nearly all Romans were Christians now, and those still devoted to the ancient pagan rites often had to hide their true faith.

Galienus Lars had hastily bandaged the wound on his leg. He knelt before a tiny statue of the god Maris[34], which he always carried with him, tied to his cingulum.

Vatinius Auruncus watched him silently. He knew of his Etruscan origins and had often noticed him performing strange rituals, though he had never seen him so deeply absorbed. He was certainly not a Christian, but it didn't seem to trouble him at all. He did not

---

[34] *Maris:* The Etruscan god of war, equivalent to the Roman god Mars. A protector deity of warriors and battles.

fear the wrath of the Church or the bishops, who increasingly persecuted pagans in various ways.

Severinus Majorianus, a fearsome optio even among the veterans, removed his helmet and ran a hand through his cropped, sweat-soaked hair. With the same hand, he wiped the mix of sweat, blood, and dirt from his face.

He took a deep breath and locked eyes with Fulcinius Agricola Statius. The two understood each other immediately. Against all those barbarians outside, there wasn't much more they could do. It was a miracle they were still alive.

Fulcinius Agricola Statius gave a barely perceptible nod before helping Auctus Tullius Plato, who was loading Drusus Variatus onto a cart to be taken to a shelter for treatment.

Gaius Octavianus entrusted himself to the healers, who were already applying ointments and compresses to his wounds.

Tarquinius Glaucus discovered an arrow lodged in the bands of his lorica, which, thankfully, hadn't pierced him. However, he cursed aloud when he noticed a wound on his thigh, raising his eyes to the heavens and shouting all his hatred at the barbarians.

What he did next was incredible.

Despite his exhaustion from the battle, he felt for the pouch at his belt containing what was left of his pay. Then, looking around cautiously to ensure no one was watching, he slipped away.

He entered the house of a prostitute directly across the street and indulged in her charms. As he crossed the threshold, he noticed Vatinius Auruncus watching him.

"If I have to die... I'll die happy!"

The young centurion couldn't help but smile.

***

The barbarian vanguard seemed to take a pause before the next attack.

They were likely waiting for the bulk of their army to catch up.

Night fell over Duro Catalaunum without any further clashes. As darkness descended, the temperature plummeted drastically.

The changing of the guard at the ramparts was arranged.

The defense of the walls was entrusted to the legionaries of the Second Century, who were rested, having not taken part in the earlier sortie. Their commander Antoninus Tacitus, however, was too exhausted to stay awake through the night. He made his way to the ramparts, wrapped himself in his cloak, and sank into a state between wakefulness and sleep.

"Call me if anything happens," he ordered before falling into a deep, dreamless slumber.

On the Walls

Legionary Ulzio Dacianus stood wrapped tightly in his sagum, a coarse woolen cloak, over which he had draped a wolf pelt for warmth. He remained a short distance from a lit brazier to avoid freezing, his eyes fixed straight ahead, as tense as a bowstring, his ears alert for any unusual sounds.

Originally from the east bank of the Liris, Ulzio Dacianus was known for frequenting seedy taverns and brothels. He loved gambling so much that the scars on his body were more often the result of disputes over debts than of battles fought. He had even been punished multiple times by General Marcellinus for being caught selling army-issued boots, tunics, and cloaks to pay off his gambling losses.

It had been more than fifteen years since he last returned home to the urbs, and he often felt a deep longing for it.

Wickedly sarcastic to the point of irritating those he spoke to, Ulzio Dacianus was merciless toward his opponents in combat. He had faced Rome's enemies at the Battle of Arles and was now a seasoned veteran, only months away from earning his honorable discharge.

What a cruel irony, he thought, to be holed up in a city that would soon be sacked by the barbarians. And the barbarians were not known for showing mercy to captured legionaries.

A few meters away from him was Christianus Caligatus and his group of Balearic archers and slingers, renowned for their deadly accuracy. Christianus chatted with his companions as they gambled away their pay over dice.

Their equipment was far lighter than that of the infantry legionaries. Their task was to unleash deadly, unerring missiles, and they excelled at it when the need arose.

Dozens of bundles of arrows lay neatly along the walkways, covered with cloths to protect them from moisture.

In His Cubiculum Aristarchos Themistocles had received Ialenia Heria, a dream interpreter. She was well-known in Duro Catalaunum for her skills, not only as an interpreter of dreams, but also as a maker of medicinal ointments, decoctions, and potions, which had brought relief to many locals during times of illness. People often turned to her for dream interpretations or remedies.

The commander recounted a dream he had had a few nights prior, seeking to understand its meaning.

From a pouch, she drew a snake and some bones. She tossed the snake into the air, observing its movements as it landed and coiled on the ground. She then shook the bones and scattered them on the table, her eyes widening as she studied their arrangement.

"The gods have abandoned you, Centurion!" she hissed, fixing her gaze on the soldier.

"I am a Christian, and my God never abandons anyone, sorceress," he replied coolly, calmly greasing the blade of his gladius.

"The temple in your dream was built in honor of Jupiter... You said so yourself. Jupiter has little love for humankind, and often leaves them to their fate, even when that fate is grim. You should know this, soldier."

Aristarchos smiled faintly. "And what did my dream foretell, then?" he pressed.

Ialenia Heria picked up the snake, which coiled around her arm, hissing softly.

"Your dream is unclear," she admitted. "However, I deduce it is a premonition—not about your life, but about the fate of this isolated border town," she said, her face taut with concentration. "Save yourself, Roman, for the destiny of this city is bleak and shrouded in darkness."

At once, the image of Placidia, the slave girl to whom he had unexpectedly grown attached, flashed through Aristarchos Themistocles' mind.

He had to remain alone.

With an imperious gesture, he dismissed the dream interpreter and began to reflect.

He lay down on his straw pallet, imprudently removing his armor and greaves. Unable to resist the fatigue of the day, he fell into a deep sleep. The water basin brought by a servant for him to wash his hands and face with sat unused in the room.

By some unexpected stroke of luck, the night passed quietly. The cries and groans of the wounded faded, and the soldiers managed to rest in organized shifts.

The citizens of Duro Catalaunum, meanwhile, crowded into churches to pray. There were even spontaneous processions, and some, hidden from prying eyes, made sacrifices to the pagan gods in hopes of saving their lives.

Vatinius Auruncus fell asleep wrapped in his purple cloak, to which he had added a woolen blanket. He took advantage of a bivouac fire fueled by furniture and anything else combustible they had managed to find. His helmet, placed on the ground beside him, gleamed in the firelight.

His right hand gripped the hilt of his gladius, ready for any eventuality.

That strange tranquility did not reassure him. The Heruli were not warriors who stopped because of the cold or darkness. They were plotting something—or waiting for the main force of their army to raze Duro Catalaunum to the ground.

The warmth of the flames provided slight comfort to his troubled, fearful spirit.

Chapter III – Siege

At the end of the Secunda vigilia[1]

The campfires of the barbarian bivouacs were extinguished one by one.

The sounds from the vast army, camped just a few hundred meters from the walls, startled Ulzio, who leaned out, straining his eyes to see as far as he could.

"This is bad..." he muttered before raising the alarm.

Antoninus Tacitus appeared on the walkways with the speed of a hawk, stopping his sprint by planting both hands on the battlements. He burped, cursing the mead he had drunk to keep warm, and narrowed his eyes to slits.

"They're coming!" he whispered, his expression instantly shifting. "Wake the others. There's no time to lose."

Ulzio turned pale, his breathing quickening, creating small clouds of condensation in the freezing air. His face, elongated by his Greek-style goatee, was flushed and congested. He signaled to a legionary below, who grabbed a large horn and blew into it with all the air his lungs could muster.

Other horns echoed in response, and soldiers and civilians alike began running in all directions.

Vatinius Auruncus broke the icy shell on the water basin with the hilt of his *pugio* dagger and, despite the bitter morning chill, plunged

---

[1] *Secunda vigilia:* From 9:00 PM to midnight.

his face into the freezing water. Fully awake, he gathered the legionaries of the Third Century by shouting at the top of his lungs and concentrated them at a point along the central street, which, during the time of the sacred Augusti, had been the *decumanus maximus.*

The archers climbed the stairs and took their positions.

The ballista operators greased the ropes.

The tension became palpable, and the officers' commands echoed everywhere.

Severinus Majorianus, the optio, was already wearing his helmet, and looked so immaculate that it seemed as though he hadn't fought in the previous day's battle. His focale was tightly secured around his neck, his lorica armor polished, and his shield spotless. He barked orders here and there, and they were executed to the letter—no one wanted to make a mistake under such circumstances. Survival depended on every decision.

Aristarchos Themistocles was awakened by his servant. The servant helped him don his lorica, fastening it tightly around his torso. Then came the belt and the cloak. The focale was secured around his neck, and finally, the crested helmet was placed on his head. He took up his *vitis*, the staff symbolizing command and respect, and made his way toward the defenses. Though it hadn't been used in years, Aristarchos and his legionaries remained faithful to the old military traditions of the Empire.

He crossed the open area of the garrison dormitories, passing in front of an ancient temple dedicated to Mars, now reduced to ruins. He regarded it with little interest.

The once-glorious decorations were now barely visible, the gold ornaments had been looted long ago, and the strong stench of urine suggested that few still considered the place sacred.

He moved into the former *decumanus maximus*, advancing against the flow of the panicked crowd. As he progressed, he noticed a woman running and pleading for God's mercy.

His optio, Marcellus Antiochus, approached him.

Looking at him, the centurion indicated he wanted a report, which he received immediately.

"Centurion, nearly eight thousand men are already positioned about a hundred meters from our walls. More mercenaries are organizing behind this first wave. The Third Century is battle-ready, and our archers are in position."

"The First?"

"They're getting organized."

"Deploy the archers to ensure continuous volleys," he ordered.

"Already done. We're ready," replied the optio, his reliability the result of many years of military service.

But a whistle interrupted them. Instinctively, he ducked, trying to take cover.

It was a flaming arrow, which lodged itself in a barrel that immediately caught fire. The unmistakable sound indicated that more were on the way.

Many more.

The incendiary arrows rained down everywhere. After a long moment of disarray, the citizens began extinguishing the flames that were already spreading. Chaos erupted in the narrow streets of the settlement. People ran in all directions, and efforts to douse the fires were slowed by disorganization and the obstacles faced by the *vigiles*—abandoned carts and all manner of belongings cluttered the paths.

Dodging fleeing civilians, the centurion *primae spatha* managed to reach the walkways, followed by Marcellus Antiochus, who shielded him with his scutum, now pierced by two arrowheads.

When the centurion peered over the walls, his eyes widened. Thousands of enemies were advancing, howling and eager for slaughter.

They were attacking from multiple directions, clearly a tactic to divide the defenders of the fortifications. He shook his head in despair, convinced that the city's fall to the barbarians was only a matter of hours.

It was clear now—there was no alternative.

Turning, he saw the legionaries around him moving frantically, trying to prepare the best possible defense.

At a distance of about one stadium, as if receiving a single, unified command, the barbarians halted almost simultaneously.

The silence that followed stretched into moments so long that even the most battle-hardened veterans felt a chill.

The tension mounted until an archer stationed on the fortifications, his nerves strained, loosed an arrow. It sliced through the air, alone, and struck against the shield of an Alan warrior.

Shortly after, Rudulfus, imposing and stern atop his warhorse, advanced at a measured pace to the head of his army. Without speaking, he looked up, locking eyes with Aristarchos Themistocles. With a malicious laugh, he made a defiant gesture and spat on the ground before raising his left hand as if demanding something.

From atop the walls, a hundred archers watched the scene unfolding before their eyes. The ranks of the barbarian army parted, allowing two mercenaries to drag forward a man clad in a purple toga—a clear sign he was a Roman legionary, and almost certainly a prisoner from the legion Rudulfus' forces had annihilated.

The soldier kept his gaze lowered, moving forward with resignation and dignity toward his fate. Even from the walls, it was evident that his hair was matted with dried blood, and his face was heavily bruised.

Aristarchos Themistocles clenched his fists so tightly that his knuckles turned white. Rage surged within him, accompanied by an overwhelming desire to tear that damned Rudulfus apart with his own hands.

The prisoner was forced to his knees as Rudulfus dismounted. A squire held the reins of his warhorse as Rudulfus strode behind the kneeling man, drawing a dagger from his belt. Grabbing the prisoner's hair, Rudulfus placed the blade against his throat, but did not press into the flesh.

The centurion *primae spatha* lowered his head ever so slightly to speak to the archer at his side.

Vunxa, the Sagittaria, nodded, her piercing gaze fixed below.

"Can you do it?" the officer asked.

"I think so…" she replied, her tone betraying some discomfort at what she was about to do.

"Do it," he ordered.

The Sagittaria nodded again. Without revealing her bow, she began to draw the string, nocking an arrow in silence.

"Don't let them see you—move as little as possible," he whispered.

"They won't see me... I'm ready," she said, her eyes locked on the Roman prisoner.

As Rudulfus began to press the blade harder against the legionary's throat, the Sagittaria raised her bow and fired so quickly that Aristarchos Themistocles' voice reached her ears an instant after the arrow had already flown.

"Now!"

"I already did," she replied as the arrow struck the prisoner square in the chest.

Rudulfus' expression shifted to one of fear and astonishment at the unexpected action. For a moment, he hesitated, uncertain whether the arrow had been meant for him instead of the prisoner.

While his elite guard dismounted to shield him, another command echoed from the walls.

"Kill that mangy dog!" ordered the centurion *primae spatha*.

Vunxa nocked another arrow and aimed for the Herulian king, seeking a gap between the guards who now surrounded him. When her fingers released the string, the arrow shot through the air, completing its swift trajectory by striking Rudulfus square in the face.

Teeth shattered and scattered against the king's armor. His eyes bulged with rage as he leapt back onto his horse, screaming curses at the Romans.

The thousands of warriors behind him roared in response.

"Kill the Romans!" he thundered.

"Slaughter them!" his warriors echoed.

At his command, the horde surged toward the walls.

Aristarchos Themistocles gave the order for the archers to fire.

Christianus Caligatus, the oldest among them, shouted to nock arrows.

The first volley arced through the air, followed immediately by a second, and then another.

Dozens of barbarians fell, but their numbers were so vast that Rudulfus remained unfazed. In fact, he smirked as rivers of warriors surged past him toward the fortifications of Duro Catalaunum.

When they reached the walls, they raised their ladders and began climbing with relentless determination, seeking to breach the defenses. Aristarchos knew all too well that the walls were not very high, and that the invaders would soon flood into the settlement.

A massive rock crashed into the walls, causing part of them to collapse. Aristarchos instantly recognized the handiwork of siege engines once belonging to the Fifth Ironclad Legion—now in the hands of the barbarians, who were using them against their former owners.

The relentless bombardment devastated everything in its path. He needed to act quickly. He ordered the Third Century to form ranks along the *decumanus* to act as a last line of defense should the barbarians break through, while the First and Second Centuries were sent to the walls to repel the attackers.

The clamor of battle was deafening. The cries of the legionaries were drowned out by the clash of iron, forcing them to shout just to be understood. The projectiles of the ballistae whooshed over their heads, followed by the crashes and explosions of the targets struck behind them. Tiles and debris flew everywhere.

Hand-to-hand combat erupted along the battlements.

Auctus Tullius Plato drove his blade into an Ostrogoth attempting to climb over the walls, then hurled another back, even as the barbarian reached for the axe strapped to his back. The man howled until he crashed to the ground below.

A third enemy managed to climb over from another ladder, engaging Plato in dangerously close quarters due to the cramped space. Battles now raged wherever a foothold could be found.

The Ostrogoth wore finely-crafted armor and a honey-colored woolen cloak. His trousers were wrapped in animal hides studded with metal. His dark hair was long, filthy, and tangled. His eyes, a piercing blue, gave an unsettling impression of transparency, while his pale complexion made him look like a corpse risen from the *mundus*[2].

Plato, in contrast, wore a segmented lorica over the short tunic of the legionaries, trousers, sandals, and bronze armguards engraved with verses he had composed himself. His focale was tightly fastened around his neck, and his helmet's cheek guards were securely strapped beneath his chin. At his *cingulum militaris*, he carried a dagger in its sheath. The ring on his right hand marked him as a member of Augustus' Eight Legion, to which he was fiercely loyal.

The barbarian shouted words Plato couldn't understand, though the soldier could feel the hatred directed at him.

Christianus Caligatus loosed arrows one after another, nearly emptying his quiver, each shot finding its mark. The ladder beneath him saw no climbers fast enough to evade his deadly aim; its base was already littered with pierced bodies.

Ulzio Dacianus recklessly climbed onto the edge of the walls, slashing the throats of barbarians before they reached the top of the ladders. Whenever he saw an enemy crash to the ground below, he raised both arms to the sky and shouted:

"For the honor of Rome!"

The armor he wore was frayed at the edges from frequent use. His intense brown eyes studied the enemies climbing furiously toward the top of the walls. His curled hair, cut neatly across his forehead, reflected the style of the time. His leather cuffs were tied with matching laces. The blade of his gladius was battered from countless clashes, and his helmet was never strapped under his chin—a personal habit. Yet, surprisingly, it never fell, not even when struck. On his finger, he wore a ring engraved with, "VRBE ROMULA," a testament to his deep attachment to Rome. The

---

[2] *Mundus:* The world of the dead. A term more commonly used by the Etruscans than by the Romans.

other soldiers came from every corner of the Empire.

Panting from exhaustion, Ulzio Dacianus stood firmly on the walls, waiting for the mercenaries.

With sticky, bloodied hands, Gaius Octavianus gripped his gladius tightly by the hilt, though it was sheathed for the moment—a habit he had whenever he needed to devise a plan. He would always sheathe his sword before thinking.

Descending from the walkways, he headed toward a construction site near the grain warehouses. There, he gathered a small group of men and instructed them to collect as many stones as possible. He then led them back to the walls.

The task was easy, given the destruction caused by the catapults.

He then ordered them to continue collecting rocks, bricks, and any other debris they could find, instructing them to bring it to the walkways without stopping until everything was used.

He muttered at two archers trying to repair their broken bows, ordering them to abandon the repairs and use stones against the attackers instead.

Together, the three began hurling stones at the mercenaries climbing the ladders. Forced to hold on with both hands, the attackers could not protect themselves with their shields.

The tactic worked—many of the attackers fell under the impacts.

Seeing the effectiveness of the idea, other legionaries began throwing stones and any materials they could find.

Unfortunately, despite their efforts, many enemies managed to reach the walkways, sparking brutal hand-to-hand combat.

Dozens of legionaries perished in the clashes. All around lay the wounded and the dead, their bodies looted of coins and ornaments by the mercenaries, who also inflicted grotesque mutilations.

"This is looking bad!" shouted Marcellus Antiochus, holding his shield high to block the long sword of a Herulian warrior who had reached the platform.

He tried to counter the barbarian's powerful blows, but his foe was far stronger and more skilled than him.

Marcellus began retreating step by step, hoping to reach a

group of legionaries for assistance. But they, too, were locked in fierce combat with other Herulians, who had reached the narrow passageways along the walls.

Resigned, Marcellus prepared for a desperate counterattack. Yet the Herulian skillfully parried the blow with his oval shield before slashing downward with his sword, striking Marcellus on the shoulder and cutting through both his lorica and his body.

The arm holding his gladius nearly detached, hanging unnaturally at his side.

Marcellus' scream of agony caught the attention of the centurion *primae spatha*, who watched from a short distance as the legionary met his end.

The towering Herulian raised his blade horizontally and delivered the killing blow.

As if this weren't enough, the barbarian removed Marcellus Antiochus' focale and tied it to his shield as a trophy. He then advanced along the walkway, cutting down legionary after legionary. No one seemed capable of stopping this warrior.

Reluctantly, the task of confronting their rampaging foe fell to Centurion Antoninus Tacitus. As the barbarian approached, Tacitus cursed his fate and hurled insults at the uncivilized barbarians and their gods.

The Herulian warrior raised his shield and long sword high into the air, roaring like a bear before charging the Roman centurion.

Antoninus braced himself, planting his feet firmly and hiding behind his shield. But the impact of the charging giant was so powerful that it knocked him backward, causing him to lose his shield. His eyes widened in shock as he realized the enemy towered over him by at least three *gradus*[3]—nearly five feet.

This was no ordinary man—he was a true giant.

The centurion tried to prop himself up on his elbows, but the Herulian pinned him to the ground, pressing a foot against his

---

[3] *Gradus:* A Roman unit of measurement equivalent to 0.741 meters.

chest.

It was over, Antoninus thought. He raised his gladius, hoping for a warrior's death.

But fortune—or perhaps the favor of the gods—was not yet done with him.

A moment later, Drusus Variatus leapt onto the giant's back, wrapping his legs around the barbarian's waist and slashing his gladius across the Herulian's neck. Blood spurted from his severed jugular as the giant fell to his knees, choking on his own blood.

As life drained from the barbarian, Antoninus retrieved Marcellus Antiochus' focale from the barbarian's shield and secured it to his own belt.

Drusus Variatus had saved his life, and the centurion's pat on his shoulder conveyed more than gratitude—it carried a glimmer of hope.

The cries of battle and the clash of weapons softened into a muffled hum, barely distinguishable.

It had started snowing.

Soon, the snowfall turned into a blizzard.

The sounds of combat grew more scattered and isolated. Snow blanketed everything, increasing in intensity and muffling the chaos. Yet despite its tranquil appearance, the battlefield remained littered with corpses and wounded men, groaning in pain.

The enemy's advance came to a halt. The snow on the ground had grown so deep it reached past the warriors' knees, hindering their movements.

Rudulfus called off the attack, grudgingly acknowledging the tenacity of the legionaries defending the small, besieged city.

But it wasn't skill or strength that had saved the crumbling, burning walls—it was sheer luck.

Everything felt surreal.

The fighting ceased everywhere.

Roman archers rubbed their arms, sore from constant shooting and stiff from the cold. Wounded legionaries were taken to makeshift shelters scattered across the city, wherever an intact roof could still be found.

The dead were piled up, waiting to be burned as soon as possible.

Aristarchos Themistocles closed the eyes of his fallen optio, Marcellus Antiochus, with his thumb and forefinger, whispering funeral prayers for him. When he finished, he signaled the soldiers to carry away the body.

They had miraculously survived the second assault, and despite everything, their losses were not as severe as they had feared. Aristarchos noticed a cut on his temple—not particularly deep, though he couldn't remember how he'd gotten it. He pressed a piece of dirty cloth, the only one he had, against the wound, cursing as he tried to stop the bleeding.

He ran toward the *decumanus*, reached the formation of the Third Century, and stopped in front of the young Vatinius Auruncus.

Their eyes locked.

The fatigue was evident in both men's features.

Aristarchos Themistocles gave a slight nod, as if confirming the gravity of the situation they were in.

He had seen this young centurion fight in many battles, always leading his men into the thick of the action. He knew what he needed to say, and he didn't hesitate.

"Centurion..." The young officer stiffened before Aristarchos could continue.

"Vatinius Auruncus, you will be in charge of defending the city once the barbarians breach the walls. Your task is to slow their advance. Deploy your maniples as soon as possible."

The young centurion paused to think. It wasn't a small responsibility he was being given—perhaps that's why his fist was clenched.

"Do you think they'll try again, despite..." he gestured toward the falling snow.

"They were just caught off guard, as we were. But they'll try again soon."

"These men haven't eaten properly in nearly two days. It'll be a real challenge for them to face that horde of butchers," Vatinius replied.

"No one has eaten properly in a long time, in any corner of the Empire, I'd wager," Aristarchos replied harshly, turning away and walking off without waiting for a response. "Follow me," he commanded as he kept walking.

When Vatinius caught up to him, Aristarchos admitted, "This snow saved us, but only for a short while. Those men out there are reorganizing, and will return. During the last assault, they nearly took the walls—they managed to create a few breaches. Next time, they'll target the gate as well. But we can make it so costly for them that we might force a truce. It's our only chance."

The young centurion was now fully attentive.

"If we hold out at the principia, defending it as best we can, we might buy ourselves time. Time to come up with another plan. Do you understand now?" Aristarchos' expression was full of hope.

"You mean to say that…" Vatinius began to interject.

"I mean that, while you of the Third drive your fine swords into those mercenaries, we'll prepare the defenses at the principia. Our barracks are as defensible as if they were a small *castrum*. Centurion…" he concluded, "…do your duty."

"I will. And the Third will do the same."

Vatinius Auruncus stood still for a moment, watching Aristarchos leave footprints in the snow until he disappeared behind a crumbling wall. He then unfastened his helmet and tucked it under his arm.

He looked at the optio, Severinus Majorianus, who had overheard parts of the conversation, and motioned for him to come closer.

Severinus stepped out of formation and began shouting at the men to get into proper order, as the centurion had something to say.

"You're always so hard on them…" Vatinius teased.

"These bastards deserve far worse," Severinus retorted.

"They're probably freezing…" Vatinius continued.

"They have good cloaks."

"And they haven't eaten in days…"

"If that's the case, I've got a surprise in store," Severinus admitted.

At those words, the two turned simultaneously, finding themselves face-to-face.

"What do you mean?" Vatinius asked.

"The bishop's granary..." Severinus suggested.

"Ah!" was all the centurion could manage as his mind raced to process the proposal.

A glint of cunning flashed in Severinus' eyes. "Give me five men, and I'll bring back some food for these starving beasts," he proposed with a sly smile.

The soldiers in the front rows chuckled.

"Silence!" Severinus barked, silencing them.

"Fine. But be quick about it," Vatinius ordered.

Severinus quickly selected five trusted men and left.

For the centurion, there was nothing left to do but prepare the soldiers for what lay ahead.

"Are you cold?" he asked, fixing his gaze on them.

No one answered.

"I want an answer—are you cold?" he repeated.

A chorus of assent rose from the men.

"That doesn't surprise me, given the snow falling on our heads," he said with a grin before asking another question. "Are you hungry?"

They all responded with a resounding yes.

"Then we'll fix that."

He was certain he had their full attention.

"Ten...ten men will go in search of anything that can burn. The rest will prepare the defenses necessary to halt the enemy's advance when they break through the walls."

The legionaries' expressions grew more serious.

"Our job is to prevent the barbarians from running free in the city until the men of the First and Second have set up a solid defense at the principia. At that point, we'll join them, fortify ourselves, and resist for as long as we can. Is that clear?"

The approval was unanimous, though one soldier raised a

hand to speak.

"Centurion...what's the firewood for?"

Vatinius smiled. "It'll be the bridge between the cold and our defense against the invaders."

The optio had a habit of never letting go of his gladius hilt and used only his left arm to gesture. His purple cloak was tightly fastened at the neck, and he often wore the hood up, hiding part of his face. Not on this day, however.

On his plate armor, he bore the image of a gorgon's head, a clear nod to Greek mythology and the virtues of courage. Severinus Majorianus was both a skilled fighter and a good husband and father. His three-year-old daughter, to whom he was deeply and affectionately attached, bore an Etruscan name, Vercna[4]. He often spoke of her, recounting amusing anecdotes about her games and growth to friends around a campfire.

In the current circumstances, his only fear was for his family, whom he had hidden in a house he owned in the Provence region. He hoped that once he obtained his discharge, he would take them back to his hometown, where he planned to sell fish along the coast of Minturnae. But the Empire was crumbling, and barbarians roamed freely across Europe, causing chaos and frequently pillaging Roman villas.

He shook his head at the thought of what could happen to his loved ones should they encounter those savages.

Distracting himself from his worries, he spoke in a low voice to the five legionaries accompanying him: "I'm certain the granary in the bishop's residence still has plenty of supplies. We just need to take what we need."

Seeing the shocked expressions of the others, he quickly explained, "We'll leave enough for those clerics to survive. What we take will be shared—some for us, some for the people."

"But...the centurion told us to take only what we needed for

---

[4] *Vercna:* A name of Etruscan origin (modern "Virginia"), meaning "Fire."

ourselves," one soldier objected.

"Pretend you didn't hear that and follow my orders," Severinus snapped.

Their expressions softened at that.

Many legionaries had families in Duro Catalaunum, and their thoughts, understandably, often turned to them rather than the Legion. Now, they would have a chance to feed their loved ones.

When they reached the entrance of the bishop's residence, the six men noticed a group of guards stationed there.

"Who's paying those men now that the bishop is dead?" one soldier asked.

"His officials, eunuchs, and whores. They're afraid for their lives and are using the bishop's treasury to hire armed men at the highest price," the optio replied.

"And now? Why don't we just kill them?" interjected Fulcinius Agricola Statius, a soldier the optio had chosen for his aptitude for combat.

"Let's try diplomacy first..." Severinus Majorianus said, stepping forward.

Standing before the guards, he introduced himself: "I am Severinus Majorianus, optio of the Third Century."

The oldest among the guards stepped forward. He must have once been a Burgundian officer, as he wore coarse wool clothing layered with the upper half of his Roman armor. Over this, a wolf pelt rested on his shoulders. His helmet had long horsehair plumes that swept the ground, and at his waist a broad leather belt supported a sword, likely once belonging to a high-ranking equestrian officer, judging by the blade's length.

In a gruff, coarse voice that reflected his hostile demeanor, the man replied, "What do you want?"

"The troops defending the city are starving. I'm certain the bishop's granary still holds ample supplies, and—"

"No one will enter the residence," the man interrupted sharply, cutting off the optio.

"But we'd leave enough food for your survival. You have my

word," the Roman pressed.

The other's eyebrows furrowed in open hostility. "Didn't you hear me? No one will pass through this gate," he said, pointing to the massive gate behind him that stood before the iron-studded wooden door.

At that moment, Fulcinius Agricola Statius stepped forward, his face twisted in a grimace of resentment as he leaned in close to the guard captain. "Why don't we just kill them all?" he asked the optio, without breaking eye contact with the other man.

Hearing those words, the other guards drew their weapons, and Severinus Majorianus had to act quickly to defuse the situation.

He pulled the soldier back by his armor, ordering him to rejoin the others, and shot him a scathing glare, pointing firmly at the spot where he was to remain still.

Turning back to the Burgundian, Severinus tried again: "You were a soldier once, weren't you? You should know what it's like to be hungry and cold. All I'm asking is for you to open the gate and let us through. I've already given you my word that we'll leave supplies behind."

"Your word means nothing, Roman!" the guard spat back, emphasizing his disdain by spitting on the ground at the last word.

With a swift, experienced glance, Severinus assessed the situation. He was facing about ten well-armed guards who were likely well-fed and rested, though they probably hadn't trained in a long time.

On his side, he had five men trained to wield their gladii against any enemy, but they were tired and hungry. He sighed before making the decision he had hoped to avoid.

"Kill them all!" he shouted.

The legionaries leaped like deer, throwing themselves at the guards and engaging them in combat.

Fulcinius Agricola Statius darted past the optio, smirking. "I told you we should've done this sooner!"

A faint smile crossed Severinus Majorianus' face. "Well, I wanted to try diplomacy…" he began to say, but his sentence was cut short as the guard captain swung his long sword over his head.

Fulcinius grabbed the captain's arms, twisting them until they dislocated. The man let out a scream of agony as the legionary finished him off with a roof tile he had picked up from the ground.

"No need to even unsheathe our swords with these ones," Fulcinius muttered, already targeting another guard.

Within moments, six guards lay dead, and the others had fled, abandoning their weapons.

From the captain's belt, the optio retrieved the keys, using them to unlock the gate and, further inside, the door.

The cloister that unfolded before them was proof that the Empire still had skilled architects and artists. A marble colonnade marked its perimeter, and in the center was a fish-filled basin.

A servant approached, likely sent by a frightened official.

"Gentlemen, may I ask the reason for your visit?" he asked in a calm voice.

Severinus Majorianus noticed that the place felt like a haven of serenity, as if untouched by the chaos outside. Only the collapsed roof of part of the colonnade brought him back to reality, reminding him of the times they were living in.

Seeing no sign of guards around, Severinus decided to act quickly.

"Listen closely. I want to be clear, so I'll show you something…" He gestured for Fulcinius Agricola Statius to step forward.

Fulcinius took two steps forward and held up a bloodied finger, still wearing its ring. He hadn't been able to remove the ring, so he had taken the entire finger.

The optio resumed speaking: "This belonged to the captain of the guards. Now, without hesitation, you will take us to the granary and the cellar. Then you will provide us with a cart. Do you understand?"

The servant turned pale, holding back a retch. He nodded silently and led the legionaries to the places they had requested.

***

Vatinius Auruncus positioned the maniples to guard the two main access points to the city.

Then began the waiting, during which the legionaries rested and tried to warm themselves as best they could near the fires. The flames rose high into the sky, making it tolerable to stay close to them.

When the optio returned, everyone sprang to their feet, curious about the outcome of the mission.

Fulcinius Agricola Statius held the reins of a bay horse pulling a cart laden with sacks and amphorae. Hanging from the right side were five or six pheasants and some small game. A large cut of pork ribs dangled from the other side.

"We have food and drink!" he reassured his comrades, who cheered in response.

Fulcinius and the others from the mission quickly began cooking the meat, while other legionaries distributed the rest of the supplies.

As the men of the Third Century enjoyed this brief moment of respite, the optio approached the centurion. "Before you ask, I'll tell you: we left part of the haul with some people to distribute it. I also sent a cart to the men of the First and Second. The centurion *primae spatha* sends his regards and gratitude."

"You were clever in disobeying orders. If we survive, you'll tell me how it all went," the centurion replied with a laugh.

"Yes, if we survive," the optio echoed.

Unable to resist a deep need, Vatinius Auruncus stepped away from the unit and leaned against the wall of a house reduced to rubble. He took a deep breath, pulling himself out of the absurdity and death surrounding him, until he regained a sense of himself.

He tore into a piece of meat, freshly pulled from the fire.

Originally from Vescinae, he had lived a simple life until he was conscripted by the Empire's soldiers. Despite the many years that had passed, he still vividly remembered his home, with its trellised vines. His family owned a vineyard spanning one *actus quadratus*[5], from which they produced Falernian wine, prized and sold even in the markets of Populonia.

The Walls, meridies[6]

The assault on Duro Catalaunum had resumed.

Ulzio Dacianus collapsed onto the ground. Two barbarians immediately pounced on him. Despite his attempts to fend off their deadly blows, he was struck hard on the helmet, and his vision blurred. Another powerful strike knocked the helmet off entirely, leaving a gaping wound on his head. The legionary tried to counter with more blows, but his eyes saw only darkness. His senses dulled, and silence and oblivion claimed him. The last thing he felt was the unpleasant taste of iron in his mouth.

Fighting erupted all along the walls, wherever there was room to stand.

Centurion Antoninus Tacitus quickly realized that the defenses had been breached, and the fighting was nothing more than a desperate attempt to slow the enemy's advance.

When the central gate was shattered by a group of Thuringians, they quickly overran the wall and eliminated the Roman garrison behind it.

The barbarian horde stormed into the city with shouts of pillage and triumph.

The legionaries of the Third Century, split into two groups, stood frozen, their hearts pounding in their chests.

It was their turn now.

Their eyes locked onto the enemy, who advanced with sinister, malevolent screams.

Vatinius Auruncus fastened his helmet under his chin. He

---

[5] *Actus quadratus:* A Roman unit of surface area, approximately 1,265 m².

[6] *Meridies:* noon.

gripped his gladius and drew it from its scabbard, silently raising it high into the air.

"Hold. Stay still."

Severinus Majorianus, commanding the other half of the century, echoed the order, urging his men to maintain tight ranks, readying them for the impact.

Vatinius Auruncus tossed his shield to the ground, picked up a second gladius with his other hand, and raised it to the sky.

"Stay calm," he said, summoning the strength to shout as loudly as he could. "Stay calm and hold your ground. Let them come closer..." He then glanced at a few legionaries stationed in the narrow, cramped alleys nearby.

The barbarians charged toward them, screaming and brandishing their weapons, confident of easy plunder.

The legionaries, however, remained motionless.

The cobblestones began to tremble under the weight of the onrushing horde.

"If they break through our lines, we're all dead. So lock your shields tight!" Vatinius Auruncus bellowed.

The legionaries obeyed, forming a solid wall of shields.

"Gallienus!" Vatinius Auruncus called, and at the mention of his name, Gallienus Lars Gracchus raised the century's standard, holding it high and proud for all to see.

The soldiers shouted in unison, "Third!"

Gallienus planted the standard firmly in the ground so it would stand upright and visible, then drew his own gladius. His contribution in the coming moments would be crucial.

The barbarians drew ever closer, and it became clear they were Thuringians. Their chainmail was made of larger rings than those used by the Heruli, and their wide leather belts cinched tightly at the waist. Most wielded double-headed axes, though a few carried swords much longer than the Roman gladii. Their helmets were pointed, some adorned with animal parts—bull skulls, or antlers from deer or oxen.

They were so close now that the front lines could distinguish the color of their eyes, shining with the desire to slaughter.

Their leader wore a well-crafted cuirass, clearly the work of a Roman artisan from Etruria, as the boss displayed an image of the god Tinia[7]. The legionaries wondered how he had acquired it.

Gallienus Lars Gracchus was more angered than the rest, suspecting the armor had been stripped from the body of a soldier from his own homeland.

The moment before the clash was unbearably long.

Then, chaos erupted.

Despite the barbarian horde's impact, the Roman front line held.

Gallienus Lars Gracchus grabbed the soldier in front of him, preventing him from falling backward or retreating. When he saw a Thuringian slipping through the formation, he struck him on the head with his sword, shattering his skull. Blood and teeth splattered onto Gallienus' armor and face—a grim sign that the battle had begun.

The fighting was ferocious beyond description.

The legionaries were driven by desperation, while the barbarians were fueled by the lust for plunder and bloodshed.

Fulcinius Agricola Statius waited until an enemy was just inches away before swiftly moving his shield aside and plunging his sword into the man's abdomen. But immediately, more swarmed in to take his place.

For some reason, Fulcinius' thoughts turned to his soldier's pay[8], and a bitter, ironic smile crept onto his face.

He had been promoted to the *primi ordines* for showing extraordinary bravery during the Battle of Arles.

"A frontier soldier," he liked to call himself.

His salary had increased, and he often spent it on women and

---

[7] *Tinia:* An Etruscan deity with control over lightning, equivalent to Jupiter and Zeus.

[8] *A legionary's pay:* A Roman soldier earned about 5–10 assarii per day (roughly 225 denarii annually). This value is approximate. A soldier from humble origins could, within the legion, rise to the Equestrian Order.

gambling. A true veteran.

He had fought in many battles, but this time, the situation was different.

The barbarians had already entered the city, and they were the last line of defense.

They would be the first to die, ahead of the townspeople—the women, children, the elderly, and the infirm. Only those taken as slaves would survive.

In that moment, Fulcinius realized that all his years in the legions had been in vain.

The Empire was gone, and savages ruled everywhere.

He wondered if his hometown even still existed. He resolved to fight only for himself and his honor.

He removed his helmet and hurled it at the barbarians, stepping out of formation and dropping his shield to the ground.

Gripping his gladius with both hands, he stood to the side, daring the enemy to face him.

With one swing of his blade, he slashed open the chest of an opponent, even as others charged at him, howling with rage.

Vatinius Auruncus pulled his sword from the chest of a Thuringian, who was still gasping and screaming.

He looked around to assess the situation, and quickly realized that he had already lost many men. Dozens of bodies lay on the ground, wounded or dead.

He spotted Severinus Majorianus facing off against an enemy much larger than himself, but far clumsier. Sure enough, the optio dispatched him moments later.

Yet more enemies kept pouring into the village.

It was all over.

The snow had built up to at least a *palmus*[9] thick on the ground.

To Vatinius Auruncus, it seemed surreal to be fighting while soft, white flakes fell, blanketing everything in sight.

---

[9] *Palmus:* A Roman unit of measurement, approximately 7.4 cm.

Everything...except the blood.

One legionary slit his own throat rather than fall into enemy hands and face unspeakable torture.

Another soldier threw himself onto his own gladius, ending his life.

Two soldiers dropped their weapons and fled. One of them, however, was struck in the back by an enemy arrow, dropping him like a hunted animal.

The other, too terrified to stop and help, disappeared behind a building.

More legionaries fell, wounded or killed. The ground was now covered in bodies.

Vatinius Auruncus' gaze met Severinus Majorianus', and they exchanged an unspoken understanding.

It was time to retreat.

The centurion signaled toward the alleyways, and two carts loaded with wood and straw were set ablaze with torches and shoved forcefully toward the mercenaries, who continued to pour in.

The first ranks stopped in confusion, unable to retreat or move aside as they were pressed by their own comrades. The flaming carts crashed into them, exploding into a whirlwind of sparks and fire that quickly spread to their cloaks and garments, engulfing them in flames as though a flood of fire had swept through.

This strategy gave the centurion enough time to regroup the remnants of the Third Century into a tight phalanx positioned in the middle of the *decumanus maximus*.

It was their last, desperate attempt to hold back the barbarian invasion.

***

From atop the walls, Antoninus Tacitus ordered the archers to keep firing, trying to bring down as many enemies as possible, while Aristarchos Themistocles frantically finalized the desperate defenses of the principia.

Amid the fighting and the burning mercenaries, a young priest suddenly appeared, clad in sacred vestments, followed by a procession of clerics and faithful carrying crosses and displaying holy relics.

They began singing liturgical hymns at the top of their voices.

The priest's face bore an expression of courage and defiance.

Behind him, a large cross was held aloft while prayers were recited.

For reasons unknown, the Thuringians appeared frightened.

They froze in place, as if they had all turned to pillars of salt.

They began stepping back, retreating slightly in the face of the improvised "procession."

Yet no barbarian had ever shown fear of Christians before. They were not monotheists, and their gods did not demand brotherhood or solidarity among men.

The legionaries wondered what was happening.

Unfortunately, they soon found out.

In the worst way.

The young priest stood ahead of the small procession, his vestments adorned with golden threads and embedded gemstones, appearing precious to the Thuringians. But that wasn't all. Behind him, two men carried a cross containing the relics of Saint James, covered in gold plating and encrusted with stunning, multicolored gems.

The Thuringians were not afraid; they simply couldn't believe their eyes.

At the sight of such riches, their lust for plunder reached a fever pitch. After a moment of murmurs and astonished whispers, they descended upon the religious procession, massacring everyone involved.

The young priest tried to flee, but was caught. Held in place, he screamed as the Thuringian leader drove his sword into the priest's abdomen, slicing downward to his pelvis.

The priest's entrails spilled out, dripping to the ground. His body collapsed onto them.

The legionaries of the Third Century were further stunned by what happened next.

A brawl broke out among the Thuringians as they fought over the gilded, jewel-encrusted cross. The quarrel quickly escalated into a full-blown melee, with the barbarians turning their weapons on each other. Many fell to blows inflicted by their own comrades.

The legionaries were dumbfounded. The barbarians had stopped attacking them and were slaughtering each other instead.

Vatinius Auruncus seized the opportunity to retreat to the principia.

By then, only about forty of them were left after their devastating losses.

The centurion called for the optio, telling him it was time to retreat.

"Are we to flee like rabbits, Centurion?" Severinus Majorianus retorted.

"Do you want to die here for an Empire that no longer exists and for an Emperor who enjoys dressing like a woman?" Vatinius locked eyes with him, hoping his meaning was clear enough.

"They won't appreciate this order. They stayed because they're legionaries," Severinus muttered, wrinkling his nose—more at the stench of burning flesh than at the command he had just received.

"They'll appreciate being alive," the centurion replied, giving him a firm slap on the shoulder plate of his lorica. "Let's move before they notice us again."

The optio cast one last incredulous glance at the Thuringians, who were still killing each other over the gilded cross.

If there was ever a time to run, this was it.

He loudly called the soldiers' attention and relayed the orders.

Gallienus Lars Gracchus spat on the ground before retrieving the standard of the Third Century.

Fulcinius Agricola Statius, shaking his fists toward the sky, shouted insults at the centurion, describing his mother as so lascivious that she had found work in the worst dance hall in Argentoratum.

Vatinius Auruncus shot him a glare that needed no words.

"Fall back. Cover yourselves and retreat!" he ordered.

From the top of the walls came ceaseless shouts of battle cries and the clash of steel, as the ferocious fighting continued. Even Ialenia Heria, the dream-reader under the command of Centurion Antoninus Tacitus, loosed arrows against the enemy.

Without ever looking away from her targets, she would retrieve the arrowhead, notch the arrow, draw the string, aim, and release.

Her tunic hung open at the shoulders and cinched tightly at the waist. The boots she wore clashed with the usual attire of women, as did the dagger always fastened to her belt, which she used to cut roots and scrape lichen for her potions.

She wore a light leather cuirass, laced at the sides, covering her torso, over which her long braid of raven-black hair fell. Tribal paint, blue and white, framed her face—a signature of Celtic women like her.

Around the campfires, stories of her mysterious origins were often told. Some claimed she was the daughter of a druid with extraordinary powers, while others praised her skills as a *medicus*.

Many legionaries sought her out for poultices or herbal concoctions.

A necklace with a crystal pendant swayed around her neck.

Arrow after arrow. She was tireless.

Each dull thud marked another target hit.

Despite everyone's efforts, the Romans were forced to retreat from the battlements.

There was nothing more to be done—the walls had fallen to the enemy.

Antoninus Tacitus blew the horns, signaling the order to retreat.

The legionaries and civilians defending the walls fled in disorder, which allowed the barbarians to swarm up the external siege ladders and breach the battlements almost unopposed.

Banners and flags were soon raised on the walls to signal to the barbarian generals—watching from their tents on the surrounding hills—which sectors had been taken and which still remained under Roman control.

Fortunately, the retreat through the city streets went smoothly, as no enemy squads or patrols awaited them there. The Third Century had done its job well.

One regret, however, gnawed at Antoninus Tacitus' stomach— the wounded left behind on the battlements.

Buried under the bodies of both comrades and enemy merce- naries, Ulzio Dacianus tried to lift himself off the ground, but his remaining strength failed him.

He managed to open his eyes for a brief moment, just enough to see the barbarians swarming nearby, elated by their advantage in the battle.

Then he fell unconscious again.

Once the legionaries regrouped at the principia, they prepared for one last, desperate stand.

The centurion *primae spatha* gathered the remnants of the three centuries and arranged them as best he could.

Addressing his men, he gave a brief speech:

"We will hold our ground here. It's the only place we can still resist. Some of you have family out there. If you wish, you're free to go to them."

At those words, a dozen soldiers ran off.

"To those who remain, I say this: we die with honor!"

"Honor!" they all shouted in response.

The soldiers finished fortifying what had already been partially secured.

They blocked the entrances with carts and piled up anything that could form a makeshift wall, creating barriers that the enemy would have to scale.

Meanwhile, the snowfall intensified, making visibility increas- ingly poor.

This fortunate turn of events dampened the barbarians' momen- tum, as their assault faltered without clear orders from their gen- erals. Before long, the fighting ceased altogether.

An eerie calm settled over the scene, broken only by the groans of the wounded and the murmurs of the Romans.

The barbarians had retreated just far enough to maintain their positions without getting too close to the enemy.

Even the looting seemed to have stopped.

Once again, the snowfall proved to be a blessing. The flakes now fell so thickly that it was difficult to see even a few *perticae*[10] ahead.

It didn't take long to station soldiers at the most strategic points.

The mercenaries would face significant challenges if they tried to attack the principia, which had originally been built like a small *castrum*.

The two watchtowers were well-positioned, offering archers a clear vantage point.

Vunxa licked the feathers of her arrows to stiffen them, ensuring they would fly straight.

She crouched beneath her cloak atop one of the towers.

Christianus Caligatus offered her a piece of dry bread. "Here, I'll split it with you. We archers shoot better on a full stomach," he chuckled warmly.

Her eyes reflected gratitude as she hungrily bit into the offered food.

"I've also got some dried fruit," he added.

"Thank you," she said simply.

"Don't you find this situation strange?" he pressed, eager to keep the conversation going.

"What do you mean?" she asked, chewing voraciously and showing little interest in his words.

"There are tens of thousands of barbarians out there who've been trying for days to capture this tiny town in the Empire's most remote province...and yet we're still alive, holding out in here."

Now Vunxa's gaze met his. That was something, he thought to himself.

---

[10] *Pertica:* A Roman unit of length, equal to 10 feet, or approximately 2.964 meters.

"This will be a snare for us, mark my words. Not even the gods will save us," she replied.

"I'm a Christian, and I believe in the one true God. But I doubt even He will save us."

They burst out laughing.

Christianus Caligatus spoke through bites of food: "Still, we might just get through this. I've heard that the Heruli and the Thuringians aim to conquer large swathes of land to settle on. That gives us hope—they don't plan to fight forever."

"So, you're a Christian?"

"My family raised me with Christ's teachings, instilling His values in me. Plus, my name is a dead giveaway," he laughed.

"Very creative," she remarked wryly.

They laughed again.

Then, suddenly, Vunxa surprised the archer. She leapt forward like a hare and extended her hand.

"You know my name already, but you don't know my story," she said.

The archer's expression invited her to continue.

"I grew up following the army. My father was a Batavian cavalryman who ended his career right here, in the *vexillatio* of Duro Catalaunum…"

Christianus Caligatus studied her peculiar helmet, adorned with a long, black horsehair plume.

"Had you fought before this?" he asked.

"As an archer with Augustus' Eight Legion. That's where I earned the name Sagittaria," she said with pride.

"Yes, I'd heard your nickname," he admitted, offering her some dried fruit.

A freezing gust swirled the ever-thickening snowfall around them.

In Duro Catalaunum, only a few scattered patrols of Thuringians roamed the streets, searching for anything to loot.

Most of the population had locked themselves inside churches or the homes that had once belonged to wealthy landowners. There were not many nobles who had chosen to live in this remote border town, but their residences were like small fortresses.

The fortified village was now covered by a white blanket of snow.

The snowfall had hidden even the bodies lying on the ground, as if the battle had never happened.

The sentinels posted on the towers kept watch over the principia, along with soldiers stationed at the most strategic points, while the rest of the troops rested around the campfires, warming themselves as much as possible.

The centurion *primae spatha* discussed his plan with the other two officers while roasting a piece of horse meat skewered on his dagger.

The horse had been the one optio Severinus Majorianus had used to transport the provisions looted from the bishop's residence, and now it served to feed the soldiers.

The firelight illuminated the faces and armor of the three centurions gathered around the flames.

"It won't be long before the mercenaries realize there's little left to loot here in Duro Catalaunum. At that point, they'll either slaughter everyone, or move on in search of what they need to survive." A spark of understanding lit his eyes. "There are tens of thousands of them—warriors, women, elders, and children—and they need food for everyone. That's a tall order in the dead of winter, especially in these times. Even for them, who take whatever they can find as they go," he said, glancing at the other two to ensure they were listening.

Vatinius Auruncus and Antoninus Tacitus nodded.

It was clear what he was explaining. That barbarian horde had only one real necessity to ensure their survival: to keep moving.

As he chewed the meat, the youngest centurion sought clarification. "You think they'll move soon, don't you?"

The crackling flames created a warm atmosphere, stirring memories of past campaigns and shared moments among the three officers.

A swirl of glowing embers rose into the air before dissipating in a gust of wind.

Aristarchos' armor gleamed in the reddish glow of the fire as he added another log.

The scent of the campfire smoke lingered in the soldiers' nostrils, while the smoke itself hovered briefly before being carried away by the wind.

Some legionaries began shoveling the accumulated snow, which had piled up significantly.

"They'll be sorely disappointed by the poverty they find in this godforsaken hole in the middle of nowhere. At that point, the generals will struggle to control their mercenaries. They'll have no choice but to move on, or they'll perish," the centurion *primae spatha* elaborated.

"Curse them, their mothers, and their accursed gods!" Antoninus Tacitus cut in. "Let's go out there and kill some more of them. You'll see—they'll leave even sooner!" he concluded, drinking directly from the jug of wine.

Vatinius Auruncus couldn't help but laugh. "Haven't you had enough fighting?"

"You can say that again!" Tacitus shot back, continuing to gulp down wine.

Even their commander, though visibly fatigued, allowed a faint smile to cross his face. He quickly wrapped up the discussion, hoping to get at least a couple of hours of rest: "Let's hold out as long as we can. It's our only hope of making it through."

Without waiting for a reply, he stood and walked away, leaving deep footprints in the fresh snow.

Sinking up to his knees with every step, he made his way to his quarters. Just before opening the door, he allowed himself a fleeting thought.

During the fighting, he had realized that it wasn't his own fate he feared, but the prospect of never seeing *her* again.

Her—the woman he had kept as spoils of war. Her—the slave who had never lowered her gaze in fear of his wrath. The woman who had tended to his wounds far too often and soothed his temper.

Aristarchos Themistocles feared losing her more than he feared the blade of an enemy sword.

Was this love? he wondered, startled by the thought.

For a brief moment, his pride as a legionary was overtaken by a greater desire—the urge to flee and take with him the woman who now occupied his heart.

And then there was that vexing sensation in his chest, as if it might explode at any moment when he thought of her.

Shaking his head, he tried to dispel those thoughts, but with little success. He, a centurion who had earned military honors, now lacked the courage to tell her he loved her.

That, he realized, was the only conclusion to be drawn. To seek what mattered most and nothing else. And now he was certain—nothing mattered more than her.

When the door opened, Placidia's eyes mirrored the joy in her heart as she began examining him from head to toe for injuries.

"What are you looking at?" he asked.

Their faces were now closer, and her lips seemed to move slowly.

"Whether you've been hurt," she replied softly.

As her hand turned him to remove his armor, the cold that had numbed his body began to fade. Pleasant shivers coursed through him, heightened by the intoxicating scent of her, which blurred his thoughts and lowered his defenses.

He, who had faced the deadliest of foes, now found his legs weak and his breath quickening, as though he feared something unknown.

In that harrowing day, he allowed himself this brief moment—when everything was centered on their eyes and their breaths.

Placidia stood still, unwavering. Her expression revealed much; her lips parted as she leaned closer with deliberate slowness.

She was honey. Blackberries from the bramble. The taste of freedom. Perhaps even blood—but the good kind, the kind that fueled passion.

Now both Aristarchos Themistocles' eyes and hers were closed. Sensations swirled—like wine being poured into a cup, like sand slipping through fingers. Sweetness and softness.

There was no need to open his eyes to feel her hand caressing his hair; the sensation was enough, more than enough. He had often watched those hands, slender and tireless.

For a moment, her lips parted from his. As if catching their breath to regain control over their seductive, mischievous, and perilous actions.

He returned her bold kiss with a look of gratitude.

Those eyes again—they were magnets, ambassadors of her desires.

All he could do was run his fingers through her long hair as it fell over her shoulders.

Her lips melted into his once more, this time more assertive, seeking a victim to consume. Stronger than a shield blow to the face.

Placidia's body fit perfectly on the *triclinus* where she lay, as though it had been made just for her, for this moment. A divine frame for the masterpiece she represented in the eyes of the commander of Duro Catalaunum's *vexillatio*.

Her bosom was a sculptor's conception, unmatched even by the frescoes adorning the grandest villas.

Her lips again. Tremors, more frequent now.

Her chest, her hands, entwined, threading through his hair. Sighs.

Now it was his senses devouring him—not the blades of enemy swords.

This was the scent of life.

The centurion *primae spatha* finally understood it.

Placidia arched her back, slightly parted her lips, and let out a brief moan. Her chest swelled, her breaths intertwined with his, merging into a single rhythm.

They were one body, flexing and stretching to its breaking point, reaching the very limits of desire—the point beyond which there was no return.

Her legs wrapped around Aristarchos Themistocles' torso, and the memory of clashing swords and searing blades faded from his mind, replaced by the dance of delight now at its peak.

***

A loud knock startled him awake.

He opened his eyes to a pleasant sight—his arms wrapped around Placidia, who was resting curled up against him.

He gazed at her face and was surprised to see, for the first time, an expression of serenity and vulnerability.

"Centurion, open up, quickly!" someone shouted from the other side of the door.

Aristarchos Themistocles rose, grabbed his gladius from its sheath, and opened the door slowly. A legionary stood before him, snow covering his armor—a clear indication he had been on sentry duty.

"Centurion…" The soldier stiffened in a military salute, barely hiding his astonishment at finding his commander completely naked.

"What's happened?" the centurion asked, sparing him further embarrassment.

"The governor and his escort have arrived at the principia. Your presence is required."

Placidia had opened her eyes. The way she looked at him revealed a hint of apprehension.

"Alright," he replied to the soldier, "I'm coming."

He closed the door with a sigh, resigned that his brief moment of peace had come to an end.

"I'll help you dress," Placidia offered, her warm voice filling his heart and giving him the energy he needed to move forward.

He was surprised by how deftly her skilled hands adjusted his focale before securing the lorica over his chest. Watching her dress a Roman soldier with such patience and expertise left him momentarily dazed.

As she carefully examined his skin for any scars, he felt a sense of being cared for, of being loved. Her concern was a treasure to his weary spirit.

Fastening his sword to his belt, he mentally locked away the precious moments he had just shared with Placidia and prepared to leave.

With both hands, he picked up his helmet, still smeared with blood, and tucked it under his arm.

He gave her one last glance of gratitude.

"I'll wait for you," she said, her words carrying the weight of a loving ultimatum.

"Then I'll make sure to return," he replied.

He walked down the narrow corridor, wondering what time it was and how long he had slept. The answer came quickly—a faint slit in the ceiling revealed no light. It was still the dead of night.

When he reached the courtyard, he found Governor Attilius Faticus waiting for him, perpetually surrounded by his personal guard, who had positioned themselves defensively, as though facing a mortal enemy.

The governor's escort consisted of Gallo-Romans and southern Burgundians. Their uniforms were a patchwork of mismatched armor. The Burgundians sported long hair and beards, while the Gallo-Romans wore imperial-style breastplates, but carried longer swords instead of the traditional gladius.

The centurion *primae spatha* felt a wave of irritation at the governor's presence. Surely, trouble had arrived with him—trouble they already had plenty of.

Attilius Faticus, with his usual arrogance, demanded an update on the situation. He seemed visibly annoyed by the Roman officer's irritated demeanor, sensing that Aristarchos Themistocles was in no mood to entertain him.

"What brings you here, Governor?" the centurion asked curtly.

"To remind you that you and your men are still under my command," came the haughty reply.

Aristarchos Themistocles scanned him from head to toe. His body wrapped in fox fur, the governor's white-gloved hands displayed massive rings, set with precious stones that reflected the light of the campfires.

"My men and I serve only the honor of Rome," the centurion began, though he bit his lip to keep from saying more, knowing it could severely worsen the situation.

"How many men do you still have at your disposal?" the governor asked, his tone dripping with entitlement.

"Not many. They're exhausted and freezing. There's little they can do against the horde outside."

"Should we surrender, then? Perhaps we'd face a better fate," the nobleman suggested.

Aristarchos Themistocles glared at him, anger flashing in his eyes. He knew this was not a question, but the prelude to a decision already made. Attilius Faticus had resolved to surrender.

"Governor, Ravenna might ransom you. We..." he turned to his soldiers, "...we would all be killed, tortured, or sold as slaves in the markets of Syria."

"Do you see another solution, Centurion?" Faticus challenged.

"No, but I will never propose surrender. It would be the end of us."

A seasoned politician, Attilius Faticus knew how to navigate such situations. If he had suggested surrender, it was highly likely a messenger had already been sent to Rudulfus to negotiate terms.

Sensing the centurion's disdain, several legionaries began approaching the governor's guard in a menacing manner. The tension became palpable, but the officer defused it by signaling his men to sheathe their weapons.

The governor's wild-eyed expression betrayed the bitter pill he was forced to swallow—he no longer had the authority to order the centurion's execution.

Struggling to maintain his composure, his face contorted with rage, he continued: "I have sent a messenger to speak with the king of the Heruli to negotiate a surrender, fair to both victors and vanquished. That is why I've come—to personally deliver the order that, should the opportunity arise, you are to surrender."

Those words echoed through the principia like blasphemy. Every legionary turned toward the source of such absurdity. The veterans spat on the ground.

Fulcinius Agricola Statius stood to his full height, pointing the tip of his *pugio* at the governor. "Say the word, Centurion, and I'll gladly cut out his tongue," he declared, showing no fear that his words might ignite conflict.

Aristarchos Themistocles stepped face to face with the governor, their noses almost touching. He waited a moment before speaking, knowing those few seconds would ensure his men would listen to what he had to say—and keep their swords sheathed, even hotheaded Fulcinius Agricola Statius.

Through clenched teeth, his eyes sparking with fury, he laid out his position: "We will not surrender. We must hope they migrate south in search of food. That's this city's only chance."

A roar of approval erupted from the principia. The legionaries began hurling insults at the governor and his guard.

Fulcinius Agricola Statius strode up to the centurion *primae spatha*, ready to ask for permission to dispatch the unwanted guests, but the glare he received sent him back to the campfire, head bowed.

Attilius Faticus' face twisted in indignation before he spoke. "I am a powerful man, Centurion. The moment I reach Ravenna, I will ensure you are sentenced to death for high treason."

With that, he turned on his heel and stormed off.

The Tent of the King of the Heruli

Gathered in council with his generals, Rudulfus abruptly raised his head when he heard shouts of jubilation coming from the Roman *principia*.

The only thing Rudulfus envied about the Romans was the camaraderie their legionaries seemed to share. It was something he had always begrudged. If his own army could achieve the level of cohesion the Roman soldiers displayed, no enemy would be able to challenge him. But his warriors were driven only by the thirst for plunder.

He glanced at a servant, who promptly poured him some mead. The cup he held in his hand was gilded and adorned with oval-shaped bone fragments, polished to a smooth finish. At feasts, Rudulfus often boasted to his companions that the fragments came from the skulls of Roman officers, personally claimed as trophies.

Even the cup itself had been looted from a Roman noble during the sacking of a rural villa along the banks of the Rhine.

"What could they possibly be celebrating?" one general grumbled, swallowing a gulp of mead.

"Don't they know that tomorrow will be their last day?" echoed another, his gaze fixed on the map spread out across the field table. He traced the only viable route for the army and its followers with his finger. Given the harsh winter conditions, migration southward was the sole feasible option. The snow would mire their wagons and slow their march considerably.

Rudulfus' voice cut through the murmurs, commanding silence.

"Marching south during such a brutal winter would be sheer madness. We'd lose countless animals and people to the cold—not to mention the shortage of provisions."

At these words, an officer named Hottentroth, whose temperament leaned more toward recklessness than reason, interjected:

"We'll plunder every town we pass! There aren't enough legions left to stop us…"

Catching the sarcasm in his tone, the other generals burst into laughter.

But the ambassadors of the other tribes did not laugh. Neither did Rudulfus, who growled before hammering down on the discussion like a massive mallet striking an iron pin:

"Roman cities are starving. There are no fertile fields or farms for leagues upon leagues. Livestock is scarce, and we'd have to mobilize the entire army just to hunt enough game to feed our people. I thank the gods they didn't choose *you* as king of the Heruli!" Rudulfus snarled at the presumptuous general.

Hottentroth, however, refused to be intimidated. He took a step forward, his posture openly defiant.

"You're getting soft—just like the Romans. It wouldn't surprise me if tomorrow your tent were filled with eunuchs," he hissed, locking eyes with Rudulfus in open contempt.

A deadly silence fell over the tent.

With deliberate control, Rudulfus let his hand drift away from the dagger he instinctively grasped at such provocations, restraining the urge to slit the insolent general's throat. Fighting the storm of rage within, he seated himself in his chair—a war trophy taken from General Marcellinus after the annihilation of the Legion.

From his seat, Rudulfus addressed everyone present, deliberately ignoring the still-seething general. His words carried a weight that no one dared dismiss.

"During the assault on Duro Catalaunum, we lost many warriors. Still, we've breached their defenses and now hold key positions within the city walls. Alongside us are the Thuringians, who also maintain strategic footholds. However, like every other border town we've sacked during our migration, this one offers little in terms of sustenance. I will not lead my people any further. Tell your kings," he said, turning to the ambassadors of the other tribes, "that the Heruli will remain here and winter at Duro Catalaunum."

He then fixed his blazing eyes on the assembled generals, except for Hottentroth, who had earned nothing but disdain:

"Does anyone have any *better* suggestions?"

The question was laced with an unmistakable threat, one that everyone understood perfectly.

All eyes turned toward the impudent general who had dared to confront the king.

"Well? Is that clear now?" Rudulfus pressed, his glare dripping with scorn.

The general, realizing he had no alternative, muttered a begrudging, "Yes," his defiance tempered by the fear of a gruesome fate.

"Good. You're all dismissed," Rudulfus concluded.

The tent emptied in moments, as everyone was eager to retreat to the warmth of a fire and escape the icy atmosphere inside. The braziers glowing in the corners of the tent barely provided any relief from the bitter cold of the night.

With a flick of his fingers, Rudulfus summoned one of his personal guards.

"My king," the guard responded immediately.

"Slip into Hottentroth's tent as soon as you can and slit his throat while he sleeps. Then hang his tongue at the entrance of my tent as a reminder to all of what happens when words are not used wisely. If you succeed, you'll be handsomely rewarded. If you fail, someone else will finish the task—and your tongue will hang alongside his," Rudulfus ordered.

"I will not fail," the mercenary promised before vanishing to carry out the command.

Rudulfus stared at a corner of the tent, lost in thought. He knew things rarely unfolded as planned, and tried to imagine what the coming days would bring.

Sleep was out of the question. His chest still burned with rage—toward the Romans, toward the insolent general, and toward the ceaseless frustrations of leadership.

The campfires of the Heruli stretched across the valley before the fortified town of Duro Catalaunum. These fires belonged only to the vanguard of the army; the rest of the host camped beyond the hills and forests.

The sprawling encampment extended eastward for miles, its bivouacs marked by thousands of flickering lights. Only the occasional braying of beasts of burden broke the silence, muffled by the heavy snowfall that blanketed the tents and trapped the smoke, making it hover like a spectral ceiling above the camp.

Principia

Vatinius Auruncus, Fulcinius Agricola Statius, and Severinus Majorianus huddled in their cloaks, trying to rest beside a fire that was gradually dying out.

Drusus Variatus and Auctus Tullius Sextus Plato stood guard alongside Christianus Caligatus and Tarquinius Glaucus, who, somehow, still managed to joke around.

To maintain visibility, they had rigged up a makeshift curtain using the banners of their military unit. This clever setup allowed snow to pile up on the fabric instead of falling on their faces, enabling them to keep their eyes alert.

Meanwhile, the resourceful Gaius Octavianus, without asking for permission, had slipped past the barricades and infiltrated the Thuringian encampments, disguised in clothes taken from a fallen enemy. He spent his freezing night gathering as much intelligence as possible.

The weary Centurion Antoninus Tacitus idly picked up a branch from the ground and smoothed it with his fingers, searching in vain for buds. Closing his eyes, he tried to get some rest.

Gallienus Lars Gracchus, the restless Etruscan, found his nerves even more frayed by the longing to leave this cursed place and return home. Still, he removed his armor, wrapped himself in a cloak, and relished the warmth of a nearby fire against his back. Yet sleep eluded him, gnawed away by an uneasy feeling in his stomach. Was it fear?

Soft footsteps crunching on the snow jolted him to awareness. He couldn't believe his eyes.

The rest of the night passed in quiet reflection for the legionaries—a night both silent and eerily calm.

From the highest remaining Roman positions, what they could see beyond the thick snowfall was chilling: thousands of campfires, stretching as far as the eye could see.

***

Ulzio Dacianus awoke, already half-buried in snow. Propping

himself up on his arms, he slowly regained his bearings. After a moment of confusion, memories of the battle and how he had been incapacitated came rushing back.

A pang of dread struck him as he realized he was alone and trapped in the section of the city now under enemy control. There were no Roman sentries or fires on the walls—clear signs that his comrades had retreated or, worse, that Duro Catalaunum had already fallen. If that were the case, its inhabitants and the soldiers of the *vexillatio* had likely been massacred.

His head throbbed, but he knew he needed to leave. If discovered, he would surely face a gruesome death by torture.

He began crawling slowly, doing his best to remain silent, eventually reaching a set of stairs. He dragged himself down, maneuvering around corpses.

Footsteps. He could hear footsteps. Turning his head, he spotted the glow of torches and strained his ears to catch the voices—they were not Roman.

Feigning death, he lay still as a patrol of Thuringians passed by, their torches casting flickering shadows.

Patiently, he waited until the patrol moved far enough away, then resumed his silent crawl.

His elbows scraped raw as he dragged himself along until he reached an ancient pagan temple dedicated to Mercury[11]. There, he retrieved a gladius, concealing it under his armor. He scavenged dried meat from the pouch of a dead Thuringian soldier, making it his desperate meal.

The cold had numbed his limbs, and his fingers moved without feeling. The temperature had plummeted, and he knew he needed

---

[11] *Mercury:* A Roman pagan god representing trade, profit, and commerce. His name likely derives from *mercator* (merchant). Due to his speed, he was also considered the god of thieves. In Rome, a temple was erected in his honor on the Aventine Hill in 495 BCE. His staff, the "Caduceus," later became a symbol of medicine. He was regarded as the messenger of the gods and was often depicted with wings on his feet.

to seek shelter before succumbing to the freezing conditions.

He dragged himself inside the pagan temple, which reeked of urine and decay, having long been used as a public latrine. Even the barbarians had chosen other places for shelter.

As his eyes adjusted to the darkness, he struggled to his feet, unsteady. In an adjoining room, he found the shattered remains of a marble statue of Mercury—only the lower half remained intact. The sculpted wings on the feet were masterfully done, though now cloaked in cobwebs. The marble walls had been stripped, leaving behind crude plaster.

A large candelabrum lay toppled on a floor littered with fragments of amphorae, vases, cups, and other debris. At some point, merchants had turned the temple into a dumping ground for broken goods.

Despite the unwelcoming surroundings, Ulzio Dacianus, a seasoned veteran, felt a sense of safety. Here, he could finally gather his wits and rest.

Deciding to leave his plans for later, he leaned against the cold wall and surrendered to exhaustion.

***

The fires were carefully kept burning, consuming everything that could serve as fuel: wood, furniture, dispatches, maps, even tents. Everything. The desperate situation demanded it.

Centurion Antoninus Tacitus made his rounds, still drowsy, to check that all the guard posts were vigilant. Drusus Variatus hung his head low, occasionally snapping it up to check that everything was in order, only to let it fall back into a defeated slumber. His right hand, however, remained firmly gripping the hilt of his gladius.

They all knew the situation wasn't as calm as it seemed. The soldiers rested, but they were still on edge, ready to spring into action at the slightest sound. The crunch of Antoninus Tacitus' boots in the fresh snow, now over a *cubitus*[12] deep, betrayed his presence. As he passed, everyone opened at least one eye to see who it was.

Christianus Caligatus, in his prudence, had collected as many arrows as he could, even those fired by the enemy, which he intended to adapt for his bow. He had suggested the same to his fellow archers, and the hailstorm of arrows that had rained down on them during the previous assault had yielded a substantial stockpile. "We'll return them to sender when the time comes," he thought with a smirk as he huddled closer to the fire, his watch just completed.

Principia, Quarters of the Centurion primae spatha

Aristarchos Themistocles stared intently at his servant.

"Kungian," he called softly.

The striking woman froze. He had never called her by her barbarian name before—only the Romanized one, Placidia.

"Kungian...turn around," he murmured warmly.

She turned slowly, keeping her gaze lowered.

"Kungian, I need to speak with you seriously. I'm certain that tomorrow, events will spiral beyond anyone's control. None of us can predict what will happen, but many of us will die, and others may face unspeakable tortures or worse. The governor has proposed surrender. We have two more hours of darkness left, during which you..." His voice faltered, his stomach knotting at what he was about to say. "Kungian...if you want, you can leave. You're free now. You have no ties or obligations to me," he said, gesturing towards the door with the finger that bore his centurion's ring.

"Placidia," she corrected him. "My name has been Placidia for some time now. I don't even know who Kungian is anymore." Her eyes filled with tears she stubbornly fought to hold back.

---

[12] *Cubitus:* A Roman unit of measurement equivalent to 44.46 cm.

He had always treated her with a cold detachment, even though she was sure he harbored strong feelings for her. And yet, here he was, showing her a loyalty and respect that no slave could ever expect.

His gaze hardened, his tone becoming firm and unyielding. "Kungian, you must go. In two hours, you could cover a lot of ground, and it'll be many more before anyone finds you. It's likely they won't harm you if a patrol catches you. You're one of them, of barbarian lineage; more than that, you were once a noble's wife. They'll probably keep you alive, maybe even marry you off to a tribal chief. Just don't tell them you were ever..." His voice cracked, and he shut his mouth tightly, realizing he was about to say too much.

But Placidia understood.

"Aristarchos, I..." she whispered, leaning closer to his ear, "I don't want to leave. I want to stay by your side."

She regretted not saying what she truly wanted—to confess her affection, her love.

The awkward pause that followed felt like an eternity. They stood frozen, as though an enchantment had turned them both into statues of ice. Placidia stared at a distant corner while Aristarchos struggled to keep himself from grabbing her and holding her close—so close that she could feel how much he longed to keep her near, for as long as possible. For forever.

But that wouldn't be in her best interest.

Only two hours separated life from death. Outside the principia, thousands of barbarian mercenaries waited to massacre every man, woman, and child in Duro Catalaunum. He was only trying to save her from that fate.

He cursed fate and the heavens for what he was about to say.

"Slave, I release you from your bonds. You're free now. Get out." His fists clenched, his jaw tightened after he uttered the words.

Placidia let out a small sob, tears streaming down her cheeks. She reached out to caress his face one last time, and he allowed it.

She gathered her few belongings into a sack.

"Wait," he stopped her. "I've packed some provisions for you, and this." He grabbed a blanket from his field sack and handed it to her. "It'll keep you warm if you can't find proper shelter. And remember…" He sighed deeply before continuing. "Head north. The way will be clear."

Her hands received the blanket, folding it neatly into her sack. She took the provisions he had prepared for her, placing them inside as well.

Then, as if performing a daily routine, she slung the sack over her shoulder and sought his eyes one last time—the eyes of the man she loved more than anything else in the world.

"Goodbye," she said.

"Goodbye."

When she disappeared beyond his quarters' door, Aristarchos Themistocles felt his legs weaken. He had just made the decision that would weigh on his heart more than anything else. He stared at the lantern's light reflecting off his helmet with resignation.

He walked down the corridor, his eyes briefly catching an ancient fresco depicting a banquet with men reclining on triclinia. Women danced sensually, and a tuba player entertained the gathering. It must have been a remnant of a bygone era.

***

As Placidia crossed the lines patrolled by the Romans, she sobbed quietly. She passed almost unnoticed through the narrow streets of Duro Catalaunum, which she knew well, and headed toward a small gate that Aristarchos Themistocles had pointed out to her some time ago. No one was guarding it, and she was able to clear away the piles of snow without disturbance. Once she opened it, she looked outside and felt a pang of fear as the dark forest, teeming with wolves and bears, stretched before her. She swallowed hard and stepped through.

This was the moment when she had to decide—whether to flee or remain and face whatever fate awaited her.

She had chosen to flee.

The darkness of the forest quickly swallowed her.

Walking forward through the cold, soft snow with almost no visibility, dodging branches that struck her face, seemed nearly impossible. With her heart pounding in her chest and temples, she summoned her courage and placed one foot in front of the other, searching for refuge in the ominous maze of trees.

The first purplish hues of dawn caught her off guard as she cautiously stepped onto the rocks, attempting to cross a frigid stream whose waters flowed rapidly and crystal clear.

The crunch of snow drew her attention.

But relief spread across her face when she realized it was a large stag drinking from the stream, not a pack of wolves ready to tear her apart.

She decided to take a moment to rest and watch it. Clouds of vapor puffed from the stag's nostrils, dissipating into the air. The animal had noticed her, yet it showed no intention of fleeing. Perhaps the bitter cold of the past days had made it more docile.

Who knows, she thought to herself before continuing her journey.

She jumped in fright when, turning around, she found herself face-to-face with a hulking man standing just a few steps away, staring at her.

His eyes were as clear as ice, and his grip was strong—so strong that it made her cry out in pain.

Chapter IV – Rudulfus

Rudulfus received the news at the first light of dawn. Stepping out of his tent, he raised his hand to shield himself from the blinding glare. The snow had stopped, and as the sun rose, its reddish light spread across the snow, making every ice crystal glisten with golden sparks.

A messenger had warned him that no delays would be tolerated, and armed with this authority, the man urged him to hurry.

The escort was already waiting for him, with nervous, snorting horses. The groom helped him mount his majestic warhorse, whose sleek coat shone brilliantly in the morning light.

Once in the saddle, Rudulfus glanced back at the entrance of his tent and noticed, hanging from a hook, the bloody head of the arrogant and presumptuous general he had confronted only hours earlier. He exchanged a knowing look with the man who had delivered this splendid gift and leaned forward in his saddle to ask him, "Do you know why you were chosen to join my escort?"

The other man replied candidly, "Because my name is Cunipert, son of the tribal chief who bears the same name, and you know how loyal he was to you."

The sharp eyes of the Heruli king softened. "You're right, Cunipert. Your noble father was like a brother to me, and he assured me you inherited his courage and strength."

"Thank you, my king," Cunipert replied, lowering his gaze in submission, though inwardly he harbored doubts, sensing the king's last words carried a hint of false pretense.

"You proved your reliability last night. I'll reward you as promised."

"I am happy to have served you well, my lord."

"Choose any of my servants who pleases you and spend the night with her," Rudulfus said with a smile.

The loyal warrior returned the smile gratefully before taking his position in the escort.

Rudulfus smirked. "Lead the way," he ordered the messenger.

The messenger spun his horse around and set off at a gallop along the snowy path. After about half an hour, the group arrived at the Thuringians' camp, which immediately soured Rudulfus' mood.

"What are we doing here?" he asked the messenger.

"Magnificent Rudulfus, I am merely a courier and do not know my king's intentions," the man replied evasively, signaling to the guards that everything was in order and that the group was authorized to enter.

Rudulfus, whose temperament did not favor surprises, cast a warning glance at his men, signaling them to stay alert.

He was led to a tent he knew all too well—the tent of the Thuringian king, whom he hated with all his heart. Rudulfus knew there was something odd about this invitation, which felt more like an order. Outside the tent, a line of heavily armed Thuringian warriors stood guard.

The messenger approached him obsequiously. "Only you, great king, may enter the quarters of the new governor of Gaul," he explained.

The Heruli king snapped his head toward the source of those absurd words. "What are you implying, you filthy worm?" he growled through clenched teeth.

The messenger bowed and stepped back two paces before answering. "The Italic rex[1], Odoacer, has appointed King Gargalico as the new governor of Gaul," he said simply, gesturing toward the entrance of the tent.

---

[1] After killing Orestes and deposing the young Romulus Augustulus, Odoacer proclaimed himself Rex.

Rudulfus shot him a furious glare, vowing silently to kill the insolent lackey. Then, lifting his chin in a display of pride, he advanced inside.

Upon entering, the Heruli king removed the wolf pelt from his shoulders, growling in anger. Until that moment, he had believed himself to be Odoacer's favored candidate for the governorship of Gaul. The news that the position had instead been given to Gargalico, the Thuringian king, sent him into a rage.

He immediately recognized the truth of the matter when he saw Gargalico seated at the center of the tent, surrounded by his personal guard, with all the generals seated in a circle before his elevated throne. The podium on which Gargalico sat was raised by several steps, symbolizing the growing distance between him and everyone else.

In a corner stood Odoacer's envoy, ready to record everything that transpired and report back to the new regent of the Western Roman Empire.

The envoy, though dressed in Roman fashion, bore unmistakable Heruli features.

With a dismissive wave of his hand, Gargalico signaled for Rudulfus to kneel.

The Heruli king remained motionless, as impassive as a statue carved from travertine.

"Kneel, Rudulfus. Rex Odoacer himself, regent of the Western Empire, has appointed me governor of Gaul," Gargalico said, pausing deliberately to heighten the tension. "... From now on, you are in my service," he hissed, pretending to examine a document.

"Can you read now?" Rudulfus mocked him.

Gargalico was not amused. "You are still standing?"

What Rudulfus did not know was that, the previous summer, Gargalico had sent spies to Ravenna, who had done their job well. They spread rumors that Rudulfus was vying for the governorship of the north and was particularly interested in the Empire's political affairs and Odoacer's moves.

This strategy ensured that poisonous whispers about Rudulfus circulated within the Sacred Palace, distancing him from Rex Odoacer.

Once this was achieved, Gargalico's trusted spies began a correspondence with Odoacer, keeping him informed of all activities along the northeastern borders. As Gargalico had anticipated, Odoacer appreciated this so much that he placed his full trust in him, appointing him to the most coveted position in the region.

A smirk spread across Gargalico's bearded face, marked by a long scar that prevented his left eyelid from fully opening. His satisfied expression betrayed his thoughts.

Rome, sacked multiple times, no longer inspired fear. The once-symbolic city of the Empire had become a crumbling collection of dilapidated buildings piled on top of one another. Its streets were dangerous—rarely could one walk them without being robbed, or even killed.

The papacy remained the only hope for the citizens, but it drained their pockets with heavy taxes, adding to the already burdensome demands of the Empire. The capital had been moved to Ravenna, primarily for defensive reasons, but the Sacred Palace had become a breeding ground for corrupt, useless officials.

These officials had devised a complex administrative system that made them indispensable, even though, in reality, they were almost entirely useless. Each of them wielded power that even the Emperor could not circumvent, allowing them to make appointments and nominations to suit their interests, fueling corruption and the exorbitant costs of the faltering state machinery.

The Emperor himself had, in reality, become little more than a symbolic figure. Everyone knew that real power was held by the magister militum, all of whom, from the time of the great Aetius onward, had been of barbarian origin. For this reason, even the legions no longer inspired fear. The Empire had lost the ability to gather armies capable of repelling invasions and pressures from beyond its borders. There were exceptions, such as Augustus' Eight Legion, which still maintained its ancient structure, though it had been reduced to a mere few thousand men. These remnants clung to the traditions of the Augustan era, proudly carrying the military reforms of the last great Emperor, Majorianus, who foresaw the need for a strong military presence along the borders.

However, a series of puppet emperors abandoned Majorianus' crucial reforms, reducing the imperial army to a horde of mercenaries loyal to the highest bidder.

Gargalico, the newly appointed governor, had understood all this well, and had taken full advantage of it. He thought and acted like a Roman, and his approach had proven successful—the results spoke for themselves.

In this era, power lay in the ability to foresee events and forge strategic alliances. Gargalico had outmaneuvered Rudulfus and other barbarian leaders with little difficulty. After all, weren't they what the Romans called "barbarians"? This thought brought a wry smile to Gargalico's face as he mockingly observed Rudulfus, who remained standing before him in silence as the entire tent fell into an uneasy hush.

Rudulfus couldn't help but notice Gargalico's drastic change in attire. The governor wore a purple cloak over a white linen tunic embroidered with gold. An ostentatious ring with a striking blue stone adorned his hand, deliberately displayed for all to see. At his feet lay his shield, placed in such a way that anyone approaching him was forced to kneel upon it—a reminder that he was still, above all, a warrior.

It was said that upon receiving his appointment, Gargalico had immediately removed his scale armor and helmet, ordering his servants to bring him the finest garments—spoils looted from the noble homes of cities sacked during the autumn campaigns. He was still a barbarian at heart, but he had managed to refine his outward appearance.

By securing his nomination, Gargalico had demonstrated sharp political instincts, as keen as an eagle's. Yet Rudulfus was certain that his emulation of Roman customs would make him despised by the tribes. With a quick glance, Rudulfus noticed that even among the Thuringians, some generals regarded their leader with disdain—likely for the same reasons.

"Kneel!" Gargalico thundered, pointing to the ground with his finger.

Rudulfus tilted his head to the side and burst into laughter, a loud and mocking sound. The defiance was evident, and Gargalico was taken aback when he noticed Rudulfus resting his hand on the hilt of his sword.

When Gargalico's guards lunged at Rudulfus, he drew his blade and immediately cut down the most reckless among them. One stumbled forward, blood spurting in all directions, before collapsing, lifeless, at the feet of the Roman envoy, staining his pristine tunic. Rudulfus' sword cleaved through another guard before he advanced, practically unopposed, toward the governor, whose eyes widened in terror.

"Son of a bitch, how dare you demand that I kneel?" Rudulfus hissed as he plunged his sword into Gargalico. He waited, unmoving, as the governor's gurgling breaths faded. The man's lifeless eyes stared at him, cold and unseeing.

Rudulfus cleaned his blade on Gargalico's purple cloak before pushing the corpse off the throne. The body tumbled to the ground.

Standing atop the Thuringian leader's corpse, Rudulfus addressed the gathered crowd. "Let Ravenna hear this: the valiant Gargalico has fallen in battle, and I was forced—grieved as I am by his tragic fate—to take up his mantle."

Fixing his gaze on the Roman envoy, Rudulfus added, "I trust this message will be delivered by someone reliable."

A sinister grin spread across his face, sending chills through the envoy, who tried to slip out of the tent as quickly as possible. He wasn't fast enough. The ever-loyal Cunipert intercepted him, stabbing him with a dagger. The envoy fell lifeless.

Cunipert dragged the body outside the tent and decapitated it in full view of the assembled warriors from all tribes. The brutal act sent a clear message: something significant was happening within the tent.

Back inside, Rudulfus pressed his foot against Gargalico's severed head and addressed the gathered leaders:

"I wish to speak plainly to all of you..."

The room fell silent. The Thuringian generals clenched their jaws, ready to act if provoked. Yet Rudulfus had already noted that none of them had lifted a finger while he killed Gargalico—a critical detail as he prepared to deliver his proclamation.

"Odoacer granted this appointment to your king..." He gestured to Gargalico's lifeless body beneath his feet. "But he placed his trust in the least suitable man—a man far too eager to adopt Roman customs."

A murmur of agreement rippled through the tent, emboldening Rudulfus. He pressed on: "The identity of our people, our traditions, and our beliefs will never take a backseat to those of the Romans—corrupt politicians and feeble soldiers, still clinging to the glories of a past that will never return."

Surprised by his own clarity, Rudulfus continued with even greater conviction: "That is why I eliminated this worm..." he gestured toward Gargalico's corpse, "...and I will do the same to anyone who follows his example."

A Thuringian general stepped forward, cutting Rudulfus off abruptly: "King Rudulfus, your words are unnecessary. Gargalico's death was tolerated without further bloodshed for one reason only—he was the worst of our kings. Weak in battle and too enamored with Roman customs. We will soon convene to elect a new leader—a noble warrior fit to guide our people. We have no interest in hearing your self-serving speech. This tent..." He spread his arms, as if to outline its walls. "... is the tent of the Thuringian king, and that behind you is his throne. So, make your proclamation and leave."

The two men locked eyes. In the Thuringian general's gaze, Rudulfus saw the confidence of someone backed by an entire army, ready to strike at a moment's notice.

"Very well," Rudulfus said. "I will make my proclamation and leave."

With slow, deliberate steps, Rudulfus ascended the stairs to the throne. He seated himself, running a finger along the armrest as if to mock its previous occupant.

Finally, he raised his eyes to the assembled leaders, who hung on his every word: "I, Rudulfus, am the new governor of Gaul. Spread this news to everyone you meet."

The tension in the room was palpable. Yet the Thuringian generals and the envoys from other tribes received the declaration without outward protest.

The Thuringians released their swords only because the man who had been slain was their most despised leader—a man who, by embracing Roman ways, had earned the scorn of his men. They had long considered assassinating him themselves. For this reason alone, they did not attack Rudulfus and his loyal guards.

Without a word, the Thuringians left the tent, one by one.

Rudulfus remained seated, watching them leave. He signaled to a servant—one who had belonged to the now-dead Gargalico—to bring him mead.

He sipped from the cup in silence, deep in thought. The news was already beginning to spread.

***

A courier departed for the capital to deliver the latest news to Rex Odoacer.

The message, of course, was a carefully crafted version of the truth: Gargalico had fallen in combat, and Rudulfus, driven by duty, had temporarily assumed his position.

It was evident that the Heruli king was aiming for a tacit confirmation of the governorship that had originally been granted to the Thuringian king.

Once Odoacer received the missive, he would undoubtedly deploy his spies to uncover the real events behind this unexpected succession. The game would be decided in that phase.

Rudulfus' own spies would need to identify Odoacer's agents, subdue them—whether by bribery or elimination—and send back a messenger to reinforce the narrative most beneficial to Rudulfus' cause.

Now self-proclaimed Governor of Gaul, Rudulfus returned to his encampment and summoned all his generals.

He ordered them to take part of the army and head to the southern borders, anticipating retaliation from Odoacer. Rudulfus needed to demonstrate his competence as a governor by making decisive moves and achieving results.

He was fully aware of Odoacer's vengeful temperament, and taking steps to prevent a military campaign was the wisest course of action. As his first major political decision, Rudulfus decided to have his people spend the winter in Duro Catalaunum. Moving such a massive population under the current harsh weather conditions would have been pointless.

The tent quickly filled with people: military officers, messengers, advisors, and the ever-reliable Cunipert, who had earned the king's full trust.

Rudulfus sat in thought, staring at a fixed point while sipping mead in silence. No one dared to raise their voice, and those present spoke in hushed whispers.

Suddenly, as if waking from a troubling dream, Rudulfus began issuing orders.

First, he turned to his officers: "Send messengers to every city. From now on, the taxes they used to send to the Emperor of Rome will flow into our coffers instead. My treasurer will forward them to Ravenna."

As he spoke the words "treasurer," Rudulfus realized his transformation into a political figure had already begun. He understood that he would need competent people to achieve his goals—individuals he couldn't find among his Heruli followers. A bitter, ironic smile crept across his face.

He would find the right men among the Romans in Duro Catalaunum.

He would, in essence, do exactly as Gargalico had done.

The strange revelation made him chuckle to himself.

When his generals eventually left, Rudulfus drained the last of his mead and bellowed, "Cunipert! Cunipert!"

The mercenary, who had stepped outside, quickly re-entered the tent.

"Bring me more mead, food... and a woman. One of Gargalico's wives—the most beautiful among them. Quickly!" Rudulfus commanded.

Under the flickering light of torches, with all eyes on him, Rudulfus savored the feeling of true power. He now controlled Gaul, and felt a surge of energy coursing through him, invigorating him with new strength and determination.

On this freshly dawning day, the Western Roman Empire's outpost of Duro Catalaunum was witnessing a sunrise unlike any other.

***

Contrary to what the new Governor of Gaul had envisioned, however, things quickly spiraled out of control.

The Alans, who had not participated in the earlier meeting, learned of the events that had unfolded and left the camp that very morning.

Their departure caused chaos among the barbarians, sparking skirmishes over the division of spoils from previous plundering campaigns.

By midday, the barbarian army was reduced—both the Alans and the Thuringians had decided to migrate southward to warmer lands.

This left only the Heruli, who still boasted thousands of warriors. However, half of them were already en route to the southern borders to prepare for the possibility of facing Odoacer's forces.

The remaining warriors were insufficient to lay siege to a city as fortified as Duro Catalaunum.

Chapter V – A New Day

Principia, Early Morning

The rising sun in the east bathed the landscape in golden light. Shades of yellow, orange, and ochre colored the white expanse of frozen snow, creating a breathtaking scene. One could feel the faint but welcome warmth of the morning sun on their skin—a warmth that revived both the legionaries and the townsfolk.

A legionary caught the attention of Aristarchos Themistocles, who had been gazing at an ice stalactite.

"Centurion, Centurion! There's something you should see!" the soldier called out.

The centurion's stern look prompted him to elaborate.

"Centurion, come see for yourself. The snow has stopped falling, and the barbarian camps in the valley are emptying out!"

The centurion's mouth dropped open.

"Emptying out?"

"Yes! The Thuringians and Alans are leaving the valley. There have even been skirmishes between the Alans and the Heruli, who are the only ones staying behind. Come and see."

The centurion quickly climbed onto the roof of a house, used as a lookout point, to see for himself.

A satisfied smile crossed his face. The plain was nearly empty, except for the Heruli. Yet something else was happening—part of the Heruli warriors seemed to be organizing themselves, preparing to leave as well.

If things continued this way, Rudulfus would no longer be

able to keep Aristarchos and his legionaries trapped like rats under siege.

Almost every soldier had climbed to a vantage point to observe the situation, and all wore the same expression of disbelief.

The noise of thousands of men, horses, and wagons moving echoed loudly even from a distance.

The Heruli had been left without allies, and half of their forces were departing southward, though no one knew why.

Aristarchos noticed Vatinius Auruncus and Antoninus Tacitus on another rooftop, also scanning the scene intently. But it seemed the surprises weren't over yet.

Gallienus Lars Gracchus climbed onto the roof and saluted in military fashion before delivering news that left everyone stunned.

"Centurion…an Heruli delegation has requested to speak with Governor Attilius Faticus."

For perhaps the first time in his life, Aristarchos Themistocles was caught off guard. He had believed this would be his last day alive—and perhaps it still would be—but something was beginning to shake that conviction.

He had to act quickly. If the Heruli were asking for a meeting, it was possible they no longer wished to prolong the siege. Either way, the request had come at the perfect moment and could not be ignored.

"Take a couple of men and go to the governor's residence. This…" he pointed to the roof beneath his feet, "this is the perfect place for the meeting."

The *signifer* looked at the indicated spot with mild curiosity before nodding and running off to carry out the order.

As the sun rose higher, warming everything and dazzling against the snow to the point where they had to shield their eyes with their hands, the centurion *primae spatha* allowed himself a moment of concern for Placidia. He wondered if she had managed to reach one of the old postal stations to find shelter from the night's cold.

The salutes of the other centurions snapped him out of his thoughts.

"Centurion."

"Centurion."

Vatinius Auruncus and Antoninus Tacitus looked at him expectantly, waiting to hear his thoughts on the unfolding events.

"It seems we'll witness a meeting between Attilius Faticus and an envoy from Rudulfus," he explained.

The younger centurion's mouth fell open. He couldn't believe that not long ago, he had been certain the barbarians would slaughter every man, woman, and child in the city. And now, with the rising sun, they were requesting a meeting with the governor!

Their attention was interrupted by the shout of Fulcinius Agricola Statius, who called up from below, cupping his hands around his mouth to amplify his voice:

"Aren't we killing the barbarians anymore?"

"Shut your mouth, fool! Do you want to be whipped?" Plato scolded him.

"What do you know about war, boy! You'd be better off reading those books you insist on lugging around in your bag...though you'd be wiser to use the space for coins to pay for tavern women instead!" Plato laughed, then muttered, "Even those cutthroat barbarians are running off like rabbits now...what a disappointment. What a huge disappointment!" He removed his helmet to scratch his head.

Aristarchos Themistocles' gaze rested on his soldiers, all cloaked in purple mantles, enjoying the view of the valley before Duro Catalaunum, now cleared of the savage tribes that had been invading the Empire.

And so they remained, gazing at the valley, in the moments before the grand arrival of Governor Attilius Faticus.

The governor was preceded by two servants carrying a seat each. Slightly behind him followed his master of ceremonies, a figure common in the company of nobles and politicians. The master of ceremonies oversaw all social matters related to his employer, and often handled tasks deemed too dirty for his superiors, such as bribing public officials or organizing assassinations.

This man hurried forward to approach the centurion *primae spatha*. Before speaking, he rubbed his hands together as if concluding a business deal:

"The governor demands the utmost respect for the delegation he is about to receive. He also insists you refrain from interfering in decisions that only he, by imperial mandate, has the authority to make," the man said, wagging a chubby finger.

The centurion's reply was swift: "And if I do interfere, will you stop me?"

As he spoke, Aristarchos grabbed the man by the collar of his toga and pulled him close. His face, weathered by countless campaigns, nights spent in the open, battles, and endless marches under biting snow and scorching desert suns, bore down on the terrified official.

The master of ceremonies tried to pull away, but the centurion's strong arm held him firm. "I no longer take orders from sweet-talking fools like you. If it happens again, I give you my word: I'll rip out your guts and feed them to my men. Is that clear?" he growled through clenched teeth.

Terrified, the master of ceremonies, tears streaming down his face, stammered, "Y-yes…of course. Now, please…let me go."

From what he observed, Governor Attilius Faticus realized the *vexillatio* commander's temperament needed to be reined in—one way or another. He resolved to address the matter in due time.

Without commenting on what had just transpired, the governor climbed onto the flat roof of the chosen house and took a seat in the chair prepared by his servant. With a clap of his hands, he ordered a cup of wine, which the servant poured from a jug decorated with images of dolphin.

With a wave of his hand, Aristarchos Themistocles ordered the guards to let the Heruli delegation through.

The Heruli general advanced under the hostile stares of the legionaries, who had crowded together to watch him. His escort was stopped, allowing only him and his servant to climb onto the roof.

When the general stood before Attilius Faticus, he muttered something in his own language that sounded offensive.

"Do you know our language?" the governor asked.

The Heruli officer's sharp blue eyes focused intently. "Yes, I learned it from my father's servant. He was a Roman soldier before being captured in battle," he replied, a comment that clearly irked the Romans present.

The governor, however, seemed oblivious to the mocking undertone of the words and responded with courtesy, "I personally welcome you to Duro Catalaunum. It is merely a frontier outpost, lacking the comforts of our cities, as you can see, but I hope you will receive all we can offer." His calm tone conveyed a sense of control over the situation.

With a glance, he signaled for a servant to pour the barbarian a cup of wine.

The Heruli general downed the drink in one gulp, wiping his mouth and long beard with the back of his sleeve.

He got straight to the point, skipping any pleasantries: "The new Governor of Gaul, the right hand of Rex Odoacer, is now your lord."

The centurion *primae spatha* eyes widened.

Had he heard correctly? Governor of Gaul?

That was an imperial position.

Noticing the centurions' expressions, the Heruli general quickly continued: "Your Emperor has been deposed in Ravenna, and Odoacer has sent the imperial crown and royal standards to Constantinople, awaiting the ascension of a new Caesar. Odoacer himself has appointed Rudulfus as Governor of all Gaul," he lied smoothly and continued, "Rudulfus requests that you, Attilius Faticus, serve as his Treasurer of Gaul, managing finances for him and the Empire. He offers you safe passage, as well as a guarantee of safety for your troops and the people. The city will be spared from plunder."

The days prior had been full of unexpected events, but that morning surpassed even the wildest predictions.

The Heruli general scanned the crowd with an intense gaze. "Those are his words. He also says that the offer is highly advantageous for you Romans, who are otherwise doomed to certain death."

Attilius Faticus' eyes glimmered with disbelief. Not only had his life been spared, but he was being offered the prestigious role of treasurer, which would grant him control over the taxes and finances of the governorship of Gaul.

This surge of excitement greatly irritated Vatinius Auruncus, who turned away in disgust—not because of the proposed truce, but because he knew that Attilius Faticus would eagerly accept the offer, betraying every principle of the Empire.

"So, as it stands, the Empire is without a Caesar, isn't that correct?" the governor asked for confirmation.

The general nodded. "Odoacer's Gothic mercenaries routed the legions stationed in Ravenna, seizing the Sacred Palace," he added, emphasizing the annihilation of the Italian legions.

When Aristarchos Themistocles noticed that the young centurion was about to lunge at the Heruli general, it was too late to stop him. He barely missed grabbing him by the arm.

"It might not be so easy to kill a legionary, don't you think?" Vatinius Auruncus growled, gripping the hilt of his gladius menacingly.

Attilius Faticus' wide-eyed expression revealed his irritation at the young centurion's rashness. Now face-to-face with the Heruli general, who had risen from his seat and showed no sign of fear, Vatinius' defiance threatened to escalate the tension further.

Narrowing his icy blue eyes into slits, the Heruli general shot back sharply: "Save your life, Roman. Flee now."

"That's enough!" the governor's voice rang out, trying to end the dispute.

Vatinius Auruncus glanced at Aristarchos Themistocles, who gave a subtle nod of assent. The young centurion reluctantly stepped back, marking the end of the confrontation.

Visibly more relaxed, Attilius Faticus stood and clasped both of the barbarian general's hands. The latter pulled back in visible disgust, his disdain for the Romans plainly evident.

With an awkward, forced smile, Attilius Faticus withdrew his hands, trying not to draw attention to the embarrassing display of submission. Gesturing as though welcoming the barbarian into a grand hall, he invited him to sit once more.

The metallic clinking of his armor plates accompanied the Heruli general's slow movements as he sat back down. Before turning his attention back to the conversation, Attilius shot one last glare at the young centurion, who returned the look with equal resentment.

"Convey my warmest congratulations to the new Governor of Gaul, and let him know I am honored to accept the responsibility he has so wisely offered me," the governor said smoothly.

"I will. He plans to settle here in Duro Catalaunum to better manage his newly assigned province. He expects your utmost loyalty."

Hearing those words, Aristarchos Themistocles felt a pang of dread. He immediately resolved that he would never submit to the Heruli king, and began contemplating his next move.

"You will have our loyalty. You have the word of a noble Roman raised to the equestrian rank," Attilius Faticus assured, his tone oozing servility.

The barbarian general rose to leave. "Very well. The governor will be pleased with the outcome of this meeting."

In moments, the Heruli party left the Roman positions.

After watching them disappear on horseback, Attilius Faticus turned to the centurion *primae spatha*, his tone now laced with renewed arrogance: "Centurion, gather the soldiers. They are to offer no resistance as the governor takes possession of his new residence. I don't want any incidents. Am I clear?"

Aristarchos Themistocles remained silent, nodding in acknowledgment. Nothing more.

Though he wanted to fiercely oppose the orders, he knew that ending hostilities would save the people of Duro Catalaunum.

He had to choose the lesser evil, especially since, if the barbarian general's words were true, there was no Emperor and no borders left to defend.

He looked up at the blinding sun and reflected: this was the dawn of a new era, one without Caesars or legions.

His thoughts turned to Placidia and how he might find her again. He resolved to procure a horse and ride to her, faster than time itself, to reach her as soon as possible.

***

The Heruli vanguard began entering the city walls shortly after midday.

In scattered groups, they conducted what they claimed were inspections of the town's alleys and homes. However, instead of ensuring safety, they overturned tables, smashed chests, shattered pottery, and looted anything of value. Anyone who resisted was subjected to unspeakable torment.

Cries of pain and despair soon echoed from different corners of the town.

Two mercenaries dragged a struggling, screaming girl out of a small doorway, her anguished cries betraying her dread at what was about to happen. Meanwhile, others restrained her father, who protested with bulging eyes filled with terror.

When the father saw them punching his daughter into submission, his fear turned to fury, and he lunged forward to help her. The Heruli pinned him to the ground, and one of them drew a dagger, severing the fingers of his hand while smirking with satisfaction at his comrade.

Finally, they took turns violating the girl until the life drained from her body.

There was no corner of Duro Catalaunum left untouched by the atrocities committed by the Heruli.

"Where is Gaius Octavianus?" asked Aristarchos Themistocles, staring at a black column of smoke rising into the sky.

Every fiber of his being trembled with rage at the barbarians, who had broken their word by looting the city and committing atrocities everywhere.

It was Antoninus Tacitus, the centurion, who answered: "He's doing what he does best. He disappeared last night to spy on the Heruli and see for himself what's really happening. You know he only trusts his own eyes."

"I know, I know..." Aristarchos murmured before adding firmly, "Bring him to me when he returns. I fear I'll need all of you before long. Stay ready. Alert your men and the archers. I don't like where this damned situation is heading."

Before Aristarchos even finished his sentence, Tacitus had already brought his forearm to his chest in a salute, signaling that the centuries would remain on high alert.

Aristarchos turned his attention to the youngest of the centurions, calling him over.

"Orders, Centurion!" the young officer replied, snapping to attention with a stiff military salute.

"Have you done a headcount?"

"Two hundred and seventy-nine legionaries, including the archers. That excludes the wounded and missing."

"The wounded?"

"Not many. Those here in the principia are fewer than a dozen. The others...we had to leave them behind when we..." he swallowed hard, "... retreated."

"If the situation allows, we'll recover their bodies," Aristarchos said, though without much conviction.

"I hope so!"

Aristarchos gave him a sidelong glance. "Ready what's left of the Third Cohort. Prepare them for a sortie," he ordered.

The thought of more fighting seemed inevitable. Upon hearing this, Vatinius Auruncus could not hide his disappointment. He had thought a pact had been struck between the Heruli and the Roman governor, but it was clear that agreement had been violated.

"I'll go give my rascals a good wake-up call," Vatinius replied, though his voice betrayed his frustration. He walked off to carry out the orders.

***

When the sentries spotted a barbarian warrior approaching, they unsheathed their gladii.

"It's me! A legionary of the First Century!" Gaius Octavianus removed a Heruli helmet adorned with a stag horn to reveal himself.

The legionaries sighed in relief, sheathing their weapons and letting him pass.

Without a word, one of them pointed to where the centurion *primae spatha* could be found.

Upon seeing him, Aristarchos Themistocles lit up. "Gaius Octavianus... You're alive!"

The legionary grasped the centurion's forearm in greeting.

"Hail, Centurion! Yes, I've been keeping my ears open and discovered some very important things," Gaius said, his voice hoarse.

The centurion *primae spatha* noticed the soldier's dry, cracked lips.

"When's the last time you had water, soldier?" he asked.

Gaius' attempt to moisten his lips with his tongue was answer enough.

Aristarchos handed him his own water flask. "Drink."

The scout clasped it with both hands and brought it to his mouth, drinking deeply, the bobbing of his throat betraying his immense thirst.

Meanwhile, a circle of soldiers began to form around them. Gaius' sharp eyes scanned the faces of his comrades, all eager to hear what he had to say—and relieved to see him alive.

Among them were Fulcinius Agricola Statius, Gallienus Lars Gracchus the *signifer*, Auctus Tullius Plato, Severinus Majorianus the optio, Drusus Variatus, Christianus Caligatus the lignum, and the Batavian Evetius Aquila.

Their weary, dirt-streaked faces lit up at the sight of him. Gaius' daring scouting missions had often saved them from ambushes or led them away from paths that would have delivered them straight into the enemy's jaws.

Behind the group, transverse helmet crests signaled the arrival of Vatinius Auruncus and Antoninus Tacitus.

Wearing a satisfied smile, Gaius Octavianus began his report: "Fortune hasn't abandoned us completely. Rudulfus killed Gargalico, the Thuringian king who was appointed Governor of Gaul by Odoacer. Then Rudulfus declared himself governor, sending a false delegation to Ravenna to deceive Odoacer. Outraged by Rudulfus' actions, the Thuringians and Alans abandoned the camp and, despite the cold and snow, are heading south for new raids and sieges. The Empire..." his voice caught in his throat, "...the Empire has crumbled, Centurion."

Though his final words were directed at Aristarchos Themistocles, it was clear the message was meant for all.

An anguished silence followed, broken only when the centurion embraced Gaius. "We know, soldier, we know. Rest now. Tonight..." Aristarchos raised his voice so many could hear, "...if the situation permits and we're still alive, I'll grant you all your discharge. Each of you can decide what to do with your life."

The soldiers were stunned. Some cried out in protest, while others felt relief at the prospect of choosing their own destinies. Recent desertions had already made it clear that such freedom was what many desired.

"Go and rest now..." Aristarchos said to the scout. "Take off those Heruli clothes. I might need you again in a couple of hours."

Gaius Octavianus started to utter his usual farewell, "Honor to Rome," but the words died in his throat. He simply nodded, exhaustion overtaking him.

He found a makeshift bed and lay down, immediately succumbing to sleep. But it was restless, plagued with dark dreams.

As Gaius Octavianus slept fitfully, Ialenia Heria passed by cautiously, pausing to watch him.

Her expression was strangely knowing, as if she could interpret his dreams. She moved her hand close to his face, without touching it, and whispered:

"Spirits...it is the spirits of your ancestors speaking to you through your dreams. They are restless and demand your attention. Calm yourself now, legionary...calm your anger. The gods have many tasks yet in store for you, and you will know them through the dreams you will have."

Incredibly, Gaius Octavianus stopped thrashing in his sleep. Ialenia gave a faint, kind smile before continuing on her way, the magpie perched on her shoulder playfully flapping its wings.

"Where are you going, Centurion?" asked Vatinius Auruncus.

Aristarchos Themistocles cast him a mocking glance. "You're coming with me."

"Ah!"

"Eh!"

They burst into laughter.

"We're going to see Attilius Faticus."

"Why do we have to deal with that scoundrel again? If the Empire no longer exists, that means we're not obligated to anyone—least of all that worm." The young centurion's disdain was clear.

Aristarchos looked at him as if he agreed, but had already resolved to go through with his decision.

"Attilius Faticus has requested my presence. But I don't feel like going alone, and..."

"Are you scared?" Vatinius mocked.

"I'm the commander of this garrison. If I went alone, I might stumble into a trap."

"And with the two of us, we're sure to be saved..."

They laughed again.

"I don't want to get you killed for an empire that's already vanished. The Heruli won't stay long. The screams you hear and the smoke rising into the sky are proof enough. They're looting the city despite the agreed truce. We must avoid another fight."

"I'll come with you," Vatinius agreed.

The two centurions left the principia, accompanied by a guard of five soldiers. Their small number ensured they would not draw much attention, yet it was enough to fend off a surprise attack or deal with minor skirmishes with the Heruli.

Fortunately, nothing happened on their way.

The commander of Attilius Faticus' personal guard led them to a large hall that Aristarchos Themistocles knew all too well.

It was the audience hall of the governor's palace, a place where Aristarchos had spent far too much time listening to the governor's unctuous nonsense.

When the massive wooden doors, studded with iron, swung open to reveal Attilius Faticus, the two centurions watched him stride toward them.

He wore a dalmatica, finely crafted by an expert tailor. The edges, embroidered with golden threads, seemed to create an aura around him, designed to make him appear otherworldly.

The heavy black makeup outlining his eyes made him look utterly ridiculous to the two veterans.

With a forced smile, he greeted them loudly: "Centurions, welcome to my humble abode. Unfortunately, I have little to offer you in these trying times."

Vatinius Auruncus bristled at the remark. Beyond the palace walls, looting was rampant, and the townsfolk had been struggling to find food for days.

Attilius Faticus spread his arms wide, attempting an air of hospitality he clearly did not want to extend.

Aristarchos Themistocles stepped forward, preempting the younger officer's likely offensive retort.

"Governor, we've come to request your intervention. The Heruli are looting everything and..."

Attilius raised both hands to signal silence. "There are ambassadors from the Governor of Gaul here... Are you trying to get me killed?" he hissed through clenched teeth.

Vatinius Auruncus barely restrained the urge to slit his throat.

Aristarchos continued, "Let's hear what you have to say, your excellency," cutting the exchange short.

At that moment, a functionary entered, wearing a long, trailing tunic and carrying two documents.

Attilius examined the documents briefly before dismissively

handing them back. "There are no longer any customs offices, and therefore no more subsidies for customs officials."

The two centurions exchanged a bewildered glance.

Attilius then turned to address them directly: "I summoned you to ask that you...," he rubbed his hands together, "...set aside any belligerent attitudes toward our new friends."

At the word "friends," Vatinius Auruncus visibly flinched. "Let me kill him..." he growled.

"Not now, Vatinius. Not now..." Aristarchos replied. "But I won't rule it out in the future."

Unfazed by the soldiers' evident disgust, Attilius continued: "For my part, you have my word that I'll ensure reciprocity. I've been summoned by Governor Rudulfus, and I'll make sure to secure excellent outcomes for Duro Catalaunum and my military forces."

Both centurions stood frozen, mouths agape.

They left the surreal meeting without exchanging a single word on their way back to the principia.

***

The streets were now overrun with Heruli.

Many were drunk, displaying their contempt for the Romans by destroying everything in their path, urinating on sacred symbols, and spitting at the townsfolk unlucky enough to cross their paths.

Despite this, the legionaries searched for their wounded comrades. This search unfolded under the watchful eyes of the barbarian warriors, leading to a few minor skirmishes.

Fortunately, no one was killed—only because neither side had any interest in escalating the conflict. The Heruli were preoccupied with plundering, so the legionaries avoided provocations.

Every Roman soldier understood the absurdity of the situation.

In the very city they were sworn to defend, their enemies roamed freely. Enemies who, by imperial decree, were no longer to be considered such.

They were fortunate they hadn't all been slaughtered.

The search for the wounded yielded poor results. Only two could still be saved; the rest—half a dozen—could do nothing but wait for the end.

As the soldiers made their way back to the principia, the booming sound of horns drew their attention. Something solemn was about to happen.

The clatter of horse hooves echoed through the air, catching the legionaries' ears.

Rudulfus appeared on the city's central street, riding his majestic horse. He moved at an excruciatingly slow pace, deliberately theatrical, ensuring everyone saw and understood the grandeur with which he assumed his new role.

His hair, unbound, flowed over his shoulders. A wolf pelt adorned his right shoulder, covering his scaled armor. He wore it with pride, showcasing it to his generals as proof that he had hunted the beast himself.

His horse snorted nervously, releasing clouds of vapor into the cold air.

His escort comprised at least twenty mounted, armed soldiers.

As Rudulfus made his way along what had once been the Cardo Maximus, he noticed an elderly man, barely able to stand, leaning heavily on a stick.

Dismounting, he strode toward the man with a haughty air, tilting his head slightly to his right shoulder as he studied him.

The old man nearly collapsed in terror.

"Feed this man," Rudulfus commanded, under the bewildered stares of the gathered crowd.

But his pretense of refined, magnanimous behavior crumbled as he belched loudly.

At that moment, the newly appointed treasurer of the province, Attilius Faticus, appeared.

Approaching his new master, Attilius cleared his throat before loudly shouting: "Hail! Hail Rudulfus the Merciful! Hail..."

But no one echoed him.

Nearly everyone in the crowd had lost family members to the

Heruli, and the idea of Rudulfus as "merciful" was impossible to fathom.

Rudulfus locked eyes with Vatinius Auruncus, their gazes charged with mutual hatred. For a few tense moments, neither looked away.

Then the new Governor of Gaul remounted his horse and addressed Attilius Faticus—and, by extension, everyone present: "I will take up residence in the principia. From there, I will begin my duties while the governor's palace is modified to suit my tastes."

Aristarchos Themistocles suppressed a gasp of rage.

The Heruli king's declaration was a bitter insult: Rudulfus settling in the legionaries' barracks.

A humiliation too bitter to swallow.

Attilius Faticus eagerly rubbed his hands together before pointing the way. "It is all yours now, magnificent Governor," he said.

Rudulfus proceeded through the crowd, which had gathered to watch him. He moved at a measured pace toward the grand gates of the barracks.

Turning again to Attilius Faticus, he added in an imperious tone, "Now. Have them vacate the principia immediately." His expression left no doubt that he would brook no opposition.

"You heard the governor! Begin clearing the principia. Move it!" Attilius Faticus bellowed, his voice straining.

Sensing the potential for resistance, the Heruli began gathering with weapons in hand.

Within moments, Aristarchos Themistocles counted more than three hundred of them.

Wasting no time, he entered the barracks and called for assembly.

"Ad signa![1] To the standards!" he shouted.

"Ad signa!" echoed Antoninus Tacitus.

"Ad signa!" joined Vatinius Auruncus, his right hand trembling with the urge to fight.

The legionaries quickly formed ranks, donning their battle gear.

---

[1] *Ad signa:* an order to regroup under the standards; to reform the ranks.

At the head of the formations stood the two centurions, their eyes on Aristarchos Themistocles, the garrison commander.

In his eyes—and in the eyes of the soldiers before him—there was no trace of surrender.

But what Aristarchos said next was far from what they expected. "Legionaries…"

In unison, the soldiers roared: "Honor of Rome!"

Aristarchos felt a surge of pride so overwhelming that it brought moisture to his eyes.

"Soldiers, I have received orders. We will vacate the principia…"

A murmur of discontent rippled through the ranks.

Raising his hands for calm, the officer continued: "The circumstances are not in our favor," he explained.

"Give me two moments of freedom—I'll kill Rudulfus, and then we'll leave quietly!" shouted Fulcinius Agricola Statius, his outburst greeted by the laughter of his comrades.

The commander pressed on, ignoring the brief protest: "I believe the time has come for your discharge. You will all receive it. However, to earn it, you must stay alive. If we were to engage these vermin here and now…" he pointed to the ground, "… we would all perish."

"It would be an honorable death, as fighters—as legionaries!" a soldier shouted from the back.

With a shiver that came from deep within, Aristarchos clenched his teeth and continued: "And yet, it would be a meaningless death! We are a *vexillatio*, do not forget that. A small detachment with limited infantry. What we have achieved, at the cost of many lives, borders on the miraculous. Repelling an assault by thousands of barbarian mercenaries capable of wiping out an entire legion is a feat worthy of heroes. That is what you should be proud of. That is what you will tell your children."

He felt as if he had violated a sacred bond.

Aristarchos had hidden his own desire to fight behind the stoic mask of command.

He had broken the code that had bound him to his men for

years. They should have fought to the end.

But as their commander, he could not allow them to be slaughtered for an empire that had betrayed them.

They would abandon the principia—that much was true. It was the final insult they would endure.

But it was nothing compared to what the Empire had done to itself.

At least, Aristarchos reflected, he would not make his men bear the weight of the failures of inept and corrupt administrators.

That, too, was an act of leadership.

The clatter of Heruli horses' hooves broke Aristarchos Themistocles' thoughts.

He didn't want the enemy entering the principia while the legionaries were still inside—tensions would almost certainly escalate into a fight.

"Legionaries, gather your equipment," he ordered swiftly.

"The men of the Third are ready," Vatinius Auruncus announced.

"The men of the Second are ready," echoed Antoninus Tacitus.

The centurion *primae spatha* looked toward the Second Century, knowing it now included the remnants of the First Century, which had originally been under his command.

"Centuriae, ordinate ad dextram!"[2] *(Centuries, align to the right!)*

The soldiers lined up to the right, forming ranks near the principia gate.

"Numerum ordinis declarate!"[3] *(Call out your ranks!)*

The soldiers' voices broke through the tense atmosphere:

"Unus!"

"Duo!"

"Tres!"

"Quattuor!"

---

[2] *Ordinate ad destram:* Align to the right (a military maneuver).

[3] *Numerum ordinis declarate:* Declare your position number (military order).

"Quinque!"

"Sex!"

Once the roll call ended, the proud commander gave his next order:

"Formate duas ordines!" *(Form two lines!)*

The legionaries arranged themselves into two rows.

"Capite scuta!" *(Take up your shields!)* He watched as the soldiers, almost in unison, reached for their shields.

"Unum gradum ante!" *(One step forward!)*

"Signa inferre pergite!"[4] *(Carry forward the standards! Forward, march!)*

Gallienus Lars Gracchus, the *signifer*, sprang into action, taking his place at the head of the column. His strong arms held the legion's eagle standard aloft—a proud symbol of their cohort and their heritage.

The legionaries advanced with disciplined steps, staring straight ahead, ignoring the jeers and insults hurled at them by the Heruli.

Some of the barbarians spat at them, but the soldiers did not retaliate. No one gave in to the provocations.

The *signifer* raised two fingers, signaling those following him to maintain their formation.

Aristarchos Themistocles marched with his chin held high, exuding austerity, pride, and defiance.

As he passed Rudulfus, Aristarchos cast him a brief, cutting glare.

Fleeting as lightning, yet sharp enough to make its meaning clear.

Rudulfus' hardened gaze followed the procession of legionaries, a mix of malice and envy in his expression.

Despite himself, Rudulfus couldn't deny a grudging admiration for the Romans' unmatched ability to organize their armies and train their soldiers.

---

[4] *Signa inferre pergite:* Advance the standards (the banners); this was the signal to begin marching.

What he witnessed before his eyes only solidified that respect.

These men moved in perfect synchrony, their motions fluid, as if they breathed as one.

Holding his horse's reins tightly, Rudulfus kept it from side-stepping, though the beast's muscles twitched in irritation at being made to stand still. He didn't move—he felt compelled to witness this display of discipline and cohesion.

After all, was it not true that a mere handful of Roman frontier soldiers had held his thousands-strong horde at bay?

That bitter truth was hard to swallow, but he couldn't deny it.

A thunderous cry from the Romans jolted Rudulfus out of his thoughts.

"Honores vexillo!" *(Honors to the standard!)* The shout echoed through the streets.

Rudulfus tightened his grip on the reins and swallowed hard, feeling another wave of burning resentment.

Under a barrage of insults, curses, and spit, the legionaries left the principia for good.

Principia, Early Afternoon

In the distance, thunder rumbled, its echo carried by a wind so cold it could freeze a hibernating squirrel in its den.

As Rudulfus entered the governor's gardens, a swarm of servants sent by Attilius Faticus greeted him, offering fruit and wine.

Step by step, Rudulfus explored spaces he was unaccustomed to.

A sense of vindication welled up in him.

These had been the barracks of Rome's soldiers—men willing to die to protect this sliver of empire and their Emperor.

Rudulfus knew he could never inspire such unconditional loyalty among his own men, and the thought filled him with envy.

The wooden training shields and swords were still neatly arranged, just as they had been left after the last drills.

On the walls, faded yet colorful murals depicted symbols of Roman pride, alongside inscriptions etched into the plaster by soldiers—expressions of their devotion to duty.

Rudulfus could read enough Latin to understand their meanings.

A gust of wind rustled the branches of a nearby tree.

Rudulfus raised his arm, halting the entourage of servants and generals who were following his inspection of the principia.

With a glance, he silently instructed Cunipert to dismiss everyone.

"The Governor of Gaul wishes to be alone," Cunipert announced with the authority of someone speaking for the highest power.

Within moments, everyone had dispersed.

Rudulfus fixed his gaze on the tree. He broke off a small branch and held it in both hands, looking skyward.

He began chanting softly:

"I call to you, great deity of the wind. Protector of earth, air, and day, I know you speak to me through these branches and the wind. Protect my life and guide my choices. Allow me to fulfill my plans. I beseech you, Mother, to absorb the blood of my enemies that I have offered and turn it into courage for my soul."

Another gust of wind rustled the leaves, causing them to tremble.

Scooping up some damp soil, Rudulfus smeared it across his face in deliberate patterns, transforming his expression into one of hunger and determination.

He then claimed the great hall, where military decisions were once made and garrison accounts managed.

Rudulfus immediately stationed his personal guard and summoned all his generals.

For hours, they pored over maps of northern and southern Gaul.

The generals murmured quietly among themselves, careful not to disturb Rudulfus' concentration.

Servants sent by Attilius Faticus brought an improvised dinner, accompanied by plenty of wine.

By the time Rudulfus finally looked up from the maps, it was the dead of night.

All eyes were on him, awaiting his words.

"We…the Heruli, will rule all of Gaul," he declared.

His generals erupted in cheers, raising their spears and swords in the air.

"Those who chose to leave have made a grave mistake. Moving thousands of people—men, women, carts, and livestock—during such a harsh winter is madness. But they don't have a king like yours…"

He clapped his hands, signaling Cunipert, who left the tent and returned moments later, dragging a chained woman to the center of the room.

The woman groaned in pain as Cunipert grabbed her hair and revealed her face: she was one of King Gargalico's wives—the most beautiful of them.

The generals burst into laughter, now understanding their king's ironic message.

"Now, after placing her virile husband in his rightful place, she is mine," Rudulfus sneered, provoking more laughter.

Some of the men mimed obscene gestures.

Exchanging a brief look with Cunipert, Rudulfus received a barely perceptible nod.

The first part was complete. He had explained his decision to remain behind while the other tribes had moved south.

It was essential to dispel any notions of cowardice among his officers. This wasn't fear—it was strategy.

While the other tribes would face the cold and starvation, the Heruli would remain within the walls of Duro Catalaunum, ruling over all of Gaul.

Now came the more delicate part: justifying his ambition to create a quasi-empire within the Empire itself.

Rudulfus envisioned a realm that even Rex Odoacer could not challenge—a dominion stretching from the Alps to the frigid northern coasts.

Even before this meeting, Rudulfus had already dispatched spies to Ravenna, tasked with preempting any moves by Odoacer.

Outside the great hall, warriors bustled about, transporting supplies and furnishings looted from Roman towns.

One of them, groaning under the weight of a sack of flour, made strange noises, as if cursing the burden.

Beneath the conical helmet was the young face of Gaius Octavianus, the Scout.

Disguised in the typical garb of the Heruli—his shoulders draped with patched wolf pelts and a long Gothic sword hanging from his belt—Gaius had spent years on the Empire's borders, and had learned the dialects of many migrating tribes.

After dropping the last sack in a storage room guarded by a squad of warriors, Gaius slipped away, careful not to draw attention.

He was inside the principia, observing the Heruli from up close. Very close.

***

The events of that day left a deep mark on the souls of the legionaries. All of them, without exception.

The realization that the Empire was now at the mercy of barbarians shattered any hope of better times. True, it was possible that the Emperor of Byzantium, if he did not support Odoacer's election, might send an army to depose the rex.

Perhaps he would even dispatch his powerful fleet to besiege the cities now under barbarian control.

But all of this would merely be an attempt to patch up a tattered and worn-out mantle.

It was clear that the Western Roman Empire had become nothing more than a complex governmental organism, tangled in corruption and palace intrigues.

As the sun set, its amber light reflected off the frozen snow, creating a beautiful shimmer. Some ice formations even took on the strange shape of roses with frosted petals.

Once the legionaries vacated the principia, they busied themselves in the streets of Duro Catalaunum.

A small detachment freed the civilians who had barricaded themselves inside the town's churches, narrowly escaping the atrocities of the Heruli. When the massive church doors were opened, people poured into the streets, crying out in joy and desperately searching for water, having gone two days without drinking during the siege.

Inside the temples, the air was unbreathable. Soldiers covered their mouths with scraps of cloth, trying to suppress the urge to vomit. The stench was compounded by the suicides that had occurred within those sacred walls—acts of despair by those who feared torture and floggings worse than death itself.

Another group of soldiers helped the townsfolk bury the dead to prevent disease from spreading. Meanwhile, the remaining centurions decided that the bishop's residence was a suitable place to shelter until the situation became clearer.

Inside the cloister, the soldiers set up a hospital for the wounded and dying, while they established their military command in Bishop Calibertus' private chapel. The soldiers themselves found accommodations in the residence's rooms.

The centurion *primae spatha* placed his command table in the apse.

The spacious area was filled with sacks of grain, potable water, and any other foodstuffs they could recover.

He had brought maps of the local area and the entire region. Under the dim light of a lantern, he studied them, deeply absorbed, trying to anticipate every possible scenario surrounding Rudulfus' ambitions, which—he'd stake his life—knew no bounds.

Running his finger south along the river Rhone, Aristarchos imagined reaching Lower Gaul, where he hoped to find settlements still under Roman control.

Perhaps, he thought, the First Flavian Legion of Peace or the Victorious Twelfth Legion were still operational, regrouping in the south to halt the barbarian advance.

These were mere hopes—he knew that—but he had to entertain every possibility to imagine a path forward.

Many of his centurions' veterans had followed their families, and their absence was now painfully apparent.

Perhaps, he told himself, if they moved south quickly, they might find more soldiers to stand against the barbarians. Or, upon reaching the coast, they could head for Minturnae, becoming deserters, but at least keeping their skins intact.

After about an hour, he decided to stop tormenting himself with such thoughts.

This…this was the moment when hope gave way to the harsh acknowledgment of reality.

Weariness made him see things for what they were.

They were few, exhausted, malnourished, and frozen to the bone.

Farther south, there were almost certainly no more legions.

The Empire was now in barbarian hands, out of control.

He sighed, rubbing his temples.

***

Hand over hand. A foot finding purchase in a crack. With the strength of his arms and legs, Vatinius Auruncus hoisted himself up onto a dilapidated *insula*[5].

Once at the top, he looked around: rubble and desolation stretched as far as the eye could see.

The metallic glow of the moon reflected off the white mantle of snow that covered the town.

Bands of looters had taken the place of the barbarians, who—

---

[5] *Insula:* A type of residential building that functioned as an apartment complex in late Republican and Imperial Rome. These quadrangular structures featured an inner courtyard (cavedius), often with a portico, from which individual living units were accessed. Essentially, they were akin to modern apartments. The ground floor typically housed *tabernae* (shops), while the upper floors contained living quarters. The higher the floor, the less prestigious the accommodation. The floors were often supported by vaults for added stability.

paradoxically—had stopped their pillaging and were now working to settle in the town.

In some areas, the streets were so clogged that hundreds of Heruli, accompanied by their families and carts, remained stuck, waiting motionless for long stretches of time.

The young centurion calculated that there wasn't enough space inside the walls for all those people; many would have to camp outside.

Turning his gaze toward the principia, he saw banners flying, celebrating the Heruli's triumph.

A pang of resentment twisted his stomach.

Then his eyes fell upon the body of a woman killed during the looting.

Crows pecked at what remained of her insides, as other flocks descended upon the corpses still waiting to be buried.

The young centurion lingered on the rooftop, staring at the stars, wishing this absurd situation were merely a nightmare from which he might soon wake.

But he knew all too well that hope often ended in disappointment.

That night passed peacefully.

Principia, Night

The gates slammed shut behind the rider galloping swiftly toward the south.

He was yet another messenger sent to Ravenna from the newly established governorship, only a few hours into its reign.

The message was a request to the new rex, Odoacer, for consent to collect taxes and the authority to enact laws to rebuild what had crumbled over the past decades.

The irony was that the one making this request was Rudulfus, the most feared barbarian of all.

With a face marked by weariness, the new governor raised a hand to his forehead.

"A messenger has arrived, my king. Our armies have settled in Gratianopolis[6] to winter there. They will be ready should Odoacer send troops against us," reported Cunipert.

Rudulfus' expression betrayed a certain satisfaction, though his gaze lingered lazily on a torch crackling nearby.

A servant handed him a cup of wine from some distant land.

Although Duro Catalaunum was a border town, it had still received numerous goods until just a few months ago, goods that helped its inhabitants endure life on the fringes of civilization.

Casting a glance out of the window, Rudulfus tried to imagine the streets bustling with life—merchants displaying their wares, shops open with vendors shouting to attract customers, children chasing one another, livestock being led to the market.

He pictured slaves scurrying about on errands for their mistresses, troops of soldiers returning from patrols, cutting through the crowd in their armor and purple cloaks.

Once again, he was struck by that irritating feeling of admiration for a people who lived in perfect harmony with their politics.

With a gesture of irritation, one that did not go unnoticed by the generals present, he acknowledged his begrudging desire to emulate them.

After all, the position he had assumed reflected much of Roman custom.

He took another sip of wine, savoring the blend of wild berries and delicate spices as it lingered in his throat and nose.

"My king..." Cunipert tried to regain his attention, his voice echoing in the disoriented silence of the hall. "It is very late..." he ventured, hoping for dismissal.

"We must rest. I know," Rudulfus replied. Then, pointing to the wife of King Gargalico, he ordered, "Take her to my chambers."

---

[6] *Gratianopolis:* The modern-day city of Grenoble. Originally a Gallic settlement, it became a Roman city in 379 and was named Gratianopolis in honor of Emperor Gratian.

As the woman was dragged away, one of the generals followed her with his gaze until she disappeared through the bronze door. It was Vaillardo, the commander of the cavalry, the most feared and respected of the Heruli generals.

Vaillardo had proven his valor every time the need arose to draw his sword and face the enemy.

"My king," Cunipert began again.

"My king," Vaillardo interrupted.

Annoyed, Cunipert raised his voice: "My king, I ask you—"

Rudulfus silenced him with a gesture, then turned to Vaillardo, granting him the floor.

Vaillardo spoke: "My king, my cavalrymen are unhappy about sharing this city's walls with Roman soldiers. I am struggling to keep them under control. I'm not sure how much longer I can hold them back," he warned.

Rudulfus smirked. "You're right, Vaillardo. But we've killed enough for now. Do not worry..." He switched to address everyone in the room. "The legionaries will get what they want: an honorable death."

The room erupted in laughter.

Then Rudulfus continued, his voice rising for dramatic effect: "Look at where we stand!" He emphasized his words with triumphant fervor. "We are deciding our strategies in the command hall of a Roman garrison. Would you have ever imagined this? We'll sleep in their quarters and feast on their tables. We'll have their women, their comforts, and they'll pay their taxes to us."

He paused briefly, ensuring he had their full attention.

"Their land now belongs to us. We will reap wealth and good harvests from it. This, I tell you."

At his final words, brimming with ardor and conviction, the generals' spirits ignited. Swords were raised toward the ceiling, and triumphant cries filled the great hall.

Cunipert smiled, his grin marred by the gaps where teeth had been knocked out in a fight years ago. But a bitter taste lingered— resentment over what had happened moments before, when

Rudulfus had heeded Vaillardo's words over his own.

He couldn't hide his growing disdain for the cavalry commander.

Chapter VI – The Shadow Empire

Ravenna, the Emperor's Palace

When King Odoacer received Rudulfus' letter—Rudulfus, who had declared himself governor—he flew into a rage. Rudulfus was not the man he had chosen to govern Gaul. That role had been assigned to Gargalico, a far more loyal subject. Enraged, he cursed and kicked over a wine amphora, which shattered, spilling its contents across the floor. Still unsatisfied, he grabbed a bronze candelabrum and began smashing a magnificent marble statue, said to have been crafted by a renowned sculptor.

He summoned Frodewin, his most trusted general. The general entered the chamber and knelt before him, bowing his head. The metallic clink of his armor brought Odoacer's thoughts back to the days when he, too, had donned battle gear.

"Your orders, my king?" Frodewin said simply.

Odoacer lowered his gaze to the purple tunic he wore, a garment he felt he had no right to don, wearing it with brazen defiance. Everyone in the palace knew the manner in which he had deposed the rightful Emperor, but Odoacer remained indifferent to their knowledge. Yet, he couldn't entirely ignore the murmurs among his generals, who criticized him as being too "Romanized." Still, he paid them too well for them to consider rebellion.

"Have you already beheaded that fool we tortured during the banquet yesterday?" he asked.

Frodewin frowned.

For a moment, he seemed unsure how to respond. Then he said, "I was thinking of keeping him as a personal slave, but if your wish is to have him executed, it'll only take a few minutes and—"

"No!" Odoacer roared, his voice echoing through the grand hall adorned with multicolored marble. "I need him alive! I've changed my mind—have him brought to me at once."

"As you wish, most noble *rex*," replied the high-ranking officer.

A few minutes later, the prisoner was brought before them in chains.

He was filthy, dressed in tattered clothes—though it was clear they had once been of fine quality. He was chubby and bald, with one eye swollen shut and bruised, and his lips split in two places. One finger was twisted unnaturally, and mucus dripped from both his nose and mouth.

Before Odoacer, he bowed his head and began to whimper.

The king of the Goths, and rex of the Western Roman Empire, urged him to speak.

"You were the most trusted minister of Orestes and the Emperor, weren't you?"

The man only nodded, still groaning. He collapsed to his knees, clutching his bald head. Black tears streaked down his cheeks from the makeup that had once lined his eyes.

"Do you still have any spies active in the region of Gaul?" Odoacer pressed.

The man nodded again.

"Name one."

The unfortunate soul mumbled something unintelligible.

"Tell me the name."

But he remained silent. He knew he was doomed—and if he had to die, he wouldn't help Odoacer on his way out.

"Then you're of no further use..." He shot a glance at the commander of his personal guard—a Visigoth nearly two meters tall, with skin as pale as milk.

The guard stepped forward toward the former minister of Romulus Augustulus, lifted his chin with one hand, and with the other, slit his throat. Then, to spare everyone the inconvenience, he dragged the body away, leaving a crimson trail across the travertine floor.

Only Odoacer and his general remained in the hall, aside from the guards standing watch.

Frodewin took on a sly expression before saying, "Someone like Rudulfus might be useful to us in Gaul."

Odoacer rubbed his chin. "And why is that?"

The general replied without hesitation, "He's a bloodthirsty bastard, and I'm sure he murdered Cunipert. But he knows how to win battles. On top of that, with the position he's taken, he'll fatten the Empire's coffers—along with his own. I believe he knows how to collect taxes from Roman nobles and the common people alike..." He paused just long enough for the words to sink in, then added, "...and when he becomes a problem, we'll send someone to get rid of him." A glint of cunning flashed in his eyes.

Odoacer still wasn't fully convinced. "Rudulfus might split the Empire—he's ambitious. He has many warriors. Tens of thousands."

The general pressed on, risking a step too bold. "Your Excellency, we command multiple armies—Visigoths, Thuringians, Alans... even the Burgundians, if we manage to make peace with them. And we still have what's left of the imperial army, with the backing of a few compliant generals. Rudulfus knows this well. He understands the limits of his own force and wouldn't dare stand against us."

"My scouts saw part of the Herulian army wintering in Gratianopolis, in lower Gaul. That means he's expecting us to strike back."

"We'll disappoint him. We won't move any armies against him. For now, we need him where he is."

Odoacer seemed to relax slightly.

He summoned a servant, who poured him some mead with practiced grace, careful not to get too close, and offered a tray filled with honey-covered dates.

Picking at the fruit with his ring-covered fingers, Odoacer dismissed Frodewin, who bowed to his rex before leaving the hall with a slow, dignified stride.

Odoacer sipped from his cup again, lost in thought. He rose from the throne and walked out to the veranda. A sharp, cold breeze sent a shiver through him. As far as the eye could see stretched the homes, shops, and churches of Ravenna. In the distance, he could make out the ships anchored offshore, shimmering against the water.

He wondered why people still clung to the word Empire, knowing full well that little remained of Rome's former glory.

A group of Visigoths were lounging in the palace atrium, burping and laughing boisterously. It was obvious they were drunk.

He considered the situation: he had deposed Romulus Augustulus and now ruled the Empire.

But the northern region—Gaul—was now under Rudulfus, who, he was sure, aimed to carve out an empire of his own. Rudulfus had even stationed troops in southern Gaul, clearly preparing for a clash with the imperial army.

A smile crept onto Odoacer's lips as he caught himself thinking like a Roman Emperor—referring to his army as the "imperial army."

What Odoacer would never know, however, was that at that very moment, the Emperor of Byzantium was receiving the embassy that bore Romulus Augustulus's crown—the same crown Odoacer had sent as a symbol of political submission.

The Eastern Emperor let out a grunt as he realized the rightful ruler had been deposed and killed by a barbarian.

His title of *rex* was never officially recognized, tainted as it was by the disapproval of the Emperor of Byzantium.

Odoacer's dark brown eyes watched as the light gave way to darkness.

He examined the fine craftsmanship of the goblet from which he sipped his mead, feeling a sense of admiration. That, too, was Rome. Every stone, workshop, palace, temple, and aqueduct symbolized the unmatched skill and ingenuity of the Romans.

A pang of envy struck him.

Pulling his purple mantle tighter around himself, he shivered slightly as a gust of wind tousled his long hair and the braided ends of his mustache.

Chapter VII – The Hour of Decisions

Fortified Village of Duro Catalaunum, Before Dawn

His eyelids fluttered open and shut, but he saw nothing. His body was numb from the cold, though the wounds no longer throbbed as they had the day before.

Using his powerful arms for leverage, Ulzio Dacianus began dragging himself toward the temple's exit, dried blood still crusted on his face. Propping himself up on his gladius, he managed to rise to his feet, taking one unsteady step after another. Gritting his teeth, he made his way to the principia, only to feel a pang of deep disappointment when he saw from a distance that the closed gate was guarded by Heruli warriors, not legionaries.

Taking advantage of the darkness, he slipped into a narrow alley, where even the cold moonlight couldn't reach. He allowed himself a few moments to think about his next move.

He was still dressed in the uniform of a Roman soldier, and he knew that as soon as daylight broke, they would catch him. If he were lucky, they'd quarter him; otherwise, he'd be tortured to death. He realized he needed to find different clothing to stand any chance of survival—or he had to escape the city and flee into the forest.

He peeked out from the other side of the alley to check. If no one was around, he'd move.

No one.

He advanced a few steps, every sense on high alert.

Cautious. Silent. Ready for anything.

Reaching the stonemasons' quarter, he crouched behind a stone workbench, taking a moment to catch his breath while frantically scanning his surroundings. Still silence. It was safe to proceed.

"Soldier!"

The voice froze him in place.

"Soldier, turn around," the voice called again.

It spoke in Latin—perhaps a Roman. Or a Heruli who knew the language.

Ulzio turned carefully, gripping his gladius tightly.

"Who are you?" the voice asked.

This time, he realized the speaker was farther away. Maybe he still had a chance to escape.

"Ulzio Dacianus, legionary of the Second Century, *vexillatio* of the Fifth Ironclad Legion," he answered.

"...My friend!"

Squinting, Ulzio made out the shapes of three men approaching. The color of their cloaks gave them away—they were fellow legionaries.

As they drew nearer, he recognized the young centurion Vatinius Auruncus. Moments later, Severinus Majorianus and Auctus Tullius Plato emerged into the moonlight, their faces now visible.

"So those damned barbarians didn't cut off your manhood after all!" the optio cackled, clapping his long-lost comrade on the shoulders.

The young centurion watched with understanding as the two seasoned veterans of the Fifth Ironclad exchanged hearty slaps on the back, clearly relieved to have found one another.

"There are Heruli everywhere in the city...does that mean they've won?" Ulzio's eyes betrayed a deep anxiety.

"The situation is even messier than it seems, my friend," Severinus Majorianus replied, supporting Ulzio by the arm, with Plato keeping a watchful eye to ensure they weren't ambushed.

"So...have they won or not?" Ulzio asked in a low voice, trying to piece together what had happened during the time he had been unconscious in the abandoned temple.

"That rotten scumbag Attilius Faticus handed over the city before they could even sack it. But, believe me...it's better if we talk about it once we've reached the quarters. We don't want to meet a grim end here."

The two veterans exchanged knowing glances.

"And what were you doing out here, then?"

"Taking advantage of the darkness to assess the situation and plan our next move for the morning. That's why we brought the kid..." Majorianus nodded toward the young centurion, who stood a few paces ahead of them.

The two veterans burst into laughter.

"I always said he'd have been better off becoming a teacher than a soldier," Ulzio quipped.

More muffled laughter, tempered by the fear of being discovered.

"Let's move now... This place has been dangerous for some time," the officer urged, ignoring the veterans' jokes. "I'll go ahead and scout the path, to make sure you bastards don't get yourselves hurt," he added, before advancing ahead of the other three, who followed more slowly, hampered by the need to support the wounded Ulzio Dacianus.

They weren't far from the bishop's residence, which had been repurposed as a temporary barracks, but caution was still necessary.

The streets were patrolled by Heruli warriors, who had ordered the citizens of Duro Catalaunum to stay locked in their homes to avoid surprises. With only three of them—one of whom was injured—they couldn't risk running into a patrol.

Still, they didn't take long to reach the residence.

The archers on guard already had their bows drawn and arrows nocked, their eyes scanning the darkness for any sign of friend or foe.

"Vatinius Auruncus, centurion of the Third!" he called out to identify himself.

The *decurion* signaled for the archers to lower their weapons, and they relaxed.

"We're home... Just a few more steps," the optio encouraged.

Ulzio Dacianus was utterly drained, though as a seasoned veteran, he did his best not to let his comrades see the extent of his exhaustion.

He dragged himself through the studded door of the bishop's residence, gritting his teeth against the pain.

They settled him into a small room, likely once occupied by a servant, but equipped with a decent straw mattress and a rough wool blanket.

The mage Ialenia Heria had already been summoned to tend to him.

She arrived carrying small pouches filled with roots, dried leaves, and various concoctions, accompanied by Gallienus Lars Gracchus, who was visibly relieved to see his friend alive and well.

Ialenia Heria, her eyes illuminated by the faint glow of a lamp, studied the wound on Ulzio's shoulder. It was deep, and the edges were swollen—a clear sign of infection. The blow to his head worried her less than the nasty laceration on his shoulder. She sniffed the wound and grimaced in disgust.

"Bad business, isn't it?" Ulzio asked anxiously.

The mysterious woman's voice was reassuring. "I have the right remedies, I think."

"What do you mean, 'I think'?"

"I think I do," she replied, irritated.

"But 'I think' doesn't mean certainty."

"If I were you..." she shot him a scornful look, "...I'd spend less time asking foolish questions and more time preparing yourself."

The injured veteran's eyes widened. "Preparing for what?"

A faint smirk flickered across her face. "Pain."

"Oh!"

"A lot of it."

"Woman, I've fought in so many battles with the legion that I don't even feel pain anymore. Beyond this life, I'll have to face the hundreds of souls of the enemies I've slain, all out for revenge—" He stopped mid-sentence as he watched her sharpen the blade of a small dagger on a rough stone. "What's that for?"

With practiced hands, the healer crushed some dried leaves and let them fall into a bowl. She added honey and a small amount of water, creating a mushy paste. From another pouch, she took out some dry moss and chalky concretions, which she crumbled into the mixture.

Ialenia Heria glanced at the legionaries. "Hold him down," she instructed.

Severinus Majorianus, Gallienus Lars Gracchus, and Plato exchanged looks before complying with her request. Their stone-like hands pinned Ulzio Dacianus to the bed.

"Are you out of your minds? Have you forgotten who I am? Don't listen to this witch! I don't need these comforts. Bring me a cup of wine instead—something to bring me back to life—for the sacred backside of the Emperor!" he protested.

The moment Ialenia Heria's blade began cutting into the infected edges of his wound, Ulzio's mouth opened in a scream that echoed through the building. The three comrades struggled to restrain him, using all their strength to keep him still.

"What are you doing to me, you damned witch?" Ulzio growled, his face contorted in pain, sweat beading on his forehead.

"Hold him steady… Don't let go. I need to remove the rotted edges," she explained to the soldiers holding him down.

The blade sliced further, slowly carving through infected flesh as streams of blood stained the straw mattress and the veteran's already tattered tunic.

"When these traitors let me go, I'll strangle you with my bare hands!" he threatened, thrashing like a wounded animal.

A bead of sweat rolled down Severinus Majorianus' forehead. Holding down the raging veteran was a monumental task, even for someone as strong as him. But he didn't loosen his grip.

Gallienus Lars Gracchus seemed to read his thoughts and nodded in agreement. He would hold on tightly.

Plato added, "You're a brother legionary, you damned boar. We'll keep you pinned until this woman finishes patching you up."

Another voice joined the fray.

The powerful hands of Fulcinius Agricola Statius joined the effort to subdue their struggling comrade. "Stop whining like a little girl. I've seen you kill dozens of Huns with an arrow stuck up your ass!"

Ulzio Dacianus' gaze hardened. He spat to the side and retorted, "It was in my buttock, not where you say, you filthy liar."

Tears of pain streamed from his bloodshot eyes.

With bloodstained hands, Ialenia Heria tossed the chunks of rotting flesh onto the floor. Using a thick needle and thread, she sutured the wound and covered it with the paste she had prepared earlier.

She wiped her hands on a piece of cloth and gave the dressing one final inspection. "The fever won't go down for a few hours, but you'll see—by tomorrow, he'll already be feeling better," she explained.

Severinus Majorianus wiped his sweaty brow, breathing heavily. "Thank you," he said gratefully.

"Just make sure he doesn't slit my throat in revenge," she joked.

"He won't," the optio reassured her.

A burst of relieved laughter filled the room.

***

"I leave command to you," Aristarchos Themistocles ordered without looking up from the maps spread across the table. "I'll try to return before midday."

"Understood, commander," Antoninus Tacitus replied, holding his crested helmet under one arm. "I hope you find her."

"Thanks… I hope so, too," Aristarchos muttered, packing a few supplies into his bag. "The horse?"

"Already saddled. I took one from the bishop's stable—it's a fine animal. That bastard treated himself well. There are about fifteen of them in the stables."

"I can believe that," Aristarchos said, casting him an approving look. "What's with that face, Centurion?"

Antoninus Tacitus lowered his gaze for a moment. "The soldiers...they're hungry. I'm not sure how much longer I can keep them from..."

"Let them slaughter them. Hungry soldiers don't fight well, and thankfully, we don't need them all. Leave four alive—they may prove useful if we need scouts or messengers."

The centurion's eyes lit up. He was already savoring the thought of roasted, flavorful meat.

"I'll inform them immediately," he said, leaving the room after saluting the commander.

Aristarchos Themistocles stepped outside, loaded his horse, and climbed into the saddle. He dug his heels into the animal's sides, and it bolted forward.

The guards opened the gates, allowing the galloping fury to pass, the horse's hooves kicking up clumps of wet earth and slushy snow.

The moon was beginning to yield to the coming day, sliding down the horizon like an indignant matron reluctantly making way for another woman.

Ulzio Dacianus' eyelids flickered open and closed, slowly bringing the room into focus.

Seated on stools or sprawled on the floor were several soldiers wrapped in cloaks, dozing.

He recognized them immediately. They were his closest friends.

Most of them hailed from the Aurunci region—they had known each other since they were boys. Now, they were all in this desolate borderland, trying to survive.

"Cursed whores, ugly as Severinus Majorianus' manhood, what are you all doing here?" he croaked, his voice thick with thirst.

The first to stir was the optio himself, offended by the remark. "They should've just cut that shoulder of yours clean off. Then you'd have to piss with one hand!" came the sharp reply.

The others woke up almost simultaneously.

Seeing all of them brought a wide grin to Ulzio's rugged, bearded face.

His eyes swept across the room, surprised to find all his friends present: Gallienus Lars Gracchus, Fulcinius Agricola Statius, Auctus Tullius Plato, Drusus Variatus, Antoninus Tacitus, Evetius Aquila, Severinus Majorianus, Christianus Caligatus, Vatinius Auruncus, and even Ialenia Heria, who had returned to check on his wound.

"Someone's missing, though…" he said, anxiety tightening in his stomach.

"They're not dead, don't worry. The commander went out to look for his woman, and Gaius Octavianus is on a mission," someone reassured him.

He pressed his lips together, showing his relief at the good news.

Vatinius Auruncus stepped forward from the others. "I'm glad to see your ugly faces grinning again, but I think it's time I take my leave. I'm going to check on the sentries and make sure they're awake. Let me remind you: the place outside is crawling with Heruli."

Ulzio Dacianus' hoarse voice called out again: "Will someone explain to me what's going on? I was fighting the enemy, and now I wake up half-dazed in the bishop's residence! And to top it off, it seems bands of Heruli are wandering freely just outside without anyone throwing a javelin up their—"

"While you were resting, your comrades kept fighting," Severinus Majorianus quickly explained. "Then something unbelievable happened. The barbarian tribes turned on each other. It seems there was a feud between their kings, which worked in our favor. Long story short, the only ones still troubling us are the Heruli, and they made a deal with our governor, Attilius Faticus, to take the city without massacring everyone."

Ulzio Dacianus' mouth opened slowly in shock.

"There's more…"

"Oh?"

"Rudulfus is now the imperial governor of Gaul."

"You're joking."

"No."

"Ah."

"Yeah."

The look of wonder on Ulzio's face didn't escape Severinus Majorianus, who seemed to take pleasure in adding more details. "You following so far?"

Ulzio nodded.

"Our beloved Emperor Romulus Augustulus has been deposed. His head is probably hanging on Odoacer's war chariot by now, and he's been sent straight to the world of the dead. Odoacer's the ruler of the Empire now. Clear enough for you?" Severinus said with a sharp grin.

Ulzio's calloused hand brushed the bandage on his shoulder. The pain had lessened, but the wound still throbbed.

"A complete mess, that's what I'm hearing. We've lost our home, and now two barbarians rule here and in Ravenna."

Every legionary in the room nodded solemnly.

"Any news of intact *vexillationes* or units?" Ulzio asked, hopeful he could join them and perhaps return to Duro Catalaunum to drive the Heruli beyond the imperial borders.

But he noticed his comrades lowering their eyes and turning their heads, avoiding the question. There was no news.

Oddly, though, a strange sense of relief settled in Ulzio's gut.

For a moment, his thoughts wandered to his hometown—a cluster of fishermen's huts along the Liris. He pictured himself as a child, running with his friends through the dense reeds, along the docks where merchant ships berthed. Slave traders, whores, cutthroats, thieves, garum merchants shouting at the top of their lungs, and countless mysterious faces just passing through—it was all there.

He could almost hear his mother calling for him, making him hopeful for an errand—usually to buy spelt cakes.

It was a fleeting feeling, but he felt free to return home, no longer bound to the army. Perhaps the Empire's collapse wasn't such a catastrophe after all, he thought with a faint smile.

"What are you grinning about?" Gallienus Lars Gracchus asked, frowning.

"I flew home... I could almost smell the camel dung on the road to the Terme Vescine, brother," Ulzio replied with a sly wink.

The room erupted into laughter.

"You said it, brother!" Plato chimed in solemnly, breaking the jovial atmosphere.

"Brother!" added Centurion Antoninus Tacitus.

"Brother!" said Drusus Variatus, hitching up his *cingulum* with his thumbs.

"Brother!" Christianus Caligatus stepped forward.

All eyes turned to the silent Batavian, who clenched his jaw as if restraining his tongue. An awkward silence hung in the air until something unexpected happened—Evetius Aquila began nodding, first slowly, then more vigorously.

"Brother!" he croaked.

Vatinius Auruncus let out a laugh. "Brother!" he echoed.

Ialenia Heria's observant eyes watched the scene unfold. At last, she spoke. "Sister, then!"

Ulzio's chest rose and fell heavily as he let out a deep sigh of relief—partly from feeling lucky to have survived, and partly from being surrounded by his legionary brothers.

***

The horse's hooves sent clumps of mossy earth and slushy snow flying as its taut muscles rippled beneath its thin coat of brown fur. Aristarchos Themistocles, his arms numb from the cold and fatigue, yanked hard on the reins, forcing the galloping animal to come to an abrupt stop.

He had taken the road leading toward southern Gaul.

The horse's hooves pressed heavily into the ground, as if trying to release the energy that had propelled it so far. Clouds of condensation billowed from its flaring nostrils, and its neck swayed as it shook off the excitement and strain, causing its long mane to ripple.

He had searched everywhere for her—at abandoned waystations, among refugees heading south, and in a few farms that had been looted and reduced to rubble and ash. But there was no trace of her—the woman he had come to realize he loved more than himself.

He cursed himself and railed against fate for advising her to leave the city. Yet at the same time, he knew he had given her the chance to escape a grim fate.

He was torn.

Her words and her voice had suddenly become essential to his existence. He had to find her, no matter where she had gone, he vowed to himself. Loosening the reins slightly, he signaled the horse to resume its march.

With the icy wind slicing his face, confined between the cheek guards of his crested helmet, he rode onward, discouraged and worried. Angry at himself.

Scanning the ground, he noticed some tracks leaving the paved road and disappearing into a narrow path through the woods.

Dismounting, he knelt down, scooping up a bit of mud that bore the imprint of a single person's passing. The tracks weren't fresh—probably from the previous day—and the size was unmistakably feminine.

In his mind, he quickly calculated how far a determined woman like Placidia might have traveled on foot, burdened and weary from the cold.

He let his gaze wander across the snow-covered undergrowth, which was marked only by the tiny prints of rabbits and squirrels. He felt relieved not to see any wolf tracks nearby.

In this cold, wolf packs grew more vicious in their hunt for prey to survive.

Remounting, he held the reins with one hand, while his right instinctively rested on the pommel of his gladius.

The horse resumed its slow, head-down climb along the trail. Sunlight pierced the dense forest in narrow beams, glittering on the icy crystals scattered across the ground.

A sudden noise made him whip around. A heavy branch, weighed down by snow, had snapped and fallen.

The horse tossed its head and neighed in irritation.

After maneuvering around a massive boulder covered in grayish lichens, the animal suddenly halted, digging its forelegs into the earth.

Not far ahead, three Heruli riders paused to see who it was. From his higher position, Aristarchos Themistocles locked eyes with them.

One of the Heruli spurred his bay horse forward, drawing his long sword from its sheath and spinning it in the air while shouting war cries.

The other two followed, one brandishing a spear and the other a double-bladed axe.

Aristarchos Themistocles cursed the fate that had led him into a Heruli patrol. Realizing he had no time to escape, he made the only sensible choice. Drawing his gladius, he pointed it toward the nearest enemy.

The Heruli snarled something in his guttural language as he closed the distance. His long sword twirled above his head, and his frothing horse snorted heavily through its open mouth.

With a sickening crunch, the head of Aristarchos' horse exploded in a spray of blood, flesh, and bone fragments.

The massive animal collapsed, catapulting the centurion forward. He tumbled for several meters, snow and ice embedding themselves in every crevice of his armor. Planting himself on one knee, he smacked his helmet to ensure it was secure. Pain radiated through his body, but this was no time to dwell on it.

His gladius lay a short distance away. He scrambled to grab it as the Heruli rider who had felled his horse wheeled around to finish him. The other two struggled to maneuver their mounts through the dense trees and now found themselves uphill, their charge stalling.

Alone, horseless, and wounded, Aristarchos Themistocles braced himself to face the three Heruli. Snowflakes fell from his mail armor as a viscous trickle of blood began to drip from his nose.

"Roman! You're about to meet the dreadful ferryman of souls!" snarled the nearest Heruli, baring his teeth and speaking in crude Latin.

He spurred his horse forward. The beast reared onto its hind legs before charging. The clanging of armor plates echoed as the animal's pounding hooves drew closer, shaking the ground beneath Aristarchos' feet and making his heart race in his chest.

A surge of fear twisted his stomach, sending a bitter taste rising to his throat. For a moment, he locked eyes with the animal, its pupils wide with the frenzy of its charge, before refocusing on the Heruli rider poised to strike.

"The sword is on the right..." Aristarchos thought quickly. "He's holding his sword on the right!"

Shouting the observation aloud, he sidestepped to the opposite side at the last moment and slashed at the attacker's leg. His blade tore through skin, muscle, tendons, and bone.

The Heruli's battle cry turned into a howl of pain as his powerful horse skidded in the slushy snow, struggling to halt its momentum.

This was the moment to act.

With quick strides, Aristarchos closed in, delivering relentless strikes at the dismounted rider, who lost his balance and tumbled to the ground.

With all his strength, Aristarchos drove the gladius into the man's neck, piercing through to the other side. Blood sprayed from the Heruli's mouth, staining his long beard.

The earth beneath Aristarchos' feet trembled again.

The other two were close. There was no time to lose.

The centurion *primae spatha* turned, spinning his gladius across the back of his hand. The fear was gone, replaced by courage.

The second Heruli rider approached, hurling his spear at the Roman officer. Aristarchos managed to dodge it and, from the Heruli rider's own saddle, grabbed a spear.

He weighed it in his hand before throwing it with force, striking the advancing warrior. The Heruli fell from his saddle, landing with a muffled thud on the snowy ground. His body rolled down the incline, snapping the spear that had pierced his sternum.

The odds were even now.

"One-on-one," Aristarchos hissed to the last remaining rider.

The Heruli gripped his axe, raising it high to show his fearlessness, but his eyes darted nervously toward the bodies of his fallen comrades lying in the blood-stained snow.

He muttered something harsh in his language, perhaps an insult, before yanking his reins and spurring his horse toward the hill's summit at full gallop.

He had fled.

Aristarchos Themistocles mounted one of the Heruli's horses, soothing it by stroking its neck. He would return to the paved road and continue south, praying that Placidia had not fallen into the hands of those damned cutthroats.

"Come on, boy, run...run!" he whispered to the horse, urging it into a gallop down the main road, leaving a whirlwind of vaporized snow in their wake.

The icy air sliced into his throat, causing sharp pains, and his eyes watered, blurring his vision. Every ache in his battered body reminded him of his earlier fall from the horse.

"Placidia..." he murmured.

He had traveled far, but still found no trace of her. The tracks he had followed had led him straight into the Heruli patrol, and now he was stranded in the middle of nowhere, too far from Duro Catalaunum.

Reluctantly, he decided to turn back.

Duro Catalaunum, Bishop's Residence, Tertia Vigilia

When Aristarchos Themistocles arrived at the *excubitores*[1] of the legionary camp, the night was still deep.

He summoned Severinus Majorianus, who was in charge of the night watch, and immediately gave orders: "Give the men two more hours of sleep. At dawn, wake the centurions and have them gather everyone for the final assembly."

"Centurion, are you injured?" the optio asked, noticing his disheveled appearance. The horse he led by the reins looked exhausted, its legs battered and bleeding.

"I've had a rough day, but it's best we skip the stories. A quick piss, and I'll be as good as new," Aristarchos said, attempting to lighten the mood.

Severinus understood, and disappeared into the milky fog to carry out his duties.

At the first light of dawn, Severinus followed through with the orders. Within a short time, the subordinate centurions began shouting for assembly.

When all the legionaries gathered, already clad in their loricae, helmeted and fully armed, Vatinius Auruncus and Antoninus Tacitus began organizing them into formation.

"*Ad signa!*" came the command.

Hearing the call to assemble, the soldiers grouped themselves behind the *signifer*.

"*Quattuor ordines!*"[2] Vatinius Auruncus shouted, raising his hand to display four fingers.

As if guided by instinct, each soldier took his position, forming four orderly lines behind the *signifer*.

---

[1] *Excubitores:* sentinels.

[2] *Quattuor ordines:* formation in four ranks.

"*Deponere scuta!*"[3]

The shields were set on the ground, held steady by hands gripping the top edges.

With the formations in place, the two centurions took up positions at the ends of the lines. Slowly and with solemn steps, the centurion *primae spatha* inspected what remained of his centuries.

Stopping in front of Gallienus Lars Gracchus, he gave him a hearty slap on the shoulder. "Does that foggy veteran's brain of yours still remember Arles?" he asked, smiling faintly from the corner of his mouth.

"I made a lot of wives into widows that day, Centurion!" Gallienus replied with a grin.

They laughed.

Among the ranks, Aristarchos noticed Ulzio Dacianus, still pale, but fully dressed in his lorica and helmet. He looked frail, as though he needed a solid meal to regain his strength.

"Welcome back!" Aristarchos called out in greeting.

"I'm just here to let you know those widows were my doing, not his," Ulzio replied, nodding toward the *signifer*, who turned around with an annoyed look.

Laughter erupted again.

Finally, Aristarchos Themistocles positioned himself in front of the assembled legionaries, standing tall and martial. He began what would be his final speech.

"Legionaries, I'll be honest with you. The Rome that once was is no more. The Emperor has been assassinated. The imperial army has scattered to the far corners of what we once called an empire. Nothing we've known makes sense anymore—not our customs, not our bonds. No one will pay us the *solidi* we're owed, nor will we receive the land grants promised by law..." He paused for a moment to ensure everyone's attention.

---

[3] *Deponere (deponite) scuta:* command to place shields down, where the legionaries would rest their shields on the ground, holding them by the upper edge.

The legionaries stared at him in silence. A few spat on the ground in frustration.

"Our army no longer inspires fear. The world belongs to the barbarians now. That is why, on this frigid morning, I grant you all the *honesta missio*—the honorable discharge you've earned as brave men, survivors of these past days' trials. Those of you who wish to may keep your equipment. Perhaps you can sell it for some coin to get by for a while," he said, clearing his throat. Then, with gravity, he delivered the most important words: "From this moment on, I will no longer give you orders."

The soldiers stared at him in disbelief, but none moved a muscle.

Aristarchos Themistocles, the centurion *primae spatha*, added one final remark:

"You fought valiantly these past days. Holding out against an enemy that outnumbered us was no small feat, and yet you did it. You were brilliant, brothers. I will remember you with pride and honor. You are free now."

With that, he concluded.

Centurion Vatinius Auruncus drew his gladius and pointed it to the sky.

Antoninus Tacitus followed suit.

"*Stringite gladios!*[4] Draw your swords! *Ostendere gladios!*[5] Show your blades!" Vatinius Auruncus shouted again.

Soon, all the legionaries had unsheathed their swords, raising them high as they roared in unison: "Virtus!"

A wave of pride swept through Vatinius Auruncus. "*Sursum capita!*[6] Lift your heads!

---

[4] *Stringite (stringere) gladios:* command to draw swords. Soldiers would unsheathe their gladii and stand at attention, keeping their elbows close to their right flanks and the blades pointed upward.

[5] *Ostendere gladios:* command to present swords.

[6] *Sursum capita:* literally "heads up." A command for formation.

Every head rose simultaneously, and their eyes turned toward their commander.

"*Honores Vexillo!* Honors to the Standard!" the young centurion's voice pierced the frigid air.

"Fifth Ironclad!" they all cried.

Vatinius Auruncus' throat tightened, making it impossible to utter the final command.

Sensing his moment of hesitation, the other centurion stepped in to deliver the order.

"*Quies!* Rest!" he barked, scratching his rear. "Did you hear me, you bastards? Rest!" he repeated.

And so, the *vexillatio* of Duro Catalaunum, the last remnants of Rome's Fifth Legion, gave their final salute.

Gallienus Lars Gracchus leaned the standard of the Third Century against a marble column whose capital had been removed and reused to build a nearby wall.

As if moved by instinct, all the legionaries removed their helmets at the same time.

After a few moments of indecision, they began to break formation in small groups. Left in the square were about eighty soldiers, talking among themselves—some to bid farewell, others simply unsure of what to do next. The sudden change had left them deeply unsettled.

Spontaneously, the group of friends from the Liris plains and the nearby regions gathered under the colonnade.

They had shared their lives for years, from the Battle of Arles to the present moment. They were bound by a connection deeper than blood—a brotherhood forged by shared experiences and survival.

Tarquinius Glaucus, always the joker, cracked one of his usual remarks: "I'll spend the rest of my days between the thighs of a prostitute."

The others laughed, but their eyes betrayed worry and uncertainty.

---

[7] *Quies:* rest. A formation command after which the soldiers remained in formation, but adopted a more relaxed posture.

A long moment of silence followed, stretching endlessly.

Severinus Majorianus, Evetius Aquila, Christianus Caligatus, Auctus Tullius Plato, Gallienus Lars Gracchus, Vatinius Auruncus, Gaius Octavianus, Antoninus Tacitus, Drusus Variatus, Fulcinius Agricola Statius, and Ulzio Dacianus formed a circle.

It was time to decide what to do.

The only sounds were the crackling of torches.

The decision had to be unanimous.

They began their deliberation with a shared understanding: now was not the time to wander alone through the shattered remains of the Empire. The land was crawling with barbarians free to pillage, torture, and kill.

If they were to return to the Liris plains, it would be best to do it together.

This group of legionaries had spent their lives serving side by side. They had grown up in the army, fought in the infamous Battle of Arles, and shared a bond strengthened by their many trials.

Severinus Majorianus was the first to speak. "I've been thinking about heading back to the Italian peninsula to..." He swallowed hard. "...to go home."

Everyone had something to say, but no one spoke.

Their gazes met, heavy with intent and expectation, but the silence stretched on.

"I agree with him," Fulcinius Agricola Statius finally broke the silence. "Let's leave this cursed place to the Heruli if they want it. Let's head back to the warm coast. My old bones can't take this gray, rainy climate anymore."

"I'm with you," Auctus Tullius Plato chimed in, toying with the tip of his *pugio*.

Gallienus Lars Gracchus and Drusus Variatus exchanged a knowing glance before nodding their agreement.

"I've got a wife and daughter at home," Drusus Variatus added. "They were supposed to join me here in Duro Catalaunum, but... I'm glad they didn't, considering how things turned out." He looked off toward a corner, avoiding their eyes.

"For the ass of that stranger who calls herself my mother, I'm in!" Antoninus Tacitus interjected.

"I'm in," Christianus Caligatus said simply, looking around at each of his comrades.

The last to speak was Ulzio Dacianus, who was chewing on dried fruit. "I can't wait to lose a few *solidi* in a gambling den!"

Everyone laughed.

"Let's get out of here, then," Vatinius Auruncus added, removing his crested helmet.

"Always together," Gaius Octavianus said, still wearing a wolf pelt cloak he had taken from a Heruli rider.

"I don't have a home or family waiting for me," Evetius Aquila said unexpectedly. "All I want is to ride a fine horse alongside my legionary brothers."

His words caught everyone by surprise, leaving them visibly stunned.

Those sitting on the low wall or on the paved ground stood up, while those who were already standing took a few steps forward.

They drew closer together, so close that they could feel each other's breath.

Vatinius Auruncus gathered their attention: "As soon as possible, we'll leave this moss-covered place. Let's get to work. We'll gather everything we'll need for the journey. Move it, you lazy bastards," he urged.

A flurry of activity followed.

They lit fires to cook their final meals at Duro Catalaunum.

Fulcinius Agricola Statius roasted the meat of one of the horses that had once belonged to Bishop Calibertus.

"Where did you get that…" Tarquinius Glaucus began to ask, only to be interrupted by a sharp elbow from Drusus Variatus.

"Do you know what'll happen if the centurion *primae spatha* finds out we slaughtered the draft horse?" Drusus scolded him, giving a pointed glare.

Tarquinius rolled his eyes, rubbing his chin with thick fingers as he mulled over the elbow he'd just received. "Fine. I take it back," he said with a laugh, then continued in mock contemplation: "Let's just hope the barbarians along the Italian coast haven't already married all the women. Otherwise, I'd be better off staying in this rat-infested hole."

Fulcinius Agricola Statius seized the moment to retort: "You'll end up hanging by your feet if you don't calm down. Every time you walk into a tavern, you start a brawl. And if they don't string you up, some jealous husband will cut off your manhood!"

Vatinius Auruncus stifled a laugh, pretending to stoke the fire.

"And what are you laughing at, Centurion? Do you think there isn't a woman in every city we've passed who weeps for my absence?"

The group erupted in laughter.

The situation was paradoxical.

In the face of their dire circumstances, they still found the strength to joke.

Severinus Majorianus and Christianus Caligatus were holding Plato, while Gaius Octavianus jammed a helmet onto his head backward, blinding him. Then they shoved him into a pile of hay mixed with manure.

"That's why the barbarians won! In the end, they were recruiting little girls into the legions!" Antoninus Tacitus cackled, pointing at Plato with his finger.

No one noticed the faint smile that crept onto the stoic face of the Batavian, Evetius Aquila.

"There's something to burn," said Vatinius Auruncus, though no one seemed to hear him. He carried two planks under his arm, salvaged from the frame of a river raft.

He tossed them onto the fire, feeding the flames, which rose quickly, crackling and sparking as they consumed the wood.

They spent these moments—the final moments of the *vexillatio* of the Fifth Ironclad Legion—gathered around the fire, joking and clinging to the hope of returning home.

Nightfall enveloped the small fortified town of Duro Catalaunum, which seemed improbably calm.

The Great Hall of the Principia

Torches cast a hesitant, reddish light throughout the room, more than sufficient for visibility. Several oil lamps had been lit and hung from decorative chains.

The Great Hall was undergoing a transformation. Once the headquarters of the Fifth Ironclad Legion, it was now taking on the appearance of a stately, princely residence.

The shelves that had once held maps and rolls of parchment recording soldiers' pay were being replaced by lavish new furniture and refined ornaments—plundered treasures from the nearby estates that the Heruli had looted.

Rudulfus now wore garments of noble quality, and seemed to revel in surrounding himself with precious objects.

He was already envisioning rooms filled with accounting ledgers that tracked the Empire's tax revenues.

As the new Governor of Gaul, Rudulfus held a critical position within the Western Empire.

He idly played with a long sword, letting its tip tap against the marble floor, producing an irritating clinking sound that grated on those around him.

How he managed the province of Gaul mattered little.

Governance during this period was no simple task. The political and social landscape was as chaotic as a storm at sea.

When his officials showed him the current state of affairs, he quickly realized that this part of the Empire was in total disarray.

Tax evasion was rampant, partly because no one was quite sure who was in charge anymore.

And Rudulfus had only managed to meet with officials from the nearest cities. The divisions and rivalries among the various factions were so pronounced that anyone could align with whichever side they preferred.

Rudulfus focused on what needed to be done.

He broadened his perspective and began to think deeply.

Since the time of the revered Emperor Majorianus, power in the West had been divided among three cities: Arles, Rome, and Ravenna.

The Roman Senate still carried some weight, though its members were thoroughly corrupt. Some supported the Emperor, others the commander-in-chief of the army, while others still shifted their allegiances depending on how much gold one side or the other could offer.

In Gaul, Arles had been the center for tax collection, bureaucratic administration, and the resolution of private disputes.

But Rudulfus' appointment had shifted the balance to Duro Catalaunum, at least for the winter.

Still, he had to account for Odoacer. After deposing the last Emperor, Romulus Augustulus, Odoacer had chosen Ravenna as his seat of power, inheriting not only an incredible number of civil servants, but also the entire bureaucratic apparatus established during the time of Theodosius.

Suddenly, everything became clear to Rudulfus.

The West was now ruled by two kings: Odoacer and himself. Though he did not formally bear the title of king, he was one in practice.

But he couldn't ignore the fact that Odoacer commanded the bulk of the military forces, while Rudulfus had only his own army.

In this delicate situation, Rudulfus decided on a middle course—not too authoritarian, which might provoke Odoacer, but not so lenient as to appear weak.

The middle path proved to be the right choice.

His first move was to summon, through Attilius Faticus, the civil servants who were already arriving in Duro Catalaunum.

Within an hour, a line of ten officials stood waiting to be received.

Rudulfus requested a report on pending cases awaiting resolution.

One by one, the officials presented the situation. The picture that emerged was alarming: the imperial chancery was sending files reporting a severe decline in tax collections.

During the recent waves of devastation and looting, many officials had abandoned public offices to retreat to their private estates or country villas, protected by mercenary militias.

Additionally, the Romans of Gaul had lost interest in holding public office. These positions had become increasingly irrelevant due to the chaos and disorganization engulfing the Empire.

It wasn't about the financial benefits—they still earned directly from tax collections—but rather the loss of prestige, as no one recognized or respected their titles anymore.

In short, the population had lost interest in the *Res Publica*.

Everyone was out for themselves, and the blame lay with the barbarian incursions and the utter lack of morality among public officials.

Not to mention the bureaucracy, which no longer served public administration, but had devolved into a perverse system designed to create obstacles. This forced citizens to pay bribes to resolve their affairs successfully.

Despite the officials' polished language, Rudulfus' mind wandered.

The first few presentations were enough for him to grasp the extent of the administrative degradation in the Gallic region.

After taking a long moment to think, he raised his hand, silencing the current speaker.

An awkward silence filled the room.

Turning his gaze to Attilius Faticus, Rudulfus gave voice to his thoughts.

"It seems clear to me that the old Emperor failed to make the state apparatus work properly. That doesn't surprise me, knowing you Romans…" His remark provoked chuckles among the officers present, while the officials exchanged worried glances.

"We need to replace the heads of many public offices, delegates, and other responsible parties. You'll handle it on my behalf," he instructed Faticus. "And remember to keep every recommendation you receive in mind. We'll need to collect favors from those we assist to secure future ones in return. Keep the old administrators in line by promising them a decent pension—but only grant it after they surrender significant portions of their properties. Let's keep them useful until we find worthy replacements."

Attilius Faticus swallowed bitterly.

He understood that "finding replacements" implied that the old administrators would be eliminated. His expression betrayed a mixture of admiration and disgust for the barbarian before him.

Rudulfus was proving to be a shrewd administrator, far more so than any Faticus had encountered in his long public career. And he had seen his share of the perverse, malicious, corrupt, and depraved.

Yet the Heruli king surpassed them all.

As the room bustled with officials, a messenger caught Attilius Faticus' attention.

The two spoke in hushed tones, their expressions indicating that the news was sensational.

The officials murmured among themselves, careful not to raise their voices too much and risk irritating the new master of Gaul.

One of them, however, seized the moment to mock Attilius Faticus, calling him subjugated by the barbarians: "There they are—the new slaves of Rome: the Romans!"

Ignoring the insult, Attilius Faticus ended his conversation with the messenger and approached Rudulfus with his head bowed.

He stood before the governor, bathed in a ray of moonlight streaming through a high window.

Only when Rudulfus gestured did Faticus lift his face to explain.

"Excellency, General Cunipert found a woman along the road to Argentoratum. She is extraordinarily beautiful, and he wishes to present her to your esteemed judgment," Faticus said, rubbing his hands together as if offering a lucrative deal.

"Why would you offer me a woman, Roman?" Rudulfus asked.

"I truly believe she is worth your attention, Your Excellency," Faticus replied, oozing flattery.

Rudulfus stroked his long mustache, which hung over his cheeks. "Let's hope this isn't a waste of my time."

At that, the chamberlain clapped his hands.

Two mercenaries under Cunipert's command entered, holding the woman tightly by her arms.

She was indeed extraordinary, and from her near-perfect features, Rudulfus immediately recognized her Frankish origins.

He studied her with an expression of fascination, a faint smile crossing his lips as he watched her struggle like a freshly-caught animal.

Behind her, Cunipert appeared, stepping forward and offering a nod of greeting. He grinned, revealing a mouth missing several teeth; a bearskin cloak was draped over his scale armor.

"My lord, this woman… I personally brought her before you to grace you with her presence."

Rudulfus snapped, "We're discussing important matters. Don't waste my time, or your tongue will hang beside your neck." He seemed to forget how many favors he had received from this officer. "I'll keep her. I accept your gift. Now take her away."

"One thing more, my king…" Cunipert dared, raising his hand as if to ask for another moment.

"What is it now?" Rudulfus growled.

A sly smile spread across Cunipert's face as his eyes narrowed in anticipation of delivering significant words:

"She is the woman of the *vexillatio* commander."

With that, he gave a slight bow and left the principia along with the others.

"Leave her here," Rudulfus' voice echoed through the expansive hall. "And everyone else—get out!"

The officials hurriedly gathered their scrolls and documents, clearing the room in an instant.

Cunipert exited with a satisfied look, knowing the king would reward him with land grants.

The enormous figure of Rudulfus rose from his seat and approached the woman.

Her long, flowing hair fell over her shoulders, dark and reasonably well-kept, though it was evident she hadn't washed it in some time. Her penetrating eyes, though tired and languid, revealed a fierce spirit. Despite her trembling—whether from cold, hunger, or both—she pressed her lips together with dignified determination.

He leaned in and whispered in her ear, "What is your name?"

"Placidia," she replied.

The back of his hand struck her so hard that she fell backward.

Rudulfus loomed over her. "You're not Roman, and I asked for your name," he snarled.

"Kungian..." she stammered, trembling in fear.

"Kungian, Kungian..." he murmured, grabbing a lock of her hair.

He began inspecting her, inch by inch, from head to toe.

At that, she snapped: "Placidia! My name is Placidia," staring defiantly at an indistinct corner of the room.

"Ah, I see. The Romans took you, and you decided to become one of their whores, didn't you?" he taunted.

Placidia remained unmoved. Her fists clenched at her sides as she struggled to maintain her dignity.

"Are you thinking of your Roman, woman?" he hissed, brushing her cheek with two fingers.

"I think of him every moment of my day," she answered, fully aware that each word she chose cut him like the sharpest blade.

"You'll learn the difference tonight. I've decided you'll lie with me," he declared, clapping his hands twice.

A group of servants emerged from behind heavy curtains to take her away.

Placidia did not resist. It would have been futile.

The king ordered her to be taken to the palace's *calidarium* to be bathed and perfumed.

With her mind crowded by thoughts and fears, Placidia submitted herself to the sequence of events she was being subjected to.

After the washing, all the slaves left the calidarium—except one.

She was a Nubian whose tongue had been cut out in the past for gossiping about the vices of a wealthy matron.

The woman finished drying Placidia with pristine linen cloths, and then fetched a tunic in classic colors. Shyly, she gestured for Placidia to put it on, and Placidia took it into her hands.

"Can't you speak? Were you forbidden from speaking to me?" she asked as she began dressing.

The slave mimed the mutilation she had endured.

Placidia's shock was evident. "What have they done to you! It... it was a punishment, wasn't it?" she asked in a trembling voice.

The Nubian woman lowered her head in resignation. She waited until Placidia was fully dressed, then gently took her hand and led her onward.

They entered a small, windowless room, where a bed was covered with a soft, warm cowhide.

The slave gestured for her to rest a while before going further.

Placidia sat, staring at her knees. A strange, unpleasant sensation crept over her, filling her soul. She had no sense of how much time passed as she curled up in the cowhide.

When the Nubian slave reappeared at the door, Placidia understood that she was being led to a terrible fate.

They walked down a corridor that opened into a wide colonnade surrounding a courtyard. At its center, a fountain gushed water from a single spout that had not yet frozen. The Nubian stopped before a large door, flanked by two hulking guards armed with swords and spears, clad in gleaming plate armor.

"Am I to enter?" Placidia asked, her heart pounding in her throat.

The Nubian nodded, leaving no doubt.

The room she entered was vast.

The walls were adorned with purple drapes and shields, suggesting that this might once have been a repository for military maps.

The shelves had been ripped from the walls, likely burned in fires to warm the hundreds of Heruli warriors still without proper quarters.

At the center stood a bed, carefully arranged. The linens had clearly been looted from some noble household, as no legionary would have had such finery.

Rudulfus awaited her, dressed in a linen tunic tailored in the Gallo-Roman style, embroidered with gold threads and laurel designs reminiscent of the Caesars' era.

The room was warmed by four lit braziers, making the air pleasantly temperate.

He ran a hand over his beard before speaking. "I've inquired about you, woman."

Placidia said nothing.

"There was a rumor about you," he continued. "It's said you fled on horseback with a Roman general during the siege of your village."

Placidia's eyes blazed, her expression hardening with defiance.

"What do you know about it? You were countless moons away when the Romans descended upon us. My husband was a Frankish nobleman who fought to the bitter end—and I fought alongside him, what do you think? I don't know what became of my sisters or my only daughter; they've likely been enslaved, as I have. Whoever spreads such lies about me will answer to the gods."

The king laughed. "I was told you were far from docile. But…" He stepped closer. "…come here now. I am not some soft Roman officer."

Placidia's anger flared at Rudulfus' spies; they had done their work well. They had learned of her feelings for the centurion— curse them! Surely some servant had spoken out to earn a small favor. She let a fleeting sneer twist her face.

Rudulfus drained a cup of wine and set it down roughly on a bench. He slammed his fist against the wooden frame of the bed, making her jump.

He reached out to touch her hair.

Placidia's eyes filled with tears and terror.

He stripped her and climbed over her immediately, beginning to kiss her neck. His excitement made him seize her face with one hand, twisting her chin.

Rudulfus knew tenderness only in this crude way.

Placidia stared fixedly at the ceiling. The expression of disgust on her face made it clear she was trying to separate her soul from her body.

When he tried to force her legs apart and met resistance, he stopped suddenly.

Placidia could feel his muscular body tense, and fear gripped her. She knew that defying him would come at a heavy cost.

And she was right.

Rudulfus raised his face, locking eyes with her.

"Are you rejecting me?" he asked, breathing heavily, his anger rising.

Placidia tried to find a way out. "Your Excellency, I have suffered much in these past days, and..."

But the Heruli king forcefully spread her legs and tried to take her, ignoring her pleas.

They struggled for what felt to Placidia like an eternity—a time that only seemed to stoke Rudulfus' arousal. He finally overpowered her, pinning her wrists.

His rough, clumsy movements were meant to demonstrate his strength, but he achieved little satisfaction.

Sensing an opportunity, Placidia decided to make one last attempt.

She leaned close to his ear and said, "Aristarchos Themistocles wouldn't have needed to struggle like this. I would have opened my legs for him willingly and taken pleasure in it. I would have run my fingers through his hair and whispered sweet words, because I love him. But you? I want nothing of you. You're a pig, capable only of grunting, lacking any true manly virtue. Perhaps you know how to slaughter, but you do not know how to be a man."

Rudulfus' sharp eyes grew wide with dull rage.

His arousal vanished, replaced by fury at her cutting words. He propped himself up on his arms and made one last attempt to kiss her and touch her intimately, but his desire had given way to wrath.

"You cursed whore!" he bellowed. "You're nothing but a Roman slut!"

He sprang to his feet and dragged her off the bed by her hair. He kicked her in the abdomen with all his might.

Placidia writhed in agony, gasping for breath. She let out a hoarse cry, more like a screech.

The blow he landed on her face knocked her unconscious.

When she came to, she began to beg for mercy, sobbing.

A shiver of excitement coursed through Rudulfus, filling him with a sinister thrill.

He began to strike her again, repeatedly, and kept going.

He roared in fury, his eyes bulging, his hands and face smeared with the woman's blood.

When he finally felt satisfied, panting heavily, his gaze fell upon the floor and the walls, both spattered with the blood of poor Placidia, who now lay motionless, curled up in a fetal position. She whimpered faintly from the torment she had endured.

Rudulfus took a deep breath, his face distorted by a deranged expression. He summoned his personal guard to have her taken away.

Afterward, he collapsed onto the bed and fell into a deep sleep, unconcerned by the brutality he had just committed.

Duro Catalaunum, Episcopal Residence, Night

In the dead of night, Vatinius Auruncus and Antoninus Tacitus entered the cubiculum where Aristarchos Themistocles was resting.

He sat up on the straw mattress, his expression groggy and questioning.

It fell to Vatinius Auruncus to explain what was happening. He swallowed the bitter taste in his throat before speaking.

"Centurion, quickly, come and see..." was all he managed to say.

"Are we under attack?" Aristarchos Themistocles asked urgently, his body instantly tense with nerves.

The two centurions shook their heads, their gazes falling to an undefined point on the ground.

The commander sensed a terrible conclusion—those expressions foretold nothing good. He knew these men; they were not the type to lower their eyes, not even in the face of fear. That left him no choice but to throw on his cloak over his short tunic and fasten his gladius to his belt.

"Lead the way," he told them.

They moved swiftly, leading him out of the rooms that had been repurposed as barracks and toward the door.

They crept through the dark, foul-smelling alleyways to a small side gate, unnoticed by the Heruli, who were likely unaware of its existence.

A narrow path led them through a clearing and into a dense forest. Grayish shafts of light pierced through the thick tree trunks.

They arrived at the banks of a small river, its pale glow shimmering as it flowed slowly. A light mist hovered half a meter above the ground, swirling quickly as the soldiers passed.

All the other legionaries were there, waiting for his arrival, their torches casting flickering light.

A low murmur became distinct as they drew closer. Now, voices could be clearly heard, and, unfortunately, they expressed opinions on the tragic events.

The frozen snow crunched beneath their feet, and the cold was biting.

When Aristarchos Themistocles reached the riverbank, the soldiers parted to make way for him.

His eyes immediately recognized the veterans of Arles—his old friends—who hid their concern beneath the hoods of their cloaks.

Kneeling beside the lifeless body, Gaius Octavianus was observing it, covered as it was with damp leaves.

When Gaius Octavianus rose to make way for the senior centurion, everyone fell silent.

Aristarchos Themistocles' gaze fell on a pale, livid hand, its delicate features unmistakably feminine. He knelt beside the body, and with a slow gesture, he brushed the hair from the face.

He was certain—it was Placidia, though she was horrifyingly disfigured by the beating she had endured.

She had been killed.

His nerves gave way, and he collapsed, burying his face in the snow and mud. He cradled her head in his hands, wiping the wet dirt and matted hair from her face.

When he lowered his head to hers, seeking one last affectionate connection, all the soldiers present understood to respect his grief. One by one, they stepped away.

Several interminable minutes passed until Aristarchos Themistocles finally rose, lifting Placidia's body in his arms. He walked through his legionaries with his gaze fixed straight ahead.

They all clenched their jaws in anger. The suspicion that the Heruli had committed this heinous act, as a final insult to their commander, seemed plausible.

He carried her lifeless body to the peristyle of the building he had used as a weapons depot within the bishop's residence. He laid her on a wooden table and folded her hands over her chest.

He whispered prayers, hoping that her soul might be welcomed kindly in the afterlife.

As a final act of despair, he buried his head in his hands.

If only he hadn't advised her to flee! he thought, tormented by guilt. Perhaps her fate would have been different, as it had been for many in the town of Duro Catalaunum who were still alive.

He looked at her fondly and thought of her life, so marked by tragedy.

It hardly seemed possible that a woman so proud and determined now bore such a peaceful and serene expression, despite the swelling and bruises.

Her wounded lip could not hide a faint, almost imperceptible smile. The commander attributed it to Placidia's defiant spirit and strong character, as if she were sending him one final message to let him know that she was now at peace.

That illusion eased his torment slightly.

Were those tears streaming down his face? Was it possible that eyes accustomed to making even the most hardened barbarian warriors tremble were now shedding tears?

He sniffed hard and wiped his face with the back of his hand in a futile attempt to hold them back.

Who could have done such a thing to her? he wondered, grinding his teeth in rage.

Vatinius Auruncus appeared in the peristyle, stopping a few meters away.

"How long have you all known?" Aristarchos Themistocles asked, referring to the fact that, if they had all stood vigil over Placidia's body by the river, it was obvious that his feelings for her had been evident all along.

And to think, he had believed he had hidden them well. He hated exposing himself before his soldiers, to avoid idle gossip.

The younger centurion's words cut through the still night air like a blade. He spoke softly, as if a louder tone might shatter the solemn grief: "We've always known, Centurion. Everyone understood that Placidia was special to you."

He nodded. "Thank you for keeping watch over her by the river."

"It was just difficult to find the right way to tell you, Centurion."

"I'm no longer your centurion. The legion no longer exists, nor do the centuries under our command. Rome no longer exists, legionary!" he snapped, his anger spilling out, for he despised Vatinius Auruncus' persistence in clinging to values that had disappeared like mist.

Vatinius Auruncus understood the commander's outburst. "Centurion, we know how things unfolded."

The other man raised his chin, waiting for him to continue.

"Let her go… Come outside. The others are waiting," he urged.

Aristarchos Themistocles stood and headed for the exit. His shadow stretched across the wall, cast by the dim, flickering light of two oil lamps hanging from chains.

Outside, in the atrium, the other legionaries stood without their armor. They all wore civilian clothes, awaiting their departure to return to their homelands.

A young boy, still wearing a toga trimmed with purple—marking someone not yet of age—stood among them.

Severinus Majorianus broke the uneasy silence. "This boy owns a boat he uses to fish in the river. Tonight, while he was loading his nets, he noticed an unusual glint in the moonlight and grew suspicious. He crept closer, hiding among the bushes, and saw two Heruli dumping Placidia's body on the ground. He recognized who she was because she often bought fish from him to cook in your kitchen. He came straight to inform us."

Aristarchos Themistocles approached the boy.

"What is your name, boy?" he asked.

The boy pressed his lips together and trembled like a leaf before finally answering, "My name is Paris Tullius Cereo. I'm a fisherman, like my father. I'm eleven years old."

The centurion ruffled the boy's hair. "You've done well. Here..." He rummaged in the pouch at his belt and pulled out some coins. "These are for you. And with them, you have my gratitude. Now go, before you're seen here."

The boy clutched the coins tightly but didn't move.

"Go!" he urged him.

Severinus Majorianus intervened, halting him: "Centurion... the boy has more to add."

Aristarchos Themistocles' eyes invited him to continue.

In the silence, they could hear the boy swallow nervously. He summoned all his courage and went on: "They spat on her, and one of them..." he swallowed again, "...kicked her."

The firm hand of Severinus Majorianus rested on the boy's shoulder. "Don't stop," he urged.

"Then a soldier on horseback arrived. He was clad in magnificent armor, all scaled, which sparkled under the moonlight. The helmet he wore had a nasal guard that split his face in two, and atop it hung a long black crest that brushed the back of the horse with its length. From atop his mount, he said something I couldn't understand, which made the other two warriors burst into laughter. Then he spurred the beast and disappeared into the mist.

"The other two started walking, and I followed them for a while— at least until I was sure they hadn't noticed me. I heard them speaking in their language, until one of them turned back toward the corpse one last time and said something in the dialect spoken by the Franks. I know that dialect. He was probably one of them, but I'm not certain," the boy said, his eyes now sharper, flashing with cunning.

Realizing that all attention was fixed on him, he quickly concluded: "'Rudulfus is a ruthless and invincible beast.' That's exactly what he said," the boy added, now searching the faces around him for gratitude.

"What a legionary you would've made! Go now! Get out of here, and don't let yourself be seen around these parts—it could be dangerous for you," Severinus Majorianus dismissed him.

They watched as he darted off like a hare.

Aristarchos Themistocles returned to the room, his anger steadily mounting.

When he walked beyond the walls at daybreak, he softly laid Placidia's body on the ground and began digging.

At one point, needing to catch his breath, he looked around.

Everywhere, other citizens and soldiers were digging graves to bury their dead.

Meanwhile, those who still worshipped pagan gods prepared funeral pyres to cremate their loved ones, believing that, along with the smoke, their souls would ascend.

It was a paradoxical sight, considering that the very perpetrators of these tragedies—the Heruli—had entrenched themselves in Duro Catalaunum.

The centurion's fingers dug into the damp earth, growing so numb that he could no longer feel them. He used a shovel to dig, but relied on his dagger to cut through stubborn roots.

When he had finished digging the grave, he set the shovel aside, gently lifted Placidia's body, and wrapped her in a white shroud.

The snow crunched under approaching footsteps. Aristarchos Themistocles turned around.

Emerging from the shadows, cloaked against the bitter cold, came the veterans of the Duro Catalaunum *vexillationes*: Antonino Tacitus, Vatinius Auruncus, Severinus Majorianus, Ulzio Dacianus, Gallienus Lars Gracchus, Gaius Octavianus, Fulcinius Agricola Statius, Auctus Tullius Plato, Christianus Caligatus, Tarquinius Glaucus, Drusus Variatus.

They were all there.

They stopped a few paces away, maintaining a respectful yet martial bearing. They hadn't lost their disciplined, upright demeanor.

Their armor, as Aristarchos Themistocles' experienced eye noticed, had been polished meticulously. The scarves at their throats were tied tightly.

Their helmets caught the faint sunlight, reflecting it like halos around the anger etched into their faces.

From among the trees appeared Ialenia Heria, holding an amulet in her hands as she whispered prayers to her Celtic gods. The blue spirals painted on her face emphasized the sacredness of her presence.

Aristarchos Themistocles looked at them all.

His hard face, marked by the scar from the campaign at the Catalaunian Plains, rose and fell slightly in acknowledgment, showing his appreciation for their presence at Placidia's funeral and the soldierly respect they displayed.

Hiding behind a large rock was the young fisherman who had recounted Placidia's fate. He sobbed quietly, his presence impossible to overlook.

***

Later that morning, the small town of Duro Catalaunum was bathed in an amber light.

The snow on the rooftops glistened like gold, but the somber funeral pyres continued to send columns of smoke skyward.

Despite the recent events, there was an impression that life was returning to normal.

Many merchants and artisans had reopened their shops.

Butchers, tanners, silversmiths, and bakers were already at work.

Though the goods on display left much to be desired, Heruli were increasingly seen bartering items or provisions, which were then resold.

A carpenter, with the help of two of his four sons, was hauling a large pine log. They had cut it in the forest and dragged it there with an old bay horse. His wife sat curled up on a stool, weeping for her other two sons, who had been massacred by the Heruli.

In the workshops, customers were received, and business was discussed.

Time passed, measured by the hammer strikes of a blacksmith, his concentrated gaze fixed on a glowing piece of iron.

A tailor stood contemplating precious curtain fragments and scraps of cloth, planning how to transform them into garments, cloaks, or drapes.

In the forum, gamblers were already busy, and a few prostitutes were scraping together a living in the shadows of narrow alleys.

The stench of urine in that area was pervasive and stomach-turning.

A Heruli mercenary lay sprawled in a mixture of mud, excrement, and his own vomit, waiting to sober up from the night's excesses.

The streets began to fill with people. Romans, Gauls, Heruli, Franks, Goths, and Burgundians went about their business, trying to communicate.

Duro Catalaunum had transformed from an imperial outpost into a crossroads for goods and people.

In what had now become his residence, Rudulfus, king of the Heruli and the new governor of Gallia Belgica, toyed with a dagger, spinning its tip on the sill of the bifora window while observing the activity below.

Without even looking at him, he listened to the reports of Attilius Faticus, who was accompanied by several accounting officials.

"More than 130 farms manage the local agriculture. By law, a third of every harvest, consisting mainly of fruits and wheat, must be deposited in the administration's granaries. Typically, the farmers have adhered to this taxation, but ever since the invasions began..." he cleared his throat nervously, "...uh, by the barbarians..."

Rudulfus shot him a withering glare. "To whom are you referring, you miserable fool?" he growled.

Attilius Faticus rubbed his hands together nervously, sweat forming on his brow. He glanced sideways at the personal guards stationed on either side of the room and sighed in relief when he saw they had not drawn their weapons.

"Your Excellency, I certainly didn't mean to refer to your noble self in such a way. I would use terms like 'strategist' or 'commander' for you. I was referring instead to other tribes, those devoid of any sense of civilization. Your nature, on the other hand, is refined and charismatic," he said, bowing his head in submission.

Rudulfus, however, did not seem satisfied. "You forgot to mention that I am also a capable administrator."

The Roman raised his eyes to the ceiling. "How could I have forgotten!" he exclaimed with syrupy self-reproach.

The entrance of a man dressed in a rough wool tunic interrupted the groveling display.

Rudulfus recognized him immediately, even though the man still had his hood pulled low over his eyes.

"Welcome back, Procopius Calibrandus!" he greeted warmly, rising to his feet and hurrying over to embrace the newcomer.

Attilius Faticus and his bureaucrats stepped aside.

Calibrandus was Rudulfus' most trusted spy. Though a skilled warrior, he was employed more for his abilities to gather intelligence than for his military prowess. He was one of the few people Rudulfus considered a true friend, and among the even fewer he trusted.

Grasping the spy's arms, Rudulfus beamed. "You look well. I'll ensure that you're treated like a king, my friend," he said with a smile. "Now, what news do you bring me from the court at Ravenna?"

Procopius Calibrandus hesitated for a moment before responding.

"Speak freely," Rudulfus reassured him, clapping him firmly on the shoulder. "Their tongues would dangle like banners if they dared reveal what you tell me."

"My king, Odoacer watches your actions with great apprehension. He fears you might grow powerful enough to consider splitting the Empire and turning Gaul into your own kingdom. He already has troops prepared to counter you should you make a deceptive move," he said, meeting Rudulfus' gaze. He continued:

"These troops consist of Gothic mercenaries mixed with remnants of the now-dissolved Imperial legions. North of Ravenna, he has stationed several contingents of Franks. It is said that the Thuringians are also aligned with him, and likely the Burgundians will follow. Their king intends to marry his daughter to Odoacer to consolidate his power in northern Italy. His military strength far surpasses yours."

Rudulfus felt the blood in his veins turn cold. Already, a motley force was being assembled to take from him what he had earned through courage and skill.

No, he could not allow this to happen—not now that he had finally become a true governor of the Empire, a capable administrator in the Roman tradition.

A bitter feeling swept over him as he realized a dream might slip away forever.

The spy noticed Rudulfus' somber mood and tried to soften the blow of his harsh news. "My king, you are the most courageous leader our people have ever known. But unfortunately, that's not all. Odoacer is issuing decrees to prevent you from retaining the tributes you collect. His officials, inherited from the deposed Augustus, are highly skilled in these matters. His secret agents and provocateurs are scattered throughout the Empire. Furthermore, he has already sent ambassadors to Constantinople, laden with gifts, to curry favor with the Eastern Emperor."

Those words made Rudulfus' hands tremble.

The king's breathing grew shallow, and his eyes burned with the fury raging within him.

He addressed the officer commanding his personal guard: "Summon the generals. Have the troops ready. Go, now."

The officer stiffened and left to carry out the order.

"My king, I deeply regret the news I've brought you..." the spy began to explain.

Suddenly, Rudulfus' expression softened. "Do not worry, my loyal friend. You always perform the tasks I assign you with excellence. How could I possibly harbor resentment toward you?"

Cunipert's legs felt like reeds.

Those words carried a clear meaning: he was no longer the king's favored one.

He cast a sidelong glance at Procopius Calibrandus, who was being served a cup of mead. Muttering bitter words under his breath, Cunipert left the room, his long cloak sweeping the floor behind him.

Rudulfus returned to the window, gazing once more at the forum below, where the bustle of activity gave life to the small border town where he had chosen to winter.

With his mind crowded by thoughts and doubts, he tried to focus on what needed to be done. Then, as if struck by inspiration, he turned to his friend Calibrandus.

"In the spring, I will establish myself in Arles. What was once Emperor Majorianus' residence will become mine, and from there, I will control Gaul."

"That is an excellent strategy. Arles is the ideal city—the previous Augusti understood that well," the spy agreed.

"I will gather the armies necessary to counter Odoacer and lead them into battle myself if he dares to move against me," Rudulfus said, his mouth foaming slightly, his face twisted with anger.

"My king, grant me leave to rest. The journey was long, and I could not always sleep in comfort," the spy requested.

Rudulfus' face lit up with a bright smile. "My servants will provide you with everything you require."

"One last thing..." the spy added hesitantly before departing.

The king's expression gave him permission to continue.

"Have your food, wine, and anything else you consume checked. Odoacer's assassins are deadly."

With that, he turned and left the room.

For a moment, Rudulfus stared into his goblet, then hurled it across the room, shaken by his friend's warning.

***

In the improvised quarters of the centuries, set up within the bishop's residence, nearly all preparations for leaving the city were complete.

Not all the soldiers had chosen to leave. Many had settled in Duro Catalaunum with their families. Others had started profitable ventures there in anticipation of their discharge, which was imminent for most of them.

Those who were preparing to leave had loaded their wagons with provisions and whatever useful items they could scavenge to face the arduous journey ahead.

The roads of the Empire were now in disrepair, and traveling with heavy wagons could be perilous. Often, travelers preferred to follow ancient forest paths and mountain trails rather than the decaying consular roads, which left them vulnerable to attacks from barbarian raiders.

Aristarchos Themistocles wrapped his vine-wood staff in a cloth. He could not bring himself to abandon it, as he considered it an important symbol.

He placed his lorica on the wagon, gently laying his crested helmet on top of it. The crest, slashed during a battle, was slightly frayed, but to him, it was a reminder of the many fights he had endured.

His heart was gripped by sorrow over Placidia's tragic end, and his gaze was heavy with rage that he had no way of venting.

No one spoke. Everyone silently loaded their belongings onto their wagons, careful not to interfere with one another's movements.

Only knowing glances and the occasional ironic remark, attempting to lighten the mood, broke the oppressive atmosphere.

Ulzio Dacianus had almost fully recovered. His round face had regained its original color, and his eyes sparkled with their usual ironic humor.

From a distance, only the calm voice of Drusus Variatus could be heard as he haggled with a prostitute over her price. The woman insisted on her due, while he tried to negotiate a discount.

The sound of galloping hooves drew everyone's attention.

Vatinius Auruncus peered over a low wall, spotting a group of Heruli horsemen heading straight toward them.

"Centurion!" he called, glancing at Aristarchos Themistocles, who immediately understood.

As though an order had been given, all the legionaries concealed their gladii beneath their tunics.

Antoninus Tacitus pushed through the men to join Vatinius Auruncus at the wall.

"Do you think they're here to kill us all?" he asked.

"They'd find us ready," Vatinius Auruncus replied.

"Leave them all to me," Antoninus Tacitus joked before spitting on the ground.

"Just leave me two," Auruncus retorted with a grin.

"Only two, though. The rest are mine," Tacitus quipped, shooting him a hungry look.

Meanwhile, Fulcinius Agricola Statius moved to the side, ready to launch a flanking attack if necessary. He quickly assessed the situation with sharp glances.

Aristarchos Themistocles raised his hand slightly, attempting to calm the men, though the tension was palpable.

The group of horsemen, about a hundred strong, stopped just short of the residence, waiting to be acknowledged.

One of them, carrying the banner of their unit, approached the camp alone.

His horse walked slowly, and tied to the saddle was a wicker basket.

Aristarchos Themistocles gestured to Vatinius Auruncus, and together they approached the Heruli horseman.

Some other legionaries began to move forward, but Antoninus Tacitus stopped them with an upraised hand.

The Heruli horseman halted his steed, waiting for the two centurions to reach him. The horse snorted through its nostrils and pawed at the ground with a hoof.

When they were face-to-face, neither spoke at first, using the silence to study one another.

The Heruli was the first to speak. "My king and governor of Gaul, Rudulfus, sends you a message," he said, struggling to keep his horse still.

The senior centurion gestured for him to continue.

"I speak on behalf of my king, who in this moment sees and hears through me. He wishes to deliver a clear warning. In southern Gaul, many scattered remnants of the former Imperial army have allied with Gothic forces hired by Odoacer, hoping for a proper wage. King Rudulfus hopes you will not make the same choice, and has sent a demonstration of the punishment awaiting any of you should you betray him," the Heruli said, pointing to the basket. "With his mercy, my lord seeks to spare your soldiers any unnecessary loss."

That last statement dripped with irony and irritation.

Vatinius Auruncus couldn't hold back. "Let's see how well you fare against my century! All it would take is for me to say…"

"Silence," Aristarchos Themistocles ordered.

When the younger centurion refused to calm down and even continued provoking the Heruli, Aristarchos repeated the command more forcefully: "I told you to shut up!"

Vatinius Auruncus gritted his teeth and fell silent, his eyes fixed on the Heruli. When the horseman shot him a smug glance, Auruncus spat on the ground.

The Heruli continued his message. "As I was saying, should you intend to disregard his advice, this is what will happen." He untied the basket from the saddle and handed it to Vatinius Auruncus, who held it with both hands.

Feeling its weight, a grim suspicion crossed the young centurion's mind.

The Heruli turned his horse around and galloped back to his cavalry unit, where an officer wearing a helmet crowned with a long black crest awaited him.

There was an exchange of threatening looks between the senior centurion and the Heruli officer.

Moments later, the horsemen disappeared from view.

The two Roman officers exchanged a glance.

"Open the basket," Aristarchos Themistocles ordered.

Vatinius Auruncus opened the lid and tipped its contents onto the ground.

The senior centurion clenched his fists and turned his gaze away, summoning all his strength to suppress the wave of nausea. He refused to show weakness in front of the legionaries watching from nearby.

Vatinius Auruncus, however, stared fixedly at the severed head of Tarquinius Glaucus, its complexion ashen.

The lifeless eyes were rolled back.

The mouth was slightly open, with yellowish mucus dripping from it.

His hands had been tied to his neck, conveying some unknown message.

The grotesque sight silenced everyone.

Antoninus Tacitus vaulted over the wall to join them, stopping a few steps away, frozen in shock. Tarquinius Glaucus had been his friend. Unable to restrain himself, he let out a cry of horror and rage.

"No one makes any rash moves," Aristarchos Themistocles said in a voice barely above a whisper. "I'm certain Rudulfus has anticipated a revolt or a show of force from us. Out there, hidden somewhere, there could be hundreds of warriors ready to slaughter us all."

Vatinius Auruncus intervened, "I'll see what I can do, but when everyone finds out what they did to Tarquinius Glaucus, it'll be hard to hold them back."

"They're legionaries. They'll obey. Was I clear?" Aristarchos Themistocles said, his tone firm.

Vatinius Auruncus glared at him, disliking the sharp tone.

"Centurion, there are thousands of Heruli out there. We're just a few dozen..."

"Understood, Centurion. Understood," Auruncus relented, moving away.

Step by step, he felt a crushing weight in his chest, as though only his ribs were holding his fury from exploding outward. His hand gripped tightly around the hilt of his gladius.

Aristarchos Themistocles watched him rejoin the others as he felt his own body trembling with rage toward Rudulfus. Yet he forced himself to appear calm. That was, after all, the duty of a commander: to turn his face into a mask of courage and composure, even when he wanted to show the exact opposite.

As the soldiers' anger over their comrade's death grew, a murmur of resentment filled the air.

They threatened revenge and death. Some questioned what was left of their honor.

The rising voices were interrupted by Severinus Majorianus, who called for attention. He stiffened, a bundle of nerves, as he recounted his experience.

"I went to the southern gate to leave the city, but Rudulfus' militia..." he spat the word with disdain, "...those barbarian bastards stopped me. They wouldn't let me through the walls. They noticed my purple tunic, whispered among themselves, and then blocked the way with their spears. Something is happening..." he concluded, hinting at some ominous development.

For Aristarchos Themistocles, it confirmed his suspicions.

Rudulfus feared that the remaining soldiers would join his enemies' forces. He had effectively imprisoned them in Duro Catalaunum, and it was likely they would not leave alive.

He realized that if they wanted freedom, they would have to earn it.

He decided to summon his officers.

"Centurions, to me!" he commanded.

Vatinius Auruncus and Antoninus Tacitus stepped forward.

"Orders, Centurion!" they both shouted, as if they already sensed his intentions.

The *primae spatha* leapt onto a carved stone marker, etched with images of an infernal chariot, a relic from the days of pagan gods. Addressing the group, he explained:

"The king of the Heruli has made his intentions clear: he wants to prevent what remains of the Imperial army from joining his enemies. He has decided to keep us confined within the city walls. It's likely the same is happening in other border towns like this one. He intends to dispose of us. Do not let your guard down, and do nothing reckless. We are outnumbered, so we must use cunning if we are to get out of here alive."

Heads nodded in understanding.

"Gather the men. I'll return shortly," he said, his voice regaining energy.

He shot a glance at Gaius Octavianus, the Scout, who approached him. Aristarchos spoke to him in a low voice.

When their discussion ended, the Scout left. It was later revealed that he had been sent to find the *signifer*, Gallienus Lars Gracchus, whom he found crouched beneath a cart hitched to an old mule.

"Legionary, I have an order from the *primae spatha*."

The *signifer* did not pick up on the irony and replied wearily, "I no longer have a centurion, and I'm no longer a legionary." He turned, smiling bitterly. "There are no more legions either, my friend. You should accept that." He laughed and coughed. "Besides, I'm leaving. I'm going back to where I was born."

Gaius Octavianus clapped him firmly on the shoulder. "Our *vexillatio* still has a few blows left to strike, soldier. Now listen—we don't have much time."

***

"Centurion, have you done the count?" Antoninus Tacitus asked with his usual irony.

Vatinius Auruncus chuckled. "We're few, but we're hungry," he replied promptly.

"Well?"

"We don't even reach ten…" He cast a shrewd glance before adding, "But we're all ready to go! Shields are hidden on the carts.

They're bulky, but they won't arouse suspicion. At the first sign of danger, we'll be ready to fight."

"We'll *be* the danger they face," Tacitus quipped.

"Oh?"

"Exactly." Vatinius Auruncus narrowed his eyes like someone about to pull a clever trick.

Aristarchos Themistocles caught the young centurion's attention and gestured for him to follow into the cloister.

Kneeling, Aristarchos picked up a stick, and Vatinius Auruncus watched him intently. He began tracing lines in the dirt.

"This is the western gate. You'll leave through here."

Auruncus noticed the word *you'll*, but chose to remain silent and listen.

"You will lead the assault on the guard garrison. You'll have all the men at your disposal. Meanwhile, Antoninus Tacitus and I will complete another mission..."

The two locked eyes, and then Aristarchos continued.

"Taking advantage of the chaos caused by your assault, Antoninus Tacitus and I will head to Rudulfus' residence. You and the others will exit the walls and, without hesitation, head for the forest. Do not immediately head south—that's where Rudulfus' trackers will look for you. Instead, go west and avoid Heruli patrols and scouts as much as possible. The Burgundians roam that area freely now. They were once allies of Rome, but it's best not to trust them. When you think it's safe, turn south. We will find you. Do not send anyone to search for us—it would only endanger your men. The two of us are not worth the lives of ten. Is that clear?"

Vatinius Auruncus recognized the tone; it left no room for argument or refusal. He simply nodded, though he couldn't hold back one question:

"May I ask what your mission is?"

"I intend to return Rudulfus' thoughtful gift to us... in the Roman way."

Though he had expected more, the young centurion only nodded again.

"Understood… looks like I won't get a moment's rest, if I'm not mistaken," he muttered.

"What did you say?"

"Nothing, nothing," Auruncus grumbled.

The scattered fires warmed the soldiers, who were trying to get some sleep.

Guard shifts had been organized.

Walking slowly, the young officer Vatinius Auruncus patrolled the walkways along the walls of the residence, his ears attuned to the sounds outside.

From his position, he could see the rooftops of many houses, except for a few insulae that rose several stories higher. Thin columns of smoke drifted upward, but dissolved into the mist that hovered over the town. The faint light of a few lanterns dotted the darkness enveloping the small settlement.

Some voices broke his quiet reverie. They were speaking the incomprehensible language of the Heruli, but as they drew closer, it became clear they were just a group of drunkards.

He saw them stagger out from a corner, swaying as they walked.

They passed beneath the walls and noticed him. They exchanged nudges and knowing grins before shouting a few mocking remarks in his direction. One of them spat toward him before disappearing into a dark, narrow alley.

Vatinius turned when he heard footsteps behind him. It was Ulzio Dacianus, smiling at him.

"What are you thinking about, Centurion?" he asked with a warm smile.

Vatinius returned the smile before answering, "I wasn't thinking—I was dreaming! Of a time of peace, without battles, without living in constant fear of being killed or maimed. You know…" he glanced at Dacianus with a kind expression, "near Minturnae[8], my

---

[8] *Minturnae:* a Roman city in southern Lazio, located at the mouth of the Garigliano River (known in ancient times as the Liris). It was crossed by the Appian

father owned a small property. Not far from where you grew up. If I make it back home, I'd like to farm it," he confessed.

Ulzio Dacianus spread his hands wide, as if to underscore the obviousness of what he was about to say. "I grew up along the banks of the Liris. What I miss most is working on the river docks. I traveled up the river many times, and my first drunken night was at a tavern right behind your house. I know exactly how you feel, Centurion."

The younger officer chuckled as he prepared to strike a playful jab. "So, it was on the Liris that you donned your toga virilis and became the fraud you are today?"

They burst into laughter. Someone nearby grumbled, offended that their rest had been disturbed.

"What were you about to tell me, Centurion?"

"I was talking about my father's property," Vatinius said, stretching his arms wide to mimic its size. "It's not very large, but it's enough for about a hundred olive trees. And that's not all…" He sighed, his gaze drifting to some far-off point. "That land produces a Falernian wine that would make even the reserves of the Sacred Augustus envious!"

The soldier rubbed his chin as if wiping off imaginary wine. "It must be good. I'd drink it in the arms of two women—but I imagine a nectar that fine deserves at least four!" His chest shook with booming laughter.

They spent a moment gazing beyond the walls in silence before the soldier broke it again.

"What's worrying you?" he asked the officer.

"I'm not worried."

"I know you well, Centurion."

The uneasy look Vatinius gave him revealed he had hit the mark.

"I'm wondering if we'll lose more men tonight."

Way—a position that reflected its prosperous economic development. The city's decline began in the early Middle Ages.

"We're used to fighting, but I think there's more to it."

Vatinius Auruncus nodded. "Rudulfus won't let us leave so easily. Even if we manage to escape the city, they'll hunt us down. Reaching the southern coast will be no small feat."

"A legionary is trained for long marches and combat. You'll see—we'll make it through this, too. If you let fear consume you, you'll remain a prisoner in this cold, damp border town. But if you find the courage to act, you'll earn your freedom," Dacianus said. From the centurion's expression, he could see the weight of his words had struck deeply.

The officer's hand rested on his shoulder. "I'll do everything I can to bring you all home."

"I'm going to lie down for what little time we have left before the assembly. You should do the same, Centurion."

With that, Ulzio Dacianus took his leave, while in the centurion's mind, resolve began to replace doubt.

***

Hiding beneath the hoods of their cloaks, the eyes of Gaius Octavianus and Gallienus Lars Gracchus followed Vaillardo, the Heruli cavalry officer, as he left a tavern accompanied by his personal guard of about five elite mercenaries.

One of the mercenaries shoved a drunk man leaning unsteadily on a stone marker. The drunk fell into a frozen puddle, breaking through the icy surface. Ignoring him, they disappeared into the darkness of a narrow alley to relieve themselves. They stood in a row, joking and laughing uproariously.

Though they were drunk, that wasn't reason enough to underestimate them. They were still skilled warriors, quick to draw their swords.

The scout and the *signifer* moved swiftly and silently, ensuring they went unnoticed. They approached the mercenaries under the cover of darkness. Then, like lightning, they drew their swords.

Each slit a throat, and Gallienus Lars Gracchus even had time to stab a third in the back, muffling his mouth with his hand.

The remaining two guards, caught off guard, turned, but they were both swiftly run through.

Without losing the element of surprise, Gaius Octavianus pointed his gladius at the throat of Vaillardo, the Heruli cavalry officer.

Vaillardo had no time to draw his sword. He found himself with his back against the wall, finishing his business in his own trousers.

Before them stood the very man who, on Rudulfus' orders, had delivered the severed head of Tarquinius Glaucus.

"What is your name? Do you understand my language?" Gaius Octavianus growled through gritted teeth.

The man nodded before answering, "I am Vaillardo, the high-est-ranking officer in the army…"

"Do you know why I'm going to kill you?" Octavianus inter-rupted, pressing him.

"Yes," Vaillardo said simply, showing no fear for his fate.

The legionary's blade sank into his flesh.

When they returned to the Roman stronghold, they entered the cubiculum where the *primae spatha*, Aristarchos Themistocles, was resting.

They carried with them a basket—the same one that had held Tarquinius Glaucus' severed head.

"Centurion…" Gaius Octavianus called, trying to wake him. "Centurion, wake up."

Aristarchos Themistocles sat up sluggishly on his pallet, looking exhausted.

"Did you succeed?" he asked.

The scout, Gaius Octavianus, nodded. Then he turned to Gallienus Lars Gracchus, who held the wicker basket.

"It wasn't difficult… These Heruli seem to have a habit of drink-ing even more than us Romans," he remarked, holding up the basket pointedly.

The commander's satisfaction was evident in the grin that spread across his face. "Now it's my turn to return Rudulfus' courtesy..." he said as he swung his legs over the side of the bed and stood.

He approached a bench where his armor lay and began fastening his focale.

When he finished donning his armor, he stepped outside, holding the basket tightly in his hands, followed by the two soldiers who had carried out the task.

He summoned the two centurions, who promptly arrived, already clad in their loricae, with transverse-crested helmets and purple mantles.

Vatinius Auruncus and Antoninus Tacitus stiffened in salute.

They had already received orders from the *primae spatha*, and knew what their respective duties were.

"So few, I see..." he muttered, swallowing a bitter gulp.

He had them put on their full equipment before addressing them.

Keeping his tone controlled and avoiding shouting too much, he explained the mission:

"Legionaries, the time has come to leave this godforsaken hole in the world and return home...if we still have a home left to return to."

Someone dared to laugh at his remark, even though it wasn't meant to be humorous.

"As you've seen..." he gestured toward the severed head of Tarquinius Glaucus, perched atop the jagged end of a broken column, "...the Heruli have no love for us. They'd rather see us die here, our bones stripped bare by these icy winds. But we're not giving them that satisfaction. We're leaving this place, and we'll march south – with haste."

There was a murmur of uneasy chuckles, though the severed head of the soldier served as a grim reminder of what awaited them should they fail.

"We will assault the garrison guarding the western gate and escape through there. Our mission is to draw attention away from the operation the commander is carrying out. The head of

Rudulfus' best officer is already sitting in the same basket that held this one," he said, pointing again to Tarquinius Glaucus' head. "Prepare yourselves. The battle is near."

Helmets nodded silently in response.

"Are you afraid?" he asked.

The soldiers shook their heads.

"Are you afraid?" he repeated, more forcefully this time.

No one moved. Their gazes remained fixed straight ahead.

He shot a quick glance at the optio, who turned sharply toward the formation.

"Well then, you sons of licentious bitches, did you hear me or not? *Unus ordo?* Form a single line!" barked Severinus Majorianus.

The soldiers quickly assembled into a long single line.

"March – and make as little noise as you can, you bastards! Move!"

He led them silently toward the western gate of the city walls. Their shadows stretched along the walls, wavering like restless ghosts.

Aristarchos Themistocles watched them slip through the gate and swallowed a mouthful of saliva, tinged with hope. He tapped Antoninus Tacitus on the armor to get his attention.

"It's our turn now."

"With pleasure, Centurion!"

They slipped into the alleys, heading in the opposite direction, eager to reach the principia.

It didn't take long for them to approach the gate. With a few hand signals, Vatinius Auruncus instructed his men to crouch low.

"What a lovely sight," optio Severinus Majorianus remarked with biting sarcasm as he observed the Heruli garrison guarding that section of the walls.

"I'll bet you've already counted them," the centurion teased.

"There are about fifty of them, with around ten perched on the

---

⁹ *Unus ordo:* formation in a single rank. A maneuver command.

rooftops, ready to rain arrows down. They've caged us in here, but we have one small advantage..."

He paused – one of those infuriating pauses he often made during his musings, which always frayed the young centurion's nerves. Knowing this, the optio had made it a habit purely for his own amusement.

"Are you going to tell me what this 'advantage' is, or should I gift your tongue to the officer on duty?" the centurion snapped.

"They're drowsy and freezing," the optio finally said, a smug grin spreading across his scruffy face.

Vatinius Auruncus studied the situation for a moment before giving another order.

"Tell the soldiers to keep a sharp eye on the ones on the walls – if we're not careful, they'll fill us with arrows. Keep tight formations and close ranks when it's time to attack."

The optio moved to relay the orders to the crouching soldiers, hidden in the shadows.

The Heruli guards huddled near their braziers, some chatting idly, others distracted by games. They were careless – some even drunk, barely able to keep their eyes open.

The young centurion glanced at his hands. They weren't trembling, even though he was once again forced to mask his fear behind the role of command.

But this time, there was no room for hesitation. He had to act swiftly and decisively.

Drawing a deep breath, he suddenly sprang to his feet, raised his sword high, and shouted:

"Legionaries, forward – attack!" He took a few steps forward. "*Formate testudinem!*[10] Shield formation! Close ranks – advance, advance!"

Eagerly, the soldiers formed a "tortoise", their shields creating an impenetrable barrier, even from above.

---

[10] *Formate testudinem:* form the testudo (tortoise formation). A command used in battle.

"Move quickly!"

"Get moving, you dogs!" the optio echoed.

The formation advanced at a light, steady run.

The Heruli turned sharply, trying to illuminate the source of the marching sounds and shouted orders with their torches.

The centurion bellowed again: "Standard-bearer, to me!"

Gallienus Lars Gracchus pushed forward, raising the standard of the Third Century high and proud.

"Kill every last one of those bastards!" roared the centurion.

When the standard-bearer cried, "For Rome!" the legionaries erupted into war cries.

"Optio, to me! Optio, to me!" shouted Vatinius Auruncus. Severinus Majorianus appeared at his side without hesitation.

"Watch the rooftops – arrows will rain down any moment now!" the centurion warned, without taking his eyes off the Heruli forming up ahead.

Severinus Majorianus moved behind the testudo, keeping an eye on potential rooftop attacks.

Moments later, arrows began to rain down. The Heruli, sluggish from the cold, loosed their shots sporadically.

"Hold the shields! Keep them tight!" the optio shouted. The soldiers pressed their shields together, forming an unbreakable barrier.

The arrows thudded against the shields, some quivering where they struck, reverberating ominously.

Vatinius Auruncus halted the formation by raising his gladius. Once everyone was perfectly aligned, he shouted the command:

"Parati ad impetum![11] Prepare for impact!"

The Heruli warriors charged at them, screaming and brandishing their weapons.

"Advance three steps. One, two, three… advance, one, two, three!" he began to mark the pace.

---

[11] *Parati ad impetum:* prepare for impact (be ready for battle).

The legionaries advanced three steps at a time, thrusting their swords through the narrow gaps between their shields. The first enemies began to fall.

"One, two, three! Advance!" the command was repeated, and the testudo moved forward, compact and lethal.

The Heruli tried to resist the Roman advance, but they were no match for the wall of shields, which became an unstoppable force. Luckily, the arrows hadn't injured any of the legionaries, but the enemies' numbers were overwhelming, and the Romans had to remain vigilant to prevent breaches in the shield wall.

Arrows continued to rain down on their heads. It was time to stop fighting and get out of that cursed village.

The optio rallied the troops to respond with slingshots against the enemy archers.

"A denarius for anyone who takes out more than one! Do your duty, you cursed bastards..." Even in the direst moments, he had an uncanny ability to joke.

The soldiers took him at his word. Those in the back ranks sheathed their swords and began using their slings.

The whistle of bronze projectiles filled the air. Enemy bodies tumbled from the rooftops, crashing to the ground.

Taking advantage of a gap in the shield wall, Ialenia Heria drew her bow, notched an arrow, and aimed high. She released the string, and the arrow found its target, piercing the eye of a Heruli archer.

Vatinius Auruncus noticed a reserve unit of Heruli reinforcements—about a hundred warriors—rushing to aid their comrades.

"*Attendite ad dextram!*[12] Watch the right flank! Legionaries, attack on the right!" he shouted in frustration at their misfortune.

He called out to the optio: "Optio! Optio, to me!"

Severinus Majorianus approached, shield raised.

"Optio..." Vatinius gestured toward the incoming Heruli rein-

---

[12] *Attendite ad dextram:* attention to the right. A battle command.

forcements. "What do you think about making a run for it at this point?"

The optio studied the situation for a moment.

"Once again, I have to get you out of trouble, Centurion?"

"What can I say? I miss my mother so much..."

An arrow struck the optio's sandal.

"You all right?" Vatinius asked, following the arrow's path.

"Why wouldn't I be?" the optio retorted, still sarcastic.

"Let's hurry, optio, or they'll overrun us."

"Fine. You're buying drinks if we make it out alive."

"We're not making it out alive!"

Fulcinius Agricola Statius tugged on Ulzio Dacianus' arm and pointed toward the roof.

"We'll never win if we don't stop those damned archers."

Ulzio nodded.

Fulcinius then turned to the centurion. "Centurion..." he gestured toward the roof. "...up there!"

Vatinius understood immediately and nodded. A moment later, an arrow struck his helmet, ricocheting off to the side.

A small group broke off from the formation and began climbing the stairs to the walkways. Their large shields provided excellent protection, though the arrows seemed to come from all directions.

The two legionaries advanced, covered by their shields. To give themselves time to climb onto the roof, they hurled their javelins, hitting two archers. A slingshot killed another, and Ialenia Heria's arrow felled yet another.

The remaining archers ducked for cover, fearing they'd be hit.

Fulcinius Agricola Statius and Ulzio Dacianus climbed onto a cart, and then onto the roof.

Fulcinius quickly killed the first two enemies and advanced a few steps ahead of his companion. The gap seemed to offend Ulzio, who turned it into a race to see who could reach the remaining archers first.

"This was my idea! I lead the way!" Fulcinius shouted, cutting down enemies as he went.

The testudo below was no longer under fire from arrows.

As Fulcinius advanced, he didn't notice that a wounded archer had risen behind him. The archer stabbed him in the forearm with a dagger.

Blood sprayed from the wound, and Fulcinius screamed in pain. His shield fell as he instinctively clutched his injured arm with his other hand.

Ulzio Dacianus saved him, killing the archer before he could strike again.

"See what happens when you try to do too much?" Ulzio chided him.

"You castrated peacock! Do you think this scratch will stop me? Just watch!" Fulcinius growled, slicing into another enemy with his sword.

With the arrows no longer a threat, they could maneuver freely below.

Principia, Governor's Palace of Gaul, Rudulfus

Moving carefully to avoid making any noise, Aristarchos Themistocles and Antoninus Tacitus crept forward. As the centurion had suspected earlier, the sentries were on high alert, given the battle taking place nearby.

They didn't need to approach the perimeter. Instead, they avoided the patrols, who moved under the faint torchlight, and reached an iron grate.

Aristarchos crouched and grabbed it.

"We're going into the sewers?" Antoninus asked, alarmed.

"There are no sewers here. The piss flows through small channels along the streets—haven't you noticed? This is a rainwater drain. It leads into the palace. Just follow me."

"And how do you know that?"

"I'm the senior centurion. Don't forget it!"

"Of course, who could forget?" Antoninus muttered, helping

lift the grate while remembering the vine-staff blows Aristarchos had delivered during training.

The sounds of the battle—shouts and clashes—could still be heard, muffled by the distance. The Heruli officers' cries to rally their men echoed through the streets.

"We need to move," the senior centurion said dryly. "Let's go down."

The two descended into the drain, which turned out to be only a few meters deep. It opened into a tunnel leading to the heart of the principia.

Without a lamp or torch, they took some time to regain their bearings.

The tunnel was low, forcing them to crawl through slime composed of moss, mud, and the remains of insects. The stench was nauseating.

"We're here..." Aristarchos wiped away the filth from the wall, revealing a mechanism. He tugged hard on an iron ring, and a stone slab slid aside with surprising ease.

They slipped out of the foul hole and into a corridor.

Antoninus Tacitus immediately drew his gladius, scanning the area for any potential threats. They were all in now—there was no turning back.

Aristarchos Themistocles moved ahead into the darkness of the hallway that led to the supply rooms. This part of the principia was unguarded, as the Heruli evidently hadn't deemed it significant.

When the legionaries had been in charge, this area housed everything—money for troops' wages and campaign costs, food stores, wine, armor, shields, weapons, jars of oil, and garum. A full squad often stood watch here.

Now, it was deserted.

They pressed forward to the quarters.

Ahead, they could see torches, held by mercenaries who were laughing and playing dice. Aristarchos realized that their target wasn't in this section of the principia; if he were, elite guards would be stationed there.

He motioned to keep going. They passed under an external colonnade to reach the opposite side of the quarters. Here, too, torches illuminated the area, but it was eerily silent.

Neither dared make a sound.

"That's where Rudulfus rests," Aristarchos Themistocles whispered.

Antoninus Tacitus nodded.

They crept along the wall.

When they stepped out into the open, the element of surprise was so complete that none of the guards had time to resist.

The senior centurion plunged his sword into the belly of the first mercenary. Moving swiftly, he pulled the blade free in a spray of blood and brought it down in a slicing arc across the neck of the second.

Antoninus Tacitus wielded a sword in each hand. He stabbed one guard through the throat and threw his other blade at the farthest barbarian, impaling him squarely in the chest and pinning him to the chair he was sitting on. Before dying, however, the man managed to let out a cry of alarm, which turned into a gurgling death rattle.

"Which door is it?" Antoninus Tacitus asked, hesitating before the three doors in front of them.

"What does it matter? Leave it and go!" snapped the other, scanning the surroundings for the inevitable danger.

"Rudulfus, this is for you!" shouted the Roman commander, making sure to be heard. He dropped the wicker basket onto the floor and then sprinted toward the exit they had used to enter.

Guards were already rushing in from every corner of the palace.

Rudulfus bolted upright in his bed at the sound of his dying guard's cry.

"What's going on?" he wondered aloud.

He shoved the woman lying next to him onto the floor with a kick, ignoring her cries of protest. He leapt to his feet, grabbed his sword from its scabbard, and held it ready. Whoever came through that door, he would face them.

"Guards! Guards... What's happening out there?" he shouted furiously.

When no reply came, he ventured to the doorway.

He saw the lifeless bodies of his guards lying in pools of their own blood and the wicker basket resting on the floor. But there was no one else.

He growled in rage and approached the basket, stopping before it.

The guards who arrived moments later, shouting encouragement, froze when they saw their king. A sinister silence fell, broken only by a few murmurs and the crackling of torches.

Rudulfus raised his gaze, locking eyes with the highest-ranking officer among his guards. He pointed at him with his sword.

"You. Open this basket," he commanded.

The officer removed his cloak, made of stitched wolf pelts, revealing an ornate breastplate crafted by Belgian artisans—likely plundered from some defeated soldier. Without objection, he lifted the lid of the basket and reached inside.

The look of disgust that crossed his face left no doubt that the contents were grim.

He pulled out a severed head, gripping it by the hair.

Rudulfus immediately recognized it: Vaillardo, the finest of his generals.

It was no coincidence that Vaillardo had been the target of this retaliation. He was the officer Rudulfus had sent to keep the Romans confined in the bishop's residence, delivering them the severed head of one of their comrades as a warning.

Now, the Romans had avenged the insult in kind.

Rage consumed Rudulfus. His fury was boundless, and he resolved to show no mercy to the legionaries.

Then, a flash of reason struck him.

Roman soldiers had infiltrated his headquarters, coming within steps of him. They had slaughtered his elite guards and humiliated him by leaving a basket containing the severed head of one of his top officers.

He pondered this for a moment.

Then, in a sudden motion, he decapitated the guard officer.

The man's head fell to the floor, while his body remained standing for a few seconds. Then, as if in some macabre irony, the mutilated corpse collapsed to its knees, still holding Vaillardo's head in its hand—a head that didn't belong to it.

"Get this out of here! Quickly!" Rudulfus ordered, shaking with rage.

Two mercenaries immediately removed the body and the two severed heads, taking them out of the king's sight.

At that moment, a young warrior burst into the room.

"My king...my king!" he shouted, gasping for breath.

Rudulfus motioned for him to speak with a tilt of his chin.

The soldier knelt. "Excellency, the Romans are attacking the western gate. A furious battle is underway, but it seems the legionaries are gaining the upper hand. We urgently need reinforcements!"

Rudulfus' eyes widened in shock. He raised his fists to the sky and roared—a sound like that of a wounded beast, freezing the mercenaries present in their tracks.

"Ready my guard immediately!" he bellowed. Then, calling for his servants, he demanded, "My armor! Quickly, you bastards!"

Four young servants, their eyes ringed with soot, appeared from every corner, carrying the necessary equipment. They began dressing the Heruli king, who burned with the desire to kill as many legionaries as possible.

The elite Heruli guard had been alerted, but it would take time for them to organize effectively. Most were drunk. Some were gambling, while others slept deeply.

Rudulfus would suffer yet another disappointment that night—one he would punish with the execution of many officers.

Meanwhile, Antoninus Tacitus braced himself with his elbows as he emerged from the tunnel he had been eager to leave. He gave himself a final push to crawl out, brushing the damp earth off himself.

Aristarchos Themistocles did the same and, once outside, inhaled deeply from the sharp, clean night air.

"We need to hurry. While the gate is under attack, we'll escape the city through the sewer runoff channel," Aristarchos said, grabbing Antoninus Tacitus by the arm and dragging him toward a dark alley. "I know the passage well—it was meant to be an emergency exit during a siege."

"But you said there were no sewers in Duro Catalaunum…" Antoninus protested.

"Exactly. It's the end of the external drainage system. Nothing like the sewers in our cities."

"Are you joking, Commander?"

"Yes—and we might have to wade through some sections almost fully submerged."

"Submerged in… what?" Antoninus asked, his voice uncertain.

The commander's face broke into a sarcastic smile.

Antoninus stared at him, saying nothing. He understood that wading through icy water would put them at serious risk of hypothermia in such temperatures.

They avoided the few areas still illuminated by the last flickering torches.

"This way…" Aristarchos urged. "Faster. Run!"

Antoninus ran as fast as his legs could carry him. The shouts of the Heruli warriors grew louder—they were everywhere now.

The manhunt had begun, and they were the prey.

At one point, they stopped and pressed themselves against a wall.

They needed to cross a wide cobblestone street—a crossing that would take considerable time without the cover of darkness.

In the distance, they heard the approach of an enemy patrol.

Had they stumbled into a trap? What if they were seen crossing? After all, there were only two of them.

Overcome by impulse, Antoninus drew his gladius. "I'll buy you time to escape and rejoin the others."

Aristarchos' reply was immediate: "Stop talking nonsense. When I give the signal, run like hell to that alley over there… see it? The one with the tannery's sign."

Antoninus nodded in understanding.

"Go, now!" the commander hissed.

Antoninus bolted, sprinting like a marathoner despite his less-than-svelte frame. As he awkwardly dashed across the wide street, a faint smile crossed the centurion's face.

Unfortunately, Antoninus entered the wrong alley.

He was running in the wrong direction, the fool! The alley curved around a few houses and reconnected with the cobblestone street—leading him straight toward the barbarians.

Luckily, Antoninus realized his mistake and doubled back. He found Aristarchos waiting, motionless, behind the wall of a crumbling house.

The senior centurion heaved a sigh of relief. He pointed toward the correct alley, just adjacent to their current position.

Antoninus grinned sheepishly, as though confessing to a prank, and nodded.

"There...that one. Go. Go!" Aristarchos urged, watching him finally disappear into the dark of the proper path.

Now it was his turn. He would need to run like lightning if he wanted to avoid being spotted.

His breathing quickened.

But it was all for naught—a group of mercenaries had already spilled into the street.

He quickly calculated their distance.

Then he bolted.

After a few steps, he ducked, hearing the whistling of arrows.

One arrow, then another, and a third grazed past him, fortunately continuing their flight without finding their mark.

"There they are! The Romans are over there!" shouted a barbarian officer. "Get them!"

The group of barbarians gave chase, while another emerged from a corner, heading straight for him.

Aristarchos Themistocles got up and tried to reach the alley, but more arrows were fired in his direction.

By the grace of the Almighty, these, too, missed their target.

He shot a sharp glance at his companion, signaling him to flee as fast as he could.

Then he dived toward the alley, narrowly avoiding more arrows that slammed into the stone walls, disappearing with dull thuds.

"Don't let him escape!" yelled an officer swinging a double-bladed axe.

The barbarians shouted war cries, hoping to catch him.

The centurion dragged himself along on his elbows until he reached the alley, just as a barbarian came dangerously close, thrusting his spear to impale him.

Out of the shadows sprang Antoninus Tacitus, who swung his gladius in a clean arc, snapping the spear shaft in two and piercing the enemy warrior.

He pulled his commander up and started dragging him away. "Let's go, or we're done for!"

"They're too close."

"And they know how to fight, Centurion."

They ran as fast as hares, but the shouts of the Heruli mercenaries grew louder and closer.

Luckily, the alley was winding and dark, making it impossible for anyone to shoot arrows effectively.

"This path will soon intersect with several others, and we'll find ourselves in a tangled maze of shadows. Stay right on my tail, understood?" the commander shouted.

Antoninus responded with a breathless affirmation.

"Turn right at the next junction."

"Got it... got it!" Antoninus wheezed.

When they reached a timber-framed house, the two stopped in front of its door.

Panting, they hesitated, unsure of what to do next.

"This wasn't here when we studied the city's defenses..." Aristarchos Themistocles muttered dejectedly. "The trapdoor was right here, and now there's an entire house in its place."

"So no freezing bath, then?"

"You'd prefer their blades, trust me."

"Are you saying that between us and our escape route is this house…which wasn't here before?"

The commander nodded.

Antoninus Tacitus threw his shoulder into the door, knocking it down.

A middle-aged man and woman, wrapped in stitched-together sheepskins, sprang upright from their straw bedding.

The pungent stench that hit the two centurions' nostrils came from a goat standing nearby. It let out a faint bleat. Evidently, the couple had kept the animal hidden indoors, unwilling to lose a good source of milk—or meat, if necessary.

The woman froze in terror, while the man grabbed a pitchfork. He leapt forward, placing himself between them and the goat, determined to protect it at any cost.

Antoninus, now standing in the center of the room, raised his hands to show they meant no harm. Realizing their appearance no longer resembled that of soldiers, he quickly added, "We're Romans… we don't mean you any harm."

Aristarchos Themistocles entered the room, closing the door behind him. Outside, the mercenaries' hunting cries echoed louder as they closed in.

The centurion signaled for silence by pressing a finger to his lips.

The homeowners complied—not out of goodwill, but out of fear of the drawn swords.

"This way, Centurion!" Antoninus whispered. "I found the trapdoor."

Descending a few steps carved into the rock, they entered a small alcove used to store carpentry tools. The trapdoor was there. They were almost safe.

Using his sword as leverage, Antoninus Tacitus lifted the cover. One by one, they climbed down into the tunnel.

More tunnels. More cold, darkness, and damp.

Both of them slid a few meters down a slope slick with moss and sewage, landing in a drainage channel. They stayed submerged for a moment before breaking the surface to catch their breath.

Each exhale formed a small cloud of condensation. The water was so icy that the pain was excruciating.

"You said there were no sewers in Duro Catalaunum," Antoninus managed to say.

"Keep moving, soldier, or you'll freeze," the senior centurion replied, forcing his body to keep going.

***

An arrow. Another. A hand reached into the quiver for another one, nocking it to the bowstring. An instant to aim, and another deadly shot flew with rapid, decisive precision.

Ialenia Heria already had the next arrow nocked, wetting its goose-feather fletching with her lips. Each shaft found its mark in the bodies of mercenaries trying to get too close to the legionaries, who were attempting to cross the gate under the cover of their shields.

One Heruli came close enough to see her clearly and was startled to discover she was a woman dressed in a studded leather corset over a cinched tunic.

That moment of hesitation cost him dearly. Ialenia Heria pulled a hidden dagger from her sleeve and drove it into him.

Then she rose and began to retreat, keeping pace with the legionaries just a few meters behind her.

Her fingers worked in a swift rhythm, plucking arrows from her quiver, nocking them, and releasing.

Dull thuds and accompanying screams confirmed her accuracy.

As she fought, memories from her childhood surged into her mind.

Her village was burning. Cries of despair drowned out the clash of weapons as her father, the druid, was tied to a tree and slaughtered.

Before he fell, he cast her a look brimming with hope, as if to say, "Run! Run, my daughter!"

Still a child, she had hidden among the ancient roots of a sacred tree.

Through tear-filled eyes, she had watched her father perish under the blades of the invaders, who mocked and defiled his lifeless body.

As this happened, a mounted officer arrived, dismounting and handing his reins to a warrior. Tied to his saddle were the severed heads of the village's men—nobles and warriors among them.

Before the druid's corpse, the officer spat on the ground.

The laughter of the men had scarred her soul.

Were they laughing at the dead enemy, or what he represented?

Other warriors dragged forth ten soldiers of the Empire, men she recognized as the garrison assigned to protect her village.

They were forced to kneel, hands bound behind their backs.

More laughter followed, this time at the sight of a hulking brute wielding a long sword—its size matching his immense frame.

With precise strikes, he killed them all.

More laughter. More screams. More flames. More pain. More tears.

That brute was Rudulfus.

She, too, had a reason to hate him.

The city gate had finally been crossed.

Centurion Vatinius Auruncus kept his shield raised, but no more arrows were coming. He kept an eye on the soldiers as they ran, ensuring they maintained their ranks and the necessary cover.

Legionaries Fulcinius Agricola Statius and Severinus Majorianus closed the formation at the rear.

The Heruli were regrouping and rushing toward the gate.

"Optio, to me!" the centurion shouted, finally regaining his grasp of the situation.

Severinus Majorianus approached. "Centurion, if they manage to reorganize in time for a counterattack, they'll tear us to pieces," he said as soon as he was close enough.

The centurion responded without taking his eyes off the walls, where stones and arrows were now beginning to rain down.

"Optio, we need to take advantage of the darkness. If we move into the forest, they won't follow us. It's still too dark, and they'd fear ambushes. We'll gain a few hours of lead time until first light. See that path over there?" He gestured with his gladius to indicate the direction.

Severinus Majorianus turned and immediately spotted the path. He clapped the centurion on the back, signaling that he understood the plan.

"Let's move!" he ordered.

At that precise moment, an arrow tore through part of his crest. The optio relayed the command to retreat toward the path:

"Shields up! Fall back! Quickly, you damned wretches, you sons of bitches!"

Moving as if guided by a single mind, the soldiers retreated step by step. Their pace and coordination made the formation look like a single block sliding toward the forest in the eyes of the Heruli watching from the walls.

Once inside the forest, shielded by the darkness, the legionaries allowed themselves a brief moment of rest.

Drusus Variatus was utterly spent. He had fought ferociously, and his arms were heavy with pain. His legs felt as though they might give out at any moment, and his breath came in short, labored gasps. To make matters worse, as he retreated, he tripped over a clump of earth and fell backward. Two arrows meant for him instead lodged themselves in the satchel slung across his shoulder.

"I can't even move anymore," he groaned.

"Don't even think about it. We'll be moving again soon," Fulcinius Agricola Statius encouraged him, even as sharp arrowheads thudded into the foliage around them.

The arrows, fired blindly by the Heruli, couldn't penetrate the dense underbrush. For the moment, the barbarians were limiting themselves to this tactic. The bulk of their forces hadn't yet come out of the gate.

Vatinius Auruncus took advantage of the reprieve and asked the soldiers for one more effort.

On the walls, torches began to multiply, their movements frantic. The Heruli were planning something. Time was running out—every second mattered now.

He raised his gladius into the air and shouted:

"Move quickly—move quickly!"

The legionaries echoed his command and began moving at a light jog.

"Faster, faster!" Vatinius Auruncus barked again.

At a certain point, the labored breaths of the soldiers reminded the young centurion that these men had been fighting and were utterly exhausted. He granted them a brief rest.

Ialenia Heria, who had followed the group like a hare, also stopped to catch her breath. She wet the feathers of her arrows with her lips, readying them to be fired again.

It was at that moment that the worst-case scenario unfolded: the Heruli poured out in force, running with weapons raised and screaming war cries.

In the blink of an eye, more than a hundred bloodthirsty enemies flooded out of the gate, with many more already crowding behind, pressing forward to join the battle.

Vatinius Auruncus was about to sit down when a searing pain in his collarbone made him gasp, leaving him breathless.

Looking down, he saw the tip of an arrow protruding from his chest.

He had been hit—and, in the heat of the fight, he hadn't even noticed. He dropped to his knees, remaining in that position until his vision blurred. The sounds around him faded, and a tingling sensation enveloped his body.

Everything went dark.

Auctus Tullius Plato noticed what had happened and called for Drusus Variatus. Together, they rushed to the fallen centurion, lifting him by the arms.

To protect them, the three veterans of the legion—Fulcinius Agricola Statius, Gallienus Lars Gracchus, and Ulzio—formed a shield wall in case any enemies appeared.

Suddenly, an eerie silence fell over the forest.

Gaius Octavianus thrust his gladius into the ground and knelt, completely spent. He was breathing heavily, his chest heaving.

He looked on anxiously at the scene unfolding before him. The wounded centurion was a grim sight indeed.

Chapter VIII – Forced March

The first light of dawn painted the sky in shades of bluish purple. A few clouds hung suspended, heavy with their leaden expanse. An opalescent mist lingered over the forest.

Only the hoots of owls broke the silence of what remained of that night of bravery and fear.

The legionaries marched in exhaustion. Their legs buckled and gave out at times. Their steps sank into the frozen snow, which crunched beneath their feet, making every step harder and freezing their feet in their studded-soled boots.

The cold had stiffened their limbs, and their muscles ached with every movement.

Each breath produced clouds of condensation, and no one felt like speaking.

Severinus Majorianus could barely keep his eyes open. It wasn't from lack of sleep, but from sheer exhaustion and numbed senses.

Taking advantage of a small clearing, he stopped and turned around. It was time to halt the march.

"We'll set up camp here. You organize the guards," he said to Drusus Variatus, who was leaning heavily against the trunk of a tree, gasping for air.

Vatinius Auruncus had been wrapped in a cloak, and was being carried on an improvised stretcher made of long branches.

The optio detached himself from the group and climbed onto a moss-covered rock, from which he had a better vantage point. He had to consider that the Heruli would waste no time; at the first light of dawn, they would begin hunting them down.

The optio ordered Gaius Octavianus, their experienced scout, to venture into the forest and survey the area.

"If they start chasing you, don't lead them in our direction," he instructed.

A brief silence followed.

"Understood, optio," Gaius replied, giving him a knowing look.

Gaius Octavianus longed for rest, but the order he'd received extended his ordeal.

As he scanned the horizon, Severinus Majorianus couldn't help but think about the grim events that were not only destroying his life, but the entire world as he knew it.

All that remained of the once-great Empire were ruins, with no prospects for the future. He and the other legionaries had been left unpaid, and there was no telling if they would ever reach their homelands.

Shaking off a shiver from the cold, he snapped back to reality and decided to return to the camp.

"Don't light any fires—the smoke will give us away. Make as little noise as possible and keep your swords out of their sheaths, ready for an ambush. Stay close to your shields."

Some soldiers dug shallow pits to lie in, wrapping themselves tightly in their cloaks. Others huddled together, sharing body heat for warmth.

Severinus Majorianus returned to the top of the rock to keep an eye on the situation. Seeing no movement, he curled up in his cloak.

The last thing he saw before falling asleep was a single leaf spiraling down, carried by the icy breeze.

***

He dreamt of his mother gently stroking his face. The surface of the Liris River sparkled with dazzling reflections as a trireme sailed upstream. The heat of the sun burned his skin so intensely that he felt like loosening his neck scarf.

The tranquility of his home was so sweet. The grapevine pergola cast a web of shadows, creating a refreshing coolness.

Once again, his mother approached, pulling at his sleeve with a worried expression. She was saying something, but her voice carried a masculine tone.

"Centurion...wake up. Centurion..." the voice insisted.

Vatinius Auruncus propped himself up on his elbows, seeing the optio gripping his shoulder and calling his name.

It was his voice. He had been dreaming. The image of his mother vanished in an instant. Reality hit him, leaving him grim and irritable.

"What do you want?" he asked the optio, who looked at him with concern.

"Vatinius Auruncus..." the optio stared at him. "The sentries have changed shifts. Let's rest for another couple of hours, then we'll move. I want to put more distance between us and those damned sons of harlots."

The centurion nodded and placed a hand on Severinus Majorianus' arm.

"All right. In two hours, we'll leave. But for now, light some fires, or we'll all freeze to death."

"I ordered against that, Centurion. I didn't want the smoke to make us visible," the optio explained.

"It's a risk we have to take. As frozen as we are, we won't even be able to hold our shields. Let's give the men some warmth; they'll recover their strength," the officer explained.

"Now, we need to deal with that wound," Severinus Majorianus said, pointing to the arrowhead protruding from the young man's shoulder.

The blood around the shaft had congealed. The area was swollen and painfully inflamed.

The centurion signaled for Ialenia Heria to join him.

The woman approached with an unnerving calmness, and only revealed her face from under her hood when she was near.

"Do you have any of your potions with you?" he asked.

"Centurion, I'm a diviner. What I know about medicine comes from what my father taught me—he was a druid. But I'm not a surgeon. I wouldn't know where to begin with that nasty wound. However, I know herbs, and I can make sure it doesn't fester," she said, raising her hands as if to clarify her point. "But someone else will have to remove the arrow—I won't do it!"

The centurion gritted his teeth.

The garrison surgeon had been killed during the first Heruli siege, and they didn't have another.

"Fine! Prepare your mixture, then!" he said, resigned.

The woman rummaged through her bag.

"I already have some of what I need. But not everything," she muttered to herself.

Without another word, she disappeared into the forest, vanishing into the thickening mist.

Fulcinius Agricola Statius and Ulzio Dacianus approached the centurion.

Fulcinius was the first to make a joke. "Don't worry, Centurion, we'll pull the arrow out for you..." he grinned, showing his brilliantly white teeth. "It'll probably hurt just a bit, but then it'll all be fine," he added, pretending to cover a laugh with his hand.

Ulzio Dacianus rolled up his sleeves and firmly gripped the arrowhead. "Hold him down!" he ordered.

The optio held the centurion tightly around the torso.

"Let's get this over with," he said.

When Fulcinius snapped the arrow's shaft, twisting it in the wound, Vatinius Auruncus opened his mouth in a silent scream of agony before losing consciousness.

He slumped into his cloak, still held by the legionaries.

Ulzio Dacianus finished the job, pulling out the remaining shaft, which was followed by a gush of blood.

He pressed the wound with a cloth. "Let's wait for the witch before we bandage it," he said, wiping the sweat from his brow.

***

As soon as the order was given, the legionaries wasted no time.

They set up two fires and eagerly gathered around them. Branches were laid across the top, covered with greenery to trap the smoke.

"Finally!" someone grumbled.

Everyone had the same idea—several pulled out pieces of salted, dried meat from their pouches. This would be their breakfast. Those without any meat of their own cleaned roots to chew on in a feeble attempt to stave off hunger. But these men were brothers before they were soldiers, so the meat was divided equally, and the roots were discarded.

Step by step, sinking into the snow, Ialenia Heria reached a tree with a trunk so wide it had split open, creating a hollow large enough for someone to take shelter from the rain. She knelt and carved druidic symbols into its bark, then placed both hands on it.

"Powerful Earth, protect our journey. Grant us your benevolence and favor while keeping adversity and evil spirits away. Be generous with us, and I shall honor your gifts," she intoned solemnly.

A gust of wind shook the snow-laden branches above.

After completing her prayer, she ventured deeper into the forest, her knowledgeable eyes scanning every nook and cranny. She stopped at a bush growing against a damp rock, knelt, and began digging. Soon, she unearthed a root. She cleaned it of soil and placed it in her satchel.

She moved to a shrub with clusters of red berries and harvested all of them.

Next, she lifted a large, smooth stone, revealing damp soil beneath. Using her dagger, she scraped away the dirt and collected the worms that surfaced, placing them in a smaller pouch.

Satisfied with her haul, she headed back.

Silent as a shadow, she reentered the camp.

When the optio saw her, he shot her a stern glare.

"You took your time."

"I needed rare roots," she replied.

The soldiers warming themselves around the fires barely noticed her return, except for Vatinius Auruncus, who was feverish and saw in her the hope of a swift recovery.

"Welcome back!" Severinus Majorianus greeted her.

Without lifting her eyes from her hands, busy preparing the salve, Ialenia Heria replied, "You can help me prepare it, if you'd like."

"I'd like to, but I can barely stand. What are you making?"

Using her dagger, she cleaned the roots further and tossed them into a bowl of melted snow. "I'm making an ointment to purify the centurion's wound," she explained.

"But…there are worms crawling out of that pouch!"

"Those worms, once boiled, release a viscous substance that binds the mixture. It will make it easier to apply," she said calmly.

During their conversation, the woman stirred the mixture as it warmed over the fire.

Severinus Majorianus offered her some dried meat and flatbread, sharing everything he had to eat.

"I have a suggestion, optio," she said.

"You have my full attention," the soldier replied, holding his helmet under his arm.

"I know this part of the forest. I used to hunt here with my people. If we reach the bed of a small stream and follow it, we can move safely, shielded from any attacks."

"How can you be so sure?"

"Because it runs through a gorge, well-hidden by dense undergrowth. From a distance, it's practically invisible. Heruli scouts won't be able to spot it unless they come very close," she explained.

After a brief moment of thought, the optio nodded.

"Yes, that sounds reasonable. You'll lead the way."

The witch allowed herself a faint smile. She was visibly pleased.

Gallienus Lars Gracchus wiped his hands on the damp grass, then looked at them and shook his head, incredulous that he had survived yet another ordeal.

When Drusus Variatus and Plato approached, he told them he was starving and had nothing to eat.

Plato handed him a piece of dry barley flatbread, which he devoured without chewing much.

"If we don't get moving soon, we'll become prey for the Heruli," he said.

"We need to recover our strength if we want to march faster—you should know that," Plato replied, drawing his gladius. "By the way, do you have any grease? I need to oil this blade; otherwise, it'll stick in the scabbard."

"I don't, but rest assured, once I hunt a deer, I'll have enough to spare," Gallienus Lars Gracchus interjected with a grin. "If we make it out of this alive and I return home, I'll buy a horse and go boar hunting. Then I'll sell the hides for a good sum. Where I'm from, there's plenty of game." His eyes stared into the distance, as if envisioning the landscapes of the Aurunci Mountains, filled with fragrant vegetation.

Auctus Tullius Sextus placed a reassuring hand on his shoulder. "We'll make it, my friend. We'll make it home."

Back at the camp, the atmosphere grew lighter. The fires were being extinguished and covered with dirt and stones. The legionaries had started bantering again, which was a good sign.

They would find food the following day, if possible. For now, they had only one task: resume the march.

✳✳✳

There were three deer, standing side by side.

The male had a grand, imposing rack of antlers. The other two appeared to be females.

The faint rustling of foliage suggested another animal was joining the group.

And indeed, it was.

A fourth deer approached, its impressive size marking it as mature. The downy fur under its jaw revealed its age.

The sun pierced through the dense vegetation, casting beams of light that made the snow glisten.

Gaius Octavianus signaled to Ulzio Dacianus to circle around the animals, hoping to capture at least one of them.

The gnawing hunger had distracted them from their reconnaissance duties. The centurion wouldn't let it slide, but maybe with the smell of roasting meat, he'd be more forgiving.

Ulzio Dacianus slowly drew his gladius and crept closer to the small herd, step by step. Gaius Octavianus picked up his sling and selected a stone, fitting it snugly into the pouch and taking aim.

He whirled the stone in the sling and hurled it toward the herd.

At the same time, Ulzio lunged at one of the deer, plunging his gladius into its back and clinging to the animal as it dragged him through the trees.

The stone launched by the scout struck true, hitting one of the females square on the head. The deer collapsed to the ground, twitching in its death throes. In an instant, the legionary was upon it, finishing it off with his dagger.

A few minutes later, Ulzio Dacianus returned, dragging his kill behind him.

"Let's head back to camp—we've got lunch!" Gaius Octavianus declared proudly.

"The centurion's going to have us flogged," Ulzio replied.

"We'll take the beating, but at least we'll be full," Octavianus shot back.

"You've got a point."

***

When Vatinius Auruncus opened his eyes, he noticed the metallic taste of blood in his mouth.

About five hours had passed since the diviner had treated him.

It was now well into the day, and the soldiers had been marching for three hours already.

"Can you stand, Centurion? We can't keep dragging you along while you nap," Severinus Majorianus asked, kneeling in front of him as he adjusted a greave.

261

"Yes, yes. I should eat something to regain my strength faster, but if I grit my teeth, I'll manage," Vatinius replied, inspecting his wound. "I hope the fever subsides. Luckily, the arrow didn't hit any bone."

"You can say that again. You'll be back in the fight soon enough. And believe me, you'll need to be."

"I can always prod the enemy with my other arm, my friend!" Vatinius shot him a grateful glance.

Severinus Majorianus didn't reply, though his smile made it clear he appreciated the centurion's gratitude.

"You look worn out, optio," Vatinius said, changing the subject.

"Rudulfus must have sent hundreds of his men after us. I'm worried, Centurion."

At that moment, something caught their attention. Severinus Majorianus shot to his feet.

"Someone's approaching the camp," he warned, moving toward the eastern side with his sword already drawn.

Vatinius Auruncus rose unsteadily, dizziness washing over him from the blood he had lost. He quickly regained his composure, resting his hand on the hilt of his gladius without drawing it.

He took a few steps toward the spot where the other legionaries had gathered, ready to face whoever was approaching.

"Raise your shields!" Vatinius Auruncus commanded, stepping into the battle-ready formation.

With a swift motion, he donned his crested helmet, securing it with a firm slap since his injured arm couldn't fasten it properly.

The bushes rustled again, and the sound of footsteps became unmistakable.

"Who goes there?" the centurion barked, gripping his gladius handle nervously.

Two weary but triumphant faces emerged from the bushes, waving their arms for help.

"Give us a hand! We've got two plump deer with us," Gaius Octavianus explained.

When the camp saw the animals, everyone rushed forward,

eager to grab a piece—even raw. Some pushing and shoving broke out, and the tension began to rise.

The soldiers were starving, and in such circumstances, fights or dangerous scuffles could easily erupt.

Aware of this, Vatinius Auruncus stepped in to restore order.

"Listen to me. All of you!" he paused, waiting until the legionaries quieted and gave him their attention. "We're resuming the march. We'll eat this meat tonight when we cook it at the next bivouac."

The legionaries stared at him.

No one openly protested, though a few grumbles could be heard here and there.

Still, an order was an order, and it had to be followed.

Ulzio Dacianus and Gaius Octavianus weren't the only ones who had approached the group of legionaries, however.

A soldier wearing armor entirely different from that of the legionaries appeared. Everyone drew their swords, ready for battle.

"Don't be alarmed. I'm alone, and I'm Roman," the stranger said.

"You're wearing Hunnic armor. You're not a Roman soldier," someone objected.

The man raised his hands in a gesture of surrender.

"I'm Gallo-Roman. My garrison was wiped out, and the only way to avoid being killed was to wear barbarian armor. While walking, I found the skeleton of a Hun in the forest and took his armor."

"So now there's a dead Hun in the forest wearing Roman armor?" Fulcinius Agricola Statius quipped, drawing laughter from the group.

"State your name, soldier!" The young centurion's voice silenced the group.

The soldier stiffened to attention.

"Quintus Faustus Esquilius, Southern Gaul Army, *vexillatio* of Dinia[1]," he declared.

---

[1] Refers to the ancient Roman name for the modern town of Digne-les-Bains, a commune in southeastern France, historically part of the province of Gaul.

"And how did you get here?" Plato asked.

Quintus Faustus Esquilius' expression darkened. "I was fleeing. Wandering, looking for a village that hadn't yet been ravaged by the barbarians. But it seems there aren't many left."

Everyone listened closely to his words. Every time the conversation turned to the state of the Empire, the news always seemed worse than before.

"We'll set out at the *Hora septima* [2], in the early afternoon," Vatinius Auruncus declared, setting the detachment back in motion. "We'll use the evening to rest and prepare camp."

Quintus Faustus Esquilius shook his head.

"Is something wrong, soldier?" the centurion asked sharply.

The two locked eyes for a tense moment.

"Centurion, I don't want to head south. Give me a portion of the venison, and I'll go my own way," the soldier said, stepping toward the deer.

"Absolutely not. That meat is for my men. You can leave if you wish, but the deer stays."

At that point, the optio stepped forward menacingly, making it clear that any dissent would not be tolerated. Ulzio Dacianus and Fulcinius Agricola Statius appeared at the scene, eager to observe the confrontation.

"Didn't they teach you that a centurion's orders are to be obeyed?" Fulcinius Agricola Statius said mockingly, flashing a grin that signaled trouble.

"I'd quite like to reach the coast as soon as possible," Ulzio Dacianus added, smoothing his beard with a threatening air as he glared at the defiant soldier.

Quintus Faustus Esquilius finally relented. "Fine. Fine, damn you bastards," he spat, stepping back and leaving the deer where it was.

---

[2] *Hora septima:* The seventh hour of the Roman day, approximately 1:00 PM in modern timekeeping. Romans divided their daylight hours into twelve parts, so the exact time varied with the season.

Vatinius Auruncus let out a sigh of relief. He was fortunate the situation had ended this way, reduced to little more than glares and muttered threats.

The soldiers began building stretchers out of branches to carry the deer, and the group resumed its march.

Duro Catalaunum, principia palace, former headquarters of the vexillatio – Afternoon

By the time the last of the royal guards had been executed, the room was littered with bloodied corpses.

A dozen officers and guards had been punished for allowing the Roman legionaries to get so close to their king's bedchamber.

Meanwhile, the high-ranking officers and generals had already prepared the force that would hunt down the fugitive Romans and annihilate them.

"My king, we're ready," one of the generals announced as he approached Rudulfus.

The king sat on his throne, stroking his beard. He was already wearing his armor, ready to lead his contingent personally.

He pressed his lips together before asking, "How many men?"

The general replied promptly: "Two hundred Heruli and a contingent of fifty Hunnic auxiliaries—expert horsemen and formidable archers."

Rudulfus nodded, grunting with a thirst for vengeance.

The general concluded his report: "My king, eight thousand warriors will remain to guard the region while we await your return." He then bowed and returned to join the other officers.

The king of the Heruli leaned back against the fabric-covered throne. "I don't want any mistakes in my absence. Is that clear?" he demanded.

The assembled officers nodded.

Attilius Faticus was trembling with terror. His wide-eyed gaze was fixed on the corpses of the executed soldiers. His lower lip quivered visibly, and when Rudulfus summoned him, he hesitantly stepped forward.

The other officers and generals regarded him with disdain, muttering their contempt for a man who had once been considered a Roman patrician of equestrian rank.

Attilius Faticus knelt, clutching the finely-embroidered blue tunic he wore. "Command me, most excellent king. I am your servant," he stammered with his head bowed.

Rudulfus' expression of disgust left no room for misinterpretation.

"Oversee the collection of tributes. Use my mercenaries if necessary, but restore the taxation of every Gallo-Roman. Understood?"

Attilius Faticus nodded eagerly, desperate to prove his understanding. "I will personally supervise the tax collectors in every corner of the region," he promised.

He retreated, rubbing his hands nervously, until he rejoined the palace functionaries.

At that point, the Heruli king stood. With the help of a servant, he donned a cloak made of wolf pelts.

He walked slowly and deliberately across the great hall, passing the assembled officers and palace administrators, his pace meant to unsettle.

Outside in the large courtyard, a groom helped him mount his horse. The animal shied slightly to one side, but the king tightened his grip on the reins, asserting control.

At a measured pace, he made his way to the front of the column that would pursue the Romans.

Holding his chin high, he raised his hand and swiftly brought it down with a decisive gesture.

The long column began to move.

As they passed through the gate where the legionaries had escaped, Rudulfus saw the bodies of his warriors strewn about.

A crow was pecking at the eye of one of the fallen.

His rage swelled uncontrollably, inflamed by the skill of those damned Roman soldiers.

But it wasn't their losses that angered him—he cared little for the fate of his men.

What he truly feared was that the remnants of the once-proud legions stationed in Gaul, now defeated and scattered, might regroup under Odoacer's banner.

And then there was the insult—those damned Romans had dared to send him the severed head of Vaillardo, one of his most trusted men, in a wicker basket.

Just thinking about how the story of that episode might spread across the Empire, tarnishing his reputation, filled Rudulfus with fury. He spat on the ground, his entire body trembling with the impatience for vengeance.

At that point, there was only one solution left: to hunt down the surviving legionaries and execute them in the most horrific way possible.

His revenge, too, would echo in every corner of Gaul.

At the mere mention of his name, Roman dignitaries and senators would cower in their fortified villas.

The horse he was riding snorted as it advanced, occasionally kicking out, its restless and untamed nature on full display. Beneath its glossy coat, its muscles twitched irritably.

The gates of Duro Catalaunum closed behind the column of warriors as they snaked along the road heading south.

The first stretch of the path was devoid of stones, which had been used by the Heruli during the siege, but beyond the forest, the road was still paved and in relatively good condition, despite years of neglect.

With each breath, both soldiers and animals exhaled small clouds of condensation—a clear sign of the biting cold.

Midday

From the top of the hill, Aristarchos Themistocles and Antoninus Tacitus spotted the legionaries below, moving through the undergrowth along a narrow trail.

"We've found them!" Aristarchos exclaimed.

"About time! I'm exhausted. Let's hurry and catch up before we lose them again."

They were chilled to the bone. Their wet clothes had frozen stiff, and only the grueling march had kept them from succumbing to the cold.

"It's not yet time to cross the threshold into the afterlife," Antoninus Tacitus muttered grimly.

"Half a day's march, and we'll reach them. By evening, you'll be warming yourself by a campfire, losing a fortune in *follis* at dice," the commander teased, laughing.

"Let's hope they've got some Falernian wine to drink—though I doubt that bunch of eunuchs has any with them," Antoninus retorted wryly.

Aristarchos laughed even louder and turned to his companion. "By now, Rudulfus must be absolutely livid…" he added with a note of humor.

Their laughter mingled in that brief moment of hope and relief.

They had pulled off a daring and incredibly courageous act. Delivering the severed head of one of Rudulfus' most trusted men to the king of the Heruli had been no easy task.

The faces of the two Romans still bore the marks of tension, despite being far from Duro Catalaunum. After catching their breath, they began descending toward the trail. They were finally going to reunite with the survivors of the *vexillatio*—their brother legionaries.

Hora septima, Early Afternoon

Centurion Vatinius Auruncus halted the group.

The optio moved closer to him. "We're stopping already?" he asked, unable to hide a trace of skepticism.

"Cold, hunger, and despair are doing nothing to help our resolve to reach the coast. And we're not just dealing with the Heruli chasing us. There are also Burgundian raiders infesting this area. If we run into one of their bands, we'll have to fight—and in our state, we wouldn't last long. We need to rest and accept the risk, my friend," the officer explained.

Severinus Majorianus gave a faint smile. "We used to be able to march until sunset... We must be going soft."

"Nothing will ever be like it was," Vatinius replied, his tone resigned. "Don't forget, we've been through several battles in the last few days. We're all completely worn out."

"So you agree with me then..."

"About what?"

"That you should have picked another profession. Being a warrior doesn't suit you," Severinus teased, barely stifling a chuckle.

"I fought at Arles, just like you. And, if I may say so, I don't think I did too badly there," the centurion shot back dryly.

"That was the exception. The other times..." Severinus pretended to hold back a laugh.

"What, do you expect a *tremissis*[3] for saving my hide?"

Severinus burst into a laugh that was far too loud, given the circumstances. "How's the wound?" he asked, still grinning.

Vatinius glanced at it, as if inspecting the injury. "Better. That strange woman must have used the right potion, it seems."

"She's a witch, maybe even a pagan."

"She has her beliefs... I know she's the daughter of a druid. Around here, they're seen as true authorities, even if the bishops don't like them."

"She's a pagan, believe me, and I don't trust her."

"You're talking nonsense."

"Ask her if she believes in Our Lord, then. Test her," the optio challenged, shooting him a quick but pointed look that carried a hint of suggestion—or so it seemed.

---

[3] *Tremissis:* A gold coin used in the later Roman Empire and early Middle Ages. It was valued at one-third of a *solidus*, the primary gold currency of the time.

"Everyone is free to believe in what they want."

"On that, I agree with you, Centurion. I also believe the Empire hasn't completely fallen apart yet," Severinus said, his tone carrying a hint of hope.

"What do you mean?"

"That Rome must still have forces left. The Army of Gaul, for example—General Syagrius is no barbarian, but a proud Roman citizen!"

Vatinius Auruncus lowered his gaze, melancholy washing over him. He appreciated that some hope still clung to the hearts of his soldiers, even if his own skepticism kept him from entertaining such optimistic notions.

He decided to end the conversation. "Optio, we don't even know if Syagrius is still alive. Let's stop here and set up camp. You're starting to sound like an old gossip!"

"Next time, I'll leave you to the Heruli, Centurion!" Severinus retorted, stiffening into a formal salute before turning and heading toward the others, barking orders left and right as he went.

The legionaries set up their bivouac. They sharpened poles to make a makeshift fence and lit a fire to warm themselves and cook the venison.

They had marched deep into the forest, so deep that it seemed unlikely anyone could spot the smoke from their fires. However, this didn't reassure the optio, who kept glancing anxiously into the trees, fearing an ambush.

Vatinius Auruncus washed his wound in the icy water of a stream. A scab had finally formed—a good sign. He no longer felt feverish.

Despite their exhaustion, the soldiers seemed energized by the prospect of a meal. When the venison was prepared, a cheer went up. Everyone worked quickly to ensure they could eat as soon as possible. Some cracked crude jokes, sparking laughter among the group.

Fulcinius Agricola Statius directed his teasing gaze toward Ialenia Heria.

"Careful," she said with a sly grin. "Or a legionary's testicles might end up roasting alongside the venison."

A playful exchange followed, ending only when the first portions of food were distributed.

Vatinius Auruncus couldn't help but marvel at how the men still found ways to entertain themselves, even in situations like this. As he polished his helmet with a greased cloth, he thought about how extraordinary it was that laughter could exist amid so much hardship.

Soon, the meal turned into a full-fledged feast. For a brief moment, the men allowed themselves to feel safe. The centurion, however, knew better. But he understood the need to push aside dark thoughts, even if only for a while.

He set his helmet down, stretched, and stood. The hearty laughter of Fulcinius Agricola Statius caught his attention.

Fulcinius, Drusus Variatus, Gaius Octavianus, Gallienus Lars Gracchus, and Ulzio Dacianus sat in a circle, tossing dice and tearing chunks of meat from a haunch.

"You lost! That's five *follis*," Drusus Variatus declared, extending his palm toward Ulzio Dacianus, who scowled in response.

"This hardly seems fair," Ulzio retorted. "Before the siege of Duro Catalaunum, I lent you two *sesterces* to buy thirty fat geese! And yet, here we are—you haven't paid me back!" He pointed an accusatory finger.

Drusus shot to his feet. "I needed those geese to sell the *ficatum!*[4] I'd have repaid you if those damned barbarians hadn't ruined everything!"

"Oh, so it's my fault now, is it?" Ulzio spat. "This is a gambling debt, and you're obligated to pay! And by the way, Duro Catalaunum is no longer a Roman outpost, in case you hadn't noticed. We're running for our lives!"

---

[4] *Ficatum:* The Latin word for liver, used here to describe a preparation of foie gras, a delicacy derived from fattened goose or duck liver. The name stems from the practice of feeding the animals figs (*ficus* in Latin) to enhance the flavor.

Drusus puffed out his chest, squaring up to Ulzio. "And what does that have to do with me? Don't treat me like I'm stupid!" he said, rolling up his sleeves before lunging at him.

Vatinius Auruncus could hardly believe what he was seeing—two grown men brawling in the snow over such a petty argument.

Ulzio grabbed Drusus by the throat, ignoring the punches Drusus landed on his ribs. They rolled in the snow, throwing wild blows at each other.

Meanwhile, Fulcinius Agricola Statius and Gallienus Lars Gracchus were already taking bets on the fight, while only Gaius Octavianus made an earnest effort to break it up, albeit without much success.

The commotion abruptly stopped when the other soldiers grabbed their weapons and took up defensive positions around the camp.

Someone was approaching.

A makeshift wall of shields formed along the rough fence encircling the camp. Drusus and Ulzio, now standing shoulder to shoulder, gripped their shields tightly.

Vatinius Auruncus donned his crested helmet, fastening it securely under his chin.

"Optio!" he called out, glancing at Severinus Majorianus, who was already in position.

"I've got your flank, Centurion," the optio replied, his tone steady.

Ialenia Heria crouched behind a tree, her bow drawn and ready. Gallienus Lars Gracchus and Fulcinius Agricola Statius held their javelins, poised to throw.

Gaius Octavianus sidled up to the centurion.

"Have they already found us?" he asked.

Auruncus shook his head. "No, that's not possible. A column of warriors would be visible from miles away. I think it's just a small group, maybe even a lone visitor."

"Let's hope so," Octavianus murmured, though his grip on his sword remained firm.

Severinus Majorianus raised an arm, signaling the centurion: someone was very close.

The legionaries fell silent, their muscles tense.

The rustle of a bush confirmed it. The damp undergrowth crackled faintly with each step of the unseen visitor.

Then, suddenly, the noise stopped.

Anxious moments followed, every man holding his breath.

"I am Aristarchos Themistocles, centurion *primae spatha* in the *vexillatio* of Duro Catalaunum. Commander of the First Cohort of the Fifth Iron Legion."

Silence persisted.

"Well? Is that not enough, or should I show you the vine staff I used to thrash you countless times?" insisted the familiar voice.

A murmur spread among the men: their commander had found them.

Vatinius Auruncus responded with a hint of sarcasm: "We're not entirely convinced... We need some tangible proof of your identity. For all we know, you could be a Herulian warrior imitating the voice of a soft-spoken commander!"

A whistle cut through the air.

The commander's gladius, with its bone handle, spun through the air and lodged itself firmly in the ground right in front of Vatinius Auruncus' boots.

The legionaries watched the scene unfold with rapt attention.

Vatinius glanced down, relieved to find that the blade hadn't severed his toes. He raised his head and shouted, "Welcome back, Centurion! Good to have you among us again. I hope you didn't come alone, though."

"I haven't left him alone for a moment, boy. Did you think I'd let these barbarians do me in?" added Antoninus Tacitus, stepping out of the brush.

An instant later, the commander himself appeared, walking forward to retrieve his sword from the ground.

"Am I mistaken, or were you two just brawling?" he asked, crouching to grasp the sword's handle.

"Not at all!" Vatinius Auruncus lied quickly.

"Must've been my imagination, then..."

The young centurion offered no reply.

Centurion Aristarchos Themistocles and Antoninus Tacitus settled by the campfire, where they were promptly handed some food. As the flames crackled, their account of recent events captured the attention of all. The tale of how they had humiliated the king of the Heruli lifted the soldiers' spirits, sparking a wave of sarcastic banter across the camp.

Laughter rekindled the vigor of the weary legionaries.

A sudden gust of icy wind swept through the camp, rustling cloaks and carrying sparks from the fires into the dark forest beyond.

***

The Heruli scouting parties returned to the main column with increasingly discouraging news.

There was still no sign of the Romans.

It was certain they were hiding somewhere in the forest, but the search had yet to flush them out.

But what if they weren't heading south? Rudulfus thought, his face dark with irritation.

Calibrandus, the highest-ranking general, seemed to read his mind. "My king, they're undoubtedly heading for southern Gaul. They know as well as we do that the north is entirely under our control. They're no fools—you've seen what they're capable of."

That last remark didn't sit well with Rudulfus. He snapped his head around, glaring at the general with searing intensity. The officer, sensing the storm brewing, quickly bowed his head in submission, avoiding what would have surely been a scathing tirade.

"Keep searching. They'll have to surface eventually," Rudulfus ordered curtly, before trotting off on his horse.

Each hoofbeat sent clumps of mud and moss flying into the

air. His hand-picked mercenaries followed closely behind, never letting him out of their sight.

As Rudulfus moved ahead, Cunipert sidled his horse next to Calibrandus'. "Lost the king's favor, have you?" he mocked.

"You're in no position to talk. Last I checked, you didn't have the stones it took for me to bed your mother," Calibrandus shot back, reining his horse to a halt.

The two generals stared each other down for what felt like an eternity until Cunipert edged closer, his horse pacing restlessly beneath him.

As their mounts shifted uneasily, the two men locked eyes.

"One day, I'll see your tongue hanging from your neck. Better find yourself a woman tonight—it could be your last," Cunipert hissed through clenched teeth, his hand gripping the hilt of his sword.

"If I were you, I'd ride hard. When Rudulfus notices you're not licking his boots, his fury might turn your tongue into a trophy for my lance," Calibrandus retorted, wheeling his horse around and galloping back toward the rear of the column.

Still seething from the exchange, Calibrandus vowed silently to settle the score.

Cunipert, too, galloped off to rejoin Rudulfus before his absence drew attention.

The barbarian column stretched along the paved road, its length a twisting serpent of warriors. Unlike the initial stretch of the road, the section they were now traversing lay in utter neglect.

On either side, remnants of once-majestic pagan temples stood abandoned—columns now served as crude benches, and their capitals lay discarded, half-buried in weeds and damp earth.

Rudulfus tightened his fur-lined cloak around his neck, bracing against the biting cold wind that tugged at his hair and long beard.

Dusk was falling.

Chapter IX – Ready for Anything

Four days of relentless marching had left the Romans exhausted. Fortunately, they had encountered no Heruli vanguards. The further south they went, the milder the climate became.

Their march had followed a strict routine: they would break camp at *Hora secunda*[1] and only stop at *Hora undecima*[2] to set up defenses and cook game.

From the top of a hill, Aristarchos Themistocles surveyed the terrain ahead, searching for the best route to continue their march.

"Where do you think we are?" he asked.

"I think…" Vatinius Auruncus began, only to stop mid-sentence when he caught the commander's sharp look.

"I mean…" He cleared his throat and pointed to the shimmering, snake-like strip of water in the distance. "That's the Rhône."

"We've come a long way, then," Aristarchos replied, his gaze still fixed on the horizon to the south.

"The men are exhausted, Centurion," the younger officer said, raising his chin slightly, as if to let the soft, fragrant southern air soothe him.

Both men shared the same concern. They were nearing the forest's edge. From here on, they would have to follow a long stretch of paved road to reach the nearest town. Without the cover of the woods, they would be fully exposed to their pursuers.

---

[1] *Hora secunda:* roughly 8:00 AM.

[2] *Hora undecima:* roughly 4:00 PM.

Scattered across the landscape, small farmsteads emitted thin columns of smoke from their chimneys. No herds could be seen—likely hidden by farmers who had managed to evade Burgundian raids. Fields once teeming with crops were now overgrown and abandoned. The passage of the barbarians had left its scars, even on these fertile lands.

The once-bustling roadside stations lay in ruins. Stables that had once cared for relay horses were overrun with weeds, and there were no innkeepers to serve warm meals to travelers, messengers, or merchant caravans hauling goods from distant corners of the Empire.

The arrival of Antoninus Tacitus broke the grim silence.

"I'm tired of shitting out venison. So, when are we reaching the coast? I could eat a mullet raw right now!" he blurted out.

"If Rudulfus doesn't plant an arrow in your ass first, you might get your wish in a few days," the commander quipped, a faint smile tugging at his lips. Despite the humor, his expression betrayed a lingering unease.

Sensing their thoughts, he added, "We must be extremely cautious now. From this point onward, we'll be visible to the Heruli vanguards."

The two officers scanned their surroundings, assessing potential threats.

"Maybe we should follow the river," Aristarchos suggested, his eyes tracing the Rhône's shimmering path.

"They'd see us," Antoninus Tacitus objected, removing his helmet to adjust his damp, sweat-matted hair.

"They'll see us regardless. A column of marching legionaries stands out like a sore thumb in all this greenery," Aristarchos countered, spreading his arms to emphasize the open terrain.

After a brief pause, the younger officer pointed to the road below. "They'll emerge from there. They've likely followed the paved roads, which gave them the advantage."

"The Rhône!" Aristarchos exclaimed, seizing on the point.

"Exactly. Their problem will be crossing it, while for us, being fewer in number, it's easier. But we must act fast, before they catch up," Vatinius concluded, gripping the hilt of his gladius firmly.

"We don't have the resources for such a maneuver," Aristarchos pointed out.

"Those sort..." Vatinius gestured back towards their pursuers with his thumb. "...never pay the ferryman. This time, neither will we," he said, his voice resolute, leaving no room for doubt.

"Let's get to it, then," Aristarchos said, turning to rejoin the soldiers descending the hill.

***

When they reached the group, Vatinius exchanged a knowing glance with the optio, who nodded in understanding. The two veterans had fought together long enough to communicate without words.

"What's the plan?" the optio asked slyly.

The young centurion smiled before replying, "We're crossing the Rhône."

"What, by selling Ialenia Heria as payment for the crossing?" the optio joked, nodding towards the druidess, who walked a few paces behind the group.

The soldiers continued their march, chatting and occasionally breaking into laughter.

However, between Drusus Variatus and Ulzio Dacianus, the tension still lingered. Their gambling dispute remained unresolved, and sharp glares frequently passed between them.

At a small riverside port, Fulcinius Agricola Statius held a fisherman at sword-point while the others boarded his boat, ready to cross.

The crossing was brief, and once on the other side, they signaled to the fisherman that they had left his boat tied up downstream.

The fisherman shouted something, presumably a curse on their mothers.

Unbeknownst to the Romans, a Heruli scouting party watched the entire scene from atop a nearby hill.

The next day, the Romans reached the gates of Aquae Sextiae[3]. The towering gates were securely shut.

Centurion Aristarchos Themistocles stepped forward and raised his hand to halt the column.

"We are soldiers of Rome! Open the gates! We are Romans!" he shouted up to the walls.

A centurion with an unkempt beard and graying hair appeared atop the walls.

"We can't let you in," he shouted down to the group. "Our supplies are already running low, and we don't need more mouths to feed. Find somewhere else to go!"

From below, Vatinius Auruncus replied irritably, "We'll only stay one night. Open up!"

The centurion disappeared, but returned after about fifteen minutes.

"You've got a prostitute with you," he called out. "If you give her to me, I'll open the gates."

"She's a…" Vatinius hesitated, searching for a way to define Ialenia Heria, "a seer." It was the best excuse he could think of.

The officer on the walls fell silent, seemingly disappointed. He turned as though consulting with someone. Finally, he called back, "That'll do. We'll let you in."

The massive bronze hinges groaned, but didn't seize up thanks to regular greasing, as the gates creaked open slowly.

A squad of soldiers immediately marched out, shields raised, maintaining a defensive formation. Caution was a must—they had to confirm this wasn't a trick by barbarians disguised as Romans.

Once the fleeing soldiers were deemed genuine, the column entered the city and discovered a far better situation than they had dared to hope for.

Tabernae[4] were open and bustling. Half of the urban layout was

---

[3] *Aquae Sextiae:* modern-day Aix-en-Provence.

[4] *Tabernae:* shops/stores, plural of *taberna.* These were often a type of tavern,

relatively modern, while the other half consisted of dense, towering insulae that blocked sunlight from reaching the streets below.

As they delved deeper into the city, they encountered a network of narrow alleys and *angiportus*[5] teeming with life. Few locals paid attention to the column of soldiers passing through.

Nearby, a *vestiarius*[6] was busy cutting lengths of fabric imported from Dalmatia, which had itself come from some distant corner of the East. His partner showcased modestly-crafted tunics of decent quality to potential buyers.

Numerous *popinae*[7] bustled with patrons grabbing quick meals, while a bronze worker, an *aerarius*[8], shaped a breastplate adorned with intricate carvings of a quadriga, its charioteer depicted in the style of soldiers from the time of the Caesars.

Despite the dire state of the Empire, the city thrived, showing few signs of its decline.

Commander Aristarchos Themistocles halted the group. "We're safe here. Let's enjoy a few hours of respite. We'll regroup and leave at first light."

The legionaries' smiles were all the response he needed.

As the column moved along the main thoroughfare, Ialenia Heria noticed the *vicus unguentarius*[9] and veered toward it.

"Ah, women!" Gaius Octavianus remarked, eliciting laughter from his comrades.

However, a single glare from Ialenia silenced them all.

---

though not always, typically consisting of a single vaulted room with a stone counter where food containers were embedded. Food could be heated, and meals often served as opportunities to close deals or forge agreements, but it was also simply a place for discussion.

[5] *Angiportus:* proper alleyways.

[6] *Vestiarius:* tailor.

[7] *Popina:* can be considered a kind of bar.

[8] *Aerarius:* bronze artisan.

[9] *Vicus unguentarius:* alley of perfume sellers.

***

"One and one makes two!" Fulcinius Agricola Statius declared as he handed over four *follis* to a leather merchant. "Can I go now?" he asked impatiently, practically bouncing on his feet.

The merchant inspected the coins before nodding gruffly and gesturing with his thumb toward the loft above his shop.[10]

There, a striking young woman with long, raven-black hair waited, reclining on a straw mattress. A sheer veil barely concealed her figure as she watched the eager soldier strip off his armor. His helmet, gladius, and pugio were set carefully on the ground, while his tunic and trousers were hastily piled atop his dusty, soot-streaked armor.

Overcome with excitement, he scooped the woman into his arms. "What's your name, beauty?"

"Lucilla Flavia Corvina," she answered.

"Flavia Corvina, eh? I paid a hefty price, but you're worth every coin!"

The two disappeared under a coarse woolen blanket.

The woman opened herself to him, her legs parting invitingly. Her hands roamed his scarred back and arms, feeling the evidence of countless campaigns.

Their mouths intertwined, and his hands hungrily explored every inch of her alluring form.

Downstairs in the shop, Christianus Caligatus waited impatiently for his turn, his gaze fixed on the loft.

He had elbowed his way past four other men vying for the woman's attention. Though they had protested, they eventually relented when he gifted them a *solidus*[11], cheerfully urging them to drink to his health.

---

[10] It wasn't uncommon for a prostitute to use a shop's mezzanine to supplement the shopkeeper's business.

[11] *Solidus:* a Roman coin. The word *solidus* is the origin of the modern Italian word *soldo* (meaning "pay" or "wage").

What they didn't realize was that the coin was a fake—an increasingly common deception in those times. Christianus Caligatus was an expert at such scams.

Meanwhile, the leather merchant continued haggling with customers, boasting about the woman's talents and charm.

***

An intoxicated man hurled a clay jug against a wall, shattering it into pieces. It was his reaction to losing a *siliqua*[12] and thirty *follis*—a debt nearly impossible to repay in those times.

Two hulking brutes roughly grabbed him under his arms and dragged him out. Just before stepping through the tavern's threshold, one of them exchanged a meaningful glance with the man's gambling opponent. With a nod of agreement, the punishment was decided.

In a narrow, foul-smelling alley reeking of urine, the two men beat the gambler until he was unconscious. Then, with a precise blow from an iron bar, they broke his arm, jolting him back to consciousness with a scream of pain. His cries dissolved into the noisy bustle of people crowding the streets.

Ulzio Dacianus and Drusus Variatus exchanged uneasy glances.

"Looks like it's best not to owe debts around here, eh?" Drusus Variatus remarked dryly.

"Just wait till I find some sucker to swindle. I'll show you how to buy a horse worthy of a cataphract officer," Ulzio hissed, scanning the surroundings for amusement. "This is my kind of place, boy!" he added, stepping inside a gambling den.

The two men found themselves seated at a wide table surrounded by other rogues engrossed in a game of tesserae[13]. A man

---

[12] *Siliqua:* a silver coin valued at 1/24th of a solidus. The siliqua was first minted under Constantine I. After the fall of the Western Roman Empire (in 476), siliquae continued to be minted up until the reign of Heraclius I (610–640) and possibly (though historical sources are unclear) until the time of Tiberius III (698–705).

[13] *Tesserae:* equivalent to dice games.

with a deep scar that tugged one side of his face, closing his left eye, invited them to join.

"I'm in," Drusus replied, casting quick glances around the room. He noticed their presence had drawn the attention of several curious onlookers.

"We're here for this, aren't we, friend?" Ulzio encouraged, lifting a cup of wine that a serving girl had just filled.

Eyeing the girl up and down with an exaggeratedly suggestive expression, he grinned, "You're a fine little thing... Keep yourself free for me when I'm rich. I'll take you to the Gulf of Lestrigonia,, and you'll bear my bastards!" He downed the wine in one gulp and exclaimed, "Nectar of the gods—warms my insides!"

On the wall, a hollowed-out die had been nailed as a warning. Beneath it hung a rotting finger, likely belonging to someone who had tried cheating in the tavern. It was a stark reminder of the seriousness with which the establishment treated its rules.

Drusus pointed to the grisly display. "Don't try any funny business here, you scoundrel. That's proof they mean it," he warned Ulzio.

Then Drusus pulled out a small pile of coins, flashing them to show he could afford to play. They were his earnings from years at Duro Catalaunum.

Ulzio glared at him. "So, you did have money after all? I swear, once we're outside, I'll slit your throat—if it's the last thing I do!" he threatened.

Drusus clenched his fist and growled, "Try it, you mangy dog!"

The tension broke as the game began.

The scarred gambler shook the *fritillus*[14] vigorously, releasing the dice, which rolled across the table and stopped just short of the edge. Cheers erupted from the excited players, drowning out every other sound.

The tavern was packed, chaotic. People shouted over one another just to be heard. At other tables, some engaged in games of

---

[14] *Fritillus:* a terracotta cup used to throw dice.

navia aut capita[15], while others faced off in *micatio*[16]. Here and there, men disappeared with prostitutes. Others simply drank themselves into oblivion, singing bawdy songs or yelling drunkenly.

The air reeked of vomit, sweat, and sour wine. Smoke from the lanterns coiled upward, acrid and black, stinging eyes and coating mouths with bitterness before settling under the low ceiling. The tavern owner tirelessly filled pitchers from large amphorae, which his wife carried to the boisterous tables.

***

Meanwhile, Vatinius Auruncus wandered through a bustling square filled with people. Weaving his way through the crowd to the other side, he felt the urge to relieve himself, and ducked into a narrow alley between a sauce vendor's stall and a fishmonger's shop.

As he ventured in far enough to avoid being seen, he was suddenly confronted by a towering Burgundian, easily twice his size.

"I've got a cow for sale—cheap price, you'll see," the giant said, stepping sideways to block his path.

"I don't need a cow. Can't you see I'm a soldier? Now get out of my way," Vatinius replied, keeping his tone steady, but feeling uneasy about the situation. Something about the man seemed off.

"Just a few coins, and she's yours. A fine breed, plenty of milk, or you could sell her for a tidy profit," the man insisted, his expression darkening ominously.

Vatinius glanced quickly to the side and noticed the alley converged with other, narrower lanes. From those shadows, three more figures emerged, edging closer. One of them, with a hand concealed inside a coarse woolen tunic, flashed a decayed grin of missing and rotting teeth.

[15] *Navia aut capita:* the game of "heads or tails." Literally, *navia* (ship) or *capita* (head).

[16] *Micatio:* the game of morra (a traditional hand-gesture game).

Realizing he'd wandered too far into a dangerous part of the city, Vatinius tightened his grip on the hilt of his gladius. His senses sharpened, readying him for a fight.

The Burgundian let out a guttural growl. "Did you make your will before stepping out, soldier?"

The cow sale was nothing more than a ruse to lure him into a trap.

Vatinius Auruncus already had his hand tightly gripping the hilt of his gladius, prepared for anything now. His gaze darted between the towering Burgundian and his accomplices, all of whom had drawn their weapons.

This was a robbery. Maybe even a murder.

The giant spoke again: "We'll settle for your coins," he said, his eyes dropping to the pouch hanging from Vatinius' *cingulum*. "Hand them over, save your life, and run back to that dog of a wife of yours," he sneered, tightening his grip on his dagger.

Rage flared within Vatinius. Was this how it would end, in such a humiliating fashion? He reminded himself he was a soldier, and if it came to it, he would die as one—fighting to the bitter end. He would not go quietly.

But before he could act, a voice from behind him broke the tension.

"And you scoundrels—did *you* make your wills? You'd best be careful, for your throats are at risk."

It was the *optio*. Severinus Majorianus stood there, sword drawn, wielding it menacingly at the would-be attackers.

Vatinius exhaled in relief, a smile breaking across his face as he glanced at his friend. With renewed confidence, he pressed the tip of his gladius to the Burgundian's throat, pricking the skin enough to draw a thin line of blood.

It was then Vatinius noticed the mark burned into the man's shoulder—a brand that read *FUR*[17]. A thief, condemned and

---

[17] *FUR:* thief. Thieves and/or slaves guilty of such crimes were branded with this word.

marked for all to see. How had he not noticed this earlier? He chastised himself for missing such a glaring warning.

"You're just two," said the toothless bandit, his jagged smile unnerving. He had now drawn a second weapon, a jagged-edged gladius. "And we're twice that number. I'd advise caution, soldiers." He moved as if to encircle them, flanked by his two accomplices.

But Vatinius stepped forward, pressing his blade deeper into the Burgundian's neck, enough to send a rivulet of blood down the man's tunic. The dagger slipped from the giant's hand, clattering onto the cobblestones.

"Do you want me to take one more step forward?" Vatinius asked, half-smirking.

For a moment, the tension hung heavy, neither side daring to move. Then, with a series of quick glances among themselves, the bandits turned and slinked off into the labyrinthine alleys.

"What are you doing here, Centurion?" Severinus asked, sheathing his sword. "A man like you should be reclining under a sycamore reading Plotinus, not wandering into some filthy *suburra*. Someone who looks more like a scholar than a soldier has no business here."

It was a common jest among the centurions—that Vatinius seemed more like a philosopher than a warrior. Yet, his valor on the battlefield had earned their respect, even if they loved to tease him.

Vatinius merely shrugged, then clasped Severinus' forearm in gratitude.

"I was just trying to relieve myself," he muttered, turning to face a brick wall. "Now do me a favor and watch my back. And you—what are you doing in this part of the city?"

Severinus scratched his chin thoughtfully. "I'm looking for a peaceful place to spend my time," he declared, bursting into a boisterous laugh. It was clear he was in search of a woman's company.

"I saw those three coming out of the alleys while crossing the square, and then I spotted the purple of your cloak. I thought to myself, 'Could it be the kid's gotten himself into trouble again?'

Then I reasoned further, 'How's he going to fight his way out with that bum shoulder?' When I heard you crying, I knew I had to step in and save you. I should be paid like a *bucellarii* for this."

"I wasn't crying."

"Sure sounded like crying to me."

"No, I wasn't," Vatinius insisted, playing along.

"Don't let those lowlifes hurt you, eh?" Severinus quipped before strolling off, disappearing into the bustling crowd in the square.

Finally emerging from the crowded and perilous district, the young centurion strolled under the porticoes. Hunger gnawed at him, so he joined a line at a *thermopolium*[18] to purchase a warm flatbread. He bit into it eagerly as he continued walking along the street, carried forward by the bustling throng pressing from behind.

The murmur of voices was so persistent and loud that it began to feel oppressive. On one side of the road stood rows of masonry benches, long abandoned. In another time, children might have sat there, learning to read and write under the stern guidance of a litterator, a tutor whose strictness was often dictated by the wealthy parents who employed him. A tutor who failed to instill knowledge could quickly fall out of favor with those in power. But those customs were relics of the past. Education for children had largely vanished decades ago, a victim of the decline of Roman society.

The young centurion reflected somberly: Roman youth were becoming more like the barbarians with each passing year. He had even seen children at play, pretending to be barbarian warriors rather than emulating the great Caesars or Roman generals of old. Shaking his head with melancholy, he lamented how education had been cast aside in a society that began its slide into decadence long before the barbarian invasions.

---

[18] *Thermopolium:* a type of fast-food counter. It had a small counter where food from the kitchen in the back was displayed and served.

Deep in thought, he noticed a girl standing with her mother in front of a fabric merchant's shop. They were inspecting bolts of cloth and arguing animatedly. The mother scolded her for something he couldn't make out. As though sensing his gaze, the girl turned and looked directly at him.

Her eyes, framed by dark makeup, glinted green and transparent—like the emeralds that once adorned the crown of an empress he had seen in an imperial procession. The wife of Augustus Julius Nepos[19] had worn a golden diadem with gems so brilliantly green and clear that the sunlight fractured into dazzling shades of the same hue. This girl's eyes possessed that same mesmerizing quality.

Her dress fit her perfectly, accentuating her alluring form, and was fastened securely at the shoulder with a gleaming brooch. Vatinius Auruncus gave her a faint smile. His appearance—dirty armor streaked with blood and mud, and a face blackened with soot—must have seemed anything but appealing. Yet the girl smiled back at him. She whispered something to her mother, who brusquely gestured toward the cloths as if to redirect her attention.

Before she turned back to the merchant's wares, the girl cast him one last fleeting glance. That look, however brief, lifted his spirits.

***

Droplets of rain began to fall, heralding an imminent storm that promised to drench the lands of Gallia Lugdunensis.

---

[19] *Julius Nepos (Iulius Nepos)*: Western Roman Emperor from 474 to 475. He was the last legitimate Western Roman ruler, holding the title until his death. Julius Nepos was the son of Nepotianus, magister militum between 458 and 461, and the nephew of Marcellinus, *comes* of Dalmatia. He succeeded his uncle Marcellinus in governing the Dalmatian region, which was formally part of the Western Roman Empire, but was effectively autonomous. He maintained close relations with the Eastern Roman Empire, served as magister militum for the Praetorian Prefecture of Illyricum, and married a niece of Leo I, Emperor of the East.

Rudulfus stood motionless, his gaze fixed on the flowing river as it was pierced by countless raindrops falling from the low, leaden clouds above. Wrapped in a waxed cloak whose waterproofing was beginning to falter, the Herulian king remained still, his emotions hidden beneath a hardened exterior.

The downpour's rhythmic patter was oddly soothing, even to a warrior as noble as he considered himself to be. Water dripped from his sodden beard, streaming over his armor and pooling at his feet. His steely eyes betrayed the turbulent rage he struggled to contain.

The affront of the Roman centurion's brazen act—approaching his very chambers to leave an insult—gnawed at him. If Rudulfus failed to exact an exemplary punishment, his reputation would suffer irreparable damage. Word of his humiliation would soon reach the courts of Ravenna and Toulouse.

Gripping the hilt of his long sword tightly with a gloved hand, his thoughts turned to Odoacer, imagining the scornful laughter of the barbarian king. Then, carried away by an unstoppable train of thought, he imagined hearing the boisterous laughter of that arrogant Visigoth king, Euric[20]—seated on his throne in Toulouse, stuffing his face with roasted meat and spiced wine. He could see him pointing a mocking finger, calling him the fool who'd been outwitted by a handful of Romans.

This same Euric, who on one hand flaunted his defiance of the Empire, yet on the other, married off his daughter to Ricimer[21], one of Rome's most powerful patricians.

---

[20] *Euric:* Visigothic king, the fourth son of Theodoric I. He became king after assassinating his brother, Theodoric II. Euric ruled from 466 until his death in 484 CE. During his reign, he rejected the authority of the Roman Empire.

[21] *Ricimer:* a politician and general of the Western Roman Empire. Of Gothic descent, Ricimer held the real power in the empire from 460 until his death on August 18, 472. Named *patrician* in 466 (a title granted to him by the Byzantine Emperor Leo I, known as "the Thracian"), he placed the compliant Libius Severus on the imperial throne to control affairs from behind the scenes.

Gnashing his teeth in fury, Rudulfus raised his gaze toward the rising columns of black smoke in the distance. Despite the hours of relentless rain, the fires burned on, signaling the devastation wrought by his band of marauders. Several villages had been looted and torched in search of any sign of the fleeing Romans, but every effort had yielded the same result: no trace of them, save for the meager garrisons guarding the towns along the Rhône Valley.

"My king..."

Rudulfus turned sharply, sending droplets flying from his sodden beard. "What is it?" he growled.

The towering Calibrandus bowed slightly in deference. "My king, one of our spies has delivered a message," he said, handing over a parchment bearing the seal of a Roman noble.

Rudulfus snatched it from his hand, scrutinizing the document. "It seems I was wise to place you among the Romans," he said, a rare note of approval in his voice. "You've spun useful webs." He referred to Calibrandus' talent for corrupting Roman nobles and infiltrating their administration.

The general acknowledged the compliment with a reserved nod. "The letter comes from a decurion who owes me a significant favor. The Burgundians seized his estates north of Arelate[22], and I interceded on his behalf. I stayed in his household for nearly two years, during which I mastered Latin and their ridiculous manners—the very ways that reduced them to weaklings. He tells me the Romans are in Aquae Sextiae."

With the message clenched tightly in his hand, the Heruli king lifted his chin arrogantly and flared his nostrils, as if attempting to inhale all the air around him. With an unexpected affability that even surprised the high-ranking officer before him, he placed a firm hand on the man's shoulder and said, "My valiant Calibrandus, once again you've proven your ability to accomplish tasks that

[22] *Arelate*: modern-day Arles in the department of Bouches-du-Rhône.

are never easy. Stay on this path, and one day you'll command an entire province."

Calibrandus nodded subtly, acknowledging the promise with measured appreciation. "What are our next steps, my king?" he asked.

"We'll flush out those Roman rats and send their heads to Odoacer and Euric!" the king declared triumphantly, turning his gaze skyward.

At first, Calibrandus didn't understand why his ruler had mentioned Euric, but clarity came during their march toward Aquae Sextiae. Rudulfus himself admitted he feared the ridicule of the opposing rulers: Odoacer, leader of the Roman remnants, and Euric, the Visigothic king. The Heruli king's pride couldn't tolerate becoming a subject of mockery in the courts of Ravenna or Toulouse.

Hidden among the shadows of a dense grove, a spy in Cunipert's employ observed the entire scene and overheard the promises Rudulfus made to Calibrandus, his rival. "Damn bastard," the spy muttered under his breath, careful not to make a sound. "Deceitful snakes," he added, already savoring the payment Cunipert would give him for this intelligence.

Aquae Sextiae, Late Afternoon

Auctus Tullius Sextus Plato climbed one of the city's watchtowers. While gazing out over the rain-soaked city, he began to compose verses in his mind, delighted with his own creativity. He had seized this brief moment of peace, knowing full well it might end abruptly.

The tower's canopy shielded him from the torrential downpour that had swept through the city. Fortunately, the rain began to ease, and as the clouds parted, a soft amber sun bathed the horizon in fiery hues. When the glowing orb dipped behind the skyline, Plato abandoned his poetry and decided it was time to find something to eat. Hunger gnawed at him, and he knew it was wise to eat well before the uncertainties of the following day.

The commander of the *vexillatio* had already made his decision: they would resume their march at first light.

As Plato descended the tower, he heard someone calling him. Among the townsfolk dodging puddles in the streets, he saw Gallienus Lars Gracchus signaling for him to come over.

"Where have you been?" Gallienus asked.

"Writing verses," Plato replied.

Gallienus shook his head. "You'll end up like that centurion who seems more like a litteratores than a soldier!"

"Do I look like a teacher to you?" Plato shot back.

Gallienus smirked and changed the subject. "I smell something good coming from that place..." He pointed to a tavern marked with a painted sign of a flamingo. "Shall we gorge ourselves and drink some wine before rejoining the ranks? What do you say?" he grinned suggestively.

"I've got a few coins left to spend before I end up skewered on a Heruli spear," Plato agreed, letting Gallienus lead the way.

The tavern keeper greeted them, rubbing his hands together. "I've got fine wine, excellent food, and a few girls who could make the gods themselves dream!" he proclaimed.

The two soldiers exchanged knowing glances and burst into laughter. They had found their sanctuary.

"Looks like you're laughing without me!" came a familiar voice from behind them.

Severinus Majorianus squeezed between them and plopped onto a wooden bench, raising his arm to order wine as well.

The tavern keeper wiped his greasy hands on his apron and called his plump wife, who brought over a pitcher of wine for the trio. Soon, the soldiers were chatting casually, their troubles momentarily forgotten, as if the past days of hardship had never occurred.

"I've got some business to take care of," Gallienus Lars Gracchus announced abruptly, his eyes fixed on a caramel-skinned girl whose Carthaginian heritage was unmistakable.

"You'd better have a sack of coins ready, my friend! She'll cost you plenty to win her favor!" Plato teased.

Realizing his limited funds, Gallienus chose to spend his money on food rather than other indulgences. The trio settled in and feasted.

***

Evetius Aquila, the Batavian, leaned against the wall of a house, his large frame at odds with the bustling crowds around him. Though accustomed to the chaos of battle, he found the crush of people in this city overwhelming.

The loud hawking of merchants grated on his surly nature. He made a half-hearted attempt to approach a baker, but quickly abandoned the effort. That was when he noticed a man with heavily-lined eyes staring at him.

Evetius instinctively reached for his sword as the stranger approached, his unrelenting gaze unsettling. As the man drew nearer, he introduced himself. "I'm Metellus, and I don't charge much."

Evetius didn't understand at first, and took a cautious step back. The stranger didn't appear threatening, but trust didn't come easily to the towering Batavian.

Metellus, unfazed, smirked at Evetius' wariness, made a lewd gesture, and placed a hand on the Batavian's groin. Evetius leaped back instinctively.

Realizing the man's intentions, the colossal soldier quickly retreated into the crowd, eager to escape the awkward encounter.

He let himself be carried to the entrance of a tavern, where he slipped inside.

He had frequented many such establishments in Duro Catalaunum with his fellow legionaries, and within these walls, he felt at ease.

He turned at the sound of someone calling his name. Gallienus Lars Gracchus, Severinus Majorianus, and Tullius Sextus Plato were seated nearby, laughing drunkenly. They waved for him to join them, and he was grateful for the invitation. He decided not to mention what had happened to him.

In the middle of the alley outside, the archer Christianus Caligatus stood motionless. Passersby had to dodge around him to continue on their way. His gaze was fixed straight ahead, but he wasn't looking at anything in particular. He was lost in thought, reflecting on his future.

As a veteran of the Legion, he had come to accept that he would never receive the honesta missio, the retirement payment due to him upon discharge. Lowering his eyes, he stared at the eagle emblazoned on his tunic, the symbol of the legion, and sighed deeply.

Many years had passed since the day when, still a young boy, he had joined the imperial army. He had done so for the meager salary, coming as he did from a family of freedmen who lived in poverty. His days had once been spent fishing for eels with his father, which they sold at the market in Minturnae. But after his father's death, other men had taken control of the eel fishing, leaving him with no choice but to seek another path.

When his skill as an archer became evident, he was noticed by an officer who enlisted him among the slingers and archers of the newly forming Fifth Legion. Much time had passed since that day. Now, as it had back then, the time had come for him to change direction.

Perhaps fate had brought him to this city for a reason. Perhaps it was here he was meant to remain. In that very moment, he decided he would not rejoin his old century. After all, one could not be considered a deserter if there was no longer an army to desert, he reasoned.

And besides, he was tired. Tired of running, of enduring the cold and hunger. A soothing sensation washed over him, as if a new life were beginning—a life that deserved to be lived differently.

Someone bumped into him as they passed by, forcing him to turn.

"Watch where you stop, stranger," the man said.

"I'm no longer a stranger..." he replied, smiling.

Aquae Sextiae, Evening

Aristarchos Themistocles sat beside the governor of Aquae Sextiae, Sulspicius Gracchus. The governor had summoned him to be briefed on the events at Duro Catalaunum. Aristarchos had no choice but to comply.

Still, things hadn't turned out so badly. Seeing the state of the centurion *primae spatha*, the governor had ordered that he be refreshed with a bath and a meal.

During dinner, Sulspicius Gracchus explained why, despite the countryside being all but abandoned and the pastures devoid of livestock, trade in Aquae Sextiae remained so prosperous. The city, he explained, was a crossroads of major routes in southern Gaul.

Despite the devastation brought by the Huns' invasion and the ongoing raids of the Burgundians, the city's economy had rebounded remarkably. But it was a superficial recovery. The merchants' profits rarely ended up in the state's coffers. To avoid taxes, shopkeepers preferred to bribe the tax collectors, ensuring they paid only a fraction of what was due.

Landowners hid much of their harvests, finding it more prudent to pay hefty tributes to the Burgundians to prevent kidnappings of their peasants and raids on their farms. As a result, the city's granaries and other storehouses were nearly empty.

Even many nobles had been forced to cede much of their estates to the Burgundians, leaving them without any source of income.

"You see, my esteemed guest, the future of this city lies in its ability to adapt to diversity. We are living in a period of transition, and until things stabilize, other cities in Gaul would do well to follow suit. Let me give you an example: look at Toulouse, the capital of the Visigoth kingdom. There, Roman nobles now serve a king of Gothic lineage whose domain stretches across western Gaul. The Sacred Augustus pretends that he has 'granted' them permission to live in these lands, but if we examine the facts, what do we see? That the Visigoths defeated many Roman armies sent against them and have taken those lands by conquest. Believe me…"

He looked at Aristarchos with an almost affectionate expression, though it was clearly insincere. "Find a place in this city to spend the rest of your days and leave everything else behind. I can, with considerable effort, hire you and a few of your trusted soldiers to serve in my palace guard. Here in Aquae Sextiae, that's all we can offer you...as soldiers, that is."

From these words, Aristarchos understood that the governor did not trust his closest associates—or even his personal guard.

"I understand your vision of the future. But if you don't organize an adequate defense soon, when Rudulfus reaches your gates, you will suffer the same fate as Duro Catalaunum. You could send messengers to Ravenna and request intervention from the Italian army, and..." the *vexillatio* commander began to suggest.

"Silence, Centurion!" the governor interrupted. "You are in no position to give me advice. I..." he emphasized, pointing to himself, "... take orders only from the Augustus himself."

"I meant no disrespect, governor. I was merely trying to warn you of a fate I consider inevitable."

Sulspicius Gracchus' furious expression softened into a smile, as though nothing had happened. He grinned broadly: "My friend, make good use of what I offer you in my humble home. Do not worry about us. Aquae Sextiae will never be razed to the ground—it's too important for anyone seeking to conquer this land. They would not dare destroy such an unparalleled source of wealth."

As he spoke, Sulspicius Gracchus watched as the servants carried platters into the hall. Swarms of them arrived, bearing roasted boars glazed with honey, pheasants, and hares. The guests applauded, delighted by the sight, and dived eagerly into the dishes, grabbing chunks with both hands.

Aristarchos Themistocles, angered by the governor's demeanor, feigned a calmness that he could barely maintain. He tore at the meat, chewing slowly. Frequently, his gaze wandered to a dancer, twisting sensuously, the jingling bells on her wrists accompanying her movements.

Flute players provided music for the banquet, officially held in honor of the legionaries who had survived the barbarian onslaught. In truth, it was little more than an excuse to gorge themselves and drink to excess.

Ignoring the centurion's warning, the governor already had a woman seated on his lap. He pulled her dress aside, exposing her chest, and began licking her breasts as he cupped them in his hands.

At his signal, a eunuch clapped his hands. From behind wide curtains, about twenty young men and women appeared, dispersing into the hall. The other guests eagerly scrambled to claim their chosen partners.

One of the governor's trusted officers ordered his men to position themselves at the four corners of the hall. No one was to attempt an attack on their master.

A wealthy landowner stopped a young servant carrying a wine amphora, forcing him to set it down. Lifting the boy's tunic and ignoring his frightened protests, he bent him over a table, shoving dishes aside with one hand. He lifted his own robe and began to abuse the boy. Amused by the boy's screams, the man's drunkenness only fueled his cruelty. He poured wine over the boy's head in a final act of contempt, drawing laughter from nearby diners.

Another guest, who had earlier been reciting passages from the writings of the blessed sages, now lay sprawled on a couch with a girl's head bobbing up and down in his lap.

Elsewhere was a decurion who had introduced himself as a scholar and pontificated on philosophy and politics, spending the meal explaining how he would liberate northern Africa, now completely under the control of Genseric's Vandals[23]. According to his absurd

---

[23] *Genseric.* (Balaton, 389 – Carthage, 477) King of the Vandals and Alans, he was one of the key figures during the final tumultuous years of the Western Roman Empire. He led the Vandals, Alans, and a faction of scattered Visigoths from the Iberian Peninsula to North Africa, founding a kingdom that quickly became one of the Mediterranean's dominant powers. In 455, he led the Vandals in the infamous Sack of Rome.

theories, it would have been enough to send an army by sea to annihilate the enemy. However, he conveniently forgot that such an action had already been attempted by Emperor Majorianus, with such disastrous results that no other emperor had dared to try again.

Now, the man sat between two prostitutes, engaged in lewd games.

Centurion Aristarchos looked around, incredulous.

He had expected the governor to investigate Rudulfus' self-proclaimed title of "Governor of Gaul". Instead, all he saw were drunkards and foolish officials feasting and reveling. Many of them had already vomited, only to continue drinking in a futile effort to regain their senses.

A young woman sat on his lap, but he remained unmoved. The image of Placidia flashed through his mind, and a wave of melancholy swept over him, leaving his spirit shattered. With gentle words, he made it clear to the girl that it wasn't the right time for seduction. She left, looking at him with gratitude.

At the start of the first watch, Aristarchos Themistocles, disillusioned by his failure to draw attention to the imminent danger, bid farewell to the governor's residence and returned to the meeting point where the legionaries were waiting for him.

As soon as he left the room, the governor summoned his master of ceremonies.

"That man brings nothing but bad luck. Keep an eye on him until he leaves the city. Go, go!" he ordered with a dismissive wave of his hand. But the man hesitated.

The governor then slipped a silver coin into his hand, which convinced him to follow the centurion.

***

Antoninus Tacitus, the oldest of the centurions, had been waiting for the legionaries at the designated meeting point. He had organized a night watch, ensuring that one soldier would remain on guard while the others rested.

Next to his bivouac was a sack containing dried meat, spelt, freshly baked flatbreads, and dates from Africa. He had stockpiled provisions in preparation for the days ahead. But there was one item he treasured above all else: a small plant in a terracotta pot.

It was a tiny olive tree, barely a sapling. If he survived, he planned to plant it on his property alongside many others, as part of a future far from battles and the ranks of the armies.

Vatinius Auruncus approached him with a friendly slap on the shoulder and a smile. "Has the centurion *primae spatha* shown up yet?" he asked.

"Yes, he's over by that fire," Tacitus replied, pointing to a campfire where their commander was warming himself alone.

"Commander," Auruncus said as he approached.

Aristarchos Themistocles turned to acknowledge him. His helmet and ornate greaves lay at his side.

"Did the governor grasp the situation?" Auruncus asked, smiling bitterly before continuing. "Or is he polishing a helmet with a horsehair crest, thinking he'll never need to use it again?"

The centurion made a resigned expression. "He's probably drunk, fooling around with some wench. And I doubt he's ever fought in a battle in his life. No one listened to me because no one cares about what's happening."

"To hell with them," Auruncus muttered.

"I noticed Christianus Caligatus is missing. Has something happened to him?"

"The men said he told them he wouldn't continue with us."

Aristarchos nodded. "At first light, we'll leave the city. The coast isn't far. We'll reach a port and…" He shrugged, as if to say there was no other option. "…we'll borrow a few ships." His expression made his intent clear.

Auruncus understood immediately. "Understood, Centurion. I'll prepare the men," he said, taking his leave.

As he walked away, he glanced back at the commander, who sat by the crackling fire, wrapped in the deep purple cloak of the legionaries. Auruncus could have sworn his eyes were swollen with tears.

He was likely thinking of Placidia—everyone knew how much he had loved her. Or perhaps it was just the reflection of the firelight playing tricks on him. After all, it would have been the first time anyone had seen him cry. Not even during the great Battle of Arles, in the harshest moments, had Aristarchos ever shown signs of despair.

But perhaps the feelings a man has for a woman can lead even the strongest to this.

Auruncus shook his head, brushing aside those thoughts. After all, this was his commander—a hardened legionary. A dear friend, just like all the others in their strange band of misfits who came from the same region and had bonded during their service in the legion.

Aquae Sextiae, Gaul, Tertia viglilia

The makeshift camp beneath the porticoes was scattered with bodies wrapped in purple cloaks. A fire, tended by Ulzio Dacianus, was about to be handed over to Tullius Sextus Plato, who would take the next watch.

At dawn, after the fourth watch[24], Vatinius Auruncus had the unpleasant task of waking everyone.

Grumbling and curses of protest emerged from every purple cloak. It was time to depart.

Some ate dried meat, while others preferred dried figs. Ialenia Heria drank sheep's milk she had purchased the previous afternoon at the market.

The centurions' orders interrupted the brief moment of peace. The scout was summoned and sent ahead to the city gate to ensure everything was in order.

About half an hour later, the unit set out. They marched along the city's main street, which had been bustling with people the

---

[24] *Quarta vigilia*: between 3:00 AM and 6:00 AM.

previous day. Now, only a few sleepy shopkeepers and their servants were removing shutters from their stalls.

A few torches, still burning, quietly extinguished themselves as daylight began to take over.

Gaius Octavianus awaited them at the gate. The guard detachment did not oppose opening the city gates early, just before sunrise.

The unit of legionaries left the city of Aquae Sextiae, heading for the coast.

The Following Evening, Near the Fortified Village of Venelles

The screams and cries were deafening.

The fire had consumed the entire village by now. Flames spiraled into the sky, twisting on themselves. Every Roman house and every Celtic-style hut was ablaze.

Some Heruli warriors were assaulting a woman, while others dragged several women into more secluded areas to commit the same atrocities.

A group of mercenaries hung a Roman soldier upside down and tore strips of flesh from him with pincers. Two others tossed around the head of another soldier, laughing as if it were a game.

Rudulfus' orders had been explicit: no prisoners and no survivors, except for two or three who would be spared to recount what had happened. Everyone would know what the new Governor of Gaul was capable of. His name would strike fear even in the hearts of the Gothic generals.

As for Odoacer, if he began to fear him, he might finally agree to endorse his title.

The surviving men were herded into a group, awaiting their fate. Some would die quickly, while others would be tortured to death that evening for the amusement of the garrison.

Some mercenaries tried to exploit the chaos, selecting young women from the captives to sell at slave markets. An officer noticed one such mercenary and approached to reprimand him, but the man responded insolently. The officer promptly drew his dagger and sliced off two of the man's fingers as a warning.

In situations like these, controlling warriors drunk on the lust for plunder was difficult, and severe punishment was the only way to maintain order.

General Calibrandus oversaw the execution of the survivors. The severed heads were piled into pyramids at the corners of the village as a warning: anyone who resisted the Heruli would meet the same fate.

The neighboring villages would learn the lesson before it even reached them.

This was how respect was earned, Rudulfus thought as he sat on his horse, watching the scene unfold with a blank expression. Even the smoke, carried by the wind and stinging his eyes, didn't make him flinch.

A farmer tried to crawl behind a barn to hide, but fate was not on his side. He was caught and pierced by the blade of a sword. Nearby, mercenaries held a man as both his feet were cut off. His screams joined the chorus of others—cries of devastation, terror, and agony.

This was Rudulfus' signature.

This was the message he wanted to spread.

Rudulfus turned his horse in another direction; the sight no longer entertained him. At a slow pace, he moved through the streets, satisfied with the outcome.

He was on his way back to camp when two warriors brought him a man with a broken hand, his fingers twisted unnaturally. The man's face was contorted in pain. He clutched his injured arm with his other hand in a futile attempt to ease his suffering.

An officer approached and asked to speak.

"Speak," Rudulfus allowed.

"My king, this man has something to tell you," the officer explained.

Rudulfus looked at the unfortunate man, waiting for his words. The man, whimpering, fell to his knees.

"Most exalted one, I...I saw something, but please, I beg you, don't torture me anymore..."

The officer kicked him, urging him to continue.

"I had my goats with me," the man stammered. "I was leading them to graze not far from the village, and I noticed a thin trail of smoke in the woods. It's unusual for anyone to travel or camp in the forest in these cold times, so I climbed a hill to get a better look."

Another kick from the officer sent the man sprawling onto his side. "Hurry up!" the officer growled.

"Yes...merciful king," the man cried out. "I saw they were imperial soldiers, but not many—only about ten of them." He trembled like a leaf, his eyes fixed on Rudulfus, silently pleading for mercy.

Rudulfus' horse pawed at the ground, snorting impatiently. For a moment, no one spoke. It was clear these were remnants of the Duro Catalaunum garrison. They weren't far.

"What should we do with this one?" the officer finally asked.

The king grimaced in disgust as he turned his gaze to the pitiful man, who whimpered and drooled, mucus dripping from his nose and mouth. Rudulfus tilted his head slightly, continuing to study him.

"You, Roman, what was your trade in this village?" Rudulfus asked.

The man scrambled to answer, seeing in the question a faint glimmer of hope for survival.

"My king, I am a builder. I know how to construct houses and shops—I'm very skilled..."

Rudulfus didn't catch the last words due to his limited knowledge of Latin, but he was satisfied with the response.

"Good, good," he said simply. Then he turned to the officer. "He's a fine reward for you. Sell him as a slave, or keep him as a servant. He'll bring you good profit," he concluded.

The officer began to protest. "But his hand is useless now! I won't get anything for this wretch, my king!" he argued loudly.

Rudulfus didn't even glance at him. He simply turned his horse and began walking slowly toward the camp.

The Romans had left Aquae Sextiae, and were very, very close.

Chapter X – The Honor of Rome

Two Days Later

From the highest hills, the sea was visible. Despite it being the middle of winter, the temperature was pleasant.

In the distance, the city of Massilia[1] could be seen. The port was still active, a sign that it had not been sacked by the barbarians.

From the legionaries' vantage point, they could observe ships docked at the harbor and others preparing to enter the bay: transport triremes, dromons, liburnians with sturdy bronze-reinforced hulls, oil freighters, biremes, and small fishing boats. However, a significant portion of the northern side of the port appeared abandoned.

Numerous hulls were clustered together, seemingly left to decay. Perhaps there were no crews to sail them, or there were no goods left to transport.

Vatinius Auruncus considered the latter hypothesis to be the most likely. Trade must have dwindled to a minimum, given the ongoing fragmentation of the Empire's territories.

At his side, Evetius Aquila, the Batavian, gazed at the breathtaking landscape with an expression bordering on ecstasy.

"You've never seen the sea before, have you?" the young centurion asked.

The enormous Batavian simply shook his head.

---

[1] *Massilia*: modern-day Marseille.

Vatinius' eyes rested on Evetius' scaled armor. It was a mishmash of styles: the body armor typical of Batavian warriors combined with a Roman *cingulum* at his waist, from which hung a fine *pugio* with a hilt shaped like an eagle's head.

"We'll cross it," Vatinius said.

But it was clear that Evetius didn't understand.

Vatinius tried to clarify. "We'll board a ship from there and sail."

"I don't know how to sail!" the Batavian replied in his usual blunt manner.

"You won't have to do anything… the wind will do all the work."

The Batavian gave him a puzzled look, unable to grasp what the wind had to do with it.

"The wind will push the sail—an enormous piece of cloth—and that will move the entire ship. If the wind dies down, we'll use oars."

"Oars?"

"Long wooden poles with widened ends that push the water," Vatinius explained.

The Batavian nodded uncertainly.

This conversation made Vatinius realize that once they reached the port, they would have to hire a crew. He wondered how they would pay for it.

A nudge from the legionary Gallienus Lars Gracchus pulled him out of his thoughts.

"Look over there, Centurion," Gallienus said, pointing to a campsite.

The young commander squinted.

"They're soldiers… Those are bivouacs, and a palisade has been built around them," the *signifer* suggested. "They must be Roman soldiers."

Vatinius nodded. "Yes, they're soldiers. And it seems they've spotted us too. A group of them is heading in our direction."

After a few moments, everyone had seen the camp nestled slightly lower down the hill. Aristarchos Themistocles called the two centurions to him. Together, they moved to meet the approaching soldiers.

The encounter took place a little further down, in the middle of a clearing.

The three waited until the commander of the small detachment of imperial soldiers was only a few meters away. He was an older officer who dismounted from his horse and approached them.

"Where are you coming from?" he asked.

Aristarchos Themistocles observed their garments and armor. They were a regiment of Gallo-Romans, covered in dirt and dried blood—they must have fought recently.

"We are the *vexillationes* of Duro Catalaunum. The north is in the grip of the Heruli. Their king, Rudulfus, commands a powerful army. A large garrison is pursuing us... they're hunting us."

The older officer frowned. "My name is Servius Augustinus. I am the centurion of the Second Cohort of the Army of Gaul. The army is falling apart; regiments have deserted, and now many of the men resort to raiding to survive. What was left of my forces was routed about a month ago by an army of Alans that fought like furies." He shook his head, as if trying to dispel the memory of that battle. Then he continued, "Down there, I have about two hundred men, plus their families. These are soldiers who will go with whoever pays them the most. For now, they prefer to stay together—they know full well that united, they have a better chance of surviving."

Aristarchos glanced toward the camp. He could make out the unmistakable imperial helmets with cheek guards, chainmail loricae, cingula, and the characteristic Roman cloaks.

Their weapons were a mix of long swords instead of the shorter gladii, and their oval shields bore the *chrismon*[2], a sign of Christian devotion.

Seeing other Romans armed for battle gave Aristarchos some reassurance, so he decided not to hide his intentions from their commander.

---

[2] *Chrismon:* a symbol used by Christian emperors, consisting of the Greek letters χ (*chi*) and ρ (*rho*) intersecting one another.

"We need to set sail. All of us are from the Liris Valley, and we're heading home. I'm considering using one of the decommissioned ships in the harbor for the journey. Once we reach the Italian Peninsula, we'll decide what to do next."

Vatinius Auruncus and Antoninus Tacitus nodded vigorously, as if the harder they moved their heads, the sooner they would board a ship.

Servius Augustinus resumed speaking with energy: "I hope you succeed, although I don't see much difference between staying in Gaul and heading to Italy. However, you should know..." he gestured inland, beyond the hills, "that there are soldiers there too. But they're not legionaries. They're Burgundians who had allied with the imperial army. Now they're waiting to be hired. There aren't more than 150 of them as far as I know. We don't trust them, which is why we've set up separate camps," he explained, removing his helmet, which was missing half of its crest—likely sheared off by a sword blow—and scratching his head. "If the Heruli you mentioned show up, we'll gladly join forces with you. Dying with honor, under the banners of Rome, is still a principle many of us hold dear," the older centurion concluded before leaving the meeting.

The two commanders had exchanged all they needed to say.

Servius Augustinus had offered his alliance in the event of a battle, although it seemed he wasn't entirely certain of his control over his men.

Aristarchos Themistocles, on the other hand, had laid his plan bare, signaling their priorities.

It was clear, then, that in the case of an external attack, the two groups would decide their course of action based on the circumstances.

***

Elsewhere, a girl collapsed to the ground, letting out a whimper of pain. One of her eyes was swollen shut and streaming tears, while the other reflected the terror that had consumed her.

Rudulfus, entirely naked, was gripping his manhood in one hand and yelling at her to come closer. The unfortunate girl retreated instead, curling up in the corner of the tent.

With his free hand, the Heruli king grabbed her by the hair and dragged her to the straw mat. He mounted her, but she turned away in disgust.

That final act of defiance sent him into a rage. Consumed by an uncontrollable surge of violence, he began beating her.

Two of her teeth flew from her bloodied mouth.

"You wretched bitch... Don't you understand what you're supposed to do? The same thing you did for that pathetic Roman husband I gutted with my own hands!"

The girl was now little more than a lifeless body, her senses nearly gone.

She was about to lose consciousness, which, in a way, was her salvation. If he killed her, at least she wouldn't be aware of it.

Still panting, his face and chest splattered with blood, Rudulfus called for his servants.

They entered, carefully avoiding eye contact with the king.

"Take her away. Get that Roman whore out of my sight," he ordered, plunging both hands into a basin of water.

"My king..." Calibrandus' monotone voice caught his attention.

A slight nod from Rudulfus signaled permission to speak.

"I have a gift for you," Calibrandus said, bowing slightly while trying to read his commander's mood.

"This is not the time."

"Have I ever chosen the wrong time, most exalted one?" Calibrandus ventured sweetly.

Rudulfus scowled. "What is it?" he asked, pouring himself some mead.

"I paid a farmer two *silique*. He revealed the location of Roman camps."

"Good. Now leave me alone."

Outside the tent, Calibrandus rummaged through the pouch fastened to his belt, just beside his long sword.

He pulled out a gold *tremissis* and placed it in the palm of one of the king's personal guard mercenaries. The man bit the coin to test its authenticity before pocketing it.

The closer spies were to those under scrutiny, the more expensive they became. This was a sacred rule for those like Calibrandus who relied on such slimy services—a rule he had never broken, and one that had brought him immense rewards.

"Alert me to everything he does," Calibrandus instructed.

"Haven't I always served you well, my lord?" the warrior replied slyly as he made the coin disappear.

"Continue to do so!"

***

By the *Hora octava* [3], an unusual calm seemed to hover over the camp.

Some men were napping, while others busied themselves with camp chores.

Gallienus Lars Gracchus, for instance, was sharpening his sword on a whetstone.

Nearby, Ialenia Heria arranged colorful pebbles into strange patterns, only to cover them with dirt.

Many watched her from a distance, wary and fearful of her peculiar divinations.

Drusus Variatus got too close, but she chased him away with a harsh scolding.

Evetius Aquila and Fulcinius Agricola Statius lay stretched out in the sun, warming their limbs after days spent in the grip of the cold.

A gust of wind rustled the leaves of a nearby beech grove, swept through the tall grass, bending its tips, and carried glowing embers from the fire into the air, where they spiraled upward before disappearing.

---

[3] *Hora octava* (eighth hour): approximately from 1:00 PM to 2:00 PM.

The plume on Vatinius Auruncus' helmet swayed gently with the breeze. His helmet was resting on a white rock, one side of which was covered with a dry crust of gray and yellow lichens. He tilted his head back, enjoying the refreshing gust.

The biting cold of Duro Catalaunum felt far behind him now.

After casting one last glance to ensure everything was in order, he stepped away and climbed to the top of a large boulder. Settling himself there, he took slow, deep breaths.

From this vantage point, he gazed out toward the horizon, where the sea shimmered brilliantly, its blinding reflections breaking over a deep, pure blue expanse.

To him, that blue symbolized freedom and salvation.

A profound sense of hope surged within him, filling him with newfound energy.

In the distance, a trireme sailed southward. It had just left the port of Massilia, its sail billowing in the wind.

"What's that savage doing?" Fulcinius Agricola Statius asked Ulzio Dacianus, who was busy skinning a hare he had caught during their march.

Ulzio looked up to see who he was talking about and spotted the massive Batavian, Evetius Aquila, lying shirtless on the damp grass. He was staring at the sky with an ambiguous smile plastered across his face.

"He's as strange as all the Batavians. Trust me on that," Ulzio replied.

"But...it looks like he's laughing," Fulcinius pressed.

"Leave him be. Maybe he's going mad," Ulzio muttered, returning to his work on the hare.

"I'm going to ask him."

"No, you're just looking for trouble, as usual," Ulzio warned, shooting him a glare.

"Look at him! Lying half-naked on wet grass, grinning at the sky. I'm telling you, I need to figure this out," Fulcinius insisted.

"Why don't you just rest, like everyone else?" Ulzio emphasized the last part.

"My friend, you lack curiosity. That's why you'll never be as rich as I will... You're not curious."

"You're not rich, either. You're a soldier, just like me, and soldiers aren't rich."

"I will be, my legionary brother. Soon, I'll be rich!" Fulcinius said with a confident grin.

Ulzio stopped what he was doing and looked at him. "What do you mean by that?"

"When we reach the Italian coast, we'll part ways. Each of us will go their own way, right?"

Ulzio nodded, but added a skeptical grimace.

"I'm going to buy a house and turn it into a shop. I'll become a merchant and swim in gold *tremisses*, my friend!" Fulcinius said, looking at him as if expecting approval.

"But we won't even get the *honesta missio*. Without the end-of-service pay, what are you planning to buy?"

"Well..." Fulcinius leaned in conspiratorially, "...during the march, I noticed something that could be very useful to us. Very, very useful."

"What is it?" Ulzio's interest was now fully piqued.

The two drew closer and lowered their voices. "The commander is carrying something valuable," Fulcinius began, pausing dramatically to build suspense.

"By Jupiter, will you spit it out or not?" Ulzio urged, scratching his stubbled beard.

"The *vexillationes* standard! It's not large, but it's made entirely of gold, wrapped in a rough cloth and tied with a cord. He keeps it hidden beneath his cloak, out of sight," Fulcinius said, raising his eyebrows as though he'd made the discovery of a lifetime.

"And how do you know this?" the veteran asked skeptically.

"I saw it with my own eyes," Fulcinius replied, pointing to his eyes for emphasis.

"But you just said he keeps it hidden under his cloak."

"Centurions have to relieve themselves too, you know! And to do that, they take off their cloaks." Fulcinius burst into laughter.

"Keep it down! Can't you see people are watching us?" Ulzio scolded, now entirely drawn into the conversation.

It was true; their laughter had drawn the attention of others nearby.

"Don't worry, no one will suspect a thing. Aristarchos Themistocles is a cunning bastard," Fulcinius said with a sly grin.

Ulzio's expression darkened. "Either way, this doesn't concern us. We can't steal it, can we? It's still a symbol, even if it no longer has meaning. No..." he shook his head firmly, as if trying to erase a dangerous idea.

"And who said anything about stealing it?" Fulcinius knew exactly how to keep Ulzio engaged. "This is about investing in its value."

"You're making my blood boil with your cryptic talk. Will you just tell me what you're thinking?" Ulzio hissed.

"You've always had a short fuse... You'll never change," Fulcinius chuckled. "What if we sold it and split the proceeds?" he proposed, wearing the face of a seasoned merchant.

"And I'm the one who doesn't keep his cool? The king of fist-fights is standing right in front of me, and he's got some nerve! And anyway, the commander will flay you alive just for thinking about it."

"In a few days, we won't have commanders anymore."

"No, we're not stealing it!" Ulzio said firmly.

"How else am I supposed to buy my shop?" Fulcinius argued.

"That's irrelevant. A shop isn't worth the *vexillatio* standard. We're talking about a symbol—something sacred. And if the commander catches us, he'll have our throats slit."

"You thick-headed fool! If enough of us propose the idea, the commander will have to consider it. We're his men, after all..."

"But you just said we wouldn't have commanders in a few days," Ulzio countered.

Fulcinius paused to think. "Maybe you're right. But mark my words, if he agrees to sell the gold from the standard, you won't get a share. Those who don't sow, don't reap."

Ulzio placed a firm hand on his veteran comrade's shoulder. "Listen to me…" He leaned in just enough to meet his gaze. "If the commander sells the standard, it'll be for a good reason—and I don't think it'll have anything to do with your shop."

"We'll see about that," Fulcinius retorted, stubbornly clinging to his idea.

Ulzio Dacianus brought his hands to his forehead. "I can't believe the thought even crossed your mind."

"Let's play a game of dice—maybe I'll take a few *follis* off you!"

The Heruli Camp, Hora nona

With long strides, Cunipert entered Rudulfus' tent.

When he reached the king, he bowed his head. "My king, the men are ready."

Rudulfus didn't even glance at him. He stared off into the distance, absentmindedly toying with the cup in his hand while using the fingers of his other hand to pluck small chunks of salted dried meat from an empty skull.

"Where are they, exactly?" His voice sliced through the momentary silence, filling it with unease.

"They've nearly reached Massilia. But…" Cunipert quickly added, "…my spies are still tracking them."

The word "spies" wasn't used casually—it was intended to highlight the king's focus on Calibrandus, his rival. Once the business with the Romans was settled, there would remain the task of dividing the prefectures, the collection of tributes, and other spoils. If the balance of power didn't shift, Calibrandus would claim the best cities, while Cunipert would be left with the dregs of the region.

Overwhelmed by these thoughts, he shot a look brimming with resentment at his rival, who pretended to be engrossed in studying a map.

"Keep it up; we'll descend upon them soon," Rudulfus said curtly, distractedly, before stepping down from his throne. He walked past Cunipert as though he didn't exist and stopped beside a cage containing a frightened bear cub.

Using his dagger, he poked at the animal, trying to provoke it. The cub whimpered in pain and curled into the opposite corner of the cage.

"Don't you notice a certain resemblance between this animal and the Romans? Both appear ferocious, yet when properly prodded, they reveal their true nature—weak!"

Everyone in the tent erupted in laughter, including Cunipert, though he shifted uncomfortably as he sensed Calibrandus' acrid gaze fixed on him.

When their eyes met, Cunipert realized Calibrandus was moving toward him with a mocking grin.

Once close, Calibrandus sneered. "So, you have spies now, too? Let's hope you know how to manage them—before they poison your food, or your water, or your wine…or maybe slit your throat while you sleep."

The threat was whispered directly into his ear.

Cunipert's hand instinctively moved to the hilt of his dagger, but Calibrandus noticed and grabbed his wrist.

"Don't even try it! You wouldn't leave this tent alive. Everyone here is on my side. Be more careful," Calibrandus warned before returning to his place.

Shaken by the threat, Cunipert noticed that two of the king's elite guards had already readied themselves to take him down. No longer the favorite of Rudulfus, Cunipert decided it was wiser to stay still. He clenched his fists, suppressing his rage.

Roman Camp, Hora decima

Everyone waited for nightfall to descend into the city and head toward the port.

As the sun set, the fire was stoked to ward off the evening chill. Massilia dimmed as lamps and torches were extinguished, and during the transition from light to darkness, campfires began to flicker across the valley and surrounding hills like stars scattered on the ground.

These were not stars, but refugees, merchant caravans, mercenaries awaiting employment, and fragments of garrisons that had survived battles of unknown origin.

The centurion *primae spatha* sat on a milestone, staring at the lights of the encampment belonging to the survivors of the Second Gallic Cohort.

He pondered Servius Augustinus' words: "I have about two hundred men, plus the families of the legionaries."

He couldn't help but think of numbers.

His own forces were small, but if combined with Servius' soldiers, they could form a solid defensive line against Rudulfus' pursuing army.

His extensive experience from numerous military campaigns told him that the Heruli king could not afford to send more than a thousand warriors in pursuit. Given the times, sustaining a larger force would be impossible.

Moreover, being a pursuit force, Rudulfus' army would need to move quickly, and would have little time to gather provisions.

The centurion made another observation: the broad hills would favor the maneuverability of Roman maniples and their disciplined testudo formations, to the disadvantage of Rudulfus' disorganized horde, which lacked structure or cohesion.

He admitted to himself that Rudulfus had become an obsession, his sole purpose reduced to avenging Placidia's death.

A cold gust of wind broke his train of thought, reminding him that it was time to rest for a few hours. At dawn, they would reach the city and decide their next move.

"Commander…"

Someone had decided not to let him close his eyes.

"I don't mean to disturb you, but…" Vatinius Auruncus began apologetically.

Aristarchos Themistocles sat up. "You've already disturbed me, Centurion, so you might as well continue…" he replied wryly.

"What are we going to do once we reach Massilia?" Vatinius asked, his expression a mix of impatience and apprehension.

Lowering his eyes, Aristarchos allowed himself a moment to think. "I'm considering storming the port," he said.

Vatinius' mouth fell open, though no sound escaped.

The commander continued. "We'll seize a ship and set sail."

Something didn't sit right. It sounded too simplistic for a man like Aristarchos, who was known for carefully calculated actions.

"What's troubling you about the concept of 'storming the port'?" Aristarchos teased, noticing Vatinius' hesitation.

"We'll need food, water, and someone who knows how to navigate. Stealing a dromon won't be enough. Not to mention the city's militia—we'd have to deal with them, too. Perhaps you've underestimated the challenge, commander," the young centurion replied sharply.

Aristarchos laughed as though he had anticipated this response. "Then we'll buy provisions at the first port we stop at. As for the crew…we'll abduct them."

"Commander…" Vatinius stiffened.

"What?"

"You already have a plan, don't you? You're just keeping it to yourself."

"That's a possibility."

"Well, may your balls fall off, then," Vatinius muttered as he left.

"Thank you—and may yours as well," Aristarchos quipped with a grin.

With the exchange over, Aristarchos Themistocles lay back down on the makeshift bed of leaves and branches he had prepared earlier.

The fire burned brightly, sending sparks and acrid smoke into the air from the damp wood.

He clutched a bundle wrapped in rough cloth and tied with a strap.

A thunderous burst of collective laughter startled him awake.

He had just managed to drift off to sleep.

The source of the uproar was Fulcinius Agricola Statius, who was enthusiastically backing up Drusus Variatus as he recounted the tale of an old battle.

Caught up in the fervor of his memories, Fulcinius leapt to his feet, shouting in his characteristic manner: "I killed dozens of those Goths, but they just kept coming. Believe me, there were thousands of them! It was no walk in the park..." His gaze grew distant as he stared into the roaring flames.

At that moment, Centurion Antoninus Tacitus interjected, eager to add his own embellishment. "At one point, I found myself facing at least..." he counted on his fingers, "five of them all on my own. They were all taller than me, wielding double-headed axes and swords far longer than my gladius, and..."

"They had everything longer!" Severinus Majorianus, the optio, interrupted, triggering a fresh wave of laughter from the group.

His suggestive remark was accompanied by an exaggerated gesture that made the men laugh even harder.

Aristarchos Themistocles cursed under his breath.

Gaius Octavianus, in turn, decided to add to the mischief by shifting the milestone that the optio was sitting on. When Severinus dropped back into his seat, he tumbled over, landing flat on his back and prompting even louder laughter and jests.

In the fire, a chunk of wood began to crackle, sending flames spiraling upward and releasing a flurry of sparks that vanished into the darkness.

Chapter XI – The Dream

The white ox with long horns was slaughtered right in front of her.

Yet, the blood hesitated to flow from the gaping wound.

The priest who performed the sacrifice chanted somber litanies, his hands and gaze lifted toward the sky.

Still, the blood would not pour.

A woman swung a bronze censer, releasing its acrid fragrance into the air.

But the cut remained dry.

Only after repeated invocations and prayers did the awaited blood of the enormous beast begin to drip, first in slow, hesitant drops, then in a sudden rush of torrents, saturating the ground below.

A raven landed in the crimson pool, dipping its talons into the blood. It approached the dying beast and began pecking at one of its eyes. It continued until the eye was reduced to pulp and ripped it from the socket, flying away with its grotesque prize.

"Ialenia Heria, wake up! Wake up, Ialenia Heria, you're dreaming! Wake up!" Gaius Octavianus shook her firmly, gripping her shoulders.

The woman propped herself up on her elbows, her forehead beaded with sweat, her breaths ragged and shallow.

Her face bore the unmistakable mark of deep agitation.

Once fully awake, she reflected on the nightmare she had just experienced: the blood that wouldn't flow and the raven feasting on the ox's eye.

It was an ill omen—there was no doubt.

She jumped to her feet, hastily gathering her few belongings into a canvas sack.

Moments later, she approached Aristarchos Themistocles.

She knew there was no time to waste. Something dreadful was about to happen—she could feel it. The dream had revealed it to her.

The gods of the forest had sent her a warning, and she was determined to heed it.

Shaking the commander vigorously, she roused him from his slumber.

It was clear now: fate had decided not to let him sleep that night.

"Commander, please, wake up!" the druid pleaded.

"What's all the yelling about, witch?" Aristarchos Themistocles asked, glaring at her with irritation for the abrupt wake-up. "Stop shouting, or you'll wake everyone," he warned, pointing a finger at her.

The woman took a deep breath, trying to calm herself before explaining.

"I had a dream..." she began. Seeing the commander's skeptical expression, she quickly added, "It was a terrible omen. We need to move quickly...to leave this place without delay. Give the order, Centurion. The others will follow you."

Aristarchos Themistocles seemed to ponder her words.

He was not one to believe in prophecies, and he didn't intend to start now.

And yet, something about her unease troubled him.

"What did the dream reveal?" he asked, finally indulging her.

She shook her head vigorously. "I don't know. I don't know exactly what it foretold, but I can feel it—something is about to happen. Something terrible. Do you understand me now?"

"I can't very well prepare everyone for battle based on a bad dream, can I?" he asked, carefully avoiding offensive words. With surprising control of his tone, he added, "Very well, witch... Go back to sleep now."

He turned to return to his makeshift bed, but Ialenia Heria stopped him.

"Commander, you must..." Her voice trembled on the last word. "You must believe me. We need to leave this place—now!" She lowered her gaze as though haunted by a terrible vision she couldn't bear to see.

"Well then?"

"I see blood...a lot of blood. It could be Roman blood—in fact, I'm certain it is. We need to flee before it's too late."

"I told you to go back to sleep," he said. "And try to dream something pleasant this time," he added, dismissing her.

Plato, who was curled up in his cloak just a few steps from their discussion, chuckled at the centurion's quip.

Ialenia Heria tried to protest, but the centurion *primae spatha* had already gone back to bed.

"You have no idea what a terrible mistake you're making," the woman whispered. "And I'm not a witch—how many times do I have to tell you that?"

Aristarchos Themistocles, however, couldn't fall asleep.

He felt restless all the same.

***

The first light of dawn began to brighten the horizon. The surrounding landscape was bathed in shades of violet, which gradually gave way to a soft, pale blue.

Then, an explosion of red spread across the scene, racing quickly toward Massilia, which shimmered in the reflection of the rising light.

One by one, the city's districts were bathed in a reddish glow.

The breaking day made the activity in the port clearly visible. Though the day had barely begun, the harbor was already bustling with energy.

A bireme had just departed, followed closely by a dromon. Both were moving slowly, their oars cutting through the water, as their sails had yet to be unfurled. Behind them, a white trail began to mark the deep blue of the sea, which looked like an endless expanse—a surface so smooth it seemed as though one could slide across it.

Severinus Majorianus began shouting to wake the troops.

The fire had nearly died out, and a thin line of smoke rose skyward, swirling gently with every puff of the morning breeze.

The soldiers, still groggy, gathered their meager belongings into their packs.

Once the unit was ready to march, the centurion *primae spatha* positioned himself at the front and gave the order to move out.

Within less than an hour, after cresting the first hill, the soldiers' attention was seized by shouts and the clash of metal.

The Burgundians, who had camped at the edge of the forest, were under attack by Rudulfus' Heruli vanguard.

They must have marched without pause to catch up to them so quickly, Aristarchos Themistocles observed, his thoughts immediately turning to the druid woman's ominous premonition.

"They've caught up to us! Run for the city—the gates are already open!" Gaius Octavianus shouted.

"Let's move it!" echoed another voice from the rear.

Murmurs of protest rippled through the column.

Antoninus Tacitus and Vatinius Auruncus joined the commander, cursing the cruel fate that had turned against them when salvation was within reach.

From the tree line at the forest's edge, more and more warriors emerged, howling as they brandished their weapons.

They thirsted for blood, and there was no doubt which they preferred: Roman blood.

The Burgundian contingent, taken by surprise, was on the verge of annihilation despite hastily assembling a defense.

The Heruli vastly outnumbered them.

Executions of the survivors had already begun—a gruesome practice.

A Burgundian had been tied to two horses, which were sent galloping in opposite directions, ripping the unfortunate man apart. His agonized screams could be heard even from their position.

It was a massacre.

"Look there, commander," Antoninus Tacitus pointed toward the Gallic cohort's encampment.

They were organizing for battle.

The centurion Servius Augustinus could be seen walking along the ranks, his hands clasped behind his back, speaking to the soldiers as they formed into maniples.

When the formation was complete, the small rectangles of men ready for combat were clearly visible.

"They won't give up without a fight, huh?" Gallienus Lars Gracchus muttered to Drusus Variatus while holding the century's standard high. Variatus nodded in agreement.

From the forest, more Heruli warriors poured out, amassing for an assault on the Gallic cohort.

Centurion Servius Augustinus donned his crested helmet, its plume running horizontally across the top.

Despite being vastly outnumbered, they were ready to fight.

At one point, among the barbarians roaring in victory over the defeated Burgundian regiment, a path opened in their ranks.

King Rudulfus emerged, mounted on an enormous, restless warhorse.

His personal guard carried the banners of Gaul, flaunting them for all to see—symbolizing not only his title as King of the Heruli, but also his self-declared position as governor of this part of the Empire. The second-highest rank in the Empire, second only to the wearer of the Sacred Purple.

"He dares to display imperial banners while attacking Roman soldiers. That vile bastard deserves to be struck down by the Almighty," Aristarchos Themistocles growled to himself as he spotted them.

His gaze locked onto the Heruli king, and he was convinced Rudulfus was staring back at him.

"Fool," the young centurion whispered under his breath.

How proud that barbaric savage must feel to have caught up with the column he had been pursuing, Aristarchos thought bitterly.

Meanwhile, dozens more Heruli mercenaries spilled out from the forest.

"We're wasting too much time! We need to get out of here!" Fulcinius Agricola Statius shouted as he broke formation.

Turning to face the commander, he yelled angrily, "What are we waiting for? For them to tear us apart? Massilia is so close—we can still make it if we move now! Commander..." He gritted his teeth. "Rome no longer exists. They..." he pointed toward the Gallic cohort, "those men are doomed. They're fighting for an honor that no longer exists."

Aristarchos Themistocles stared at him.

He was a bastard, but, the commander had to admit, he wasn't entirely wrong.

Still, Aristarchos couldn't ignore the reality that even if they combined their forces with the Gallic cohort, they would remain outnumbered against the enemy.

He took a moment to consider.

Abandoning the Gallic cohort to be massacred without offering any help weighed heavily on him.

Antoninus Tacitus and Vatinius Auruncus, on the other hand, were seething with rage. Their desire to strike at the Heruli burned far stronger than any fear they might have felt.

***

Rudulfus stared intently at the column of Romans. He was eager to crush them.

Calibrandus approached to inform him that the Visigoth auxiliaries, who had been marching in the rear, had now joined the main army. The force was finally complete.

"Where did you find the Visigoths?" Rudulfus asked.

"I have friends in Toulouse, near the royal court. I promised them a hefty reward," the general revealed.

"I'm always impressed by your resourcefulness. However, I'd advise you to only pay their officers. That way, you'll save my money while still ensuring their loyalty," the king suggested.

"As you wish, my king."

Rudulfus barely managed to keep his restless horse still, as it snorted and pawed at the ground with its front hoof.

Calibrandus stepped forward to update the king on the Gallic cohort, which was positioned in battle formation, ready to resist the assault.

"They're nothing but frightened Gallo-Romans. Soldiers in retreat, nothing more. They even have their families in tow. They'll scatter like deer the moment they're overwhelmed," he declared with a sneer.

Rudulfus listened to his words, then burst into laughter. "Give the general order. Send in the vanguard and annihilate that band of desperate fools."

Calibrandus tugged at his reins and galloped off on a sturdy brown horse with short legs. He relayed the king's orders to the vanguard officers.

The barbarian horde began their advance toward the Second Gallic Cohort.

Centurion Servius Augustinus stood motionless before his ranks.

They were ready for the fight.

***

Aristarchos Themistocles had little time to decide.

They were so close to safety, yet something within him compelled him to rush to the aid of the Second Gallic Cohort.

The shouts of the Heruli mercenaries, rallying for battle, broke his concentration.

This was no longer about the honor of Rome or respect for an empire that had crumbled into pieces. It was about a sense of belonging—a visceral pull that twisted his gut when he saw fellow legionaries in trouble.

No, Rudulfus would not massacre those soldiers without consequence.

He had made up his mind.

Climbing onto a rock, he called for the attention of his legionaries.

In the distance, the war cries of the Heruli vanguard, charging the Gallic cohort, grew louder and more distinct.

"Legionary brothers. Free men. We are but a step away from safety, and you can see it for yourselves. However, I ask you for one final sacrifice."

The centurion *primae spatha* held his crested helmet under one arm, pausing to underscore the gravity of the moment.

Gallienus Lars Gracchus, the *signifer*, understood the significance of those words, and raised the standard of the Third Century as high as he could.

"I know the barbarians are many, but if we can reach the Second Gallic Cohort and join forces, we'll have a better chance of retreating safely to Massilia. Within those walls, we'll be secure. The Heruli don't have the numbers to launch an assault on the city walls, nor do they have siege engines with them."

He paused again, giving his words time to sink in.

"Let's strike these barbarians and lend a hand to those brave soldiers of Rome!"

Finishing his speech, Aristarchos descended from the rock and donned his helmet. He fastened it tightly under his chin and began marching forward.

For a moment, no one moved.

They were so close to salvation, yet they were turning their backs on fortune to face death.

Then Aristarchos marched alone for about a hundred meters before the others began to follow.

"Well, at least we'll hit them hard," quipped Gaius Octavianus.

The hobnails of their sandals struck the ground in unison—they were once again heading into battle.

From a distance, Centurion Servius Augustinus saw the Roman column advancing and realized they wouldn't face the Heruli alone. He was relieved.

Even Rudulfus noticed the maneuver.

To counter the move, he ordered the auxiliaries to attack the column of legionaries and crush them.

Five hundred Visigoth cataphracts[1], armed with javelins and mounted on their warhorses, charged.

The thunder of hooves shook the ground.

Aristarchos Themistocles felt the earth tremble beneath his feet. The charge of the Visigoth cataphracts was terrifying. They fanned out into a wedge formation and bore down on his men.

He halted the column and shouted, "Centurions, to me!"

The two officers joined him.

"Form a testudo! Have them kneel under their shields!" he commanded.

The centurions relayed the orders. The legionaries knelt under their shields and held their positions, bracing for the attack.

As the cataphracts came within range, they began hurling javelins while continuing their charge.

The sound of the spears striking the shields was demoralizing. In mere moments, the cavalry would overrun them.

From their position, it was hard to grasp the full extent of what was happening.

The hail of javelins was relentless.

The Visigoth cataphracts grabbed javelins from their quivers and hurled them nonstop. The Roman soldiers tightened their shields as much as possible to prevent any sharp points from slipping through the gaps.

Aristarchos Themistocles watched the enemy advance through a small gap in the shields. They were dangerously close—nearly upon them.

"Hold... hold... wait for my command..."

He waited a few heartbeats longer before initiating the counterattack.

---

[1] *Cataphract:* A cavalry soldier equipped with armor made of overlapping metal scales.

When the enemy cavalry reached the kneeling formation, they were caught off guard.

With the legionaries crouched and shielded, the javelins were ineffective at close range.

The horses, now in full gallop, had no choice but to veer around the low testudo formation, as their riders received no clear orders.

The cataphracts hesitated, unsure of how to act, their long swords held at the ready.

Aristarchos seized the moment of confusion and shouted, "Attack! Attack them now!"

The legionaries sprang to their feet and engaged the cataphracts in close combat.

They dragged the riders from their mounts and impaled them.

Within minutes of fierce fighting, the enemy was halved in number and still lacked any coherent strategy.

The Romans had closed in on the remaining cataphracts, leaving them no room to maneuver their horses.

One officer found a gap between the Romans and spurred his horse to flee.

When the other cataphracts noticed his cowardice, their morale crumbled further. They began to drop their weapons and attempted to flee.

The Romans raised their swords in triumph as they finished off the remaining enemies.

Rudulfus was consumed with rage. He donned his battle helmet, ready to deliver the decisive blow to the small band of legionaries that had caused him so much trouble.

He was more restless than his own horse, which snorted and pawed the ground.

The auxiliary militias had been annihilated within minutes, and they had constituted a significant portion of his forces.

The clash of metal and the cries of battle drew his attention.

His vanguard had engaged with the Second Gallic Cohort, and a ferocious fight had erupted.

"Good, now we're in the thick of it," he growled, raising his double-headed axe.

"Advance!"

The Heruli ranks began their descent toward the Second Gallic Cohort, a tidal wave of warriors ready to crash down upon the thin Roman formations.

Calibrandus, commanding a regiment, advanced more cautiously than the others, attempting an encircling maneuver.

He acted on his own initiative, confident in the favor he currently enjoyed. If successful, he would only receive praise.

Meanwhile, Cunipert's men charged recklessly down the hill, eager to overwhelm the enemy.

Cunipert gripped his reins tightly, digging his heels into his horse's flanks to spur it forward. From atop his mount, he shouted promises of rewards and glory to his troops.

Occasionally, he glanced at the opposite flank to observe the movements of his rival general, noting Calibrandus' measured advance.

"That coward is dragging his feet—too afraid to clash swords with the Romans. I hope that idiot Rudulfus notices..." he muttered to himself, satisfied by what he assumed to be his rival's cowardice.

The king's magnificent armor gleamed in the sunlight as he galloped ahead, sword pointed at the hated Romans.

Behind him, his cataphracts and infantry thundered forward, their war cries echoing through the valley.

Through the ornate golden engravings of his helmet, Rudulfus' eyes spotted Calibrandus' maneuver. "Good, you clever bastard! Surround them and crush them!" he said, pleased.

The massive horde descending upon the Gallic cohort was a terrifying sight, even for a seasoned centurion like Servius Augustinus.

His front line had already clashed with the enemy vanguard, holding its ground surprisingly well.

However, the sheer number of enemies soon began to tilt the scales in their favor.

Things were taking a grim turn.

The *vexillatio* from Duro Catalaunum was still too far away, and, to make matters worse, they had been attacked by the Visigothic cataphracts.

If the forces didn't unite soon, they would all be slaughtered.

Aristarchos Themistocles pulled his sword from the chest of a Visigoth, taking a moment to regain his bearings.

Thanks to his strategy of kneeling under the shields, his men had routed the attackers.

The few surviving auxiliary cataphracts were now fleeing, and the legionaries celebrated their victory.

Covered in blood, dirt, and sweat, the centurion *primae spatha* wiped his face with the back of his hand.

He reassembled his unit and jogged toward the embattled Gallic cohort.

Vatinius Auruncus and Antoninus Tacitus panted with exertion, exchanging glances of satisfaction mixed with worry.

They were charging headlong into Rudulfus' army, which vastly outnumbered them.

They were only about a hundred meters away from the raging battle now.

As they approached, the clash of metal and the shouts of combatants grew deafening.

Servius Augustinus had expertly positioned his centuries, which held their ground against the barbarian onslaught.

But it was clear that the overwhelming number of enemies would soon envelop the Roman formation in a pincer maneuver.

What the approaching Romans saw was horrifying.

The Second Gallic Cohort was surrounded by Heruli, who relentlessly tried to break their ranks.

Many legionaries fell, but their comrades immediately filled the gaps, maintaining the formation.

Vatinius Auruncus reflected on the value of ancient Roman combat techniques.

The old testudo formation, preserved despite the misguided reforms of emperors who lacked military knowledge, was proving its effectiveness once again before his very eyes.

His thoughts were interrupted by the commander's voice.

"Centurions, to me!" Aristarchos shouted.

The centurion *primae spatha* summoned his officers.

They needed to come up with a plan as swiftly and decisively as an eagle swooping down on its prey.

The eagle of Rome was preparing to strike its final prey.

Aristarchos first turned to Antoninus Tacitus.

"They're encircling the centuries, so we'll hit them from behind."

"Understood, Centurion!" Tacitus replied.

Next, Aristarchos addressed Vatinius Auruncus: "Reach the centuries, take command of one, and advance on the left flank. Our maneuver will draw at least a hundred of the enemy toward you. Your task is to hold them off and slaughter as many as you can."

"With pleasure," Auruncus grinned.

Aristarchos fixed his gaze on both officers, ensuring they understood.

"At my signal, we charge."

"Honor of Rome!" Vatinius Auruncus roared.

"Honor of Rome!" Antoninus Tacitus echoed.

Both returned to their positions, shields raised as they ran.

When Aristarchos raised his gladius high in the air and then brought it down, the legionaries surged forward with a battle cry.

The wedge formation was designed so that the flanks were shielded while the tip pierced deep into the enemy's ranks.

Like the tip of a spear, the Roman formation drove into the thick barbarian horde, cutting them down and throwing them into disarray.

Without clear orders, the Heruli were forced to fight on two fronts, but their lack of coordination quickly proved their downfall.

Vatinius Auruncus slipped between two Roman shields and reached Servius Augustinus.

"Give me a century!" he demanded.

"I'll be halving my force if I do..." protested the senior centurion.

"You have to trust me if we want to survive!" Vatinius shouted.

Reluctantly, Servius Augustinus nodded, though his conviction was weak.

This was no time to waste on hesitation—the battle raged on, and the surprise attack's effectiveness would not last much longer.

Vatinius raised his gladius and positioned himself behind the first rank.

"Form a square!" he bellowed, his voice carrying over the chaos.

For a moment, the soldiers hesitated, unsure of what to do.

Then, recognizing his transverse crest and the distinctive armor of an officer, they obeyed.

A moment later, a square formation of shields broke away from the main line.

The warriors, driven back by the manipular force from Duro Catalaunum, retreated to the left and crashed directly into the shield wall of the century now commanded by Vatinius Auruncus.

Caught between two fronts and leaderless, the Heruli began to fall beneath the Romans' blows.

Swords darted out through gaps in the shields, striking down enemy after enemy.

It was a devastating defeat for the Heruli, both in casualties and morale. The Romans were decimating them.

Standing upright in his saddle, Rudulfus observed the chaos and realized that Cunipert's men were taking the brunt of the Roman assault.

Unable to anticipate the clever Roman tactics, Cunipert had failed—and that enraged the Heruli king.

Shouting at the top of his lungs, Rudulfus roared, "Reform the ranks!" But amidst the deafening din of battle, his messengers couldn't hear him.

Then it happened.

For an instant, which to both men seemed to stretch into eternity, their eyes met.

Rudulfus' icy blue eyes locked onto the brown, defiant gaze of Aristarchos Themistocles.

The mutual hatred between them was palpable, almost tangible in the air, and tasted like iron.

Aristarchos Themistocles broke through to the ranks of the Gallic cohort and reached its commander.

Servius Augustinus was a bundle of nerves—his face taut, dripping with sweat and blood.

"Hail, Centurion!" Aristarchos called, his voice rising above the cacophony of battle.

"Well met," replied Augustinus. "But we won't hold against the cavalry—they're charging straight for us."

"We've stopped their encirclement. Now we need to fall back and blunt the momentum of the Heruli charge," Aristarchos explained, his expression making it clear they had little time to act.

But before they could organize, the Heruli cavalry smashed into them, shattering the Roman formation.

Aristarchos Themistocles was thrown to the ground, narrowly avoiding being trampled by a horse.

Nearby, a Roman soldier collapsed, half of his face missing.

All around him, the battle devolved into chaotic, individual skirmishes. The formation was broken—each man now fought for his own survival.

Through the fray, Aristarchos spotted Rudulfus dismounting from his horse.

The Heruli king, wielding his double-headed axe, pointed it toward the Roman and growled, "Roman, prepare to be ripped apart!"

Aristarchos rose to his feet, adjusted his helmet with both hands, and charged at his adversary.

He had longed for this moment so much that he feared it might be a dream he'd suddenly awaken from.

For a moment, the battle around them seemed to freeze.

The remaining Heruli cataphracts—the king's personal guard—

ceased fighting and regrouped. There were only six of them left, two visibly wounded.

The impending duel between Rudulfus and Aristarchos captured the attention of those nearby.

This was the decisive clash.

Rudulfus discarded his shield, gripping his axe with both hands. His sword remained strapped to his back.

Aristarchos, not to be outdone, also cast aside his shield to level the playing field. However, he picked up a second sword from the ground to better counter his opponent's weapon.

For a few tense moments, the two combatants studied each other, their eyes locked, anticipating the other's first move.

Rudulfus was almost twice the size of Aristarchos—a mountain of muscle.

His braided hair, tied with colored ribbons, spilled out from under his ornate helmet.

His icy blue eyes were as cold and emotionless as his expression.

His armor was a masterpiece, crafted by expert artisans from bronze and adorned with golden plaques, likely commemorating past victories.

Aristarchos, by contrast, wore a dented lorica. One of the lion heads once affixed to his shoulders had been lost during earlier skirmishes. His tunic was tattered, and his cloak torn. He bore little resemblance to the noble Roman officer he had once been.

Rudulfus spoke in surprisingly fluent Latin: "Roman, I must admit, you have a talent for causing trouble."

Then, like a beast, he attacked without waiting for a response.

For a time, the only sounds were the clash of metal and the labored breaths of the fighters.

Onlookers, cheering for their respective champions, watched a spectacle of equal skill and exceptional ferocity.

It was a surreal scene—a gladiatorial duel amidst a raging battle.

The fight was relentless, each man parrying the other's strikes and launching counters with techniques honed over years of campaigning.

For Aristarchos, the challenge was compounded by the length of Rudulfus' axe, which allowed the Heruli king to strike from a distance, exposing the Roman's flesh to danger.

Only by crossing his two swords was Aristarchos able to block a downward strike that would have split his skull like firewood.

The exchange of blows was unending.

The Roman officer could feel his heart pounding in his temples, his short hair soaked with perspiration.

Rudulfus was a fearsome opponent, Aristarchos thought.

For his part, Rudulfus was blinded by rage.

The man before him had caused him so much grief, and he relished the thought of ending him.

The expression on his face revealed a man accustomed to combat—showing no fear, only a sadistic pleasure in war.

"Roman, are you already tired? Taking after your emperor, who plays with eunuchs and turkeys?" Rudulfus jeered.

Aristarchos, ironically, couldn't disagree with the insult. He truly was exhausted.

A faint smile crept across his face before he retorted: "I'll have to find your mother and make sure she never spawns another mangy dog like you."

He broke into laughter, though it quickly turned into a cough from the strain of battle.

Rudulfus was eager to finish him.

Dark clouds rolled in overhead, and a distant thunderclap shattered the unnatural stillness between them.

Rain began to fall as the two resumed their fight.

Rudulfus delivered a crushing blow, forcing Aristarchos to block with both swords, though the impact sent pain shooting through his forearm.

Aristarchos countered with a thrust at Rudulfus' side, but the king's armor absorbed the blow.

The rhythm of combat demanded a swift follow-up, and Rudulfus swung his axe down again. Aristarchos barely dodged it, only to be knocked backward by a powerful kick to his chest.

One moment he was fighting; the next, he was flat on his back, one sword lost.

Rudulfus was proving himself worthy of his fearsome reputation.

Another blow from Rudulfus forced Aristarchos to roll away just in time to see the axe embed itself in the ground.

Then, everything went black.

Rudulfus had landed a vicious kick to his face, rendering him unconscious.

Now, the Roman centurion lay defenseless before his most formidable enemy.

It was an opportunity Rudulfus wouldn't waste.

The axe tore through Aristarchos' armor, sinking into his chest.

The Roman arched his back and opened his mouth in silent agony.

With a mud-caked hand, he reached for his fallen sword and made a desperate attempt to strike, but Rudulfus coldly kicked him again, sending him sprawling.

The first to notice what was happening was Ulzio Dacianus.

He let out a cry so anguished that it drew the attention of everyone fighting nearby.

A cry of victory rose from the Herul ranks as Rudulfus' axe fell once again on the chest of Aristarchos Themistocles, whose body ceased to move. Antoninus Tacitus finished off an opponent by impaling him, swiftly withdrew his sword, and dashed toward the commander.

He saw him lying on the ground, motionless. Rudulfus knelt down and began removing the helmet from Aristarchos Themistocles' head—a Roman commander's ultimate humiliation in defeat. Arrogantly, Rudulfus lifted the helmet high, showing it to all. He had vanquished the Roman leader and wanted everyone to see.

It was a moment not to succumb to emotion. Protected by the shields of the century he now commanded, Vatinius Auruncus swallowed the bitter pill of their loss. The death of their commander was the most demoralizing blow to the Roman soldiers.

He had to restrain the urge to rush at Rudulfus and gut him on the spot. Instead, he focused on staying clear-headed—exactly what the situation demanded.

Some legionaries had become isolated from the formation and were battling multiple enemies. Vatinius witnessed the martyrdom of a soldier struck by two spears, which were now cutting his throat. Only reason kept him from ordering an advance. He couldn't act rashly. His priority was to keep the formation intact and move deliberately.

Ulzio Dacianus had dropped his shield and was trying to reach the body of Aristarchos Themistocles, but enemies swarmed him, forcing him to fight his way forward. He met the Herul warriors head-on, slicing with his sword and delivering killing blows with his dagger.

Vatinius Auruncus parried the strike of a mercenary with his shield and drove his sword through the man's neck, thrusting it between the gaps in the enemy's shields. Beside him, a legionary fell to a blade, his helmet's shattered fragments scattering across the ground.

Fulcinius Agricola Statius and Gaius Octavianus fought back-to-back, facing more opponents than they could handle, yet responding to each attack with vigor. Gaius Octavianus had lost his helmet to a blow that narrowly missed decapitating him. He was now defending himself from a barbarian wielding an axe that had nearly splintered his shield. After a few more strikes, the shield shattered completely. Grabbing a javelin, Octavianus thrust it into his attacker's abdomen, piercing through chainmail and flesh alike.

"Come at me, cowards! Hurry to meet your sacrilegious gods—I'll send you there myself!" he snarled.

Fulcinius Agricola Statius wrestled with two Herul warriors. They rolled in the mud, clawing and striking each other with whatever they could grasp, even stones. Though his forearm was gashed, the adrenaline of battle dulled the pain. He pummeled one mercenary unconscious, breaking several fingers in the process, but refused to relent. He retrieved his gladius from the mud and ran it through the second warrior, who had managed to grab a large hammer.

Drusus Variatus, Auctus Tullius Plato, and Centurion Antoninus Tacitus held their shields tightly together, advancing step by step and fending off enemy attacks. They were desperately trying to rejoin Vatinius Auruncus' century.

"Get back in line! Move it!" shouted the young centurion.

Quintus Faustus Esquilinus, a Gallo-Roman legionary who had rejoined the *vexillationes* of Duro Catalaunum after fleeing through the forest, was overrun by enemies. One grabbed him by the neck while another drove a spear into his abdomen. His intestines spilled onto his legs in a grotesque display of agony, leaving him no chance to survive.

The Herul assaults were losing intensity as fatigue from the battle began to weigh on them. Still, the Roman legionaries struggled to maintain their formation and repel the pressure. A retreat had to be initiated immediately, or it would be too late.

Vatinius Auruncus summoned Severinus Majorianus. "Listen to me—take a handful of men and regroup those in the Gallic cohort. They're falling apart," he ordered. The optio darted off immediately, gathering ten soldiers for the recovery effort. He ducked as a javelin flew at his head, narrowly missing him.

Meanwhile, Ialenia Heria's arrows rained down on the advancing enemies, keeping them at bay. Her deadly accuracy caused bodies to collapse to their knees or tumble backward, pierced by the relentless projectiles. When the soldiers returned to the ranks of the II Gallic Cohort, Rudulfus realized his warriors were struggling to break through the Roman shields.

But Rudulfus still had most of his cavalry. The death of the Roman commander had filled him with renewed vigor, and his thirst to annihilate the legionaries was insatiable. He called for the cavalry and launched them into a full-scale assault on the Roman formation.

Vatinius Auruncus' heart sank as he heard the elite guard's war cries and the thundering hooves of their horses growing louder, striking fear into the remaining Roman soldiers. He shut out everything—the battle, the cries of the wounded, the clash of weapons—all of it faded away. Even Rudulfus' shouted orders became silent movements of his lips. Vatinius' mind worked furiously to find a way to counter the sudden charge. The shields would be useless against the cavalry. The beasts would trample anything in their path.

Then, in a flash of insight, he shouted, "Open the ranks! Open the ranks!" at the top of his lungs. The soldiers parted, creating a wide corridor into which the Herul horsemen charged. Rudulfus realized the Roman strategy too late. He tried to rein in his horse, but the momentum of the charge carried them forward, the trained warhorses unwilling to stop.

The Roman legionaries began to strike at the barbarians' flanks, dragging them off their mounts. Gallienus Lars Gracchus spotted a rider urging his horse straight toward the centurion. Clumps of dirt and grass flew from the animal's hooves as it sped forward. The rider's intent was clear: kill the Roman leader and throw the remaining troops into chaos.

The Etruscan knelt, bracing his javelin for a devastating counter. He planted the weapon firmly into the ground and took position. But as the horse's approach shook the earth beneath him, he shifted his strategy. Leaping to his feet, he adjusted his grip on the short spear, took aim, and hurled it with all his might.

The javelin whistled through the air and struck the horse in the chest. The beast stumbled a few more steps before collapsing in a heap, tumbling from the force of its charge. Its rider was flung forward, and Gallienus Lars Gracchus ended him with a precise thrust of his gladius into the man's heart.

Breathing heavily from the exertion and tension, he realized how close he had come to death.

Due to the reckless maneuver Rudulfus had made earlier, his cavalry had been left isolated. Around fifty cataphracts were testing their mettle against the soldiers and legionaries of the *vexillatio* of Duro Catalaunum.

From atop their horses, the barbarians fought with the advantage of elevation. However, the Romans, well-versed in combating cavalry, knew how to turn this strength into a liability. They pressed their attacks against the horses' flanks, striking at the legs of the riders or bringing the horses down, toppling the cataphracts in the process. Once the cataphracts were on the ground, they were swiftly finished off.

Ialenia Heria wielded her long spatha with precision, crippling horses one after another and sending them crashing to the ground. The length of her Celtic blade allowed her to maintain a safe distance from the animals' flailing movements while targeting their legs. It was then up to the legionaries to complete the task.

Many horses were already writhing on the ground, emitting agonized neighs that filled the air. The blood soaking the earth drove the surviving animals into a state of madness, making them uncontrollable.

Unbeknownst to Ialenia, a rider was closing in on her. She was crouched slightly forward, her spatha held in both hands as she panted for breath. Her arms ached with exhaustion, and every breath brought a sharp pain to her chest.

"Watch out! Hey, druid, watch out!" shouted Ulzio Dacianus, who noticed the danger despite being locked in combat with Drusus Variatus against a cataphract officer.

It was nothing short of a miracle that Ialenia avoided being decapitated by the rider's devastating weapon—a chain with a lead weight at the end that destroyed everything in its path. She ducked just in time, dodging the deadly swing.

She watched as the rider yanked hard on the reins, halting the horse's momentum. As the beast turned to prepare for another charge, Ialenia braced herself, digging her feet into the ground and preparing to repel the attack.

The cataphract shouted something in his native tongue, likely a curse, before driving his heels into the horse's flanks, sending it charging at her once more. The foaming at the horse's mouth revealed its exhaustion, yet it galloped toward her with eyes wild with fury.

The chain's lead weight spun ominously over the rider's head as he bore the expression of someone who believed victory was within reach.

"Damn bastard, you won't give it up, will you?" Ialenia hissed, her voice trembling with fear and exhaustion. She struggled to steady herself despite the trembling of her legs.

As the horse neared, she sidestepped at the last moment and thrust her blade at the rider's flank. The strike, however, was absorbed by his scale armor, which held firm. Fortunately, the rider's attack also failed to land.

Once again, the horse charged toward her, the chain swinging menacingly in the rider's hands. This time, he released the chain earlier, allowing the lead weight to sail through the air and strike her square in the chest. The impact hurled her backward at least two meters, and she landed hard on her back.

Her spatha fell from her grip as her eyes rolled back. The Herul rider's laughter pierced the tense air as he urged his horse forward, approaching the fallen Ialenia Heria at a slow trot. She tried to move her fingers, her chest rising and falling in ragged gasps. Her mouth opened and closed as though she couldn't catch her breath.

The barbarian reached down, grabbed a javelin from his saddle quiver, and balanced it in his hand before driving it downward. The javelin pinned Ialenia Heria to the ground.

"Your gods of the underworld will welcome you like the harlot you are," the cataphract sneered.

It was Plato who noticed first. Ialenia was gripping the javelin that had pierced her, her body writhing in agony. He knelt beside her, taking her hand.

"You won't go alone," he whispered, trying to comfort her.

Meanwhile, the Roman ranks had reformed, retreating slightly from the corpses of the cataphracts and their horses. Vatinius Auruncus had been left outside the formation. Clutching his gladius with both hands, he waited for a horse to approach and slashed its throat with a single, precise stroke.

The rider was thrown several meters, but quickly sprang to his feet, charging at the centurion as though nothing had happened. He howled with rage, and the centurion mirrored his charge.

The barbarian's cloak billowed with each movement, revealing scale armor scarred with deep grooves—memories of past battles. The Heruli warrior swung a heavy, slashing blow that struck the young centurion's helmet, sending it flying and leaving his sweat-drenched head exposed.

The force of the next blow forced the centurion to brace his gladius with both hands, struggling to hold his ground.

To counter his opponent's strength, Vatinius Auruncus pushed hard with his legs and launched himself inside the adversary's defenses, leaving the Heruli warrior with no choice but to watch the tip of the gladius pierce through his abdomen. A gush of blood spurted out before the Heruli fell forward.

The effort was immense, and the young centurion's knee buckled. He had to plant the tip of his gladius in the ground to steady himself.

"Centurion, get back in formation!" Plato shouted with all the strength he could muster.

Vatinius Auruncus' eyes darted left and right, quickly assessing the situation. The enemy was disorganized and scattered, lacking leadership. He needed to seize the moment to reposition the Roman formation, but his legs wouldn't allow him to stand. The wound Ialenia Heria had tended to so diligently had reopened during the fight, causing him excruciating pain.

Thankfully, his optio came up behind him, helping him to his feet. Shielding him with his own body, the optio supported the centurion as they returned to the ranks.

The battle had reached a stalemate. The Herulians were attempting to reorganize, while the Romans began to fall back.

"Centurion...look over there," the optio said, pointing.

The fighting had momentarily ceased. Roman soldiers turned

their attention to a specific spot. Vatinius Auruncus followed their gaze.

Servius Augustinus, commander of the II Cohort, was kneeling alongside three other soldiers. Heruli warriors stood over them, swords drawn and ready to strike.

Then Cunipert stepped forward, advancing slowly until he was just a few meters from the Roman formation. "Who commands now?" he shouted.

Vatinius Auruncus pushed his way through the shield wall and stood before him. "I do."

The two locked eyes, their hatred palpable. If their gazes could kill, they would have struck each other dead on the spot.

Cunipert spoke first. "Roman, what you are about to witness will be your end. Governor Rudulfus is willing to spare your lives in light of the position he now holds in the Empire."

The centurion didn't flinch. "Rudulfus is asking for a surrender because this century…" He gestured behind him. "…has given you more trouble than you can handle, despite your superior numbers."

Cunipert's face darkened. "You're throwing away your only chance to leave this battlefield on your own two feet, Roman."

"I see your legs in far greater danger than mine, General," Vatinius replied, provoking murmurs of approval from the Roman soldiers.

A long silence followed.

Cunipert turned and walked back toward the prisoners. He cast one last glance at Vatinius Auruncus. "Watch closely, Roman."

With a nod of his chin, one of the Heruli warriors slit the throat of the first Roman soldier, who fell forward onto the ground. A rumble of anger passed through the Roman ranks. Then the second soldier was executed, followed by the third.

Only Centurion Servius Augustinus remained. He stood tall, showing the Heruli how a soldier of Rome died.

Rudulfus approached the grim spectacle, though he stayed at a distance. It was a calculated maneuver, designed to ensure all Roman soldiers saw what awaited them. His intent was to shatter the resolve of the exhausted legionaries, who had already watched their comrades die. Rudulfus offered them a way out—blaming their fate on their commanding centurion.

On the Roman side, Vatinius Auruncus had to act before the Heruli plan came to fruition.

"Optio, to me!"

In an instant, Severinus Majorianus was by his side. "What are your orders, Centurion?"

Without taking his eyes off the execution site, Vatinius commanded, "Make sure he doesn't suffer."

The optio clenched his jaw, nodded, and ran to the rear to relay the order to the archers. Three of them took aim, pulling their bowstrings taut. At the optio's command, they released their arrows. With three muffled thuds, the arrows struck Servius Augustinus in the chest. The centurion, moments from death, nodded in silent gratitude.

Cunipert, caught off guard, leapt back. Two of his guards stepped forward, raising their shields to protect him from further attacks.

Vatinius Auruncus bellowed, "That's how a legionary dies!"

Hearing those words, the Roman soldiers erupted into a roar of defiance.

"Optio!" Vatinius shouted again.

Severinus Majorianus was already behind him. "Let me guess—slingers?"

Vatinius smiled. "They'll create the confusion we need to retreat toward the city gate."

"Of course, it's up to me to do all the hard work," the optio quipped, rushing to the rear lines once more.

Cunipert barely managed to raise his shield in time as a stone ricocheted off it and fell to the ground. The sound of the sling-stones striking flesh and bone was eerily reminiscent of an axe splitting dry wood. Bones, teeth, flesh, and even armor shattered under the onslaught.

The Heruli general tried to rally his mercenaries, urging them forward. But most of them sought cover from the deadly hail.

A second volley followed moments later, claiming more lives. Horrified by the grotesque mutilation of their comrades, many Heruli warriors fled toward the forest.

Cunipert's officers tried to stop the retreat, shouting threats and curses. "Cowards! Attack! Don't run! Advance, damn you! Advance!" Cunipert screamed, holding his shield above his head.

Two stones struck his horse, which stumbled before collapsing. After tumbling to the ground, Cunipert scrambled to retrieve his shield and resumed barking orders. "Where do you think you're going, you sons of swine?" he yelled, watching his forces fall back.

The Romans' counteroffensive had thrown the Heruli ranks into disarray, but Cunipert saw an opportunity amid the chaos. Acting quickly, he called for one of his most trusted mercenaries.

The warrior approached, ducking to avoid the rain of sling-stones. His mail shirt was patched in several places and almost completely rusted, and a coarse wool cloak hung from a heavy torque around his neck, likely stolen in some raid.

"I have something very valuable to offer you," Cunipert said, producing an oval-shaped crystal gem. "Complete a mission for me, and you'll be rich. It's dangerous, but as you can see, the reward is substantial." His tone suggested the offer was too good to refuse.

The mercenary gave a slight nod, waiting for the details.

Cunipert's voice grew softer. "You must kill General Calibrandus. Once the task is done, return to me, and you'll flee with this gem, which will make you wealthier than you ever imagined."

The mercenary grinned, revealing several missing teeth. "I'll be your assassin, General. But if you don't keep your word, you'll meet the same fate as your target. That, I guarantee."

Cunipert's expression betrayed his displeasure at the threat, but he concealed his irritation. "My noble word is always backed by action," he replied, dismissing the mercenary.

He watched the man disappear into the fray. If the mercenary succeeded, Rudulfus would believe him to have died in combat, paving the way for Cunipert to rise to the highest rank.

But a series of shouts drew his attention, making him realize that the outcome of his plans was far from certain.

Noticing the Herulians' hesitation, the Romans attempted a sortie. A group of about twenty imperial soldiers charged at the scattered enemy warriors, intent on massacring them.

"They'll strike like lightning," Vatinius Auruncus murmured to himself, watching the optio lead the detachment, just a few steps ahead of the others.

The Heruli enemies were in disarray, and Rudulfus' generals struggled to reorganize their forces. Sling projectiles rained down on the Heruli warriors, and those who failed to take cover behind their shields were struck down. The survivors were finished off by Severinus Majorianus' unit.

The tide of battle had turned. Now it was the Romans hunting down their enemies.

Cunipert tried desperately to regain control, shouting orders to regroup his forces.

Vatinius Auruncus, his heart pounding in his chest, made up his mind about how to lead the battle. He gathered another detachment and ordered the optio to fall back into formation. As Severinus Majorianus' men returned, Vatinius' group surged forward, launching their own attack.

It was a slaughter. The disorganized enemy stood no chance.

Amidst the fighting, Vatinius spotted General Cunipert rallying his troops. Vatinius knew that confronting and defeating him would decapitate the Heruli chain of command, plunging their forces into total chaos.

The two officers finally stood face to face.

The Roman centurion held his gladius in his right hand and his shield in his left, though much of the shield's surface had been hacked away by an axe. His imperial Gallic-style helmet was dented, its transverse crest half-shorn, and one cheek guard had been torn off. His focale scarf was stained with blood and sweat, and a brooch held his purple cloak over his shoulders.

General Cunipert wore a domed helmet that framed his pale,

weathered face, lined by years of exposure to the elements. His armor was a masterpiece, its scales meticulously crafted. Beneath it, a fine chainmail shirt was visible. A broad belt secured his scabbard at his waist.

"Roman, invoke your blessed martyrs and your Redeemer," Cunipert taunted in surprisingly fluent Latin. "They will welcome you with honor soon enough."

He struck first, demonstrating remarkable skill with the sword. The Heruli general launched himself at Vatinius without giving him a moment to think.

Vatinius closed ranks, raising what remained of his shield to deflect the first blow. The impact shook his entire body, and his wound throbbed painfully, but he forced himself to endure.

Cunipert's relentless attacks left him no time to strategize. The Herulian struck repeatedly—overhead, to the side, and with straight-on thrusts—forcing Vatinius to block each blow with quick, instinctive movements. He barely had time to glimpse where the next strike would land.

Anticipating the next attack, Vatinius braced himself. Cunipert aimed a powerful downward strike, intending to shatter his helmet and skull. Vatinius sidestepped just in time, causing Cunipert's momentum to unbalance him, his muscular, scarred body lurching forward.

This was the moment.

The Roman's gladius came down on Cunipert's shoulder, slicing through his armor, flesh, and bone. The Heruli general fell to his knees, clutching his mangled shoulder. His mouth hung open, more in shock than pain.

Vatinius plunged his gladius deeper into the gash, driving it to the hilt. He pressed harder, tearing through Cunipert's flesh and crushing the internal organs beneath.

Cunipert's eyes rolled back as his pupils disappeared.

As Vatinius called his detachment to regroup with the Roman lines, the Heruli warriors under Cunipert's command began abandoning their weapons and fleeing. Leaderless, they sought only to escape.

The legionaries of the *vexillatio* of Duro Catalaunum celebrated the victory as vengeance for the death of Aristarchos
Themistocles.

Rudulfus, on the other hand, saw the events as a grim omen
from the gods. He pulled on the reins of his warhorse, turning
it around, and fled at a gallop, followed by the few surviving
cataphracts.

The Romans cheered in triumph as the king of the Herulians,
cursing loudly, retreated to the rear of his army.

With the Heruli in retreat, the Roman withdrawal proceeded
more swiftly. The barbarians covering Rudulfus' escape launched
only a few arrows, offering no real resistance. The absence of
leadership was evident.

The shrewd Calibrandus, observing from his position, had
already ordered his regiment to fall back. As he leaned from his
saddle to get a better view of the enemy lines, a warrior approached
him from behind.

Calibrandus was alone, without his usual retinue, as they were
all occupied carrying out his orders.

The assassin sent by Cunipert, unaware of his employer's grim
fate, pretended to belong to Calibrandus' regiment. As he moved
closer, he rested a hand on his dagger.

The assassin was moments away from earning the precious
gem that would secure him a life of luxury.

He drew the weapon—a small, discreet blade, but sharp enough
for its purpose. Just a few more steps, and the mission would be
complete.

But as if sensing the hostile presence, General Calibrandus
spun around, catching the assassin mid-thrust.

With lightning speed, Calibrandus' sword lashed out, slicing
through the top of the assassin's head. The would-be killer crumpled to the ground.

It was unclear how Calibrandus had sensed the attack, but it
was very clear who had ordered it. Everyone present thought of
the same name: Cunipert.

Cunipert had planned Calibrandus' murder to eliminate a rival in the eyes of the king—or perhaps he had also plotted the king's assassination. No one would ever know, as the only two people aware of the plot were dead.

"Search him. See if he carries messages or anything linking him to his employer," General Calibrandus ordered his officers, looking down at the body in disgust.

Nothing was found to incriminate anyone, but everyone would have wagered two gold coins that Cunipert was behind it.

Massilia

The archers and slingers, perched atop the city walls, provided cover for the retreating Roman legionaries as they reached the shadow of the fortifications.

The battle between the Romans and the Heruli had been observed from the safety of the city's stone defenses, but the commander of the local garrison had deemed it unwise to launch a sortie to assist the Roman soldiers. Once the legionaries reached the safety of the walls, however, an order was given to the archer units to provide them with protective fire.

Finally, the massive gates began to groan open. The Roman soldiers entered the city without significant interference from the Heruli mercenary regiments. The great wooden doors closed behind them with a deafening crash, raising a vast cloud of dust.

The enemy, aware of their vulnerability, had kept a cautious distance, remaining beyond the range of the city militia's arrows. Behind the monumental wooden gates, shielded from the muffled cries of the Heruli outside, the legionaries stood frozen. The eerie stillness felt almost surreal, but it signified only one thing: safety.

They had made it.

One by one, the soldiers sank to the ground, gasping for breath. A crowd of curious onlookers had already begun to gather, eager to see the legionaries who had fought against a barbarian army far larger than their own and had given their enemies a fierce challenge.

The news of the battle's events had spread quickly throughout the coastal city. Children peeked timidly at the soldiers, who were covered in dirt, blood, and grime. Their tattered uniforms and broken armor told the tale of their ordeal.

Suddenly, the crowd parted to make way for the prefect of the city's militia. He was flanked by dignitaries and decurions, surrounded by soldiers and attendants.

"Who is in command here?" he asked firmly.

Two centurions stepped forward at the same time.

"Hail, Prefect! My name is Vatinius Auruncus, centurion of the *vexillatio* from Duro Catalaunum," said one.

He stiffened into a salute, though the shoulder strap of his armor hung loosely, his right eye was swollen shut, and his left forearm was bruised and battered. Sweat trickled down his dirt-streaked, blood-crusted face.

"Hail, Prefect! Antoninus Tacitus, centurion of the *vexillatio* from Duro Catalaunum," echoed the other.

His lip was split, his helmet dented, and his armor caved in at several points. His left hand trembled uncontrollably from exhaustion and tension.

The prefect, clad in a finely embroidered dalmatic with purple and gold trim, invoked the Virgin and the blessed Martyrs.

"Do not mourn for your fallen comrades. They now dwell among the serene and the righteous. The Lord will care for them as a good father cares for his most beloved children," he began, raising his eyes and hands to the heavens.

The two centurions stood motionless, staring at him in silence.

The prefect quickly added, "You had a tough time out there, didn't you?"

Vatinius Auruncus, his tone tinged with resentment, replied, "Yes, but so did they," gesturing with his thumb toward the gates. His comment drew laughter and murmurs of approval from the soldiers, who were still recovering from their ordeal.

"Do not worry, my dear men. The surgeons will tend to the wounded, and all of you will be given food and rest. I will meet with your commanders tomorrow at vespers. I will also arrange a banquet in their honor," the prefect concluded.

Without waiting for a response, he turned on his heel and departed, followed by a train of officials who lavished him with compliments and words of praise for his leadership.

Meanwhile, a group of town criers loudly proclaimed that the prefect's careful but painful decision not to assist the Roman soldiers in battle had led to divine intervention. According to them, the blessed martyrs had interceded on his behalf, bringing calamity upon the enemy horde and forcing them to retreat.

Vatinius Auruncus watched the prefect's retreating figure with disdain etched across his face. Exhaustion had aged him visibly.

"Let it go. Let's focus on getting some food and rest," said Gallienus Lars Gracchus, placing a reassuring hand on his shoulder.

It wasn't long before help arrived. A procession of servants and slaves emerged from a nearby alley, carrying jars of fresh water and baskets of fruit.

Chapter XII – The Heat of the Day

Heruli Camp, King Rudulfus' Tent

Rudulfus sat on his throne, draped in deer pelts. His complexion was ashen, and sweat glistened on his hollowed cheeks, brow, and face, pooling in the hollow of his neck. His fury at having lost the battle against the Romans was palpable, and none of the officers dared to make a sound.

Only General Calibrandus broke the silence, instructing the scribes to ready themselves. His was the sole voice audible in the tent.

Rudulfus leaned against the armrest, his fist pressed against his forehead. He was lost in thought, grappling with how to salvage his reputation in the face of the humiliating feat accomplished by those damned legionaries. He still couldn't believe it: a mere handful of Roman soldiers had stood their ground against his entire horde of warriors.

In the brazier at the center of the tent, logs burned steadily, warming the room. Two of the king's armors were mounted on wooden posts planted in the ground. Candleholders illuminated the space from every corner.

On the table sat a pitcher of mead and several finely-crafted cups. Strips of roasted meat lay in an overturned skull, waiting to be eaten.

Calibrandus approached Rudulfus and whispered in his ear, "My king, I have dispatched two spies disguised as merchants to Massilia. They will report back on the Romans' retreat."

The Heruli king nodded, but gave no verbal reply. With a wave of his hand, he ordered everyone to leave, allowing only Calibrandus and a scribe to remain.

"Can we trust him?" the officer asked, gesturing toward the scribe.

"He's a monk I captured from a monastery I set ablaze. He can read and write, and he will be of great use to us. He won't live to leave our service," Rudulfus reassured him.

"Then have him draft a letter."

The monk, without waiting for further instruction, dipped his quill into ink and poised himself to write.

"Inform King Odoacer that the rebellious commander of the *vexillationes* from Duro Catalaunum has been killed. Emphasize that I will personally take on the responsibility of governing Gaul, managing its tax collection, and defending its borders."

The scribe set to work feverishly, transcribing the message.

Calibrandus read between the lines of the dictated letter. The Heruli king was distorting reality, spinning the narrative so that Ravenna would hear of the battle as a punishment for a rebellious Roman commander, rather than as a humiliating defeat.

Rudulfus had received the severed head of one of his generals in his own tent, been bested in battle by a small Roman force, and yet was now writing of a brilliant victory.

A shrewd move.

But Calibrandus wondered, Would Odoacer believe these words, or would he trust the reports of his own spies? This, Rudulfus likely hadn't considered.

Still, Calibrandus decided to keep his doubts to himself, given the current tension.

Massilia

A surreal peace blanketed the city. A gentle breeze had swept the clouds away, and now the sun warmed the skin. The azure sea sparkled with blinding reflections, while flocks of seabirds soared toward the marshlands visible near the Iberian Peninsula.

The fragrant scents of Mediterranean flora filled the air.

Vatinius Auruncus watched with amusement as the usually stoic Batavian, Evetius Aquila, paced restlessly. His newfound curiosity drove him to pester his comrades with questions about everything that seemed odd or unfamiliar to him.

Most of all, he appeared terrified of the sea. He'd never set foot on a ship, and his apprehension was evident in the way he often glanced anxiously at the moored vessels.

The centurion's attention shifted to a pink flamingo strutting nearby with a regal gait, reminding him of the pompous prefect who had welcomed them to the city.

A sudden greeting interrupted his thoughts.

"Hail, Centurion!" A soldier waved broadly to catch his attention.

Vatinius nodded in acknowledgment.

"The palace messenger says the prefect will see you at the *prima vigilia* [1]. Try to look presentable," the soldier added, eyeing Vatinius' battered armor with a smirk.

"I'll be there," Vatinius replied curtly.

He knew the audience would serve as the prefect as an opportunity to glean information about the northern border—knowledge he could flaunt to Ravenna as proof of his expertise in the region's affairs.

Massilia Port, Hora octava

"I want my money," Drusus Variatus complained, eyeing a stray dog nosing through the cracks in search of food.

"You'll get it when I sell my helmet and shield," snapped Ulzio Dacianus, rolling his eyes.

---

[1] *Prima vigilia* (First Watch): Roughly between 6:00 PM and 9:00 PM.

"Gambling debts are a matter of honor. They must be paid."

"I know what they are, but in case you haven't noticed, we're no longer getting paid as soldiers," Ulzio shot back with a glare.

"Then you shouldn't have gambled," Drusus quipped.

Ulzio clasped his hands together dramatically, as if appealing to the heavens. "I'll feed you to the fish."

"We'll end up on the other side of life together, then!" Drusus retorted with a grin.

"How about another roll of the dice?"

"Do you even have one?" Drusus craned his neck as if trying to peek into his bag.

"I kept one just for the moment I take even your tunic," Ulzio joked.

The two burst into laughter.

Antoninus Tacitus leaned closer to Vatinius Auruncus and murmured, "I can never tell if those two are seriously arguing over that debt, or if they're just doing it for fun."

"They've been at it since we were conscripted as boys. They've gambled away every last *follis* in every corner of the Empire," Vatinius replied with a chuckle.

He then changed the subject. "The prefect summoned me." He glanced at a bruised finger, suspecting it might be fractured.

"It seems we can't even find peace in Massilia," Antoninus remarked wryly.

They both sat on the bases of crumbled columns that had likely fallen ages ago.

"I'd better go. I don't want to cause any animosity now that we're so close to setting sail."

"Wise move. Better to avoid trouble..." Antoninus cleared his throat. "I've heard the soldiers of the Second Cohort are seeking contracts here in Massilia. That's good for us. The prefect will gain reinforcements for the city's defense and won't notice us slipping away."

Vatinius understood the implication. The prefect could still prevent their departure, as they were technically still soldiers of Rome. They needed to leave unnoticed.

In confidence, Antoninus unwrapped a cloth, revealing an object. "Inside here," he began, "is the standard of the *vexillatio* from Duro Catalaunum."

They stared at each other in silence for a moment.

Vatinius couldn't hide his astonishment. "I thought it was lost during the siege..."

The vexillum, made of brass, bore a central gold plaque engraved with the word *Vexillatio*.

The young centurion's wide eyes betrayed his surprise. "It's made of gold," he said simply.

Antoninus hastened to explain. "I found it in Aristarchos Themistocles' baggage. He probably kept it to use at the right moment."

"Do the others know?"

"No...I don't think so."

"He'll pay for the ships, trust me," Ulzio Dacianus was explaining with a patience he didn't truly possess.

Fulcinius Agricola Statius snapped back, his signature arrogant smirk spreading across his face: "I propose we melt it down and divide the gold equally. After that, each of us will be the master of our own destiny once we reach Italy."

"What are you all talking about?" Drusus Variatus interrupted, momentarily distracted as his eyes followed a woman carrying a water jug balanced on her head.

The woman stopped and asked for news from the northern territories. Many others approached the soldiers with the same curiosity—some driven by concern for relatives or interests in those regions, others out of sheer curiosity, and the more cautious ones out of fear of what might happen.

"So, that standard is made of gold. Let's melt it down and split the proceeds," Fulcinius reiterated.

"I asked what you're talking about," Drusus repeated, his curiosity now fully piqued.

"The *vexillatio* standard—we have it with us," someone answered.

Those words caught the attention of every surviving legionary of the *vexillatio*.

Now they all sat around the fire, which was fed by old doors and a pair of broken stools they had found nearby.

"Will it weigh down the ship?" Evetius Aquila asked, his fear of the sea evident.

"It's the size of an arm and as thin as an apple peel. It won't sink the ship, you damned barbarian," Gallienus Lars Gracchus replied, inspecting the wound on his thigh. Fortunately, it seemed to be healing well and wouldn't cause further issues.

"But what if a sea monster attacks our ship?" Evetius' face betrayed utter terror.

"Sea monsters don't exist," the *signifer* retorted.

"They do exist. I've heard many stories," the Batavian shot back indignantly, resenting the other's disbelief.

"Those are just sailor tales told in taverns after drinking an amphora of wine," Tullius Sextus Plato interjected, dismissing the topic with a wave of his hand as if to emphasize the absurdity of the conversation.

"Our weapons won't be enough to protect us. We need to load plenty of javelins onto the ship. It'll increase our chances," Evetius insisted.

The *signifer* sighed loudly. "Enough already. We're better off bringing amphoras full of food and water!" He shook his head before continuing. "I'm telling you, sea monsters don't exist."

At that moment, Ulzio Dacianus, lounging on coiled ropes while basking in the pleasant sun, interjected: "Once, a giant sea serpent sank an entire fleet. It was during the time of the Caesars... Want me to tell you how it happened?"

Evetius' eyes widened so much that they seemed ready to pop out of their sockets. He was utterly horrified.

"Stop scaring him," Gallienus Lars Gracchus ordered.

Ulzio's laugh echoed in the air.

"Were you mocking me?" Evetius snapped, unimpressed by the humor.

"With someone as big and burly as you, if a sea monster shows up, we'll just sacrifice you to it! Don't worry, it'll eat its fill and leave the rest of us alone," Plato teased, earning laughter from the group.

***

In the vast chamber, a whisper was enough to create an echo. The red and black marble floor, outlined in white, gave the space a cold atmosphere that was only slightly mitigated by the warmth of two braziers. The walls were draped with richly-woven, finely-embroidered fabrics.

A falcon perched on a stand, tethered by a chain around its leg. Shafts of light filtered through the grated windows, dissolving into faint glimmers that illuminated the dust particles suspended in the air.

The master of ceremonies, wearing a thick black wig, eyed Centurion Vatinius Auruncus with disdain. Heavy black makeup surrounded the man's eyes, giving him an almost theatrical appearance. His expression reflected disgust at the sorry state of the centurion's armor and garments.

"He doesn't seem to appreciate your tattered lorica," a Gallo-Roman officer quipped beside Vatinius.

"Maybe it's the stench of rotting fish coming from you that bothers him," Vatinius shot back.

"You think you smell like exotic perfumes from the East?"

The exchange of provocations had begun, and it was becoming dangerous.

"You'd look good wearing makeup like that clown over there," the centurion muttered, nodding toward the master of ceremonies.

The Gallo-Roman, named Agostino, couldn't help but laugh, defusing the tension.

"I'd advise some composure. You'll be meeting the prefect shortly," the master of ceremonies interrupted in a slightly shrill voice, as if even speaking strained him.

Vatinius' eyes narrowed like blades. His life of battles and scars left him ill-disposed to tolerate rebukes from a pompous fool like this one.

357

The master seemed to read the unspoken threat in Vatinius' expression and glared back. "If I were you, brave officer, I'd change my attitude. It's not uncommon for palace walls to hide dangers far greater than any battlefield."

That was too much. Vatinius despised being threatened, especially by a slimy bureaucrat. "In other circumstances, I'd hang your tongue from my *cingulum*. Consider yourself lucky..." he growled, holding the man's gaze.

The clattering of the prefect's personal guard's armor announced his arrival.

A servant stepped forward, drawing back a gleaming curtain to reveal the city's governor, who advanced and took his place on a marble seat.

The servant exchanged a knowing glance with the master of ceremonies, who began to proclaim with a voice as grating as a harp: "The most excellent Prefect Caeso Oranius Tiburnius, governor of Massilia!"

Vatinius' mouth fell open.

Caeso Oranius Tiburnius feigned deep concentration, pretending to study dispatches handed to him by a train of officials.

Finally, after a seemingly endless wait, he addressed the centurion without looking up from the documents. "I personally appealed to the bishop to thank the Blessed Virgin for preserving your precious lives," he began. "A trusted agent of ours, working in secret, has sent a message that I believe will be of great interest to you. King Rudulfus, your pursuer, has requested reinforcements from his southern army. I don't think it will be long before they arrive at the walls of this city."

Vatinius' chest heaved as he inhaled deeply, the grim news draining the last remnants of his optimism.

The prefect resumed speaking.

His voice, syrupy yet commanding, continued to echo through the chamber:

"Only the Lord knows how the difficult situation in northern Gaul will unfold. However, I will not hide my great concern from you—I fear that those lands are lost forever. Messengers struggle to reach them, often returning without delivering their dispatches. And as for goods, they are frequently intercepted by Burgundian raiders, who, as you well know, can be ruthless towards Roman citizens when they aren't properly paid. I deemed it a waste of resources to deploy cataphract detachments to secure the communication routes. Instead, I dispatched a unit of infantry composed entirely of Sciri warriors, who, it seems, are behaving worse than the raiders they were sent to stop."

Vatinius Auruncus, despite his irritation at the prefect's verbose nature, found himself agreeing with the substance of his words.

"Meanwhile, the news from Ravenna is no better. Odoacer has deposed the Sacred Augustus of the West and declared himself rex. It was a politically shrewd move, as he knew the holder of the purple in Constantinople, being of barbarian descent, would never recognize him as a legitimate emperor. Thus, there was no point in aspiring to sit in the sacred palace. By presenting himself instead as the regent of the Empire, Odoacer has secured the goodwill of the Eastern Augustus, and consequently, the highest authority in Italy and Gaul."

The centurion nodded as the prefect laid out his explanation.

"I believe it is wise to begin seriously organizing a Gallic army to confront the looming threats, which I foresee will arrive sooner rather than later," the prefect concluded.

At last, the prefect ceased speaking.

"I request permission to speak, Prefect," Vatinius Auruncus' voice rang out, piercing the silence and shocking the dignitaries and officials present.

The master of ceremonies flailed his pudgy hands, the sleeves of his dalmatic rustling as he protested: "Do not interrupt!"

With a look that could intimidate even the fiercest enemy, the centurion silenced him. "I am a Roman officer, and I will speak," he declared, his jaw tightly clenched. His patience had reached its limit.

"Speak, Centurion," Caeso Oranius Tiburnius said, his voice echoing through the marble hall.

"Forming a Gallic army is our only chance of survival. Otherwise, every city will fall, one by one. I have seen with my own eyes tens of thousands of barbarian warriors. They are human waves, driven by hunger and the desire to plunder," Vatinius explained.

The prefect nodded, acknowledging the point, then added: "I suspect you have no intention of staying here. Am I wrong?"

"You are not wrong. My soldiers and I wish to reach Italy and return home," the centurion admitted, watching the prefect closely, hoping he hadn't revealed too much.

"The soldiers of the Second Cohort have all been enlisted. Your men would make no difference. You may leave Massilia. That is my decision," the prefect stated firmly, leaving no room for argument.

With an air of austere authority, he left the chamber.

The master of ceremonies stepped forward, heralded by the cloying fragrance of his perfume-soaked robes. His expression radiated smug satisfaction as he declared: "You may leave the palace."

He rubbed his hands together as though he had struck a profitable deal, trailing a few paces behind Vatinius Auruncus as he escorted him out. In the palace's peristyle, Vatinius stopped abruptly and turned around. Caught off guard, the master of ceremonies felt the metallic taste of blood in his mouth before realizing two of his incisors were gone. Vatinius had taken his revenge.

***

At the port, where his men had gathered, Vatinius Auruncus leapt onto a section of a crumbled column.

He called for attention and motioned for Antoninus Tacitus to approach.

"Give me the standard."

The centurion's rough hands handed over the bundle. Vatinius untied the laces, revealing the golden standard of the *vexillatio* of Duro Catalaunum.

When no murmurs of surprise arose, the two centurions exchanged a glance.

"Did they already know?" Vatinius asked.

"I didn't think so..." Antoninus Tacitus replied, attempting to justify himself.

"Look!" Fulcinius Agricola Statius elbowed Ulzio Dacianus. "I told you! They'll sell it and split the gold."

"Let's hear what he has to say first. But I don't think it'll go the way you're hoping," Ulzio retorted.

"He'll melt it down and use it to pay for our honorable discharge," Fulcinius speculated.

"We'd better buy a ship with that gold. If we don't, we'll have to walk home—and with all the barbarians out there, we won't make it past the coast of the Ninth Region of Italia[2]," Ulzio added.

"You might be right..." Fulcinius admitted, scratching his forehead.

"Silence!" Drusus Variatus snapped, his eyes fixed on the shimmering standard.

Vatinius addressed the men: "Brothers," he began, "This standard needs no introduction. You have served and fought under it too many times already." He paused as nods rippled through the group. "I know how much this symbol means to some of you," he continued, giving Fulcinius a sharp look, "but we must sell its gold. With the proceeds, we can pay for passage on a ship. We must act quickly, before the prefect changes his mind about granting us our freedom. Soon, the Heruli will attack Massilia, and no soldier will be allowed to leave—mark my words."

It was a moment of intense emotion. The surviving legionaries of the *vexillatio* embraced one another.

The two centurions watched, surprised, as memories of frost, snow, rain, terror, steel, and blood surged in their minds. Yet here they were, standing under the coastal sun, their skin warmed, their clothes dry—and their heads still firmly attached to their bodies.

---

[2] *IX Regio Italiae* (Ninth Region of Italy): Refers to Liguria, a region in northwestern Italy.

Vatinius ordered them to stay put at the port, while he and Antoninus Tacitus ventured into the bustling alleys, where merchants shouted loudly, displaying their wares. Brightly colored canopies created a kaleidoscope of hues that animated the narrow streets.

"Who are we looking for?" Antoninus asked, striding confidently and shoving his way through the crowd, occasionally bumping into stocky figures to assert his strength.

"Enough of that," Vatinius admonished. "This isn't the time to start a brawl."

"I know how to handle myself. I don't need a rookie like you telling me what to do," Antoninus retorted.

Vatinius sighed, rolling his eyes. "If you start a fight, we won't finish our mission."

"Then I'll finish the fight quickly, so we can get on with it."

"No brawls. Stop talking nonsense."

"If I don't find anyone else to hit, I'll use you as a punching bag, you little teacher's pet," Antoninus shot back.

"Who'll patch you up afterward?"

Their banter ended abruptly when they stopped in front of a blacksmith's shop.

"This is the place," Vatinius said with certainty.

Inside, they descended two flights of stairs carved into the rock, arriving in a vaulted chamber.

Slaves toiled in the heat, wearing only soot-blackened loincloths. Some split wood, piling it high, while others fed the furnace. A hood vented the smoke outside.

The blacksmith appeared—a stocky man of about forty, his teeth reduced to a single molar. "What do you need?" he asked, sizing them up.

Vatinius opened the bundle, revealing the golden standard. "I need you to melt this down and forge it into an ingot."

Though hesitant, the promise of gold finally swayed the blacksmith. Moments later, the last remnants of the *vexillatio* of Duro Catalaunum were reduced to molten gold.

It was the final act of the *vexillatio's* storied legacy.

Chapter XIII – Dawn of Hope

Through unwavering negotiation, Vatinius Auruncus secured ownership of a trireme that had been anchored and abandoned at the port for what seemed like an eternity. The deal, though not overly complicated, came at a steep price. Aristarchos Themistocles had carried the *vexillatio* standard, fully aware of the high cost of corruption in the Empire.

The port official, knowing full well that selling ships was prohibited, nonetheless acted based on his intimate knowledge of the bloated and corrupt city administration. He reasoned that the vessels, docked in a decaying row, would eventually rot in the water. If one went missing, who would even notice? Furthermore, the gold he gained from the transaction was simply too tempting to refuse.

Without a second thought, he permitted the legionaries to take possession of the trireme. As the two centurions walked away, the official weighed the small gold ingot in his hand, thoroughly pleased with the deal.

When Vatinius Auruncus first laid eyes on the ship, his thoughts were blunt: "It's in such poor condition that it's practically a favor to remove it from the harbor."

On the pier, the legionaries stood silently, staring at the dilapidated wreck before them. All except Evetius Aquila, the cautious Batavian, who stayed safely back.

Even without the expertise of sailors, it was clear to all that the ship required extensive and grueling repairs.

"When we take to the sea... we'll shake in fear... until we sink and drown, my dear..." Plato improvised on the spot.

The rhyme drew laughter from the group.

"Who's going to break it to Evetius Aquila that we're going to drown?" quipped Ulzio Dacianus.

Scratching his backside, Fulcinius Agricola Statius added, "By the time he realizes it, he'll already be fish food."

Gallienus Lars Gracchus shook his head, rubbing his forehead in exasperation.

Ulzio Dacianus laughed nervously, though it was clear to everyone that his apprehension about their upcoming voyage matched their own.

Leaning closer, Antoninus Tacitus whispered to Vatinius Auruncus, "We won't even make it to that rock over there, if you ask me."

"This is the kind of trial that tests one's faith, my friend," Vatinius replied with a wry smile.

The legionaries immediately set to work. Their first challenge was replacing the rotten ropes, but the jingle of coins once again proved useful.

A customs bureaucrat granted them access to a warehouse previously owned by an Egyptian exotic animal trader who had disappeared from the Massilia port years ago—likely a victim of misfortune.

No one cared about his exotic creatures anymore, and if he ever returned, the stolen supplies could easily be blamed on unknown thieves.

Repairing the hull and planks turned out to be less complicated than anticipated. While the results were far from visually appealing, they were functional and effective.

However, a pressing problem remained: they needed water amphoras and a sufficient supply of dried and fresh food.

The solution was straightforward. They would have to steal them.

Much of their remaining resources had already been spent on purchasing sails.

With the moon shining brightly and casting silvery reflections, work continued late into the night. No one dared to light a torch, for fear of drawing unwanted attention.

As expected, Fulcinius Agricola Statius and Drusus Variatus were assigned the theft.

Unfortunately, the moon shone especially brightly that evening, complicating their mission. Hidden behind a pile of coiled ropes, they observed their surroundings.

"Why are there sentries?" Fulcinius whispered.

"How can you be so stupid?" Drusus snapped in frustration.

"And how do you know so much?" Fulcinius shot back, irritated.

"It's obvious. Right now, port supplies are a valuable asset for the city. Sailors need them and are willing to pay a fortune."

Fulcinius stared at Drusus, impressed. "When did you become an expert on port economics?"

"Stop flaunting your ignorance and just look over there."

Fulcinius followed Drusus' gaze and saw two sentries sitting down, drinking from a flask.

"Looks like they're just passing the night."

"Should we put them to sleep ourselves?" Fulcinius asked.

Drusus gave him a withering look. "That was the plan."

Moments later, after subduing the sentries, Fulcinius couldn't stop kicking one of them.

"Why are you still kicking him?" Drusus asked, baffled. Fulcinius slowed his assault and locked eyes with one of the sentries. "They're not our enemies. We just need some supplies for the galley," he explained.

The other sentry, grateful for the clarification, chimed in, "He's right! We're not your enemies!"

Bound and lying on the ground, the sentries posed no further obstacle.

Still brimming with adrenaline, Fulcinius cast one last glance at them before heading into the warehouse.

The two legionaries worked quickly, loading a cart with anything edible they could find.

When the cart was full, they wheeled it past the tied-up sentries.

"They didn't even wish us a safe journey," Fulcinius quipped sarcastically.

"You kicked them. What did you expect?" Drusus retorted dryly.

The gangway connecting the quay to the ship was a constant flurry of movement as legionaries hauled aboard the necessary supplies.

Centurion Vatinius Auruncus supervised the operation, meticulously recording the stowed items on a scraped parchment to keep track of everything already on board.

The faint glow of the oil lamp cast a flickering shadow on the wall of the ship's only cabin, where a writing desk was set up. For a fleeting moment, the thin wisp of smoke rising from the lamp seemed to him like the flowing waters of the River Liris, a sight he hoped to see again soon.

The creaking of the hull grew louder as the modest vessel filled up, the movements of the men shifting and settling the planks of wood.

Signifer Gallienus Lars Gracchus, tasked as the quartermaster, checked on the stowage. Two large jars of salted fish needed to be repositioned to balance the ship's load. He decided to place them adjacent to the inner walls of the keel. The sacks of grain posed no issues, unlike the fruit, which needed to be kept in the coolest corner of the hold.

"I told you I'd win," quipped Ulzio Dacianus with a grin.

"May Jupiter Pluvius drown your house!" retorted Drusus Variatus, never missing a chance to express his disdain for embracing the new monotheistic faith.

"Luck's not on your side today, it seems..." Ulzio Dacianus burst into laughter, which quickly turned into a fit of coughing that nearly choked him.

"Keep your voice down! Do you want to get caught? You know what the commander would do to us if he found us sneaking off to gamble with these dried figs?"

Ulzio Dacianus' face twisted in irritation. "You think we've done too little up until now? Look at this," he said, pointing to a wound he had received at Duro Catalaunum, still not fully healed. "This scar will spell the word 'sacrifice'. I've nothing to apologize for, and I never will. Now, come on, let's continue."

"Ship!"

"Heads!"

The coin was tossed into the air, and as it landed, it revealed the result.

"Ship! Unbelievable—how are you this unlucky?"

Drusus Variatus' outburst drew the attention of Gallienus Lars Gracchus, who was applying waterproof pitch to the hull. Peering past the crates and ropes, he discovered the two idlers, who looked back at him, speechless and embarrassed at being caught red-handed.

"But..." Drusus Variatus began, trying to protest before being cut off.

"Don't even try to spin this. Those are dried figs, and the food supplies are off-limits. The centurion was clear," Gallienus Lars Gracchus said, his expression promising trouble.

"Don't be a..." Drusus Variatus started again, but wisely stopped himself. He knew well that legionaries didn't betray one another—especially not friends who had grown up together, long before becoming comrades in arms.

"Come on, let's go. There's still the whole starboard hull to coat," urged the *signifer*, shooting them a sideways glare to ensure they followed.

The two exchanged a resigned pat on the shoulder before standing up to join him.

"What are you thinking about?" Antoninus Tacitus asked.

"Not thinking...imagining. A house and peace. I'm tired of this life," Vatinius Auruncus replied, his eyes fixed on the sea, which shimmered with the silvery light of the moon.

He wrapped his cloak tighter around himself, seeking refuge from the chill of the starry night.

"A house, huh? You sound like a Roman matron."

"And you'll look like one after I cut off your dick," Vatinius shot back.

"I didn't mean to offend you. I meant...well, you sounded like a Herulian woman," Antoninus said, scratching his chin.

They burst into soft laughter, hoping no one would hear them.

Below the hull, the water lapped gently, cradling the quiet of those who had finished their tasks and now sat gazing at the stars. The air was sharp, and the dampness made it necessary to pull their heavy cloaks tightly around themselves.

Vatinius Auruncus' hands moved deftly along the ship's rail.

"What are you carving?" the other centurion asked.

Vatinius' right hand gripped the dagger, while his left smoothed the surface each time wood shavings covered the carving.

"What are you carving?" the optio asked, stepping closer.

"Neptune," Vatinius replied, blowing away the wood curls.

"Neptune?"

"Yes."

"What will the others think? It's a pagan symbol—they won't take it well," Severinus Majorianus teased.

"Why should anyone care about what I carve?" retorted the young centurion, clearly annoyed.

"Why? You know full well that before setting sail, the sailors invoke the Blessed Virgin—not illegal pagan gods," the optio pointed out.

His gaze lingered on the carving, which was beginning to take shape: Neptune, trident in hand, pointing toward the bow.

"What does it matter? It's just a sculpture."

"But you know how superstitious soldiers are. They might see it as a bad omen."

"Then they can get rid of it," Vatinius said curtly.

"Unless we've already sunk by then!" the optio protested, pulling his cloak tightly around himself as he turned away.

When even the optio fell asleep on deck, the two centurions were left to decide how to handle their final task.

"Have you spotted him?" Vatinius asked.

"Yes. He's snoring with the other sailors under those covered passages," his companion replied, pointing to a spot not far away.

"Do you think he'll agree?"

"I spoke with him a few hours ago. He said he'd do it for two tremisses."

They exchanged a knowing glance.

The clatter of a sack, dropped into the hold by Fulcinius Agricola Statius, caught the attention of the Batavian Evetius Aquila.

"What's inside?" he asked, trying to squeeze his large frame out of the cramped space.

"Weapons—daggers, swords, an axe," Fulcinius replied nonchalantly.

"Where did you get them?"

"At the warehouse…"

"The commander gave strict orders not to bring anything aboard except personal equipment. He was very clear about this."

"What's in there is my future. As soon as we land on the coast, I'll look for a market. There, I'll sell the weapons—just watch, it'll be a great deal," retorted the Roman, his tone brimming with confidence. "After that, I'll head back to my village. Somewhere out there, I should still have some sort of family. A child, at least… as far as I can remember. If his mother hasn't found a man with a… well, let's say, a stallion's endowment to keep herself entertained, then maybe I'll consider settling down."

For a brief moment, his gaze dropped, betraying a flicker of melancholy.

Evetius Aquila, seemingly oblivious to the other's mood, drew the long sword from the sheath strapped to his back and inspected it. "Could I make some money with this?" he asked. "It'd be a good start."

"Of course, kid. Stick with me, and you'll be rich."

The Batavian didn't bother to hide his hesitation.

"What are you two talking about?" Auctus Tullius Plato interjected, carefully placing down an amphora filled with fish sauce and salt.

"Business," boasted Fulcinius Agricola Statius. "We're planning a future where we won't die on some battlefield of honor."

"Ah," was all Plato said.

"I'm selling my sword," the Batavian explained, showing the weapon to the newcomer.

"And why would you do that?"

"To make a lot of money."

"But…it's just a sword," Plato objected.

"A Batavian sword!"

"A sword is a sword."

"Let it go, Aquila. Everyone knows Plato has no sense for business. All he cares about is scriptures and verses," Fulcinius Agricola Statius interjected.

"Not at all! I just didn't want him to get his hopes up…that's all."

"What am I hoping for? I've got a sword, and I'll make a profit."

"See? He's already deluded," Plato muttered.

"He's just showcasing the goods."

"Exactly…my sword. It's killed many enemies, so it's worth more."

"Not at all! Aquila, be reasonable. They'll buy the sword for what it's worth, not a *follis* more," Plato said, spreading his arms in resignation.

"Aren't you being a bit much?" Fulcinius Agricola Statius' patience was wearing thin.

"I don't want to hear another word… Am I clear?" Centurion Antoninus Tacitus growled, silencing them all. "The others have finished their work and are trying to rest. We'll be departing soon."

The three exchanged glances before sitting on a coiled rope.

As Antoninus Tacitus walked away, he let out a loud fart.

"His ass has the same voice as his mouth!" hissed Fulcinius Agricola Statius, making the others chuckle softly.

***

It was the *Hora secunda* when the ship finally cast off its moorings.

The sun was beginning to warm the air, and a light breeze promised to aid their maneuvers along the coastline.

Flocks of birds streaked the sky, and a few seagulls perched on the railings.

Once they left the port, the oars were drawn in, and the sails unfurled.

The ship began to pick up speed, gliding over the water.

Looking ahead was almost impossible; the sun's glare on the azure sea was so intense that the surface seemed ready to burst into flames at any moment.

The trireme's bronze ram sliced through the water, sending white froth and effervescent spray cascading along the hull, which the mild breeze scattered into mist.

The taut ropes creaked under the force of the wind driving the sail.

The wooden hull groaned under the strain, as if emitting a growl of exertion.

Some attributed the smooth voyage to the Christian God, while others believed it was Aeolus hurling the ship toward the shores of *Regio Campania Felix,* taking advantage of the calm sea.

The salty air stung the skin and filled the breeze with its briny aroma.

Vatinius Auruncus paused to observe his comrades.

They were all veterans of the Battle of Arles, men with whom he had forged a brotherly bond over the years.

Some were now in the realm of the dead, and their absence was felt even more keenly on this return journey home.

But each had fallen in legendary battles, and for a legionary, no better death could be granted.

On the ship's deck, however, the atmosphere was bustling with activity, keeping nearly everyone occupied.

The good spirits were infectious, and sporadic laughter mingled with the whisper of the wind. The shouts of the eccentric sailor hired by Antoninus Tacitus shortly before leaving the port of Massilia were beginning to disrupt the pleasant quiet.

All that was known about him was his name—Kos—and that he was of Greek origin. He had an unusual way about him.

He would sprint to the bow, appearing as though he were sniffing the air. In reality, he was narrowing his eyes to better focus on the horizon, compensating for the failing vision caused by his advanced age. Then, he would run back to the helm, adjust its alignment, and hand it over to Ulzio Dacianus, who would take charge from that point on.

To the legionaries, his behavior seemed peculiar, to say the least.

Not to mention his attire: a tunic cinched at the waist with an oversized belt, from which hung two large iron rings. The soldiers couldn't figure out their purpose, unaware that Kos used them to secure himself on the ship in case of a storm.

His trousers ended just below the knee, leaving his calves and feet bare. He moved around the deck and along the ship's rails barefoot, his soles hardened into thick calluses, as durable as sandal leather. His olive-toned skin enveloped a wiry, bony, yet sturdy frame. His body was a tangle of muscles that tensed visibly when he hauled on ropes during difficult maneuvers. The skin of his face resembled that of a tortoise—weathered and rough, marked by a life spent outdoors and exposed to the elements.

"Do you think we made the right choice?" Antoninus Tacitus asked, his stomach uneasy despite the calm seas.

"I think so. He seems capable," Vatinius Auruncus replied, observing the sailor's movements.

"He's running back and forth. It's hardly reassuring."

"He's alone, doing the work of an entire crew."

"True..."

"We have to trust him. And if he doesn't lead us to our shores, I'll personally see to it that he's hanged."

Plato and the Scout were managing the sail.

Kos had explained how to monitor it and, at his signal, they would tighten or loosen it as needed.

The two exchanged comments, pretending to be experienced sailors.

In reality, it was Kos who issued clear instructions, and the legionaries simply followed his advice.

During maneuvers, Plato would occasionally slip away, sitting down with his knees drawn up to unroll a parchment and jot down his thoughts.

"Bah! A soldier writing poetry. No wonder we've ended up like this..." Fulcinius Agricola Statius would mock him.

"When you're swimming in *sesterces*, you'll send a servant to fetch me to recite them at one of your grand banquets," Plato shot back, not missing the chance to subtly jab at Fulcinius' ambition of getting rich by selling weapons looted from the port warehouses.

"Bah! Intellectuals… They call themselves learned and then mock business," Fulcinius muttered, cutting the conversation short.

The wind suddenly changed direction, now coming from the east and growing steadily stronger.

Vatinius Auruncus called for Kos.

He asked if this change would cause any problems, and the sailor answered honestly.

He explained that the sea was unpredictable, but he had weathered so many storms that it no longer worried him.

Taking advantage of the moment, Kos recounted his past, explaining that he had served in the Dalmatian fleet until just a few months earlier.

But the naval force stationed at Salona had been gradually dismantled amid the turmoil with Odoacer, Orestes, and the court of Julius Nepos.

Without regular pay, many sailors began secretly selling whatever they could salvage from ships or customs warehouses.

Some were caught and punished, while others, like Kos, managed to escape and fled far away, seeking work in other Mediterranean ports.

Kos went on to say that, to flee Salona, they had stolen a Liburnian ship that had been left to rot at anchor. They loaded it with casks and set sail.

The fugitives—about twenty in all—came from a variety of backgrounds: Egyptians, Persians, Greeks, Italians, and even a Vandal who had deserted from the fleet of Genseric, the fearsome immortal king of the Vandals.

Finding refuge in the port of Massilia, Kos began sailing for anyone who could pay him.

It was almost evening by the time the first day of navigation came to an end. A sudden gust of wind caused the sail to billow out violently. The trireme slowed before resuming its pace.

Concerned by the unexpected wind change, Kos reached into the pouch strapped to his belt. He pulled out a small, carved, painted wooden statue with a broken base.

"What are you doing?" Vatinius Auruncus asked, worried that Kos might be preparing to make a sacrifice to some ancient deity.

Most of the legionaries on board were devout followers of the True Faith, and despised idolaters. Such a situation would undoubtedly spark unrest. Kos' response reassured him.

"It's a statue of Blessed Erasmus[1]," he said, placing the object in the center of the deck at the base of the mast. "He's the protector of sailors and seafarers."

The soldiers approached, still wary.

Their cloaks flapped in the strengthening wind, which was now whipping fiercely as the sea began to swell.

"Don't be afraid. This is Saint Erasmus of Formia. He suffered martyrdom under Diocletian, and has since offered his protection to the sea. We sailors invoke him when storms are near, and…" Kos looked up at the clouds gathering overhead, "I believe this is one of those times."

Fear gripped the legionariesa, and many began to kneel—even those who weren't Christians. At the word *storm*, Vatinius Auruncus felt a chill run down his spine.

"Pray to Blessed Erasmus and join the voices of all sailors who, at this moment, call upon him for mercy and salvation from the sea's wrath. May he intercede with Triton and calm him, for we are but miserable beings in the grand design of the Divine!"

The young centurion looked up.

Kos had unleashed a stream of words that ultimately amounted

---

[1] *Saint Erasmus of Formia*: A bishop of Antioch, Saint Erasmus fled for seven years to a cave during Christian persecutions. Discovered and imprisoned for refusing to offer sacrifices to pagan idols, he was later freed, and began converting many people. He is also credited with miracles. After further persecution, he ended up in Formia, where he died a few days later (possibly seven). Tradition suggests he was a bishop of Formia and was martyred under Emperor Diocletian.

to nonsense—mixing a Christian martyr with Triton, a god from the Caesars' era, and even with the Christian God.

Still, he chose not to point it out, noticing that all the men were respectfully, even devoutly, silent.

"Now, brothers of the sea, let's get to work. Soon, we'll have plenty to worry about. But if you follow my advice, we might just have a chance to make it through."

"Why does he say 'a chance to make it through'?" Evetius Aquila asked nervously.

When no one answered, he repeated the question.

Still, he received no reply.

The soldiers scattered, hastily setting to work.

In his years of battle, Vatinius Auruncus had never seen his men so frightened.

The swelling sea made them uneasy, and some began to feel the queasiness of their stomachs betraying them.

The surface of the water had turned black, and the waves grew increasingly massive.

The keel groaned under the strain of the relentless motion, and keeping the course was becoming a struggle as the helmsman fought to hold the rudder steady.

"We need to lower the sail and secure it to the mast with ropes. Quickly," Kos suggested.

Before he even finished speaking, a handful of legionaries rushed toward the mast to carry out the maneuver.

"Are you scared?" Kos asked the young centurion.

"A little…"

"Pray to Saint Erasmus."

"That wouldn't be enough to calm me."

"Uncertainty is part of every sailor's life."

"Exactly. For sailors. I just want to go home," the officer retorted curtly.

The ship tilted sharply, one side crashing onto the water as it rode the crest of a massive wave that spilled onto the deck.

The hull skidded uncontrollably, and while the men scrambled to regain control, Vatinius Auruncus noticed that Ulzio Dacianus had been thrown to the ground by the rudder bar.

The rod had slipped from the legionary's grip, striking him with such force that he now lay on the deck, rubbing his head.

Kos admired how Vatinius Auruncus managed to keep his composure, even in the face of a storm that would terrify any man.

The leaden sky darkened further, hastening the arrival of night.

Grabbing a lantern, Kos waved it toward another ship not far away, also visibly struggling against the storm.

The other vessel returned the signal.

The light from their lamps was barely visible through the heavy rain that now poured relentlessly.

"What are you signaling to them?" Vatinius Auruncus asked.

"We need to find shelter. This wind is pushing us toward the Iberian Peninsula, but we can use it to sail toward Corsica. We'll aim for Centurinum[2], in the land of the Venacini[3]. There, we'll find refuge from the storm until it passes."

"How long will it take?" Vatinius Auruncus asked, his tone tinged with hope.

"We've covered a lot of distance with the favorable wind. We were already in sight of Tugullium, so it shouldn't take long... provided Triton wills it, of course," Kos explained while securing a rope to a bitt.

Vatinius Auruncus considered asking why Kos prayed to both Saint Erasmus and Triton, but he decided to keep his doubts to himself.

In the midst of a raging storm, it hardly seemed important.

His musings were abruptly interrupted when Fulcinius Agricola Statius vomited on his feet.

---

[2] *Centurinum*: A Roman settlement in northern Corsica, located at the tip of the peninsula known as the "finger of Corsica".

[3] *Venacini*: The inhabitants of northern Corsica were referred to by this name.

"Forgive me, Centurion..." Fulcinius muttered before clinging to the railing and retching again.

Looking down, the officer noticed the deck was littered with vomit.

The legionaries were not sailors.

He considered it fortunate that the peaks of the crashing waves occasionally washed over the deck, cleaning it.

Kos stopped Gallienus Lars Gracchus, who was trying to fit an oar into a slot. "Go to the galley and grab some salted fish to distribute to the men. It'll help with their seasickness," he instructed before turning to Vatinius Auruncus. "I can't have everyone falling ill—I can't sail this ship alone!" Kos spat to the side and then ran back to the helm.

He began explaining the route to Ulzio Dacianus, pointing to a specific spot.

Vatinius Auruncus couldn't hear what they were saying over the howling wind.

The other ship was no longer visible, which greatly worried the young centurion. He kept searching for it, his eyes straining to see it through the towering, dark waves that rose and fell ceaselessly.

***

A pleasant breeze tickled his face.

A young woman was stroking his hair, her expression ambiguous—was it attraction, or annoyance?

The sunlight created a soft halo around her face as her lips moved.

She had a familiar face, but he couldn't remember who she was.

He recognized the slow flow of the Liris River, snaking its way toward the sea.

He was home, but when he tried to reach out his hand, it wouldn't respond.

The woman continued to stroke his hair, biting her lower lip...
"Centurion..."

It was strange to hear a man's voice coming from her mouth.

"Centurion, we're safe now."

And yet, those beautiful lips...

"We've reached the harbor at Centurinum... We made it."

The voice sounded like Antoninus Tacitus.

He wondered why the girl's arms were so hairy.

Then, looking closer, he noticed she wore a scarf and had a long, soaking-wet beard.

"You're beautiful, but I don't remember your name..." Vatinius Auruncus said, his lips dry and his throat parched.

"Beautiful?" Antoninus Tacitus frowned. "May Saint Apollinaris help you regain your senses. Are you feverish?" he asked, scratching the back of his neck.

As Vatinius Auruncus focused on his surroundings, he realized he was lying down, his head cradled in Plato's arms.

In front of him stood Antoninus Tacitus, staring at him as one might look at a sword about to strike their head.

That girl wasn't there with him, and he wasn't at home.

He forced himself to accept reality, repeating the facts to himself.

"What happened to me?" he asked, propping himself up on his elbows.

"Praise be to the Blessed Virgin! You've come back to your senses, Commander. We were caught in a sudden storm... Kos says it's not uncommon in this part of the sea. We took advantage of our proximity to Corsica to seek shelter, and now we're waiting for the storm to pass. Once it's over, we'll resume our voyage. We shouldn't be too far from the Italian coast."

Vatinius Auruncus got to his feet, noticing that everyone was watching him, even as they pretended to busy themselves with the mooring ropes.

"Why did I lose consciousness?"

Antoninus Tacitus pointed upward toward the yardarm. It lay broken in half, and a couple of soldiers were cutting away the ropes still securing the sail. It would need to be replaced before they could sail again.

"It fell on you and that other poor soul," he said, gesturing with his chin toward Gaius Octavianus, who was rubbing his head. "You weren't killed by sheer luck—the rolled-up sail cushioned the impact," he explained.

The commander silently thanked fate.

Then he asked about the other ship they had encountered during the storm.

"It's anchored behind that Liburnian vessel. They were just as lucky as we were."

Hearing those words, he fully regained his composure. "So, we made it."

Antoninus Tacitus nodded, scratching his backside.

"Did we suffer any losses?"

"No. Fortunately, none."

"Good. At least that's something."

Almost simultaneously, the soldiers' eyes turned toward the pier.

"Trouble's coming," Antoninus Tacitus said, gripping the hilt of his gladius and sliding it slightly from its scabbard.

Seeing him, the others also reached for their weapons.

Despite his aching body and pounding head, Centurion Vatinius Auruncus rushed forward to see what was happening.

When his eyes focused on the pier, he saw about twenty customs guards. Their officer was speaking to Kos, who had approached the railing. The officer was asking to come aboard.

The two centurions exchanged a brief but meaningful glance. They needed to be ready.

After a brief conversation with the officer, Kos approached them.

"Commander, the customs officer is asking permission to board."

"For what reason?"

The Greek's face twisted into a mask of irony, not unlike a theatrical mask. "Customs always inspects ships. And there's also a docking fee to pay," he explained.

"But we're taking shelter from the storm, and we have damages to repair..."

"Precisely why..." Kos interrupted in a tone that sounded more

like an order than a suggestion, "...we can't set sail in this condition. And, in case you haven't noticed, those men now serve the
kingdom of the Vandals, not Rome. They don't take kindly to
imperial soldiers, though they might turn a blind eye if we were
just a cargo ship."

"We're not a cargo ship," the commander stated, trying to anticipate the Greek's thoughts.

"Exactly..." Kos nodded in agreement.

"What do you suggest we do?" Vatinius asked.

"Be very persuasive," Kos replied.

"I understand."

"I'm sure you'll handle it," the sailor said, stepping aside, but
keeping his eyes fixed on the commander.

Antoninus Tacitus interjected, "Do we head down there and
string them up with their own guts?"

"No. At least, not for now."

"Then?" he asked, scratching his neck and beard. "What do you
want us to do?"

"Call Fulcinius Agricola Statius," Vatinius Auruncus ordered,
his eyes still fixed on the customs guards, who were now being
reinforced by another ten heavily-armed men.

The new arrivals still wore Roman armor and equipment,
though they were now clearly in the service of the Vandals.

"I'm already here," Fulcinius announced, stepping forward after
overhearing the commander's request. "What can I do for you?"
he added with a hint of sarcasm.

The commander didn't waste time. "They say you have a dagger
with an ivory handle among your weapons."

The legionary began shaking his head. "I don't know who's
spreading such rumors, but..."

"Hand it over," the officer cut him off.

"But it's the finest piece in my collection! Without it, I'd lose
the main profit of my new business," Fulcinius protested, already
guessing what the commander intended to do with it.

"Either your dagger, or all our throats. Out there..." the commander gestured toward the open sea, "…the storm that nearly sank us is still raging. And over here…" he pointed to the customs guards, whose numbers were still growing, "…we have them." His sharp gaze locked onto Fulcinius. "Your dagger gives us an opportunity."

"What a shame—you're about to lose the crown jewel of your shop!" Ulzio Dacianus laughed.

Fulcinius shot him a glare so menacing that it silenced him immediately.

"Fine! I'll do it for you, my brothers-in-arms," Fulcinius grumbled, clearly displeased. "May the god of the abyss curse this island!" he muttered as he reached into his armor and pulled out a rough cloth bundle tied with a leather strap.

He handed it to the commander.

"I kept it with me for safekeeping."

"Say goodbye to it," Ulzio Dacianus quipped.

"Let's hope they pick you as a slave," Fulcinius shot back.

"Let's hope this works. Go greet the customs militia," the centurion ordered.

"Let's hope…" Fulcinius muttered as Vatinius Auruncus took the bundle.

The commander then rose and, with a gait that was anything but steady, approached the railing.

Feigning a friendliness that was far from genuine, he addressed the customs officer. "You may come aboard," he said, granting permission to the armed men on the pier.

The officer introduced himself.

His thin, pointed nose resembled the tip of a threatening weapon. His helmet covered a face that, despite a forced smile, exuded cruelty. He wore a Roman officer's lorica, but the tunic beneath it betrayed his Alanic origins.

It was clear that he had been placed in charge of Centurinum's customs by Genseric's administration, as part of the Vandal king's meticulous control over his territories.

Many Alanic officers, cast adrift after the fall of the Roman

Empire, had allied themselves with Genseric, who rewarded them with authority in peripheral settlements like the small port town of Centurinum.

This officer, the commander deduced, was one of them.

"Welcome to the port of Centurinum," the customs officer said, opening with a friendly tone that was clearly intended to set the stage for his demands.

"And welcome to my ship," Vatinius Auruncus replied. "I offer you my courtesy," he added, surprised at his own words.

The officer seemed to recognize the lack of genuine warmth behind the facade and got straight to the point.

"In this condition, your ship cannot return to sea, and out there, the god of the abyss has yet to calm his wrath. To remain moored in my port, you must pay a docking fee of one *siliqua* per day," he said, pausing deliberately to study the Roman commander's reaction.

"Additionally, I must inspect your cargo and review some administrative matters, which may result in significant and tedious delays to your journey."

"I'm confident your work will be meticulous and respectful of the duties your role demands," he acquiesced.

"I'm pleased to see I'm dealing with a reasonable man. It will make my job easier, and I'm certain the Regent of Italy will be glad to have his ships of soldiers set sail without undue delays," he remarked with a disdainful glance toward the legionaries.

The expressions of the legionaries, however, betrayed anything but goodwill.

The customs officer had the air of someone skilled at creating obstacles and fabricating bureaucratic issues to secure personal gain on top of collecting what was owed.

Vatinius Auruncus had encountered plenty of such individuals, and knew only one way to make them stop dragging their feet. A method with deadly efficiency.

He accompanied the Alan customs officer through the inspection. First, he showed him the storage areas, which contained only the provisions needed for the journey, except for the weapons of Fulcinius Agricola Statius—though the officer paid no attention to those. Then, he invited him into the ship's sole, tiny cabin, where he presented the scroll that ordered them to leave the port of Massilia.

The customs officer weighed the scroll before unrolling it, noticing something else inside. Something heavy. Perhaps valuable.

He unrolled it, retrieved a package wrapped in coarse cloth, and pretended to examine the seal before voicing his opinion: "I'm well-versed in port seals, and this one seems...irregular." He unwrapped the bundle, revealing a dagger with an ivory handle.

"It belonged to a noble Goth. Its value is considerable," interjected the Roman commander.

"There are still some missing customs formalities," the Alan feigned a closer inspection of the seal. "For example, this document does not indicate that the departure tax has been paid. This minor issue must be resolved before you can disembark to gather what you need for your ship's repairs," he said, his tone flat and emotionless, though his words concealed the demand for a more generous bribe.

A wave of anger gripped the Roman, who longed to tear out the tongue of the corrupt bastard, but he continued to feign compliance.

"That is for a Roman port, while this is the port of Genseric's kingdom. Whether a Roman tax has been paid or not shouldn't matter," he said in a tone that encouraged further listening. "I was just suggesting that offering this dagger to someone powerful could open many doors. It's a rare and precious weapon. The scabbard is entirely made of carved briarwood." He restrained himself from stabbing the officer then and there if he voiced even the slightest further objection.

Instead, the customs officer nodded eagerly. Perhaps the prospect of profiting from the dagger had finally unlocked something.

"I believe you're right, Roman! These documents are perfectly in order for this administration. You'll only stay as long as needed to repair your ship. In the meantime, I wish you a pleasant stay in Centurinum. However, only four men are permitted to disembark, no more. I trust I've made myself clear."

"That's perfectly fine," the Roman replied.

"Good," the officer said, bowing slightly in farewell.

The centurion felt a surge of nausea as he watched the officer hide the dagger within his armor.

The customs officer disembarked under the watchful eyes of the legionaries, who were left wondering what had transpired in the cabin. They saw him dismiss the customs militia, who dispersed into groups of five or six among the bustling sailors.

Fulcinius Agricola Statius approached the commander. "Did it work?" he asked.

"You'll see—the others will appreciate it," replied Auruncus.

"The others haven't lost a fortune," Fulcinius grumbled.

Vatinius Auruncus chose not to respond. Fulcinius' frustration was justified.

"Let's get ready," Auruncus said, addressing Kos.

***

Four men disembarked. Even one extra would have been cause for a new bribe.

The group consisted of Severinus Majorianus, Gaius Octavianus, Gallienus Lars Gracchus, and Evetius Aquila. The latter stumbled as he set foot on land, still unsteady from the ship's rolling motion.

Small houses built from distinctive black stone rose up along the modest port of Centurinum. Their windows and doors were framed with white paint. Thin columns of smoke rose, defying the drizzle that had taken the place of the downpour from hours earlier.

A milky fog rested on the forested peaks of the nearby hills.

The scents of cooking wafted through the air, mixing sharply with the stench of waste flowing through a small ditch in the middle of the paved road that wound through the houses.

"What is that horrid smell?" Plato asked, pinching his nose with his fingers.

"Tanners," Severinus Majorianus explained. "They boil animal hides to make leather."

"And how do you know about this?" the young soldier replied.

"It's called tanning. First, they salt the animal's hide, and then work it. With the rot, you can imagine the fragrance!" The optio watched him for a reaction.

"What's our task?" asked Gaius Octavianus, who carried two large axes.

"Find a nice, big tree...up there, in those mountains."

"Are you going to help cut it down, or will you just give orders as usual?" Gaius sneered, looking at the others. "You know how optios are, right?"

They chuckled, Evetius Aquila's laugh standing out.

The massive Batavian turned his head this way and that, studying the small houses and every detail that caught his eye.

"Centurions give orders. I only make sure they're carried out. I don't recall..." he gave Gaius a hard look, "...ever backing down in battle."

They passed the last house of the modest seaside village and entered the wet forest.

The path climbed steeply.

A large stag paused to watch the group for a moment before darting away, crashing through the undergrowth.

"Did you see how big it was? And those antlers!"

"That's a full-grown male, meaning meat and a nice warm hide. Isn't that right, Gallienus?" The optio anticipated his approval.

"Can I split off from the group?"

"Not alone. You'll go with Gaius Octavianus."

"I'll bring back plenty of tasty meat."

"We'll bring it back," Gaius interjected.

"Evetius Aquila and I will find a suitable tree. But you'll help us carry it back to the ship."

At that, the group split up. Two followed the tracks of the large animal, while the rest searched for the tree.

After some time walking, they found themselves in a much denser thicket.

The trees were so tightly packed that, over the years, they had grown upward in search of sunlight. The little light that managed to filter through the dense branches dissolved into the mist lingering in the air.

"It's not even cold..." Severinus Majorianus quipped, shivering as he set down the two heavy axes and patted a massive trunk with his hands. "We'll warm up cutting down this big tree."

"You're like a matron on her fifth marriage," Evetius Aquila scoffed, inhaling deeply to fill his lungs with the icy air. "Hand me one of those axes, and I give you my word: before nightfall, we'll have a new beam ready."

It was clear that the Batavian had never built a ship's hull and had no idea how long it would take to prepare the necessary components. He would be in for a rude awakening when, as night fell, it became clear they'd have to spend the night out in the open.

As he swung at the trunk, he noticed the optio setting up a makeshift camp.

"What are you doing?"

"Preparing a shelter for the night, hoping the branches will provide enough cover if the rain picks up again."

The Batavian froze in place.

"Cutting down a trunk isn't enough. You have to strip all the branches, and we won't be done before dark," Severinus Majorianus hurriedly explained.

Meanwhile, Gallienus Lars Gracchus' hand grabbed Gaius Octavianus' arm, his eyes signaling him to look down the slope, through the mist.

The imposing antlers of a stag were barely visible, and as the fog shifted, parts of the animal came into view.

The two legionaries locked eyes, trying to communicate silently, knowing even the slightest noise would send the animal fleeing.

As if speaking without words, each man took a position. They were setting up a pincer maneuver to surprise the stag, which seemed to be enjoying the cool evening air.

Gallienus Lars Gracchus crouched behind a bush to get a better look at the creature. Its slender body was muscular and well-developed.

Its broad chest, raised haunches, and long, powerful neck supported a regal head, fitting for such a noble animal. Its smooth, grayish-brown coat extended down to its tail, and long bristles framed its eyes.

This male sported a mane around its neck, making it appear even more majestic.

The stag stood motionless, savoring the freshness of the air and the tranquility of this corner of the forest, where the trees had grown twisted and ghostly over time.

It waited for nightfall to begin its search for food—fresh, tender grasses, young leaves, and twigs. But this would not be as easy as in summer. The ground was covered in moss and rotting undergrowth. With little grass and no leaves on the branches, it would have to settle for bark or roots, digging them out with its hooves.

At the precise moment the stag turned its head sharply, it spotted Gallienus Lars Gracchus behind the trunk of a fir tree. The legionary's javelin flew through the air with a hiss, cutting the silence and ending with a loud crack.

The stag leaped downhill, maintaining its usual elegance despite the Roman spear lodged in its sternum and the two legionaries in pursuit.

In a gully where a clear, fast-flowing stream ran, the exhausted stag crouched on its hind legs. Its breathing became labored as it desperately tried to gather the strength to rise and flee to safety.

But it had lost too much blood. Its forelegs gave out again, and its gaze darted around, searching for its fate.

It didn't have to wait long.

"Roast meat tonight!" Gaius Octavianus declared, his face beaming with satisfaction.

Gallienus Lars Gracchus drew his pugio from its sheath and

finished the animal with a precise stab to the heart. "Such a beautiful creature didn't deserve to suffer," he explained. "We'll need sturdy branches to carry it."

"I've already spotted one. We'll find the other," Gaius replied.

The two stripped two long, sturdy branches and tied them together with vines to create a sort of stretcher for their prize.

They rejoined the others by following the smell of burning wood.

The cold was starting to seep through their waxed cloaks, chilling them to the bone.

"About time you brought us dinner!" Severinus Majorianus protested, wasting no time in beginning to skin the carcass.

"Can I keep the hide? I'd love to make a nice shoulder cloak out of it," he asked while expertly separating the skin from the muscles with both hands.

Evetius Aquila, evidently starving, had spent the wait sharpening sticks to skewer the meat for cooking. As he prepared them, he passed the skewers to his companions, who roasted their food over the flames.

The evening passed with hopeful discussions about reaching the Italian coast, which, from what they understood, wasn't far away.

"I'll sell the antlers to Fulcinius Agricola Statius—he can make handles for some stunning hunting daggers," Gaius Octavianus proposed.

Centurinum, Prima vigilia

The Latin muttered inside the tavern was barely intelligible to Centurion Vatinius Auruncus.

He had decided to disembark despite the customs officer's prohibition.

He climbed the alleys winding up from the port, scaling the steep cliffside of the town. The maze of archways, underpasses, spiral staircases, and dark, narrow tunnels reeked of waste and rotting fish.

The dim, reddish light seeping through the tavern's foggy windows was inviting—a chance to warm up with some hot food and, more importantly, to overhear rumors about the two storm-tossed ships docked at the port.

He removed his hood, not wanting to give the impression he was hiding his face, and found a seat in the corner of a rough wooden table.

A lively fire crackled nearby.

He was served shellfish he'd never seen before, a bit of garum, and some hot soup with meat.

The tavern's patrons were a mixed crowd: Greek sailors, Egyptians, Gallo-Romans, and Vandals.

Most were locals spending their last evening hours—and much of the night—gambling with dice and drinking themselves into a stupor. Others were soldiers from King Genseric's fleet, stationed in Corsica.

Vatinius had noticed the Vandal navy's *liburna* docked in the port, and hoped there would be no clashes between his men and the Vandals.

He observed that the locals' accents were harsh and drawn-out in their pronunciation of certain words.

Most of them were fishermen and shipyard workers.

He had only counted two ships; after all, the port was quite small.

The wine tasted unusual compared to what he was accustomed to, but after traveling far and wide across the Empire, he had come to realize that wine's flavor depended greatly on where the vines that produced it were grown.

His attention was suddenly captured by a song extolling the greatness and invincibility of the Western Roman Empire.

It didn't take him long to realize it was a mocking satire, directed precisely at the Romans from Provence. They were talking about his group.

He had made the right decision to step into that tavern. This was the kind of place to gather useful intelligence.

One of them, a Scirian judging by his appearance and clothing, stood up with a cup overflowing with wine, holding it aloft as if preparing for a toast. His eyes had a translucent hue, and his long reddish mustache was tied behind his neck. His helmet lay on the table in front of him.

"In just a few months," he began, "I've held coins in my hands bearing the image of Romulus Augustulus, and others with Julius Nepos. Rome no longer has a Sacred Augustus, yet it keeps minting tremisses with emperors' faces on them—when they should start stamping coins with the faces of palace eunuchs instead," he said, mimicking a lewd scene of sodomy.

The laughter of his traveling companions and others in the tavern drowned out the usual murmur of conversation.

Vatinius Auruncus studied the man's attire. He was no sailor—clearly a warrior. Undoubtedly, he had disembarked from one of the ships docked in the harbor.

Perhaps a mercenary hired to protect the cargo from the pirates that infested the seas.

The warrior continued speaking: "While the Romans fuss over their fine tunics and their useless laws, the so-called barbarians are taking over every corner of the Empire... Empire, indeed!" He spat on the floor. "Tell me, does any territory, barely held together by the whims of the gods, still deserve to be called an Empire? Italy is in the hands of Odoacer, who pretends to be the Regent of the Republic while everyone knows he aims to be nothing less than a king. Dalmatia is under Julius Nepos, who claims to be the only legitimate ruler. The two watch each other from a distance while the situation remains unresolved. Both, they say, have sought approval from the Eastern Augustus, sending ambassadors to Zeno's court. And Zeno, for his part, has managed to displease neither, recognizing Julius Nepos as the Sacred Emperor while imposing the patrician Odoacer as supreme commander of the Italian army," he concluded with a belch.

"A clever political move," echoed a sailor who appeared to be a Vandal.

More laughter followed, along with another mock hymn to Rome's greatness—an excuse to drink more wine.

Most of the tavern's patrons were already drunk.

A warrior, now completely intoxicated, stumbled over to where Vatinius Auruncus was sitting. He grabbed the pitcher of water meant for the centurion's meal and began urinating into it.

The centurion barely restrained the urge to gut the man with his pugio. Staying incognito was more important than defending his honor.

But he flinched when he recognized the man as a Herulian.

His heart pounded in his chest. He forced himself to remain calm, continuing to eat without raising suspicion.

But it wasn't enough.

"Hey, that guy's pissing in your pitcher!" someone shouted.

Laughter erupted in the tavern.

Vatinius realized he needed to feign outrage, or they'd start suspecting him.

He stood up and changed seats, resuming his meal as though nothing had happened.

The Herulian warrior set the pitcher back on the table, tucking himself back into his breeches. Then, he snatched a cup from another patron and downed its contents.

"You're a coward! I'd have pissed in your bowl too!" the Scirian jeered.

The Roman officer pretended not to hear and continued eating.

The Herulian soon distracted the crowd's attention.

So drunk he could barely stand, he tripped and fell into the soup pot.

The innkeeper intervened, dragging him outside.

The commotion helped everyone forget what had just happened, and Vatinius Auruncus breathed a sigh of relief.

But he realized he had been noticed. Deciding to turn the situation to his advantage, he asked, "How do you know so much about the state of the Empire?"

He saw the mercenary as a good source of information.

The man gave a sly grin under his ruddy mustache. "I left from the port of Classe. The ship I sailed on went to Provence, and from there, I traveled up the river to Arles. What I know, I've learned from the locals. I've noticed that crossroads are under inspection by the soldiers of Italy's army, which has been under Odoacer's command since the young Emperor was killed alongside his father. They're making sure no contingents loyal to the Herulian king Rudulfus are on the move. He's now also the Governor of Gaul. The situation is tense, my friend..."

At the mention of Rudulfus, Vatinius felt a jolt.

"Odoacer has border garrisons, then?"

"Just small outposts with few men. The Heruli are running rampant in the north and in Gaul—also along the peninsula and, judging by the latest news, even at sea now!"

That last remark caught the centurion's full attention.

"At sea, you say? What do you mean?"

The mercenary, now the center of attention, reveled in the moment as everyone listened.

"Tonight, two ships docked here, caught in the storm while they were at sea. One is full of cursed Romans, probably fleeing given the state of their vessel. The other is loaded with Herulian warriors, who are already causing trouble everywhere."

Vatinius Auruncus swallowed hard, his chewing halted.

Now it was clear—the other ship had been pursuing them.

Worse yet, it was docked in the same port.

He needed to warn the others and set sail as soon as possible.

But the Scirian, now suspicious of his curiosity, narrowed his eyes into slits.

He didn't trust him: "I see the purple cloak that covers the tunic of Rome's soldiers. Your belt confirms what I suspect, and I find it hard to believe that an imperial soldier wouldn't know the state of the Empire to which he swore loyalty."

Things were taking a bad turn. He decided to fix it. "My men and I..." he chose not to hide that he had other armed men in Centurinum "...come from a remote corner of Belgic Gaul, where news hasn't reached us promptly for a long time. Connections to the rest of the Empire are often cut off because of the uncertainty along the borders. We were soldiers of Rome, but no longer," he carefully avoided the word "barbarian" to prevent a fight.

The Scirian drew in as much air as he could, gulped more wine, and replied, "So, Roman…" he emphasized the last word, "I'll take on the burden of explaining to you the shame your immortal Empire has fallen into."

Those words triggered more laughter, but Vatinius Auruncus decided to endure it and feigned amusement at whatever the man was about to say.

Out of the corner of his eye, however, he noticed three Heruli entering the tavern. Three warriors.

"When the brave Emperor Julius Nepos decided to leave Ravenna—not of his own accord, of course…" he chuckled, provoking more laughter and sarcastic remarks, "Orestes decided to elevate his son to the purple. A beardless boy some have called a coward," more laughter followed. "Meanwhile, Julius Nepos was hosting sodomites, eunuchs, and deacons within the sacred walls of Salona's palace. At that point, Odoacer, who had received little from the Empire's division, decided to use the loyalty of the barbarian troops stationed on the peninsula to his advantage. At Pavia, he defeated Orestes and killed him," he mimicked a decapitation with a hand gesture. "Now there's an Emperor, but he's holed up in Dalmatia, while Italy is in chaos—or rather, under Odoacer's rule. And Gaul? That's in the hands of Rudulfus."

An awkward silence followed.

The Scirian savored the expression on the Roman commander's face, while Vatinius Auruncus struggled to suppress a curse.

The latter ended the conversation with a gesture that would allow him to leave the tavern without causing trouble.

"I'll buy you a cup of wine to drink with my best wishes, warrior," the officer said.

The Scirian offered a slight smile before resuming his parody of the Empire's state.

Wrapping himself in his waxed cloak and pulling up his hood, Vatinius Auruncus stepped out into the night.

***

He ran back to the ship.

He roused the sleeping figures huddled under their cloaks.

"Have you become an insomniac, you damned know-it-all?" Antoninus Tacitus growled at him.

"The other ship..." he pointed three ships over, "...it's full of Heruli."

"By the Holy Virgin of—"

"Don't swear!" Drusus Variatus snapped, silencing him.

When everyone was awake, Vatinius noticed someone was missing.

"Fulcinius Agricola Statius..." he muttered.

Auctus Tullius lowered his gaze, a detail that didn't escape the centurion. "Where is he?" Vatinius demanded.

Plato remained silent.

"Soldier, where is he?"

Forced to speak, Plato spilled the truth: "He went ashore to find more weapons to sell once we're home..."

Vatinius Auruncus erupted with fury.

"Listen up! It won't be long before the Heruli discover we're here. We have to stay vigilant."

Everyone nodded.

Then he addressed Auctus Tullius Sextus directly: "Head into the mountains and find the others. Tell them to return quickly. If you can't find them, come back before dawn."

Plato immediately set off on his mission.

"Everyone else, stand guard," Vatinius ordered.

Centurinum, end of the Tertia vigilia.

Plato followed the scent of burning wood. He climbed a path, hoping it was the right one. He carried a torch that crackled and illuminated his steps.

A herd of wild boars crossed his path, but fortunately, they paid him no mind, and he continued his ascent.

The smell of smoke grew stronger and stronger until it became overpowering. If it wasn't another campfire, he would find his fellow legionaries.

He extinguished the torch and cautiously approached. He waited for his eyes to adjust to the darkness and, by the light of the moon, he spotted Roman armor.

He moved closer, identifying himself to avoid being cut down before he reached the fire.

The four soldiers jumped to their feet, weapons tightly gripped.

"Plato, what are you doing here, for the heart of Saint Maurice[4]?" exclaimed Severinus Majorianus, still catching his breath.

Plato quickly explained the situation, and in no time, the five of them were running back down the trail.

"And the trunk?" the Batavian asked as he leaped over a rock.

"We'll find one at the port…" Severinus Majorianus quipped.

At those last words, everyone understood.

Some other ship would "lend" its mast to the Roman trireme.

They dashed down the path and arrived at the port, crouching behind a crumbling wall.

The Heruli were sitting on a bench outside a tavern.

But they didn't seem to be hunting Romans. Their demeanor was relaxed.

Plato whispered, "Their ship sought refuge from the storm, too. They docked far from ours, and are wandering around these parts without suspecting we're here."

The optio signaled for the group to bypass the tavern unnoticed.

When they reached their ship, they found the other legionaries waiting, fully armed and wearing their armor.

---

[4] *Saint Maurice*: A Roman general born in Thebes in the 3rd century, Saint Maurice died between 286 and 287. He served in the Theban Legion and refused to persecute Christians, for which he was executed by order of Emperor Diocletian.

Centurinum, mid Quarta viglilia of the night [5]

"…So we need a mast…" Severinus Majorianus concluded his tale.

His bony hand scratched his chin as Kos reflected aloud, "This is a small trireme. We don't have enough manpower to row, so we can only rely on the wind. A mast is indispensable." He pursed his lips, thinking. "But it doesn't need to be a large one…" His eyes drifted toward the nearby *liburna*.

All eyes followed his gaze to the indicated ship. It didn't take long before the sailors aboard it found themselves under the threat of drawn swords, while Severinus Majorianus and Gaius Octavianus were already sawing the mast at its base.

"Not a sound," warned Evetius Aquila, holding the tip of his sword to a crew member's throat.

Fortunately, the winter delayed the arrival of dawn, giving them the cover of darkness to transport the mast to the trireme and begin installing it.

"What about the sailors?" Ulzio Dacianus asked, craning his neck to check on their fate.

"Tied up tight. We've got until morning—then someone will notice and raise the alarm," Evetius Aquila replied, surprisingly talkative for once.

Everyone worked to position the mast, adapting it to the ship's deck. It had been roughly cut, but they hoped reinforcing it would be enough to withstand the wind.

***

In a raucous hall, hours later, a Scirian warrior was recounting events to the gathered crowd.

"That Roman pissed himself like a coward…looked just like the Emperor wetting himself when he saw Odoacer ready to cut his—"

---

[5] *Quarta vigilia noctis:* From 3:00 a.m. to 6:00 a.m.

A man stood up.

He took a few steps and positioned himself in front of the Scirian. Beneath his mustache, he seemed to be growling.

"Roman, you said?" he asked, glaring, the muscles in his face twitching with irritation.

The Scirian, puzzled by the man's demeanor, retorted, "Sit back down if you want to hear the end of the story." He shoved the man lightly, holding a cup in his other hand.

When the cup hit the floor, the Scirian glanced down at his abdomen. A dagger's blade was pressed against his stomach. A moment later, more swords were drawn and pointed at him.

"What do you want from me? I was just—"

A hard punch to the gut silenced him.

"My name is Calibrandus, general of the Heruli armies. Tell me about the Roman."

The Scirian gasped for air, straightened himself, and spoke, "He was at this inn, eating. He wore a purple cloak..."

"Go on," Calibrandus pressed, nudging the dagger's point closer.

"There's a ship docked in the harbor. They sought shelter from the storm."

That was all Calibrandus needed. He and his men left the inn while the trembling Scirian collapsed into a chair.

"Trouble," Ulzio Dacianus muttered softly.

He was staring past the ship's bulwarks. Antoninus Tacitus didn't immediately understand, but the other man quickly made it clear.

"They're coming."

Gestures replaced words as the crew prepared for another assault.

The Heruli came charging. They didn't care for subtlety or surprise.

"They're attacking!" Antoninus Tacitus shouted at the top of his lungs.

"Legionaries, shields up!" Vatinius Auruncus ordered.

But he quickly noticed that everyone was already armed and shielded. They needed to set sail—and fast.

One of the sailors from the ship whose mast they had stolen had managed to free himself and was now shouting, "The Romans are here!"

"They already know, so shut up!" Severinus Majorianus mocked.

Despite the tension, laughter erupted among the group.

"By my mother's generous womb, there are so many of them!" Centurion Antoninus Tacitus groaned, scratching his bristly beard as he fumbled with his helmet.

"When are they ever few?" Gaius Octavianus grumbled.

Vatinius Auruncus scanned his soldiers, already in full battle formation. "Raise your shields!" he ordered.

The command came just in time as slingshot projectiles began raining down on the ship, hurled by the advancing enemy soldiers, who now shouted battle cries.

"There are too many," Kos muttered, terror in his voice. He was a sailor, not a soldier.

"We're used to this," Vatinius Auruncus replied. "Take cover below deck. Up here, it'll be a massacre soon."

No sooner had he spoken than another volley of projectiles struck the shield wall. Thankfully, the barrage caused no damage, but Vatinius was certain: the slingers were only covering the enemy's approach.

"Don't let them breach the shields!" he bellowed.

All heads nodded in agreement. They were ready.

A faint light broke through the low-hanging clouds.

Dawn was approaching.

The moon reflected on the sea's surface, as if trying to guide the Romans to salvation while they were under attack. The storm had nearly subsided, and its calmness was a signal worth considering.

Another volley of slingshot fire cracked against the shields and the ship's bulwarks. Vatinius Auruncus silently thanked fortune for sparing them any losses. The enemy's shouts echoed just beyond the dock. The clash was only moments away.

The hail of projectiles ceased—clearly, the slingers didn't want to risk hitting their own comrades. The sound of ladders scraping against the ship's hull marked the beginning of the battle.

"Hold your ground!" shouted Vatinius Auruncus, keeping his eyes locked on the enemies climbing aboard. "Shields tight... hold steady. Steady..."

The Heruli swarmed up the ladders, screaming war cries.

"Hold!"

The attackers were nearly on deck.

"Stay firm..."

When the first weapons struck against the Roman shield wall, the familiar clanging sound reverberated among the legionaries, who didn't retreat a single step.

When the initial charge faltered against the shield wall, the young centurion gave the next command: "Now!"

Blades flashed out from between the shields, stabbing the first attackers to reach the top. Their bodies fell back onto the dock. Cries of pain mingled with the battle screams.

"Close the shields!" came the next order.

A second wave of attackers smashed into the Roman wall, only to falter once again. Wounded enemies collapsed on the trireme's deck and the pier below.

"Centurion..." the optio pointed at something.

Vatinius Auruncus opened his mouth but couldn't utter a word.

Fulcinius Agricola Statius was gesturing from behind a row of barrels. The centurion wanted to reprimand him—or even flog him—but that would have to wait. Statius seemed to be signaling something urgent.

Auruncus didn't understand, and before he could, Statius disappeared.

The battle raged on as the Heruli tried to force their way onto the ship. The legionaries fought fiercely to keep them at bay.

Auruncus yanked his gladius free from the shoulder of a fallen warrior at his feet and immediately slashed downward, slicing into the ribs of another who was attacking from above.

The man's scream rose above the din of battle.

"Don't break formation!" Auruncus shouted with every ounce of his strength, trying to assess the situation.

Blood splattered across his face. He felt no pain, and realized he wasn't wounded. But then, to his horror, he saw Antoninus Tacitus on his knees, clutching his abdomen.

Scarlet streams stained Tacitus' tunic and the deck below.

"Centurion..." the wounded soldier croaked before his voice failed. Auruncus moved to help him, but was intercepted by an enemy wielding a harpoon.

Tacitus, meanwhile, braced his gladius against the deck and used it to push himself upright. Unsteady on his feet and with one hand pressed to his wound, he raised his weapon and shouted something at the attackers.

Two enemies lunged at him, stabbing him in the side and abdomen. Before collapsing, the centurion managed to impale one of them.

The deck was now swarming with enemies, pressing hard against the Roman shields. Their resistance was beginning to falter, and it was clear that if they didn't find a way to set sail soon, they would be overwhelmed.

Suddenly, the enemy's momentum wavered.

Something was distracting them.

A growing light illuminated the scene, coming from the very ship the Heruli had used to pursue them.

"That son of a brothel maid, Fulcinius Agricola Statius!" Severinus Majorianus bellowed, his armor soaked in enemy blood.

The legionaries raised their swords to the sky and roared.

The Heruli stopped climbing the ladders, and some began running back toward their ship.

The centurion called for Drusus Variatus, Ulzio Dacianus, and Evetius Aquila.

"Commander..." Ulzio Dacianus waited for orders, glancing sideways at him.

"You two," he pointed at Dacianus and Variatus, "protect Evetius Aquila with your shields while he cuts the mooring lines. We need to get this ship out of here before it's too late."

A slingshot struck the helmet of the large Batavian soldier, but he didn't so much as flinch.

Ulzio Dacianus and Drusus Variatus exchanged a glance. Seeing that Aquila hadn't lost consciousness, they jumped down from the ship, holding their shields high as Aquila crouched behind them, hacking at the ropes with his long sword.

The Heruli were in disarray. Without orders—Calibrandus had run toward their burning ship—they hesitated, launching only half-hearted attacks at the Romans' shields.

"Hurry up, you muscle-bound giant! Cut those ropes!" Ulzio Dacianus shouted.

Evetius Aquila grunted, gripping his sword tightly and slicing into the thick mooring line.

"Care to explain how someone like me is supposed to hold a shield high enough to protect a giant like him?" Drusus Variatus grumbled.

"I'll knock some debt off your tab if you manage it," Dacianus quipped, deflecting a harpoon strike and sinking his blade into his attacker's ribs.

"If I operated like a loan shark, by now I could've bought Tiberius' villa, eel pool included," Variatus shot back.

The Batavian led the charge, with the others sticking close to him as he severed the ropes. One stern line was already cut, freeing the rear of the trireme from the stone cleat embedded in the dock.

Only two ropes remained—the starboard mooring and the prow line.

As they moved toward the center of the ship, a scream from Drusus Variatus made Aquila and Dacianus whirl around.

Fulcinius Agricola Statius had been struck by an arrow as he ran toward the ship.

He collapsed to the ground, clutching his back with one hand.

He staggered to his feet, trying to reach the hull, but a second arrow hit him, again in the back.

His body arched.

A third arrow whistled through the air and embedded itself squarely in his spine.

The last thing Fulcinius Agricola Statius saw was the anguished roar of Vatinius Auruncus.

The terrible sight of their fellow legionary's death froze the scene.

At that moment, a warrior stepped forward and struck at Ulzio Dacianus, who shielded himself. The blow was so strong that the legionary fell backward.

Evetius Aquila intervened, grabbing the enemy by the throat and ripping him open, letting his entrails spill onto the dock. Then, he tossed the body aside as if swatting away a mosquito.

The glance he exchanged with Ulzio Dacianus said it all: *"I've got your back."*

From a distance, Heruli archers lined up, drawing their bows and releasing a hail of arrows. From the ship, their comrades yelled at them to hurry and climb aboard.

It took four powerful sword strikes to cut the final mooring line. Evetius Aquila's task was done—they needed to get back aboard.

"To the oars!" shouted the sailor.

There were few left to row, so Vatinius Auruncus ordered Plato and Gallienus Lars Gracchus below deck to man the oars while the others scrambled aboard. Auruncus himself stayed to protect Kos as he performed the necessary maneuvers.

Meanwhile, Evetius Aquila and Drusus Variatus had climbed aboard and were waiting for Ulzio Dacianus, who struggled to move behind his shield, now riddled with arrows.

The starboard side of the hull was bristling with dozens of shafts, and the whistling of arrows never ceased. Meanwhile, the Heruli ship was now engulfed in flames, with fire spiraling into the sky and scattering embers into the air.

"That damned bastard saved our skins," Vatinius Auruncus muttered aloud, referring to Fulcinius Agricola Statius.

The Heruli were now running back, furious, seeking vengeance for their burning ship. But the trireme had already begun pulling away from the dock.

Ulzio Dacianus tried to climb aboard, but the relentless rain of arrows kept him pinned. Evetius Aquila shouted for him to move faster, but three warriors closed in on Dacian.

Ulzio Dacianus, a seasoned veteran skilled in close combat, managed to hold his ground against the three for a time. But a blade struck his calf, severing the muscle and forcing him to his knees.

Another enemy sword found its way through the tattered remains of his armor, worn thin from the countless battles. His strength gave out, and his comrades watched as he fell under the Heruli's blows.

Vatinius Auruncus was left with the grim task of ordering Evetius Aquila and Drusus Variatus to take up the oars. The ship began to pick up speed as Kos steered them away from the cursed port.

Once they were clear of the other ships, the sailor unfurled the sail, hoping the newly installed mast would hold under the strain.

As they pulled farther away, the Heruli ship could still be seen burning in the distance, the flames now just a faint glow.

Now, all the survivors stood on deck, their gazes fixed on the shrinking inferno.

Off the western coast of Corsica, Hora quinta

Kos explained that it would be safer to sail around the Corsican peninsula again, rather than navigating southward around the island, as those waters were teeming with ships from the Vandal fleet.

No one stood vigil over the body of Antoninus Tacitus. Spirits were crushed. Even Vatinius Auruncus, for a while, pretended not to notice the still figure of his fallen comrade.

At least until the optio approached him.

"Centurion."

"What?"

"We need to take care of Antoninus Tacitus now. We can't just leave him there."

Auruncus knew he was right. He allowed himself a moment to think of the best way to proceed.

He approached his fallen comrade and wrapped him in the rough wool of his purple cloak. That alone was enough to draw the others closer.

Kos took over the tiller from Drusus Variatus, who also came forward. Evetius Aquila and Plato lifted the centurion's body and let it fall into the sea.

Weighted down by his armor and weapons, the body sank quickly into the depths.

A profound silence descended over the ship, heavy with grief.

Vatinius Auruncus never thought he'd see legionaries with tears swelling in their eyes.

The moment felt like a doorway through time, connecting their past to the painful present.

It was as if they were back on the docks of Portus Setre[6] as boys, waiting to be ferried away by a boat to join the army. Those same boys, now seasoned veterans, had barely survived King Rudulfus' ruthless vengeance.

Each legionary saw the man and the warrior in the others, but all they could think of was the boy they had been.

Exhausted from the fighting and crushed in spirit, they exchanged glances.

Severinus Majorianus clenched his fists and sniffled, trying in vain to hold back his tears. Gallienus Lars Gracchus, on the other hand, let his tears flow freely down his cheeks.

Drusus Variatus gave a bitter smile to Tullius Sextus Plato, who just shook his head in disbelief.

Even Evetius Aquila showed a rare hint of sorrow. No one could have sworn to it, but it almost seemed like he was moved.

A long time passed before anyone spoke again.

---

[6] *Portum Setre*: A small pier on the banks of the Liris River, now within the municipality of Castelforte (LT).

In the meantime, the ship moved steadily forward, leaving behind a faint trail of white foam that blended into the deep blue sea.

North of Corsica, Hora octava

"I share your sorrow for the loss of your men," Kos said, his voice carrying respect more than pity.

"This night, I lost brothers. I shared with them the dream of freedom," Vatinius Auruncus replied, his voice hollow.

Kos pointed toward the horizon. "Do you see that headland?"

The young officer nodded.

"We're not far from rounding Corsica. In two days, we'll reach Etruria. With this current, we're traveling well, and the coast of Latium won't be far after that," he explained.

Hearing no reply, Kos turned to look at the officer, finding him sunk in deep despair.

The sailor, with the wisdom of experience, chose his words carefully. "Your brothers are drinking wine in the Field of Honors now. They lived their last days as free men—don't regret their end. You're a good commander..."

Vatinius Auruncus was grateful for those final words.

Seeking solitude, he shut himself in the cramped cabin of the ship. His mind was clouded by the events of the previous night. He turned his gaze to the small window, just large enough to offer a view outside.

It seemed impossible, but the sea still managed to inspire a sense of peace, even under such circumstances.

He tried to recall the faces of Antoninus Tacitus, Ulzio Dacianus, and Fulcinius Agricola Statius, imagining them proud in their plated armor. But the image soon blurred.

His eyelids grew heavy, and his strength began to fade. He let himself drift into sleep.

Onboard, life went on.

Severinus Majorianus' first order was to wash the deck, leaving no trace of the blood spilled during the battle. Then, he organized guard shifts to keep watch over the sea and prevent any surprise attacks or unwelcome visits from Imperial ships.

Drusus Variatus sat next to Plato. Together, they ate dried meat that, despite its age, still had a tolerable taste.

From time to time, they exchanged glances, as if on the verge of asking a question, but neither spoke.

"What are you staring at me for?" Drusus Variatus growled.

Plato bristled. "You're the one staring at me!"

"Listen to this guy!"

"I thought you wanted to ask me something..."

"I have no questions for you. Let's just keep eating. My guard shift starts soon," Drusus Variatus said, resuming his meal.

A brief silence followed.

"Drusus..."

"What now?"

"What if I wanted to ask *you* something?"

"Then ask it already."

Plato took a deep breath, as though trying to gather all the air of the morning. "Where do you plan to settle? I mean, once we land in Minturnae?"

Drusus stopped chewing and looked up. "I was thinking of going back to my old home, but...I don't think anyone's waiting for me after all this time."

"Got it."

"Why are you asking?" Drusus raised an eyebrow.

"I have the same fear. I don't think anyone's left waiting for me. Who knows how much has changed..."

Third day at sea since leaving Centurinum, Hora undecima

"That's Etruria!" Kos said, pointing to the barely visible coastline.

Faint violet hills outlined the border between land and sea.

A flock of seagulls perched on the water, gently bobbing with the waves. The sun reflected off the sea's surface, creating blinding flashes of light.

The breeze was pleasantly warm, and filled the sail just enough to keep the bow slightly above the waterline.

"Good!" Vatinius Auruncus exclaimed. "Fill the sails. Keep us far out of sight of the watchtowers," he ordered.

"What? We're not docking? Not even for some fresh food..." Kos began to protest, but a stern glare quickly silenced him.

Off Populonia, start of the Tertia vigilia

No lights were visible, except for the height of Populonia, which stood tall atop the promontory. Below the settlement, in the gulf that had once been an Etruscan harbor, the faint glow of lanterns on ships anchored in the port or bay could just barely be made out.

To avoid the Vandal ships prowling the waters, they decided to keep only one lantern lit at the center of the deck. This gave the legionaries just enough light to see on board.

Drusus Variatus manned the tiller, steering along the route Kos had indicated.

The others rested.

Except for Vatinius Auruncus, who was gazing at the stars.

He had never really paid attention to them before, but they seemed to ease the knot of anxiety twisting in his stomach.

It felt as if the stars drew some of his fear out of him, letting it dissipate.

The creaking of the ship's timbers helped relax his tense limbs, and his mind wandered back to his old home in Vescia.

Vescia no longer existed—not since Rome had destroyed the Pentapolis Aurunca—but the area was still called by that name. All that remained of the ancient city were fragments of walls, almost entirely absorbed into newer buildings.

He thought of the house where he had spent his childhood.

He remembered vividly the light filtering through the vineyards. His father leading a massive bull into an enclosure. Other children chasing after a colt.

He imagined a gentle hand tracing a caress across his face. It felt tender, but in his mind, the hand belonged to a young boy, not the weathered face he had now, with its unkempt beard and the years of Rome's campaigns carved into it.

He marveled at how real memories could feel.

Looking around, he noticed Kos' peculiar way of resting.

The sailor kept a lantern close by and wrapped himself tightly in a cloak, leaving only his bony feet exposed.

Kos' sleep was not entirely peaceful—every so often, he would rise, gaze out at the sea and stars, and walk the length of the deck, still wrapped in his cloak. Then, he would return to sleep.

Their ship wasn't the only one at sea, Vatinius Auruncus was certain of it.

All vessels sailed with their torches extinguished, as they themselves did, to avoid detection.

He wondered if among those ships was Calibrandus, still pursuing them. The image of Rudulfus' sneering face flashed before his eyes, mocking him after killing Aristarchos Themistocles.

The thought forced him to reflect. He began to suspect that the Heruli king might be crossing the peninsula by land while his most trusted general pursued them by sea.

Trying to think like a cunning politician, he imagined Rudulfus and Odoacer feasting in Ravenna, discussing the division of the Empire.

A bitter bile rose in his throat, driven by resentment.

Fleeing without being able to run his blade through that bastard was an unbearable torment.

It was nearly morning when he decided to rest.

***

The following days passed peacefully at sea. As they sailed past the promontory of Caieta[7], everyone gathered at the bow.

What they saw was the coastline of *Latium Novum*, the territory that had been added during Rome's early conquests in southern Italy.

The legionaries' breaths were short, their faces taut against the brisk air.

"Are we stopping at Minturnae? Are we docking?" Tullius Sextus Plato could barely contain his excitement.

Drusus Variatus chimed in, "The first *tabernae* I find, I'm gorging on eels!"

Severinus Majorianus' gaze was fixed on the coast. It was clear he couldn't wait to set foot on land.

Kos, however, had a different expression.

He was about to ruin the mood. Years of sailing had taught him that if you wanted to land unnoticed, you had to do it at night—not in a port.

Vatinius Auruncus placed his hands on the rail. "Keep us offshore," he said simply, staring at the city of Minturnae, which was becoming more and more distinct.

He could feel the disapproving stares behind him. It was best to explain his reasoning.

He turned to his comrades. "It's been thirty years. Every corner of the Empire is at the mercy of barbarians. We don't know who holds power in these lands, where we'll be seen as soldiers gone astray. Don't expect anything else."

Severinus Majorianus stepped forward. "You're probably right, Centurion, but what difference does it make if we land now or at night?"

Auruncus appreciated that the optio had voiced his doubts. "Ports and coasts are the most closely monitored by customs mili-

---

[7] *Caieta*: The modern Gaeta (LT). In *The Aeneid*, Virgil attributes the city's name to Caieta, the nursemaid of Aeneas, whom he buried there. Diodorus, however, links its origins to the myth of the Argonauts, specifically Aietes, the father of Medea.

tias. We can't rule out the possibility that Rudulfus has spies there as well. At Duro Catalaunum, many knew of our origins, and the Heruli spies proved how good they are at their work. Let's not forget—they were able to track all our movements to Massilia, thanks to the information their agents gathered in the places we passed through."

Those words ended the conversation.

Everyone found something to occupy their time, trying to make the hours pass more quickly—until night fell.

Tertia vigilia of the night, coastline near Minturnae

Rowing, they approached the shore. The trireme moved slowly until its keel scraped against the sandy bottom. The water was so shallow at that point that the seabed was visible under the moonlight. The sky was clear and starry.

One by one, the legionaries jumped from the ship, the water reaching their chests. They waded ashore.

The waves were gentle, almost as if helping their landing by making as little noise as possible.

Despite the winter season, the air wasn't too cold—nothing compared to the freezing temperatures of Duro Catalaunum in the far north of the Empire's borders.

The soldiers' emotions were evident on their faces.

Returning to their homeland left them feeling disoriented.

Even after all these years, the emotion of setting foot on this soil again pierced through the emotional armor they had built during years of military campaigns.

Kos, the sailor, kept a respectful silence. He understood that the unusual quiet among these hardened men was due to their state of mind.

Evetius Aquila, the Batavian, scanned the surroundings, but said nothing. Though that was nothing new.

Vatinius Auruncus let seawater trickle through his fingers.

He had always assumed he would die in battle in some far-flung corner of the Empire.

He still couldn't believe he was walking so close to the place where he had been born.

He approached the optio. "We'll reach the Liris River, then everyone can go their own way."

"I agree, Centurion."

With that, they set off along the Appian Way, the ancient road built by Appius Claudius[8].

They reached the city of Minturnae, but didn't even attempt to enter through the *Porta Gemina*[9]. It was wiser to take the paths that would lead them to the paved road connecting to the Vescia region.

The legionaries' eyes fell on a stone inscribed with the number *xcviii*[10].

Evetius Aquila asked what it meant.

Vatinius Auruncus satisfied his curiosity: "It's a milestone. It indicates the number 98. In ancient times, they placed these stones along roads to show how far travelers had come and how much farther they had to go."

The Batavian nodded in admiration.

A few steps further, the moonlight illuminated what looked like a city almost abandoned.

It was inhabited, as could be guessed, but it lacked the splendor they remembered from their childhoods, when they would visit for markets or to see the goods brought by traders and sailors.

---

[8] *Appius Claudius Caecus:* A Roman military leader and politician born around 312 BCE. He was consul in 307 and 296 BCE and defeated the Samnite army in 295 BCE. He initiated the construction of the Via Appia around 312 BCE, beginning with the restoration of the road connecting Rome to the Alban Hills.

[9] The Via Appia entered Minturnae through the *Porta Gemina* and exited through the western wall. It reached Minturnae at the 98th Roman mile (1 mile = 1,481.50 meters).

[10] Mile marker: A real milestone discovered precisely where the aqueduct meets the city of Minturnae.

"I used to come here as a boy to watch the animals being unloaded from ships coming from Africa," Drusus Variatus recalled.

Normally, this would have prompted a sarcastic comment comparing the soldier to some exotic beast. But in this instance, curiosity about their surroundings took precedence over humor.

A sentry on a wooden tower noticed them, but paid them no attention. They reached the banks of the Liris River and stopped.

Vatinius Auruncus stepped ahead of the group and turned to face them. He climbed onto a half-buried marble statue. Looking down, he realized it depicted a soldier wearing a *lorica*.[11] He considered it a good omen. He took a deep breath, drawing in as much air as his lungs could hold. Placing his palm on the hilt of his gladius as though drawing courage from it, he began to speak.

All eyes—Severinus Majorianus, Drusus Variatus, Auctus Tullius Sextus Plato, Gallienus Lars Gracchus, Gaius Octavianus, and Evetius Aquila—were fixed on him. They stood still and lost in thought.

"It seems we made it," he began. "We're home!"

The men nodded silently.

"I hope each of you finds your families still alive, and that..." he swallowed hard, "...they remember us. This is the place we begin again. We're free now. The Empire didn't repay us for the years we gave to Rome's armies, but at least now we're masters of our own lives. From this moment, brothers..."

Vatinius Auruncus unsheathed his gladius and raised it.

The others followed suit, crossing their blades.

The centurion continued, "Legionary brothers, forever!"

"Forever!" Drusus Variatus echoed.

"Forever!" Severinus Majorianus added.

"Forever!" Tullius Sextus joined in.

"Forever!" Gallienus Lars Gracchus followed.

---

[11] The description draws inspiration from a statue of Caligula wearing a *lorica* (Roman armor), discovered during excavations of a temple (possibly dedicated to Rome and Augustus). The statue is now housed in Naples.

"Forever!" exclaimed Gaius Octavianus.

Noticing the silence, the legionaries turned toward Evetius Aquila.

With all eyes on him, the giant Batavian hurriedly spoke in his peculiar accent: "Brothers forever!"

Kos couldn't help but let out a laugh, revealing his missing teeth.

"Good luck, legionaries," Vatinius Auruncus concluded.

That was the moment when they each took their own path, disappearing into the darkness.

Aletrium[12], Hora septima[13]

He crossed the hall in long strides. Rudulfus was waiting for him, his usual calmness utterly absent. He had heard about the destruction of the ship pursuing the Romans and demanded answers from the one responsible for the disaster, who stood before him moments later.

The room fell silent.

Rudulfus' master of ceremonies pressed his back against the wall, ready to leave the room if things turned dangerous. Calibrandus, Rudulfus' closest general, had brought his elite guard with him. A dozen Vandal mercenaries stood ready to draw their swords.

"Did you recruit them in the same port where the Romans sank your ship?" the Heruli king sneered, baring his teeth.

The palace guards were already preparing for a clash with the Vandals.

Calibrandus grabbed a stool and sat across from the king.

For a moment, their eyes locked in tense silence.

"Are you trying to make yourself king?" Rudulfus prodded again.

Calibrandus didn't take the bait.

---

[12] *Aletrium:* Modern-day Alatri (FR).

[13] *Hora septima:* from 12:00 to 1:00 p.m.

"I could become king, yes. Instead, I bring you news," Calibrandus challenged.

Rudulfus' patience wore thin. "I could dine on your skull if I wanted. Delay telling me what you're talking about any longer, and I will—make no mistake."

The general laughed. "You'd choke on my teeth."

Rudulfus' upper lip curled in anger. "One more misplaced word, and I'll gut you myself."

"My spies have located those damned Romans. They've returned to the Liris River, where they came from. That's where they set out to join the Imperial army, and as we learned from Duro Catalaunum, that's where they've returned."

"You're good at using spies...less so at killing legionaries, apparently."

The jab hit home.

Calibrandus stiffened, flaring one nostril in an effort to suppress his urge to draw his sword.

Despite his irritation, he replied calmly, "What's the point of continuing this hunt? Let's return to Gaul and—"

"You were about to say 'govern,' weren't you?" Rudulfus was on his feet now, his temper flaring.

Calibrandus held himself in check and lowered his gaze.

It wasn't a gesture of submission, but a calculated move to avoid escalating the situation into a direct confrontation.

Noticing this, the Heruli king clenched his jaw and took a moment to reflect.

"Odoacer—and even you—might seize this opportunity to humiliate me in front of the army. At that point, it would be easy to overthrow me. But it's my head that wears the Heruli crown, and I will put an end to this matter by killing that damned centurion myself. I'll personally deliver his head to Odoacer."

Calibrandus understood the shrewd political reasoning behind Rudulfus' decision.

He decided to feign compliance. At the first opportunity, he planned to have Rudulfus assassinated.

Rudulfus continued, reasoning aloud: "Things have changed dramatically. Odoacer has decapitated every army, replacing their leaders with generals loyal to him. There's an advantage we can gain from this..."

General Calibrandus pushed his cloak back and took a few steps forward. "Command me, my king," he said, feigning servitude.

"Take these men..." Rudulfus gestured to the Vandal guards. "...and go to the Liris. Carry out my orders."

Rudulfus laid out his plan.

When the meeting concluded, the general strode across the hall with long steps and passed through the door.

***

The first dawn arrived. The higher the sun rose, the more the surface of the land sparkled.

Vatinius Auruncus, utterly exhausted, reached the place that had once been his childhood home.

The boundary of the property was marked by a low stone wall, with stones carefully fitted together.

The door opened, and a curly-haired servant girl emerged, chasing after a small goat.

Vatinius froze, unsure of what to do. He couldn't move a muscle, and he felt his heart pounding fiercely in his chest.

When the servant noticed him, she immediately ran back into the house.

An elderly woman emerged, wearing a mantle patched in countless places.

Vatinius Auruncus saw his own eyes reflected in hers.

The woman's legs gave out beneath her, and it was sheer luck that the centurion caught her in time before she could fall.

They exchanged a long, lingering gaze, brimming with emotion.

Vatinius' finger gently wiped away a tear that had traced a line along one of the woman's wrinkles.

She was frail and delicate. Her bones were visible beneath her thin, almost translucent skin.

"Mother…" he managed to say, his voice faltering.

"You've come back?"

He nodded.

"You're…you're still alive. I can hardly believe it," she sobbed.

It seemed impossible, but to this woman, the figure before her was not a centurion but a child—the same boy she had watched march off to join the army so many years ago.

Chapter XIV – The Line of Honor

Time had begun to pass since the legionaries returned to their homeland.

It was the day after the *Nones*[1] of September, during the *Hora octava*.

Warm air from Africa stirred his short tunic, tied at the waist with a leather belt from which his inseparable pugio hung—a lasting connection to his past. With the back of his arm, he wiped the sweat from his brow, which trickled down his back.

The basket carried by the donkey wouldn't be enough to hold the harvest from the row of Falernian grapes cascading down the gentle hill in front of his house. He would have to make another trip, but it was better to wait until the end of the *Hora decima* if he didn't want to bake under the sun.

Reaching the porch of his house, he unloaded the heavy basket. "Vatinius Auruncus..."

The man turned, looking for the voice that had called him.

It was a servant, pointing in a specific direction.

"Look..." her small finger gestured southward.

A group of about ten horses was galloping through the dust, coming up the dirt road flanked by grapevines. It was a detachment of Gothic cavalrymen.

As they came to a halt, one rider advanced alone. He was an

---

[1] *Nones:* A peculiar name for a day in the Roman calendar. In September, it falls on the fifth day. Thus, "the day after the Nones of September" refers to September 6th.

officer, wearing a conical helmet topped with a flowing plume of horsehair that brushed the back of his steed.

His armor was made of engraved metal plates. Two ornate dragon heads served as brooches, clasping his long red cloak—the only color marking his affiliation with the regiments of the Italian army.

The man's piercing blue eyes bore into him.

His long, drooping mustache was tied at the ends with small blue ribbons. His pale skin was sunburned in places, like the tip of his nose and his cheekbones: clearly unaccustomed to the sun, as were his men.

He wore unusual trousers that tapered at the ankles, paired with hobnailed sandals in the Roman style.

In a language that vaguely resembled Latin, he addressed him while struggling to steady his powerful warhorse. "Vatinius Auruncus?" he asked.

"That's me," came the terse reply.

In the meantime, Ostilianus, a freedman who cultivated the neighboring land, had approached with a dagger hidden beneath his short tunic.

With a glance of understanding, Vatinius signaled for him not to make any rash moves.

They were dealing with professional warriors—cutthroats for a handful of *follis* coins.

"My name is Edelrich, and I have been sent by the *decurion* of the *Palatium Praetorium* to inform you that the Sacred Palace of Ravenna has issued a decree approved by the Senate. One-third of the land belonging to every Roman citizen is to be confiscated and ceded to the soldiers of the Italian army, who will settle here," Edelrich growled, more like an animal than a messenger.

The barbarian was referring to Odoacer's decree, which mandated the division of properties into three parts: one portion for high-ranking warriors, another for the state treasury.

The horse sidestepped, forcing the man to tighten his grip on the reins.

"Not from my land...Edelrich."

A tense silence followed. The officer caught the vitriol in his words, and didn't seem to take it well.

"No one would be foolish enough to cause trouble for soldiers of Rome. I'll pretend I didn't hear that," he replied.

At those words, Vatinius Auruncus was overwhelmed by an uncontrollable urge to rip the barbarian apart.

But he managed to restrain himself.

He tilted his head to one side, feigning ironic resignation.

The Gothic mercenaries cast challenging glances from beneath their conical helmets.

Edelrich spoke again: "This is a law of Rome."

Vatinius raised a finger toward him. "You're not Roman. I don't see any Romans on those horses."

"I am an officer of the Italian army. I represent the Empire," Edelrich retorted, pulling out a rolled parchment secured with a strap. He tossed it to the ground near the centurion's feet.

"This is the confiscation order issued by the *decurion*. Read it. You cannot oppose the law," Edelrich sneered, his eyes gleaming with provocation. "Roman!" he jeered.

The others echoed his laugh.

At that moment, another voice joined Edelrich's. From among the Gothic mercenaries, another rider came forward.

It was Calibrandus, the general of Rudulfus.

Instinctively, Vatinius' hand moved to his pugio.

Out of the corner of his eye, he saw the servant and his mother retreating, terrified, into the house.

He wouldn't put them in danger, so he let go of the dagger's hilt.

Vatinius' eyes locked with Calibrandus', who challenged him from atop his horse.

"This is my land. I served Rome my entire life, and I was an officer of the Third Century of the Fifth Ironclad Legion, stationed in Gallia Belgica. Now," he gestured toward Edelrich, "that man will not take it."

"This was ordered by Odoacer, and you cannot oppose it," the

Heruli general taunted.

"Leave! Tell Odoacer that no one will confiscate my land—not even a barbarian."

The two men stared each other down for a long moment.

Edelrich then reached into a pouch secured at his belt.

He pulled out a coin and held it between his fingers.

He tossed it toward Vatinius, who caught it mid-air.

"Do you know who's depicted on it?" Edelrich asked, smirking on one side of his face.

Vatinius recognized the coin—it had been minted in Ravenna.

The face on it was Odoacer's, portrayed with his long mustache in the barbarian style—a subject of much controversy.[2]

"Why show me this?"

"He is your king. You owe him obedience," Edelrich said, pausing for effect to ensure he had everyone's attention.

"As you can see, Edelrich, he's not Roman," the centurion replied, his voice laced with irony and challenge.

The riders laughed.

"They say Zeno, the Sacred Augustus of the East, doesn't entirely agree," Vatinius Auruncus pressed.

"Rumors. Odoacer is subject to Zeno, who granted him regency of the Empire."

That word again—"Empire"—coming from that man's mouth, made no sense at all.

"I repeat, Edelrich," Vatinius said, emphasizing the name, "you will not take my land."

"You'll be the first to choose that, Roman."

"Neither you nor that swine dressed as a warrior," he said, nodding toward Calibrandus.

"You'll pay dearly for this refusal."

"Is that a threat?"

---

[2] In 477 CE, a coin was minted in Ravenna featuring the face of Odoacer, depicted with a long mustache.

"I could make it one."

"I'm not afraid of you."

"Your loss."

Vatinius Auruncus shrugged. None of the three spoke further.

Digging his heels into the sides of his splendid horse, the Gothic officer turned and rode off, followed by his detachment, leaving a swirling cloud of dust in their wake.

Calibrandus, however, remained for a few moments longer, never taking his eyes off the Roman centurion.

Vescinae[3], residence of Vatinius Auruncus, beginning of the Secunda vigilia of the night

Vatinius returned from the Chapel of Saint Luke[4], where he had gone to pray. He had felt the need, overwhelmed by the unexpected visit from Calibrandus.

Since returning to Vescinae, he felt an even stronger desire to pray.

He crossed the threshold of his home, which was pitch black.

"Vatinius, the others are exhausted," Ostilianus' deep voice greeted him, as usual.

Vatinius' gaze swept across the porch.

The farmers who had worked the fields sat with their backs resting against an ancient fallen column, using it as a bench.

From a pouch, he pulled out a handful of *follis* coins and handed

---

[3] The current thermal baths of Suio, located in the municipality of Castelforte (province of Latina, Italy).

[4] Likely built on the ruins of a temple dedicated to the goddess Marica, protector of sailors. This ancient temple was located near the *Porto delle Galere* (modern-day Porto Galeo in the municipality of Santi Cosma e Damiano, LT). Sailors would place offerings there for good fortune in navigation. Traces of a wall that served as a "pier" are still visible, as the course of the Liris River has changed over time. The area of San Luca still exists today.

them to the freedman.

Ostilianus distributed the coins to the workers, who left one by one, nodding to Vatinius in thanks as they went.

"Are you worried?" the freedman asked.

"Quite a bit. Calibrandus will return and finish what he started."

His eyes fixed on an indeterminate point in the distance.

The days of the legion seemed far away, and only God knew how much he longed for his brothers to be here by his side again, with their polished helmets and armored lorica.

Their purple cloaks fluttering in the wind.

Their shields raised, forming a wall—impenetrable by enemies or even time itself.

A wall that would block out regret, memories, farewells, and the passage of years.

With them, he wouldn't fear the assault he felt certain would come at any moment.

"I need to stay awake. The Goths are deadly in nighttime raids," he said, avoiding any prediction of the bloodshed he anticipated.

A faint breeze stirred the humid air of that wretched night.

"Finally, some fresh air..." Ostilianus said, wiping his bald, gleaming, sweat-drenched head.

"Go to bed. Tomorrow you'll oversee the work in the vineyard."

"I'd rather stay up with you. Your father granted me my freedom just before he died. He gave me the land where my house now stands, and to him—only to him—I owe my fortune..." He locked eyes with Vatinius before finishing. "I won't let anything happen to his son."

Those words struck the centurion deeply, though he managed to suppress his emotion.

"Very well... I'll fetch some focaccia and figs to keep us company."

But along with the food, Vatinius returned with a sword.

He handed it to Ostilianus.

"Take this as a gift. Because with that thing," he said, gesturing to the rusty dagger at the freedman's belt, "you wouldn't even be able to cut an eel."

They both burst into laughter.

Since Vatinius had known Ostilianus, the man had proven himself an able wine trader, managing to ship his goods as far as Provence by sea.

His robust frame hinted at his past, back when he was a Vandal warrior before being captured in Iberia.

They ate and talked until late into the night.

Fortunately, a breeze cooled the air.

Ostilianus' eyelids grew heavy, and eventually closed.

Vatinius Auruncus' eyes wandered to the fireflies sparkling in the vineyard.

It wasn't long until dawn when the first laborer arrived to begin work in the vineyard.

The man exchanged a quick greeting with Vatinius as he picked up a pair of pruning shears.

Another worker followed shortly after.

Then, it happened.

A strange gurgling sound caught Vatinius' attention.

The first laborer clutched his throat and fell to his knees. An arrow had pierced his neck, sending jets of blood spraying out.

"They're attacking! Ostilianus..." he shouted, rousing the freedman.

The horses, which had been kept at a distance to avoid detection, were now galloping rapidly toward the estate.

A volley of arrows rained down on the colonnade, but missed their mark this time.

Another servant began to sob, a streak of urine trickling down his thigh.

A flash of rage lit Vatinius Auruncus' eyes before he turned to Ostilianus.

"Ostilianus, I think this is going to be a job for the two of us," he said wryly.

The freedman simply nodded and returned his attention to the darkness, watching for the Gothic riders to emerge.

"Stay under the porch. They can't enter on horseback, so they'll have to dismount. That's when we strike," Vatinius ordered.

Ostilianus nodded again.

When the detachment emerged from the shadows, Vatinius Auruncus saw that Edelrich had brought at least twenty men with him.

Calibrandus didn't appear to be among them.

But perhaps not all hope was lost.

The riders crowded in front of the colonnade, their movements hindered as they jostled each other for space.

It was at that moment Vatinius Auruncus shouted the order: "Now!"

The two of them charged at the Goths, striking wildly.

"Aim for their legs!" the centurion yelled as he tried to unseat an opponent.

He blocked a downward blow with his gladius, then grabbed the enemy by his armor and dragged him to the ground, finishing him off with the point of his blade.

Ostilianus' powerful arms struck relentlessly, severing tendons, muscles, and breaking bones, rendering the enemy warriors helpless.

The Gothic riders were still clustered near the entrance of the house, their movements awkward and restricted.

Vatinius Auruncus observed Ostilianus' combat style and thought he must have been a skilled warrior in his past.

A shout, however, broke his concentration.

Edelrich was regrouping his forces. He called his mercenaries back to him, preparing them for another assault—one he knew would be decisive.

For a brief moment, their eyes locked in a silent, defiant exchange.

The Gothic officer pointed his finger at Vatinius in a clear warning.

"Come on, then…" the young centurion muttered under his breath. "Come on."

Moments later, the Goths launched their attack.

About a dozen of them dismounted and entered the estate with little difficulty.

During the brief skirmish, Vatinius turned to Ostilianus and said, "Go to the stable and take my horse. Get away from here. Go—don't waste any more time."

He swiftly plunged his gladius into a mercenary's shoulder, eliciting a roar like that of a lion.

"I can't leave you here..." Ostilianus protested.

"Go, I said! They'll kill you anyway. At least this way, you can regroup and deliver justice," Vatinius' voice trembled, but his expression left no room for argument.

Ostilianus saw in Vatinius' face the despair of a man who had only ever known battle, and who now saw the destruction of his home as the crumbling of a fragile hope.

In those days, many homes were attacked, families torn apart by public administration and sold into slavery.

This often happened when they couldn't pay their debts or failed to comply with Odoacer's new laws. The decurions and their allies had turned this into a profitable enterprise.

"Go!" Vatinius Auruncus shouted again as he fought off three Goths at once.

Ostilianus' blade slit the throat of one of his attackers before he sheathed it.

As he disappeared into the darkness, he cast one final glance at his friend. The message in his eyes was clear: *Stay alive.*

An instant later, he was sprinting toward the stable.

Vescinae, residence of Vatinius Auruncus, morning

The elderly mother of the centurion sat so hunched over that she seemed like a bundle of bones wrapped in clothes.

She was visibly terrified, yet her gaze defiantly met that of the Gothic officer.

Edelrich sneered at her. "Your son is nothing like the soldier he once was. Look at him now—bound and battered."

The woman remained dignified, lifting her chin.

Her body trembled, but her face was resolute as she glared at

Edelrich. "You should count yourself lucky my son is in chains. Otherwise, I'd see your tongue nailed to my door!" she growled.

Edelrich laughed heartily before turning his attention elsewhere.

He inspected the captive farmer, prying his mouth open to examine his teeth, then running his hands along his body to assess his strength.

"This one, I'll keep," he declared.

Then, turning to a soldier, he commanded, "Bring me my bow."

The warrior fetched a bow and an arrow from Edelrich's saddle and handed them over.

Edelrich nocked the arrow, drew the bowstring, and fired, striking the old woman in the back.

Vatinius Auruncus choked back a scream of agony as he tried to leap to his feet, only to be kicked back down savagely.

"Kill everyone in the house," Edelrich ordered.

With his mouth full of blood and dirt, Vatinius struggled against his chains, but they were too strong. His head throbbed, one eye was swollen shut, and his upper lip was split.

"You bastards!" he managed to slur.

"You don't seem to want to stay alive," Edelrich mocked.

"Give me a gladius, and I'll show you my answer," Vatinius retorted, bile rising in his throat.

"You'd give yourself the death of a soldier, and I won't allow it. What I want is for you to watch—so you'll carry the memory of what Edelrich, son of Vitfila, is capable of doing," the Gothic officer said, lifting his chin ever so slightly.

At his signal, two warriors dragged the servant woman into the peristyle. She thrashed and screamed in terror.

"No!"

"Vatinius, help me!" she cried between sobs.

The centurion's eyes burned with fury as they locked onto Edelrich. "Let her go, or I'll chew your guts while smiling at you," he snarled.

A sharp kick to his head silenced him, knocking him unconscious.

Late Morning

"Father…"

The old man moved his lips, but no sound came out.

"Father, I can't understand what you're saying…"

His bony hands revealed a small sheath that Vatinius immediately recognized.

It was the sheath of his first dagger—a gift from his father on the day he wore the *toga virilis*.

Vatinius Auruncus felt tears streaming down his cheeks as he woke with a start.

He tried to free his hands, recalling that his arms and legs were bound in sturdy chains. The image of his father from his dream faded after a moment, even though his uninjured eye was already open.

Still, the dream brought back the words his father had spoken when giving him the dagger: *"Son, every time you look at this weapon, you'll remember what it takes to survive."*

Sensing his son didn't fully understand, his father had added: *"To know how to defend yourself and, when necessary, attack."*

Despite the pain in his face, a faint smile crept across Vatinius' lips.

His father had been a good man—he had to admit that.

The memory infused him with a flicker of hope.

He glanced around, trying to gauge how long he had been unconscious.

Sunlight filtered through a grate, so it was still daytime.

He discovered he was in a cell, with several other men around him.

He was relieved—pleasantly so—to find that none of them were his fellow legionaries.

Two mercenary guards stood nearby, calmly chatting in their native tongue.

A body hung by the neck, its legs visibly broken.

A wave of anguish struck Vatinius as he recalled the arrow Edelrich had fired into his mother's back.

"The daylight woke you, I see," came the sharp, grating voice of Calibrandus, echoing from beyond the bars.

His thumbs hooked into the belt holding his sword, while beside him, Edelrich casually sipped from a cup of wine.

Vatinius summoned his strength, suppressing the rage that burned within him. He knew this was the time for reason, not blind vengeance—vengeance that would only lead to his death.

And a meaningless death wouldn't allow him to settle the score with Calibrandus, Rudulfus, and now Edelrich. Imagining their severed heads was the only solace he could find.

He simply nodded.

"Do you know why I'm sipping wine, Centurion?" Edelrich asked.

Vatinius fixed his uninjured eye on him.

"I'm tasting yours..." Edelrich raised his cup. "*My* wine. Excellent. I must say, it's excellent. I'm sure I'll make good money selling it," the Gothic officer taunted.

"Where are my legionaries?" Vatinius cursed himself for asking the question, knowing he had just revealed his true feelings to this bloodthirsty beast.

Edelrich burst into laughter. "Legionaries? You mean those? We're hunting them down. It's only a matter of time before we hang every last one by the neck," he said, locking his provocative gaze on the chained centurion. "I'm not even sure if they're still alive, honestly."

Vatinius flexed his arms, straining against the chains. If only he could break them...

"I'll personally report your inglorious end to King Rudulfus, Roman centurion!" Edelrich sneered, emphasizing those last words.

The guards' laughter echoed even louder.

Vatinius' open eye seemed as though it might burst into flames at any moment.

Calibrandus turned and began striding away, his cloak billowing with each step.

Edelrich, however, stepped closer to the bars. "Starting tomorrow, you'll work. You're nothing more than one of my slaves now," he said with a shrug, as if advising him to be patient.

Vatinius couldn't hold back a wave of nausea. He retched once, then again, before his head spun violently, and he lost consciousness.

Minturnae, along the Trajan Aqueduct, eight days later

The steady rhythm of pickaxes striking rock marked the passage of the day. Carts laden with stone were pulled by strong white oxen with long horns. Some slaves mixed concrete for the repairs to the aqueduct, a project funded by the public administration.

Taking advantage of the opportunity, many *decurions* and *melloprossimi* had grown even wealthier. The funds from Ravenna had been allocated for the work, but through the patronage system, much of the money had ended up in the coffers of officials at the *Palatium Praetorium*.

Edelrich had also profited, as he oversaw the restoration of the section connected to the city.

Without pause, Vatinius Auruncus hauled bricks from a cart and carried them beneath the aqueduct's arches.

A hand with a weak grip rested on his shoulder. It was the *aquarius*, the overseer of the aqueducts, who worked alongside the engineer to supervise the repairs.

"Vatinius, I need you over here now. Let the others handle the bricks," he said.

"Fine," Vatinius replied. "What do you need?"

He bore no ill will toward the *aquarius*. The man had treated him respectfully, unlike the foreman, who often ordered his henchmen to use the whip.

"You'll need to repair that pillar," the overseer said, pointing to a load-bearing section of the aqueduct. "Start with the *opus* using stones, then finish the upper part with bricks."

The centurion nodded, but paused to voice his curiosity.

"Why are you pulling me from the hard labor?"

The *aquarius* spoke honestly. "Your mother and mine were sisters. We played together as children in the eel pond. But it's been so long..."

Memories flooded Vatinius' mind.

"Quirinus!" he exclaimed.

"The very same."

They exchanged smiles.

"Quirinus the *aquarius*..."

"The one you pushed into the pond in the dead of winter. That's me..."

They laughed quietly—no one could suspect they knew each other.

"In my current condition, perhaps it's better if I just call you *aquarius*... I wouldn't want anyone spreading rumors about us being friends. If Edelrich found out, you'd certainly have problems," Vatinius said earnestly.

"I'm the only man around here capable of restoring running water to the forum. I'm carrying out an order from Odoacer himself—no one will dare harm me, you can be sure of that."

"But Edelrich doesn't strike me as someone who forgets easily," Vatinius replied as he began mixing concrete prepared by the other workers.

"Do you want to know more?" Quirinus' eyes sparkled.

"About what?"

"About Edelrich."

"What purpose would that serve?"

The *aquarius* raised his hands. "That bloodthirsty barbarian was an officer under the patrician Flavius Orestes. One of his most trusted, no less. But during the Battle of Pavia, Edelrich realized Odoacer's forces were vastly superior, so he negotiated a surrender. In exchange for his life, he pledged that his regiment of Gothic cavalry wouldn't take part in the battle. As a result, Orestes lost about three hundred men—one-third of his cavalry.

"Odoacer demanded Orestes' head at all costs, but granted Edelrich safe passage, along with a hefty sum of *solidi* coins, which, ironically, bore the image of Romulus Augustulus—Orestes' own son."

"Quite a story, I must admit," Vatinius said, processing the tale.

"And that's not all..." Quirinus added with a sly smile. "It seems that at some point, Edelrich ran into serious trouble with his own mercenaries. Odoacer wasn't interested in hiring his regiment, and with Orestes' body already sealed in a tomb, the cost of keeping more than three hundred warriors was simply too high."

Now Vatinius Auruncus' full attention was on the *aquarius*. "Go on..." he urged, intrigued.

"So Edelrich gathered his most loyal cutthroats and fled south—to Minturnae, as you've likely noticed. For years, they holed up in the mountains, descending to the valley only to raid and plunder. Then, Rudulfus' arrival in Aletrium was a godsend for him. Rudulfus, who is also the Governor of Gaul, has vast resources.

"Edelrich personally approached him and is now his 'bulwark on the banks of the Liris River and the river port," Quirinus concluded, wearing the expression of someone who had just unveiled a mystery.

"That's how Calibrandus found me," Vatinius realized.

"I don't think Edelrich deserves all the credit. I'd say they already knew where to look for you."

Vatinius Auruncus was astonished at how much Quirinus knew about the situation.

Quirinus seemed to read his thoughts. "For a handful of *follis*, people around here would sell their own mother. Chaos reigns, and many families have moved toward Capua, where there's still a semblance of the Empire left."

With a faint smile, Vatinius replied, "I'd better get back to work before they whip me raw."

"Vatinius..." Quirinus' tone suddenly turned serious.

"What?"

"I heard about what they did to your mother..."

The centurion's hands trembled, and the stack of bricks he was carrying fell to the ground. "Yes..." he whispered, his voice pleading.

Long tears traced lines through the dust on his face.

To Quirinus, it seemed strange how a man accustomed to the brutal campaigns of the legions could be so deeply affected by his mother's fate—a mother he had only recently found again after years of war.

"I want revenge on Edelrich more than anything," Vatinius admitted.

Quirinus raised his hands, urging him to lower his voice. "You'd need mercenaries for that."

Vatinius locked his gaze onto Quirinus'. "I have the legionaries from my century still in the area. I just need to find a way to free myself."

Quirinus grew even more cautious. "Let's not draw attention to ourselves. The foreman is one of Edelrich's spies. We could get into serious trouble."

Vatinius nodded. "What are you trying to tell me?" he whispered.

Quirinus' expression turned conspiratorial. "There's a garrison of customs guards at Portus Setre. Their barracks are near the *tabernae*[5]. You could find weapons and equipment there if you manage to regain your freedom. That's all I know."

"That's more than enough for me. Thank you," Vatinius said, gratitude evident in his voice.

Quirinus lowered his hand. "Get back to work now, or we'll both be in trouble."

***

At dusk, all the slaves were loaded onto carts and taken back to their cells.

Along the stone-paved road built by Emperor Septimius

---

[5] *Tabernae:* the present-day area of Taverna Cinquanta, near the Liris River, in the municipality of Santi Cosma e Damiano (LT). This was once home to one or more taverns where travelers could rest and spend the night before crossing the river or boarding a vessel.

Severus[6], the tips of the cypress trees swayed in the wind. The sun dragged away the amber veil of light that had covered everything.

Shadows stretched out, resembling ghosts waiting to merge with the darkness.

The guards escorted the small convoy. Quirinus, riding his horse, passed alongside the cart where Vatinius Auruncus and his fellow unfortunates were chained. The two exchanged a glance of understanding and a barely perceptible sign of greeting.

When they reached the *Thermae Vescinae*[7], they were unloaded and, as usual, led to the cells beneath a crumbling tower by the riverbank.

Two guards distributed the rations.

One of them, an older man, wore a leather apron over the front of his tunic. Bits of dried food stuck to it, and even to the long, curly beard that obscured his scarred face.

He was missing most of his teeth, and his breath reeked terribly.

The second guard appeared to be no older than twenty. He had only one eye, having lost the other in a gambling den.

He wore a segmented lorica, likely stolen from some imperial army depot.

The food consisted of a mushy slop of indeterminate origin.

Since arriving at this forgotten hellhole, Vatinius had only eaten meat once.

Thermae Vescinae, Slave Cells, Night

He couldn't sleep. He stared at a trickle of thermal water rushing toward the river.

He didn't know how to vent the rage eating away at him.

---

[6] *Septimius Severus*: A general who became Emperor in 193 CE. He increased the number of legions to thirty-three, totaling around 400,000 soldiers (encompassing the entire Roman military force).

[7] *Vescinae Baths*: The ancient Vescinae thermal baths correspond to the modern Suio area in southern Lazio, in the province of Latina.

After a life spent on the Empire's borders, battling countless brutal enemies, he had finally found peace—but it had lasted only a short while, burned away in a matter of months.

His tranquil life with his mother had briefly rejuvenated him, but that solace had been shattered in the worst way imaginable.

Now, his stomach felt as if it would explode with an uncontrollable thirst for revenge.

His thoughts were interrupted by a scream that broke the oppressive monotony of the cramped cell.

A dull thud followed another, slightly muffled, cry.

"Are you planning to get up, or would you prefer to stay in this damp, dark hole a little longer?"

That voice... It sounded familiar. But it couldn't be...

Then Severinus Majorianus' figure appeared beyond the bars. "Severinus! But...how?"

"This isn't the time for questions. We need to move before the rest of the guards realize we're escaping," the optio said urgently, fumbling with the lock using a key he had retrieved from the table where the two guards had been playing dice.

Once outside the cell, where over twenty men had been confined, Vatinius Auruncus motioned for the others to follow him.

But none of them had the strength to move.

Regretfully, he pressed on, knowing he couldn't waste time.

Slowly, they made their way toward the exit.

The torches mounted on the walls cast a reddish glow, their flickering light illuminating the prison walls as the shadows of the escapees trembled along them.

The two guards lay sprawled on the floor, blood pooling beneath their lifeless bodies.

Before leaving the building, Vatinius Auruncus stopped Severinus Majorianus with a hand. "The soldiers' barracks are up there—see that light among the trees?" he said, pointing.

The optio reassured him. "We're not afraid of them..."

He used the plural. "We? Who else?" Vatinius asked, his curiosity piqued.

"Me…and I'm not afraid of anyone!" Drusus Variatus interjected, urging him to leave the old tower.

A shiver of joy ran down the young centurion's spine. The two embraced, tears welling in their eyes.

"There are also…the others," Severinus added.

"Others?" Vatinius asked, astonished.

Laughter from behind made him turn abruptly. They were all there, standing side by side.

The familiar grins were unmistakable: Gallienus Lars Gracchus, the *signifer*; Auctus Tullius Sextus Plato, sporting a thick beard; Gaius Octavianus, the scout; Evetius Aquila, the Batavian; and even Kos, the sailor.

"When do we fight?" Drusus Variatus asked, clapping him on the shoulder.

"Hard labor has done you good. You no longer look like a tutor for rich kids," teased Gallienus Lars Gracchus, flashing a wide smile and eliciting laughter from everyone.

"Brother!" greeted Tullius Sextus Plato.

"Brother!" echoed Gallienus Lars Gracchus, the *signifer*.

"Brother…" added Gaius Octavianus, the scout.

Evetius Aquila said nothing, but gave a curt nod, his usual manner of greeting.

Severinus Majorianus and Vatinius Auruncus exchanged a meaningful look.

"Brother," Severinus said simply.

Overcome with emotion, Vatinius couldn't bring himself to speak.

Every word seemed to vanish in the lump forming in his throat. He managed only to pound his fist against his chest three times, mimicking the clash of a gladius against a shield.

"We need to move," came another familiar voice from behind him.

Turning, Vatinius saw Ostilianus, the freedman, his face illuminated by torchlight.

"You?!"

"You told me about your brothers in the legion. I found them, and now they're all here," Ostilianus said, a spark of determination in his eyes.

"How did you find me?"

The freedman replied, "We have a mutual friend—Quirinus the *aquarius*. He told me where Edelrich was holding his slaves. Then I tracked down your legionaries, and now we're here wasting time instead of getting out of here."

They took his words to heart.

Moving as silently as foxes, they slipped into the woods lining the riverbank.

Moonlight cast silver reflections on the water, which lazily flowed toward its mouth.

A flock of slender-beaked waterfowl rested in the center of a cove where barges were moored.

The long roots extending into the river took on an eerie appearance in the night, making the trees seem like ghosts ready to ensnare the superstitious or faint-hearted.

Another flock of pale-pink waterfowl, illuminated by the moonlight, skimmed the water's surface before settling weightlessly on it.

The legionaries were reunited once more.

They gathered around their rediscovered friend.

"How did you end up like this?" Severinus Majorianus teased.

Vatinius Auruncus spread his arms wide. "To tell you the truth, I've been cursing my luck since the day I saw that damned Calibrandus show up at my doorstep."

One thing that defined this group of friends was how years of military campaigns and border patrols had hardened them, enabling them to bounce back from every defeat.

"So, what's the plan now?" Drusus Variatus asked, munching on an apple.

Evetius Aquila and Tullius Sextus Plato remained silent, waiting for someone to make a decision.

Meanwhile, Ostilianus and Kos busied themselves inspecting barges, looking for one without rotted beams.

The centurion took only a moment to think.

"When Rudulfus hears about my escape, he'll unleash Calibrandus and Edelrich again. They'll hunt us down until we're dead. There's only one way to end this."

The optio chimed in. "We find Rudulfus and do Odoacer a big favor by eliminating him."

"I've heard Rudulfus is in Aletrium. We need to get there before word reaches him. We'll catch him off guard," the centurion ordered.

"And what about Edelrich and Calibrandus?" Ostilianus asked, frowning.

"They're a problem I'll deal with once Rudulfus is out of the picture. If we cut off the resources feeding Edelrich's Gothic warriors, they won't want to die for a king who can't pay them. At that point, Calibrandus and Edelrich will only have their personal guards left. That'll give us a better chance of taking them down for good."

As he reflected on those words, Ostilianus understood why these soldiers shared such a deep bond with the centurion. Vatinius Auruncus knew how to make the right decisions in critical moments, and this was another example.

"Very well. You can count on me," the freedman concluded.

Their attention was soon drawn to Kos, who was waving his arms enthusiastically. He had found a suitable barge for their journey up the Liris.

Once they cast off, the barge drifted away from the bank.

Kos unfurled the sail and angled it to catch the wind, allowing them to tack upstream.

When a cloud obscured the moonlight, the stars shone even brighter, surrounding them in a luminous trail as the slow journey continued.

As the barge moved forward, the legionaries gathered around their reunited friend.

"Ostilianus told us everything about what you've been through, Centurion. But there's one thing we don't understand," Severinus

Majorianus said. "Why does Rudulfus, who could rule the Gauls undisturbed, care enough about us to stay in Aletrium instead of returning north?"

Vatinius Auruncus stared at the planks of the barge and answered without lifting his gaze. "We're caught in a much larger scheme, unfortunately. Rudulfus knows he can't rule over Gaul because Odoacer has a far larger military force. The Heruli don't have a true organized army—they're just a collection of tribes fighting for survival. If they lose even the slightest fear of their king, it's very likely they'd defect to Odoacer, who maintains some semblance of stability in the Empire. Crude as it may be, it's still stability.

"We are a mark of disgrace for Rudulfus. A handful of legionaries who humiliated him at Duro Catalaunum and continue to do so. These things weigh heavily on the opinions of the various Heruli chieftains. Until Rudulfus can show them our heads on the tips of his lances, proving that anyone who defies him will meet the same fate, his power of intimidation will remain weak. That's why he won't stop hunting us."

Everyone listened intently to the centurion's words.

"But he could keep chasing us from Gaul, sending that cutthroat Calibrandus after us. Why stay in Aletrium?" Tullius Sextus Plato asked, raising an important point.

Vatinius Auruncus clarified. "He's bought Odoacer's cavalry, and Edelrich's Goths are working for him now. And don't forget the importance of this river. Several million *sesterces* worth of goods flow through here. Now, with his Gothic cavalry, Rudulfus controls these river ports. By doing so, he's squeezing Odoacer from two fronts—Gaul and the Liris.

"With control of river commerce, he'll be able to pay more mercenaries. Alongside the Goths, other scattered factions will join him. With a mercenary army in the south and his troops in the north, Rudulfus will gain an advantage over Odoacer. And let's not forget—Odoacer isn't happy about Rudulfus proclaiming himself Governor of Gaul. He knows it's a thinly veiled attempt to establish a kingdom."

A heavy silence followed his explanation.

Rudulfus' political strategy couldn't have been more clearly laid out.

Drusus Variatus broke the tension with resolute words: "We'll have our revenge."

"Brothers forever," Evetius Aquila added.

All eyes turned to the Batavian, stunned by what he had just said.

"Aquila?" Drusus Variatus asked, grinning. "And here I thought you were emotionless, and had a manhood worthy of Neptune's trident!"

Laughter erupted, quickly muffled by hands over mouths.

They couldn't risk being discovered—surely by now, Edelrich and his men had realized Vatinius Auruncus and the other escaped slaves were gone, and were searching for them everywhere.

"We need to avoid that ship," Ostilianus said, pointing to a bireme docked nearby.

Drusus interjected, "I didn't know biremes docked this far inland."

"These biremes escort cargo ships. Five or six at most, all anchored along the river, far from the sea. Better to lose oil ships that have already unloaded their cargo than to risk losing warships—that's the philosophy of the *Cosa Pubblica*," Ostilianus explained. He paused, pointing to a small landing spot. "That little beach will do."

Kos directed the barge there, securing it to a tree.

After they disembarked, the group moved toward the small town of Aletrium.

They followed a paved road bordered by sections of fallen columns, now overgrown with thorny vines. The area, like so many others, was in a state of neglect.

Walls that had once boasted fine opus reticulatum masonry were now crumbling in many places.

Even the temple, once dedicated to the triad of Jupiter, Juno, and Minerva, stood in ruin, with only two of its main columns still standing.

A few ancient milestones marking distances remained visible, but they were far outnumbered by funerary stelae.

Drusus Variatus paused to read one aloud: "I am Calliope, wife of Flavius Statius. I loved my husband, and if you are reading this stele, you know I have finally joined him." He continued to another: "In life, I was a Praetorian guard in the service of the great Septimius Severus. I would have defended him at the cost of my life." His fingers brushed the cold stone, coated with the patina of centuries—likely carved over six hundred years ago.

As they walked, they drew closer to the city.

Another stele caught Drusus' attention: "The wife of Domitianus the Aedile praised my manhood, deeming it more effective than her husband's." He smirked. "I wonder if Severinus Majorianus has a stele like this one at home."

"And what's so funny?" the optio asked, turning to him.

"I was wondering if the same inscription is carved at your place," Drusus quipped.

Severinus paused to read the stele, but simply shook his head. "Such wasted breath in the mouth of a eunuch," he retorted.

Drusus, offended, shot back, "I have a manhood that looks like two!"

But Severinus was already ignoring him, confident he'd struck a blow to Drusus' pride.

The city's massive wooden gates were slightly ajar.

Two guards sat drowsily by a fire, barely paying attention.

"Do we just go in?" the optio asked, clearly unsure.

"Not yet. First, we get some clothes," the centurion replied, making a statement that initially made little sense.

Their expressions betrayed their confusion.

Vatinius Auruncus clarified with a quick nod toward a group of merchants sleeping beside their cart.

Drusus Variatus was the first to understand, and moved toward them.

Tullius Sextus Plato followed.

Gaius Octavianus grabbed a stick and joined the others, trailed by Gallienus Lars Gracchus, Evetius Aquila, and finally the centurion himself.

Ostilianus and Kos stayed behind, still unsure of what the others were planning.

The methods used to relieve the merchants of their cloaks were far from polite—brutal, even.

The unfortunate merchants were tied up, gagged, and sent southward on their own cart.

As the cart disappeared over a hill, the legionaries donned the waxed, hooded cloaks, while Kos and Ostilianus assumed the guise of servants.

Near the still-closed tabernae, some exhausted prostitutes were dozing after a long night's work.

One of them caught Tullius Sextus Plato's eye and beckoned with a curled finger, her expression inviting. "Traveler, care to start your day off right? I'll send you away satisfied..." she purred, licking her lips in a way only a skilled seductress could.

The legionary's eyes widened. "If I understand correctly, we'll be facing half a regiment of Heruli in a few hours," he said, stroking his chin thoughtfully. Then he turned to the group. "If I'm going to die, I'd rather do it after..."

The centurion cut him off. "We don't have time."

"I liked you better when you were a prisoner of the Goths," Plato grumbled under his breath.

Surprisingly, that gave Vatinius Auruncus an idea.

"Legionary, if you promise not to take too long, I'll let you fulfill your wish. But on one condition..."

Plato couldn't believe his ears. "What do I need to do?"

"Get information."

Moans of pleasure from the woman soon reached their ears.

"She's faking," Severinus Majorianus remarked.

"Can I try getting information, too?" Evetius Aquila asked, disappointed by the lack of response.

"She's going to bleed him dry for a bunch of bronze coins," the optio laughed.

"Not a bad idea, really," the scout Gaius Octavianus added. "Too bad I don't have any *sesterces* on me."

They all laughed.

"I'm telling you, she's faking it," Kos said knowingly, with the air of a man well-versed in women.

It wasn't long before Plato reappeared.

Hurriedly, Plato threw on his cloak, pulling the hood over his head.

"The palace where the Heruli are stationed is down there," he said, striding ahead as though he had completed the most important mission of his life.

As they walked, Gaius Octavianus nudged him. "Don't get too proud of yourself—she was faking," the scout teased.

"I'm pretty sure I was her best client ever," Plato retorted.

***

The torches crackled against the stone walls.

Next to the table, a brazier radiated warmth.

Rudulfus picked up the message again, handing it to the master of ceremonies to reread. He desperately hoped he had misunderstood its contents.

But even as the words were pronounced slowly and clearly, their meaning remained unchangeable.

Odoacer had declared himself King of the Heruli.

Some of the troops stationed in southern Gaul had defected to Odoacer, joining him in Ravenna.

He cursed aloud.

Springing to his feet, Rudulfus paced across the hall. He inhaled deeply, trying to resist the urge to take out his rage on a servant.

Stopping abruptly in front of an unlucky attendant, he debated whether to kill him as an outlet for his anger, or let him go.

The servant's rapid breathing and muffled whimpers betrayed his terror.

Another messenger entered the hall, this one from Casilinum[8].

He handed the letter to the master of ceremonies and bowed his head.

With a nod, Rudulfus permitted the letter to be read.

The master of ceremonies' pudgy hands opened the parchment, his eyes widening as he scanned its contents—a detail Rudulfus didn't miss.

"Read it," he ordered impatiently.

The master cleared his throat before speaking: "Zeno, the Emperor of the East, supports Odoacer. He has allocated significant funds to appease the Gothic troops scattered in the south. A contingent under Odoacer is marching north, joined by the Heruli forces that rallied to him in Ravenna."

Folding the message, the master of ceremonies fell silent.

Rudulfus turned his focus to the maps on the table. His territories were now threatened by Odoacer's advancing army, particularly in Gaul, where many of his own forces were stationed.

The bulk of Rudulfus' troops were still at Duro Catalaunum, where he hadn't been in far too long. He realized he would need to return quickly.

To make matters worse, Zeno's envoys would soon arrive at the Liris, distributing funds to sway the scattered Gothic troops away from Rudulfus' service.

He shifted three small lead rectangles on the map, each representing Odoacer's forces.

Placing them strategically, his expression transformed from one of concern to outright fear.

If he didn't return to Duro Catalaunum, Odoacer would almost certainly make a move to kill him.

A third messenger entered the room.

Weary, Rudulfus slumped into a red marble chair, averting his

---

[8] *Casilinum:* An ancient river port of Roman Capua, located in what is now Capua, in the province of Caserta (CE).

gaze to the window, where a single beam of sunlight fell onto the floor.

The master of ceremonies cleared his throat again. "Centurion Vatinius Auruncus has escaped from the prisons at Vescinae. Edelrich and Calibrandus are on his trail, but neither he nor his comrades can be found."

This was the final straw.

A servant holding a jug of mead dropped it in terror and tried to flee, but two Heruli guards seized him.

Rudulfus stormed over, grabbing the servant by his curly hair and dragging him toward a candelabrum.

He seized the heavy object and began beating the man with it, shattering his skull.

Blood, bone fragments, and brain matter spattered Rudulfus' face and beard. Yet even this failed to quell his rage.

He knew all too well that news of yet another humiliation at the hands of the Duro Catalaunum legionaries would soon spread across the Empire, prompting even more troops to defect to Odoacer's forces.

A grim silence fell over the hall, broken only by Rudulfus' labored breathing.

The doors to the chamber opened once more.

Five hooded figures entered, carrying bolts of fine fabric draped over their arms.

Rudulfus' piercing glare sent an officer running toward the sentries at the door, likely to question how these men had been allowed into the king's chamber.

But the officer didn't get far—he noticed the sentries lying on the ground, their throats slit, just as Gallienus Lars Gracchus appeared and dragged him aside, slitting his throat with a dagger.

The two Heruli bodyguards unsheathed their swords, but hesitated to act.

The five figures stood motionless at the center of the room.

"Who are you?" the master of ceremonies stammered, fear thick in his voice.

The first to remove his hood was Vatinius Auruncus.

"Vatinius Auruncus, centurion of the Third Century, *Vexillatio* of the Fifth Ironclad Legion."

The others followed suit:

"Severinus Majorianus, optio of the Third Century, *Vexillatio* of the Fifth Ironclad Legion."

"Drusus Variatus, legionary of the Third Century, *Vexillatio* of the Fifth Ironclad Legion."

"Gaius Octavianus, legionary of the Third Century, *Vexillatio* of the Fifth Ironclad Legion."

"Auctus Tullius Sextus, legionary of the Third Century, *Vexillatio* of the Fifth Ironclad Legion."

"Gallienus Lars Gracchus, legionary of the Third Century, *Vexillatio* of the Fifth Ironclad Legion," Gallienus announced from the doorway, keeping it covered.

Rudulfus flinched, startled.

The master of ceremonies tried to slip away to summon the Heruli bodyguards but collapsed to his knees as Drusus Variatus' sword pierced him.

The guards in the hall finally attacked, but the legionaries dispatched them almost immediately.

Now only Rudulfus remained.

Vatinius Auruncus drew his gladius and stepped forward.

The Heruli king unsheathed his own sword, advancing toward the Roman.

Their blades met, their movements measured as they studied each other, waiting for the moment the true fight would begin.

The clashes of swords were swift and resolute.

One would strike, the other would parry and counter.

Rudulfus was a masterful warrior, but the centurion was accustomed to facing opponents far stronger than himself. There came a moment—a moment that seemed to last an eternity—when Rudulfus' arm fully extended, his sword becoming a seamless extension of his body. It was a strike of sheer mastery that, had the centurion not dodged in time, would have surely pierced him through.

But the momentum of the thrust carried Rudulfus forward, his entire body propelled by the lunge. His cloak billowed as it filled with air, and his finely-embroidered tunic fluttered in the gust of his movement. For an instant, the two combatants looked like a marble statue capturing a scene of battle.

Vatinius Auruncus first sidestepped the fearsome thrust, then crouched down to deflect another blow with his gladius raised to shield his head. That defensive position proved crucial for the centurion, as he darted his sword forward, driving its tip into Rudulfus' sternum. The Heruli king clutched at the wound, as though trying to hold his soul inside his body.

The two warriors locked eyes in a glare of mutual hatred as their battle briefly resumed. But Rudulfus was losing his strength. Blood poured freely from his wound. Staggering back, he collapsed onto his marble throne. Blood, mingled with mucus, dripped from his beard.

Vatinius Auruncus stood before him, his gaze sharp with vengeance.

"You're dying, you mangy dog," he growled.

Choking on a wet, gurgling cough, Rudulfus laughed hoarsely. "You Romans...always aided by your gods."

A voice rang out across the hall: "Finish him! What are you waiting for?" urged Drusus Variatus.

But Vatinius Auruncus ignored the call. Instead, he summoned a messenger.

The young man approached hesitantly, fearing he had been called to meet his own end.

The centurion moved to the ceremonialist's table, retrieving a parchment. On it, he wrote:

"Rudulfus, king of the Herulians, has perished in Aletrium. Northern Gaul is now leaderless. Centurion Vatinius Auruncus, Third Century, *vexillatio* of the Fifth Ironclad Legion."

He then picked up a jeweled chalice and handed it, along with the message, to the trembling messenger.

"Take this to Ravenna and deliver it to Odoacer's court. This chalice is your payment—worth more than you could earn in a lifetime. It belonged to a king. Now, go..."

The messenger could scarcely believe he would walk away alive. Hiding the chalice in his satchel, he slipped away through the doorway.

Once that was done, Vatinius Auruncus approached Rudulfus again. The king had slumped in his seat, and death was closing in. Their eyes met for the last time as the life drained from Rudulfus' body.

"Let's leave this place before the entire Herulian rabble shows up to skewer us," urged the optio.

Outside, they found Ostilianus and Kos waiting with horses.

"And where did you get these?" the centurion asked instinctively.

"They were...lent to us," replied his helper curtly.

Drusus Variatus let out a laugh.

"So now, on top of the Herulians, we'll have their rightful owners chasing us, too. Lovely..." quipped Gallienus Lars Gracchus.

A few minutes later, they were galloping along the paved road, the sunlight slicing through the cypress trees that bordered the path. They reached the ferry without incident, discarding the horses and the merchant disguises before casting off.

The full sail caught the wind, propelling the ferry along the slow current of the river. Everyone slept, except for Kos, who manned the tiller, and Vatinius Auruncus, whose gaze remained fixed on the shimmering surface of the water.

"What are you thinking about?" asked the Greek sailor, tying the rope to secure the sail.

The centurion dipped a finger into the water, watching the ripples that spread out behind the boat.

"My destiny..." he muttered, nodding toward the others. "Their destiny. A lifetime of fighting, and still no end in sight."

Kos knew that Vatinius' thoughts didn't rest only on that.

"It's a soldier's fate...and you're a soldier," Kos said plainly.

Vatinius Auruncus almost replied, but chose to stay silent. Kos was not to blame for what was happening.

With a resigned expression, the centurion added, "I don't think I'll ever live a peaceful life."

The sailor chuckled at the remark.

The keel slid smoothly through the water, rocking the legionaries to sleep as the two continued their quiet conversation.

"Defeat Calibrandus and Edelrich," Kos said, "and you'll see—you'll return to your life. You'll tend to your vineyard and live out happy days." His words came with a knowing grin, the kind of grin only a man who had seen too much could give.

Night, Hora prima diei[9]

Gaius Octavianus returned after about an hour.

"From what I saw, Edelrich has around thirty armed men—Goths, of course. Their horses are in the stables. The rest of his forces are camped in the hills. They're mostly mercenaries looking for work, and if we take down their leader, they'll scatter."

He waited for the centurion's nod before continuing: "However, we've got a real problem if we don't find proper equipment. Those barbarians only know how to fight on horseback. If we can get some armor and shields, we'll give them hell on foot."

Everyone understood.

Another battle was coming.

"I know where we can find the equipment," Ostilianus interjected, immediately commanding everyone's attention.

"There's an old barracks nearby. It's manned by river guards who spend their days idling about and mostly extorting tolls from incoming shipments. I doubt much of what they collect ever reaches the public coffers. They don't seem like men of integrity."

Vatinius Auruncus fixed him with a sharp gaze.

---

[9] *Hora prima diei* (the first hour of the day): Refers to approximately 6:00 AM in the morning.

"Your mother used to bribe them just to load wine amphorae onto the ships. Otherwise, not a single one would've left the docks," he added.

The centurion's face twitched in irritation.

"Take us to that barracks."

"Are we stealing again?" grumbled Tullius Sextus Plato.

"Write a poem, use your fancy words, and ask them to lend us some armor and shields," Severinus Majorianus mocked.

***

They spotted them—a group of about ten.

The guards were wearing chainmail shirts, not full armor, but it would suffice for the legionaries. Their shields were long and oval, equipped with a prominent boss at the center.

"When do we start stealing?" Plato asked, clearly unhappy.

"Go on, recite Plotinus' *Enneads*[10] to them!" the optio teased.

Everyone laughed—except Plato, of course.

At the river dock, a ship was moored, and one of the guards had boarded it to inspect the cargo. The guards wore coarse, brown wool cloaks that draped over their chainmail. Their pants were tucked into their rounded-tipped boots—boots that lacked the studded soles of legionary footwear. Their swords were long and wide, nothing like the gladii the legionaries favored in combat.

Though the gladius had fallen out of use centuries ago, Aristarchos Themistocles had insisted that his centuries continue wielding it. Since then, his legionaries had mastered its use in battle with remarkable results.

Vatinius Auruncus carefully studied the layout of the customs guards. One was counting amphorae aboard the ship, while the others stood guard behind him. The guard inspecting the cargo

---

[10] *Enneads:* A series of 54 philosophical treatises written by Plotinus and compiled by his student, Porphyry.

handed one amphora to his comrades, a necessary "toll" for the crew to unload the rest.

Gallienus Lars Gracchus stepped aboard, seized the amphora from the guard, and returned it to a sailor. In an instant, the guards had surrounded him.

"I'm not just taking the amphora—I'm taking everything else too..." the legionary declared, pointing at their chainmail shirts.

"And so the stealing begins!" Plato lamented.

There was no time to process what was happening before the attack commenced. Drusus Variatus, Plato, and Evetius Aquila confronted the guards on the dock, swiftly dispatching them. Meanwhile, the centurion, Ostilianus, the optio, and the scout boarded the ship to finish the job.

Under the stunned gaze of sailors and dockworkers, the legionaries stripped the guards of their armor, throwing their naked bodies into the river.

Vatinius Auruncus watched as the corpses drifted away, carried off by the slow current.

At the old barracks, they encountered the customs commander.

"I'll handle this," the centurion said, stepping forward.

The commander was a stout man, clearly a former soldier. A long scar ran from his eye to his chin, marking his history as a warrior.

"I was born here. Did you know that?" Vatinius asked.

The man swallowed hard before replying, "I...I don't understand. Where are my men?"

"They're floating..." Drusus Variatus interjected.

"And we stole their armor and shields," Plato added sarcastically.

Everyone laughed—except Vatinius Auruncus and the commander.

"I can give you this..." The commander pulled out a small chest and revealed its contents: coins.

"It's stolen money. We don't want it," the centurion replied coldly.

"Forgive me, but I'm confused..." Plato said earnestly, this time without sarcasm.

Severinus Majorianus couldn't help but laugh.

At that point, there was only one course left: a fight.

With a sudden leap, the customs commander initiated the battle. A flurry of strikes and parries followed.

The centurion was at a disadvantage, exhausted from recent events, while his opponent suffered from years of inactivity. He hadn't expected the centurion to wield his gladius so deftly, forcing him into a defensive stance, while a pugio in the centurion's other hand suddenly pierced his side.

The commander collapsed against the wall, his eyes fixed on the chest of coins.

"Take the armor and shields. Let's go," Vatinius Auruncus ordered.

"What about the money? Aren't we taking it?" Plato asked.

Without receiving an answer, he grabbed a handful of coins and stuffed them into his pouch.

Severinus Majorianus picked up the chest and carried it outside the barracks. Placing it on a marker, he called for the others' attention.

"Split it among yourselves," was all he said.

"What do you mean, split it?" Plato protested.

The optio shot him a sidelong glance. "This is your moment—start reciting your verses!"

"Honestly, after all this effort to steal, and we're just taking armor? Nothing else?"

A sharp smack to the back of the head from Vatinius Auruncus silenced his protest as they walked away.

They had the equipment they needed. Now, only one task remained: preparing for the final confrontation—the battle that would end this ordeal once and for all.

Night fell.

The campfire's flames warmed the chilled bodies of the legionaries.

They had taken refuge in one of the cryptoportici of an old rural villa. The chainmail shirts they had acquired were hidden in a strigulated sarcophagus, its lid broken who-knows-when. Nearby, the Liris River flowed slowly, while the distant cries of waterbirds echoed through the air.

"These walls were built long ago," Vatinius Auruncus remarked, using a stick to trace a crude sketch of the fortified villa they planned to attack in the dirt.

"There's a rock outcropping here," he continued, pointing with the stick. "Above it, a small tower has been erected. I'll bet Edelrich has posted someone there to keep watch." He marked an "X" on the spot to indicate the tower.

"Gaius..." The centurion turned to him. "Can you handle it?"

The scout understood immediately. "I'll go see what's there," he said, rising to his feet and disappearing into the night.

"When do we settle the score?" Severinus Majorianus interrupted.

"I'm more eager than you are," replied the young centurion, his thoughts flashing back to the memory of his mother's lifeless body being carried away on a cart.

The fire had begun to die down, and Ostilianus tossed in some dry branches gathered from the nearby woods. The flames revived and swirled, sending sparks into the air.

Vatinius Auruncus stood, raising his hands as if pressing down the air, signaling for everyone's attention. "Listen to me. Tonight's mission will pit us against superior numbers..."

"And what's new about that?" Plato quipped.

"Shut up!" Severinus Majorianus punched him in the leg.

"You don't need to keep reminding us that we're always outnumbered. It's been that way since Duro Catalaunum. I've stopped counting!" Gallienus Lars Gracchus chimed in.

Despite the stifled laughter—kept quiet to avoid making noise—the centurion pressed on.

"We'll be facing Gothic cavalry. Many of them. That means skilled warriors. But we also know that without their horses, they lack the mobility we have. They'll be expecting an attack, so we won't catch them off guard. We'll have to improvise. But when the fight starts, I want you to stay together. No wild swings—make quick strikes that allow you to get back behind your shield. Strike and retreat. Don't let them predict your moves. Swords out and back in. Got it?" His sharp gaze swept over each soldier in turn, a look they all knew well.

Heads nodded in silent agreement.

They rested for a couple of hours, though no one truly slept.

Severinus Majorianus chewed on a twig, gazing at the stars. Gallienus Lars Gracchus lay with his head resting on a stone, his cloak insufficient to keep him warm. Drusus Variatus lay on his side, his mind drifting to thoughts of what he might do once this cursed ordeal was over.

Evetius Aquila sat near the fire, idly poking it with a stick while listening to Ostilianus and Kos share stories of their lives.

Vatinius Auruncus, meanwhile, traced the villa's perimeter in the dirt, deep in thought about their plan of action.

Toward the end of the Quarta vigilia of the night

"Let's go!" the commander ordered, standing and checking that his gladius was securely sheathed at his belt.

Gallienus Lars Gracchus retrieved the gear from the sarcophagus.

"We're ready," said the optio, taking a few steps toward the equipment.

"Not yet," Vatinius Auruncus said, gripping the hilt of his gladius. "I just wanted to thank you..." He bowed his head.

As they filed past to collect their gear, each soldier clapped his forearm into the legionary salute, pounding his fist to his chest in silent respect.

The night sky was filled with stars. The moon's silvery light, unbroken by clouds, threatened to reveal the legionaries' shadows. To avoid detection, they crouched behind every available cover—trees, rocks, anything that could shield them.

"The tower is low, and there's only one sentry," the scout announced as he emerged from a bush, smiling as he added, "A mounted patrol just rode out. I don't think they'll be gone long."

Hearing this, Vatinius Auruncus nodded. "Here's the plan." He called the legionaries close and laid out his idea.

The scout vanished again, his target the sentry on the tower. He would do everything in his power not to fail.

The optio and the standard-bearer took positions near the fortified villa, waiting for the patrol to return. They crouched behind a dry stone wall, their swords sheathed to avoid noise, opting instead for their daggers to dispatch the enemies quietly.

"There they are," Gallienus Lars Gracchus whispered.

Severinus Majorianus nodded, holding up two fingers to indicate the number of riders.

They flattened themselves even further, hoping to remain unseen. The riders advanced cautiously, speaking in their own language, their pace slow and watchful. Taking them by surprise would not be easy.

The sound of hooves signaled that the patrol had stopped right in front of them. Fortunately, the wall's shadow concealed them. Without it, they would have been exposed.

One of the riders dismounted, propped his spear against the wall, and positioned himself to urinate—right over the wall where the legionaries were hiding.

The two men stayed completely still, even as they became unwitting targets of the Gothic mercenary's relief.

Only after the sentinels resumed their march did Gallienus Lars Gracchus whisper, "That German cutthroat just pissed on us!"

The optio's glare said it all: "Let's return the favor."

The two climbed over the wall, silently closing in on the guards. The sound of the horses' hooves masked their approach. Swiftly, they grabbed the sentries, dragged them to the ground, and slit their throats.

"Done?" the optio asked.

"Not even a whimper," the standard-bearer confirmed.

With the patrol eliminated, the two stripped the bodies and donned the stolen clothes.

"We're Goths now," the optio said with a grin, mounting one of the horses.

At a slow pace, the two riders approached the gate.

Everyone needed to be ready. The moment was at hand.

Drusus Variatus loaded his sling.

The two mounted soldiers entered the villa and dismounted their horses. As the guards began to close the gate behind them, Severinus Majorianus and Gallienus Lars Gracchus swiftly struck, driving their blades into the guards' throats and silencing them before any alarm could be raised.

At the very moment the gate reopened to allow the patrol inside, a sling spun through the air, and a sharp thud followed. The sentry crumpled to the ground, his face shattered.

They were in.

The gate was quickly shut to avoid suspicion, and the bodies of the guards were hidden. A drowsy warrior wandered out to relieve himself, but Gaius Octavianus, who had entered through the tower, took care of him before he could react.

"Do these Goths do nothing but piss?" Gallienus Lars Gracchus muttered under his breath, still bitter from earlier events.

"Get ready..." the centurion ordered, knowing it was only a matter of moments before their presence would be discovered.

Ironically, the first to notice the Roman intruders in the fortified villa was none other than Calibrandus. He stepped out onto a terrace, locking eyes with Vatinius Auruncus, who stared him down.

"The Romans!" Calibrandus shouted.

"It's time," the centurion murmured to himself.

Almost immediately, a dozen enemies poured out from a nearby door, and more shouting signaled reinforcements converging from all sides of the villa.

"Shields up!" Vatinius Auruncus commanded, his posture rigid, a statue of vengeance.

The shield wall rose tall.

The optio leaned close to Vatinius Auruncus and whispered, "You'll avenge your mother soon, Centurion."

"There's nothing I want more," he replied.

The Goths charged, wielding axes, spears, and longswords. Their battle cries echoed through the colonnades of the rural villa. However, their fighting style quickly proved inadequate. Their strikes were absorbed by the broad Roman shields, while the legionaries' gladii darted through the gaps, striking with deadly precision.

A sharp whistle cut through the air. Instinctively, Evetius Aquila raised his shield, and the arrow meant for Vatinius Auruncus embedded itself into it.

"There's an archer," the centurion muttered, scanning for the sniper.

Another whistle came, this time softer, followed by the sickening sound of impact and a pained scream.

Evetius Aquila was thrown backward, his long arms and legs flailing. A massive double-headed axe had torn through his chainmail, striking him square in the chest.

The large Batavian coughed blood, struggling to rise, but failing. The shield he had raised moments earlier had saved Vatinius, but had cost him dearly.

"Aquila is down!" Vatinius Auruncus shouted, just as a well-aimed shot from Gaius Octavianus' sling struck the archer, taking him out of the fight.

The Roman formation now found itself trapped between two groups of attackers, but the centurion, experienced in such situations, remained unfazed.

Suddenly, Gallienus Lars Gracchus was sent flying through the air, landing several meters away from the formation.

The massive warrior responsible was the same one who had felled Evetius Aquila with the axe. His piercing blue eyes now locked onto the standard-bearer, who knew this would be no easy fight.

The giant Goth discarded his axe and drew two swords from the sheaths strapped across his back, their leather harness crisscrossing his chest.

In rough Latin, he growled, "Prepare to die, Roman!"

"Maybe. But you'll pay the ferryman's toll before I do!" Gallienus retorted, rolling to one side to avoid the first strike.

He blocked the second sword with his gladius, his arms trembling from the sheer force of the blow. The Goth pushed his blade wide, keeping Gallienus' sword at bay, and dropped one of his own swords to seize the Roman by the neck.

Gallienus Lars Gracchus gasped for air, his mouth wide open, as the crushing grip made him feel as though his throat would be torn apart.

"Call upon your god. Warn him of your arrival," the Goth snarled through clenched teeth. Blood began to trickle from his mouth, staining his long, reddish beard.

The giant's gaze slowly lowered, realizing too late the depth of the pugio blade the standard-bearer had driven into his side.

Summoning all his remaining strength, the Goth tossed away his other sword and clamped both hands around Gallienus' neck, determined to crush him completely.

The Roman's vision began to darken, and the sounds of battle around him faded into a distant hum. His companions' voices grew distorted, echoing strangely in his ears.

Gallienus felt his strength leaving him. For a brief moment, he wondered if this was how he would die, crossing into the world of the dead. This wasn't how he had imagined it.

In a final, desperate effort, he twisted the blade still lodged in the Goth's side and drove it upward.

The giant's eyes widened in shock as his grip loosened.

Gallienus had won.

He realized it with immense relief as the lifeless body of the Goth collapsed to the ground. Gasping for air, he massaged his bruised neck and quipped in a hoarse voice, "Let's hope I don't meet him again in the Underworld..."

As his hearing returned, so did the chaotic sounds of the battle raging around him.

The Roman formation had fallen into disarray, and now everyone was fighting for themselves. But the centurion, with his wealth of battle experience, called out the command: "Lock shields!"

"Centurion..." Gaius Octavianus shouted, gesturing toward the fallen body of Evetius Aquila, sprawled on the ground.

Vatinius Auruncus shook his head—a gesture more eloquent than words.

The battle raged on, and no one could tend to him. These were the decisions that had to be made instantly. There was no room for emotion; only combat mattered.

The Goths had realized that charging into the Roman shields was futile. Around them lay the bodies of those who had tried. But now the enemy was regrouping, preparing to launch new attacks.

"Advance! Force them inside the building!" Vatinius Auruncus ordered, anticipating the enemy's next move.

"Is he out of his mind?" Plato protested.

"Inside the walls, they won't have enough space to maneuver," the optio quickly explained.

Step by step, protected by their shields, the unit pressed forward, crossing the threshold of the villa and reaching the peristyle. Once inside, the legionaries re-formed into a tight group.

Already, they were surrounded by enemies.

"Push them to the walls!" Vatinius Auruncus commanded, his eyes burning with determination to end this battle.

He frantically searched for Edelrich among the chaos. Finally, he spotted him, flanked by two of his cutthroats, their swords drawn.

From the colonnade, Gaius Octavianus noticed the centurion's intent. "Centurion, I'll handle those two," he said.

A single look of understanding passed between them before they both sprang into action.

The Gothic warriors were now leaderless, their attacks sluggish and aimless. They merely struck at the Roman shields without strategy or coordination.

Gaius Octavianus took down the first man with a shield bash that crushed his jaw, sending teeth and blood spraying from his bearded face. The second warrior proved craftier, dropping his shield and sword before fleeing deeper into the villa. Watching him retreat, several others followed, abandoning their weapons in the process.

Now, only Vatinius Auruncus and Edelrich faced each other.

Taking advantage of the brief pause, a spear hurled from the internal terrace pierced Ostilianus through the chest, throwing him backward. The freedman died instantly.

The fighting resumed with renewed intensity. A powerful blow knocked Plato's shield from his hands, sending him sprawling onto his side. The enemy closed in for the killing strike, but Severinus Majorianus' gladius struck first, carving a deep gash into the attacker's side.

"You owe me a jug of Falernian wine!" the optio quipped.

"If we steal and don't even keep a single *sesterce*, what do you expect me to offer?" Plato shot back.

"Fight together! Shields up!" Vatinius Auruncus shouted, even as he clashed with Edelrich.

"The worst is over. Almost all of them are dropping their weapons," the optio observed, panting with relief as he watched the enemy flee.

"Why are they running? There are still far more of them than us," Gallienus Lars Gracchus said in astonishment.

"Just watch," the optio replied, nodding toward Vatinius Auruncus.

The centurion was relentless, raining blow after blow onto Edelrich's shield. The Gothic commander struggled to defend himself.

Vatinius' fury finally found its mark—a powerful diagonal strike ripped Edelrich's shield from his grasp, sending it clattering across the floor.

Left unprotected, Edelrich lunged forward in a desperate attempt, aiming for the Roman officer's neck. But his reckless move exposed him, allowing Vatinius' gladius to drive deep into his torso.

In a last, desperate act, Edelrich clawed at Vatinius' arm, as if trying to cling to life. A moment later, he collapsed to the ground.

Too soon, Vatinius thought, still catching his breath.

He had died too quickly, robbing Vatinius of the satisfaction of delivering a slow, painful end. For a moment, he simply stared at the lifeless body, his chest rising and falling as he regained his strength.

Noticing Edelrich's cloak clasp, adorned with the insignia of an imperial officer, Vatinius knelt and tore it away.

He looked around at the blood-soaked, wounded legionaries still standing. Then his gaze shifted to those who had fallen—Evetius Aquila, one of their own, and Ostilianus, who, though not a Roman soldier, had demonstrated the heart of a true warrior.

Seeing their leader defeated, the Gothic mercenaries bolted for the exit. Without an officer to guarantee their pay, it wasn't worth risking their lives.

As the first rays of daylight filtered through the rows of cypress trees, they heralded the beginning of a new chapter.

"Centurion!" Severinus Majorianus called out, catching everyone's attention.

They all gathered to see it:

Calibrandus, the Herulian general, had been killed. His body sat slumped against the wall, a dagger buried in his heart. The act had been committed by his own elite guards, who now presented his corpse as an offering in exchange for their lives.

With the tip of his sword, Vatinius Auruncus motioned for the Herulian mercenaries to leave.

The peristyle emptied.

Only the legionaries remained.

Severinus Majorianus the optio, Gallienus Lars Gracchus the standard-bearer, Gaius Octavianus the scout, and Tullius Sextus Plato surrounded their centurion.

No words were spoken; their glances alone reflected the depths of their emotions.

Even Kos, the sailor, stood silently in the background, savoring the taste of victory.

Vescinae, 487 CE

Velia struggled to keep up with her father, who handed her figs one by one. Her small hands carefully gathered them and placed them in the basket.

"Are you tired? It's very hot…"

She shook her head from side to side, her long hair swaying.

"At least wear a hat. The sun is strong," he sighed, his words gentle but concerned.

"Father, I'm fine," she replied with her usual bold expression.

He ruffled her hair affectionately.

They spent their days happily along the banks of the Liris River, near Minturnae.

It had been some time since the day Vatinius Auruncus had fought against Edelrich's Gothic mercenaries—the decurion of the small town along the Appian Way. To commemorate that event, Vatinius had placed a marker in his home to remind himself of the path that had led to his freedom.

The Vescinae area felt like home to him, erasing the weight of the many years spent following the Roman army. He had returned to tending his vineyard, even though the Goths had ravaged it during their invasion.

Rebuilding was a long process, but now he could ship amphorae of wine as far as Regio Septima Etruria.

The affairs of the *Cosa Pubblica*—the Roman state—were of little interest to most people now, and the peninsula was slowly fracturing into autonomous regions.

Bands of Suebi, Heruli, Sciri, and Goths roamed aimlessly across Italy, seeking work or farms to plunder.

Odoacer had gained the Senate's support and introduced significant administrative reforms, continuing to distribute land to his followers with little resistance. Around this time, he led a large army into Dalmatia to conquer the region after the legitimate Emperor had been assassinated by the generals Ovida and Viator.

In places like Minturnae, local patricians retreated to their fortified rural estates, hiring mercenaries to safeguard their properties. Aqueducts, neglected for years, ceased to function, including the one that once supplied Minturnae. Many had collapsed in multiple places.

It became common practice to repurpose the stones from aqueducts to build churches, public buildings, and even private homes.

"Can I go now?" Velia's small voice dissolved her father's gloomy thoughts.

Her eyes sparkled with the excitement of joining her friends.

"I'll manage," Vatinius Auruncus allowed, giving her a soft smile.

He watched as she ran toward what was left of the forum in the small town of Vescinae, greeted by the high-pitched laughter of the other children.

From the terrace where he stood, his gaze stretched to the horizon. The blue of the sea sparkled with dazzling light, blending with the sandy strip of beach fading into the north. It was the very spot where he and his comrades had landed on a cold night years ago.

Memories rushed into his mind like sparks from a fire. He realized in that instant that the melancholy of reminiscence would accompany him for the rest of his life.

A falcon soared, undeterred by the blazing sunlight. A soft breeze stirred his toga at the knees.

He knew the hand that passed him the cup.

Severinus Majorianus stood beside him, also watching the falcon. "It's free," he said, taking a sip from his cup.

"So are we, now," Vatinius replied.

Two more cups joined theirs.

There was no need to speak or turn to look. Gallienus Lars Gracchus and Tullius Sextus Plato filled their cups and drank.

"Gaius Octavianus is missing..." Vatinius commented, though he already knew why.

The optio pointed with his finger. "There, that white sail. He's fishing with Kos. His wife is waiting for him at the fish market."

"That woman's his new centurion!"

They all laughed.

"Have you tasted the garum he makes?" Plato interjected. "Only the northern sailors buy it. None of us locals would stick a finger in that sludge."

More laughter followed.

"Another round?" Vatinius Auruncus asked, holding the pitcher firmly, his expression making it clear he wouldn't take no for an answer.

Once all the cups were refilled, Vatinius raised his and spoke: "Brothers…"

They all lifted theirs in unison.

"To the Third Century of the *vexillatio* of the Fifth Ironclad Legion!"

"Third!" they echoed together.

They stayed on the terrace, talking about everything and nothing, their laughter echoing down to the ground floor, where Rometruda, the woman Vatinius had fallen in love with, emerged.

Velia was the result of their union. Her birth marked the end of his days as a legionary.

Though he hadn't shared the most painful moments of his career with her, Rometruda understood the inner turmoil that sometimes gripped him.

"Are those rascals you're sitting with staying for dinner?" she teased, inviting the legionaries to join the meal.

"Have her whipped!" Gallienus Lars Gracchus joked.

"I've got a couple of servants who wouldn't take money to whip you, standard-bearer!" she shot back, hands on her hips.

Vatinius gave her an admiring look.

The optio nudged him with an elbow and smirked at Gallienus, as if to say he'd just been bested.

"Where'd you find her? In one of the animal cages from Portus Setre[11]?" Gallienus couldn't resist another jab.

---

[11] *Portus Setre:* A river port area currently located in the territory of Castelforte (LT).

But the centurion's reply was sharp: "She could train those beasts, and not even a testudo formation could stop her!"

They burst into laughter.

They dined at a rough wooden table under the portico.

Everyone except little Velia, who had fallen asleep curled up on a large cushion.

From the conversation, it was clear that the most precious thing they had gained from their freedom was a sense of lightheartedness.

Each of them had taken up a trade.

Severinus Majorianus and Tullius Sextus Plato had started crafting tiles, *fistulae*[12], amphorae, and dolia[13] in an area called Viarum, known for its inns and a massive grain mill. It was close to the paved road built by Septimius Severus, which gave the area its name.

Gaius Octavianus had turned to fishing and eel farming with Kos. His wife managed a stall at the river port, with a small space behind it where sailors could eat.

Drusus Variatus, using his combat skills, had become a weapons instructor for the sons of local patricians, earning a handsome income. He had purchased a house on a hill called Cescus.

Gallienus Lars Gracchus, the standard-bearer, had briefly served as a personal guard for a patrician, but left the position when he realized he'd only exchanged one army for another, albeit a smaller one. Now, he worked at a farm, caring for horses.

Vatinius Auruncus watched them leave his home, laughing and stumbling as they went.

He returned to his terrace, seeking solitude. His gaze fell on the river below, winding its way through the landscape, shimmering under the moonlight.

---

[12] *Fistula:* A pipe used to channel water, employed in ancient Rome and the Castelforte area (in the province of Latina, Lazio). In the Middle Ages, fistulae directed water from terraces to underground cisterns.

[13] *Dolium* (plural: *Dolia*): A large terracotta container used to store food, wine, and oil.

Rometruda joined him, wrapping her arms around him from behind.

"Are you happy?" he asked her.

"With you," she replied, running her finger along the scar on his neck. "I was looking at the vineyard…"

"And?"

"If the weather holds, we'll have a good harvest."

"It won't change," he reassured her.

The centurion turned, gently lifting her chin with his finger.

"Are you about to kiss me, Centurion?" she teased.

"And if I were?"

Rometruda's hands moved to undo the belt around her waist. Then, they slipped to her shoulders, pushing her dress down until it pooled at her feet.

That unrepentant sensuality, with which she always drew him in, overwhelmed him every time.

She reached out, caressing the back of his neck, pulling him closer.

Bringing her lips to his ear, she whispered, "Are you worried because you've never faced an opponent as dangerous as me?"

Vatinius Auruncus smiled faintly and pressed his lips to hers.

Author's Note

The Last Soldiers of Rome – Vexillatio 476 CE is a historical novel born from my imagination. However, the historical and strategic context of that turbulent period serves as the framework for the events narrated.

The story begins with the act by which the barbarian general Odoacer (believed by the Byzantine historian Theophanes[1] to be of Gothic origin) deposed the Western Emperor, Romulus Augustulus. Odoacer declared himself *rex gentium* and pledged allegiance to Zeno, the Eastern Emperor. In doing so, he avoided following the example of previous barbarian generals such as Ricimer and Gundobad, who had elevated "puppet emperors" to secure formal legitimacy for their ambitions.

Odoacer's move was a shrewd political maneuver, presenting himself as an agent of the imperial court and military commander in the Italian peninsula.

It was the year 476, and the Western Roman Empire had reached its twilight after years of decline.

To better understand the events leading to the tragic end of that year, it is necessary to trace the Empire's final decades.

By this time, the population had largely lost interest in the *Res Publica*. Much of the blame for this collapse lay with corruption and the complete lack of morality among officials. The state admin-

---

[1] Theophanes (Constantinople, 758 – Samothrace, 817), known as "the Isaurian" or "the Confessor," was a Byzantine historian and aristocrat. He wrote the history of the Roman-Byzantine Empire from the year 284 to 813, spanning the reigns from Diocletian to Leo V.

istration had become oppressive, targeting everyone except the aristocracy with heavy taxes. Bureaucracy, far from serving the public administration, had transformed into a perverse system that created inefficiencies, encouraging bribes from those hoping for favorable outcomes in their affairs.

Everything was left to decay—roads, postal stations, aqueducts requiring constant and costly maintenance, buildings, and agricultural or commercial resources.

Vast regions of Europe, once under imperial control, were now dominated by barbarian peoples: Thuringians, Heruli, Alemanni, Ostrogoths, Franks, Burgundians, Visigoths, Sciri, and others. Their incursions into imperial territory in search of easy plunder caused widespread devastation and misery.

These groups vied for territory and power, often at each other's expense and sometimes at the expense of the imperial court. The pressure on the borders became so great that the Empire had to rely heavily on foreign contingents to support the regular armies.

One emblematic figure of this period is Avitus, who was sent to secure allies among the Visigoths on behalf of Emperor Petronius Maximus. At the court of Theodoric II, Avitus received news that the emperor had been killed during the sack of Rome by the Vandals in 455. Ironically, Avitus was crowned Western Emperor among the Visigoths. The Visigoths then gained significant advantages from their privileged relationship with the court at Ravenna.

Later, Libius Severus granted the Visigoths the province of Narbonnese[2] Gaul—clear evidence of the Ravenna court's loss of control over Gaul. At this point, Gallo-Roman elites began integrating into the administrative structures of the Visigoths (or other barbarian peoples) to retain important positions and protect their own interests. Thus, Roman commanders began appearing among Visigothic, Frankish, or Thuringian troops.

---

[2] *Narbonnese*: Gallia Narbonensis, a Roman province located in what is now Languedoc and Provence in southern France.

It becomes clear, then, that even before 476, Roman officers were leading foreign troops. This phenomenon is understandable, considering that during the Empire's decline, many Roman contingents were isolated in territories no longer under imperial control. These contingents sought alternatives to survive, adapting to the new conditions.

During the height of the Empire's decline—before, during, and after 476—many Roman soldiers entered the service of barbarian peoples. It is natural to assume that commanders often led their troops into these new allegiances.

Looking closely at the organization of armies in this period, we see that their Roman elements were modest, besides the banners they flew. Technically, the armies in Gaul during the late fifth century had not changed significantly from earlier decades. They retained Roman combat methods, equipment (including distinct weaponry), and a structure that included officers at various levels. Even when serving barbarian forces, they likely continued fighting in the Roman style.

Procopius[3] provides a notable account of a Roman contingent that joined the Franks. He describes them as distinct units organized by their original legions, advancing in battle under Roman standards and still wearing Roman-style uniforms.

Gregory of Tours also recounts in his *Life of Saint Eptadius* the existence of a contingent entirely composed of Romans, fighting for the Burgundian army during the transitional years between the fifth and sixth centuries. It is within this historical context that my novel takes shape. The initial inspiration came from a historical event, documented in the sources and described by Eugippius[4] in his *Life of Saint Severinus*. He recounts that, in the

---

[3] *Procopius*: Procopius of Caesarea (circa 490 – Constantinople, 565) was a military historian and politician. He served as an advisor to General Belisarius and accompanied him during the Iberian War (526–532) against the Visigoths.
[4] *Eugippius* (465 – after 533), an ecclesiastical writer and author of the *Life of Saint Severinus* (*Eugippii Vita Sancti Severini*).

years following the deposition of Romulus Augustulus, all that remained of the Roman army in Noricum was a contingent under the command of a tribune and a garrison stationed at Batavis. The other surrounding cities had already fallen under barbarian control. Despite being isolated and unable to receive their pay, the garrison at Batavis sent a detachment to Italy in the hope of recovering their overdue wages. Tragically, the detachment was annihilated. The remaining soldiers in Batavis, now reduced to only about forty men, were overwhelmed by a barbarian attack on the small city. As for the contingent under the tribune's command, it is likely that it disbanded, with many soldiers being absorbed into the barbarian forces that came to dominate those lands.

In my novel, I situate a similar scenario, but shift it to the small fortified town of Duro Catalaunum (modern-day Châlons-en-Champagne) as the primary setting. I initially reference the Battle of Arles and Emperor Majorianus, one of the last Roman emperors worthy of the ideals he represented. In 458 CE, he personally led his army into Gaul and defeated the Visigothic forces of Theodoric II, driving them beyond the borders. The protagonists of the story all fought in that epic battle, led by a centurion *primae spatha*. Allow me a creative liberty here—this designation is my invention, intended to "elevate" the figure of their commander. From that point onward, their friendship will forge a bond as strong as iron, even as they are reassigned to the *vexillatio* in Duro Catalaunum, at the northern borders of the Empire.

In such contexts, I have taken another creative liberty. I chose to revive the figure of the centurion, even though it is believed that this role had been replaced by the *centenarius*. However, I liked the idea that, just as Roman contingents of the period preserved their traditional methods of combat and their deep sense of attachment to their legions, there could still be units that referred to their commanders as centurions. Some historical sources indeed indicate their continued presence. For example, the mosaic of the Villa del Casale (Piazza Armerina) depicts a centurion from the early fourth century. Similarly, a *centenarius* from the fifth-century Imperial infantry is depicted in the mosaics of Santa Maria Maggiore, wearing an Attic-style helmet with a silver crest adorned with multicolored plumes (one such helmet was actually found in Richborough, England). The mosaics of Villa del Casale also feature a *Centurio Ordinarius* from Constantine's army, wearing the *pileus pannonicus*[5], a cap typical of late-era soldiers. There is also the funerary stele of the centurion Fulcinius Aulucentius of Claudius' Eleventh Legion. This officer is depicted wearing a fringed cloak and a simple tunic, but holding the *vitis*, the staff symbolizing his rank.

In the late Imperial era, at least until the third century, ancient ranks and their respective titles still appear in historical sources. After the military reforms introduced by Emperors Diocletian and Constantine, who ruled from 284 to 305 and 306 to 337, respectively, the rank of centurion remained integrated into the complex military structure of the late Empire. Thus, ancient units such as legions (*legiones*) and cohorts (*cohortes*) maintained their organization until the seventh century. Ammianus Marcellinus[6] mentions the distinction between cohorts, centuries, and maniples, with their officers continuing to be referred to as tribunes, centurions, and decurions. In the late fourth century, Vegetius[7] mentions the *ducenarius*, ranking between the *centenarius* (centurion) and the *primus pilus* of his *Legio Antiqua*. The rank of *centurio* or *centenarius* is cited in the early fifth century in both imperial armies (Western and Eastern Empires). In the late fifth century, the *centurio* or *centenarius* commanded one hundred men. Vegetius also describes the crest on the helmet as a distinguishing feature of the rank. Regarding shields (*scutum*), the use of rectangular ones is confirmed up to the third century, while

---

[5] *Pileus pannonicus:* A quilted tunic, crafted and decorated.

[6] *Ammianus Marcellinus* (Antioch, Syria, 330 – Rome, after 397), a Roman historian of the late Imperial period.

[7] *Publius Flavius Vegetius Renatus* (late 4th century – early 5th century). His original name was likely Publius Vegetius Renatus, with the honorific "Flavius" added later. He was a Roman writer belonging to the upper echelons of late Imperial aristocracy.

oval shields from the late third and fourth centuries were also used by *centenarii* of the infantry. Artistic evidence from the fourth and fifth centuries depicts the use of long-sleeved chainmail, sometimes muscle cuirasses, leather armor, and greaves.

Forgive my use of the term *gladius*, as Roman soldiers of the fifth century actually used the *spatha*, a longer sword. However, I thought it essential to portray the protagonists of the novel as so attached to classical military traditions that they would even carry the older, iconic swords.

The *pilum*[8] had fallen out of use by this time, though some variants still existed. In the story, I simply refer to it as a javelin, avoiding further complications with technical terms such as the *angon*, a type of heavy javelin used during that period.

Deliberately, I sought to recreate the settings as vividly as possible, allowing readers to immerse themselves in the events and feel as if they were truly living in that era, almost as if they were watching a film.

The Romans divided the day from the night regardless of whether it was summer or winter. As such, the length of the hours was variable. The daylight period, from dawn to sunset, was divided into twelve hours (*horae*). The *hora prima* corresponded roughly to 6–7 AM, the *hora secunda* to 7–8 AM, and so on until the *hora duodecima*, which covered 5–6 PM.

The night was divided into four watches (*vigiliae*): the first watch (*prima vigilia*) from 6–9 PM, the second (*secunda vigilia*) from 9 PM to midnight, the third (*tertia vigilia*) from midnight to 3 AM, and the fourth (*quarta vigilia*) from 3–6 AM.

Marco Vozzolo

---

[8] *Pilum:* A javelin used by the Roman infantry.

Acknowledgments

This novel is set during a period when the Western Roman Empire was experiencing its darkest days, as everything it stood for crumbled under the weight of barbarian invasions, political corruption, and the betrayals of military generals—most of whom, by then, were themselves of barbarian origin.

It is in this historical moment that a group of legionaries proves faithful to the only things they deemed important: honor, courage, and friendship.

These heroes, however, have a modern dimension to them.

Imagine, in today's world, people for whom keeping their word still matters.

Imagine, too, people who have the courage to speak out—even when doing so would provoke a devastating backlash today.

And imagine people who stand against the malice and deceitfulness of human behavior.

The group of legionaries in this book is inspired by courageous individuals who have stood up for what is "right".

I rarely lend anything personal to my characters, but in this case, I make an exception for Centurion Vatinius Auruncus.

I like him very much as a protagonist.

He knows how to think, and though he often waits too long to act, when he does, he follows through. He bears the consequences—or reaps the rewards. He follows his destiny and, even when backed into a corner, reacts with determination.

More often than not, he draws his courage from his own fears.

And, as you'll have read, it's not an easy path for him.

Believing, hoping, and always rising again—this is the true message of these pages.

You might be wondering: so who does the author thank?

That's easy.

I thank the pure of heart.

I also thank those who wake up at five in the morning, dragging their exhaustion to work.

Who do I not thank?

The elite, perched up high and looking down on everyone else.

For them, there is space in this book—but only as the negative aspect of the story.

Lastly, thanks to you, dear Readers. I hope this has been an enjoyable read.

Contents

7   Prologue
11   Chapter I – Departure
18   Chapter II – Vexillatio, 31 Years Later
91   Chapter III – Siege
138   Chapter IV – Rudulfus
148   Chapter V – A New Day
177   Chapter VI – The Shadow Empire
182   Chapter VII – The Hour of Decisions
254   Chapter VIII – Forced March
276   Chapter IX – Ready for Anything
304   Chapter X – The Honor of Rome
318   Chapter XI – The Dream
351   Chapter XII – The Heat of the Day
363   Chapter XIII – Dawn of Hope
417   Chapter XIV – The Line of Honor
466   Author's Note
472   Acknowledgments